the Actresses

Barbara Ewing is a New Zealand-born, UK-based actress and novelist. She trained as an actress at RADA where she won the Bancroft Gold Medal, and has starred in film and TV, including *Dracula Has Risen From the Grave* with Christopher Lee, and Granada TV's award-winning series Brass. She is the author of seven historical novels including *A Dangerous Vine* which was longlisted for the Orange Prize, and *The Petticoat Men* which was short-listed for the Ngaio Marsh Award for thrillers.

Praise for *The Actresses*

'Ewing... weaves a plot as complex as fair-isle knitting, darting teasingly between past and present, and fastens off all the threads so that the pattern is satisfyingly complete.'
DAILY TELEGRAPH

'An excellent account of the late middle-aged antics of the class of '59... big emotions, moving (and sexual) moments and a terrific insight into actors' childish psyches.' *SUNDAY TIMES*

'This enjoyable book combines elements of courtroom drama and comedy of manners, as well as sharp insights into the harsher realities of theatrical life.' *THE TIMES*

'A fascinatingly interwoven story... the most accurate study of an actor's world that I have ever read.' SHEILA HANCOCK

'Brilliant... a fascinating novel.' PRUNELLA SCALES

Praise for Barbara Ewing

the Actresses

BARBARA EWING

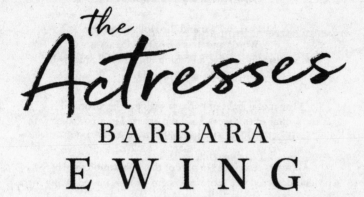

HEAD OF ZEUS

First published in 1997 by Little, Brown and Company
This edition published in 2018 by Head of Zeus Ltd

9 7 5 3 1 2 4 6 8

A catalogue record for this book is available from the British Library.

ISBN (PB): 9781788544658
ISBN (ANZTPB): 9781788544641
ISBN (E): 9781788544634

Printed and bound by CPI Group (UK) Ltd, Croydon, CR0 4YY

Head of Zeus Ltd
First Floor East
5–8 Hardwick Street
London EC1R 4RG

WWW.HEADOFZEUS.COM

For Lesley and Dick

'The important thing in acting
is to be able to laugh and cry.
If I have to cry I think of my sex life.
If I have to laugh I think of my sex life.'

Glenda Jackson

 # ONE

    In the Dorchester Hotel in London, in a suite at the top overlooking the dry parched grass in Hyde Park, a blonde-haired American woman aged fifty-six sat in a low-cut black petticoat expertly putting on make-up at six o'clock in the morning. She wore her glasses, to see clearly what she was doing.

A startling purple dress lay spread out on the bed: she had had it designed and made in New York, especially for this day.

It was already very hot and there was no breeze, no draught, no movement of air at all, just the heavy scent of expensive make-up and expensive perfume hanging there in the dark-panelled room in the early morning. Hardly a sound from Saturday morning traffic in Park Lane reached into the sealed suite.

The woman stared at herself for some time in the ornate mirror. Then she picked up the telephone and dialled the number again. A voice told her that Terence

Blue was unavailable at present but perhaps she would like to leave a message after the bleep.

The woman hung up. As she always did.

'I think,' said Pauline Bonham to her husband, who was putting molasses on his head, 'that I won't go today, after all,' and the morning sunshine streaming in through the open windows of their bedroom caught the blue silk of her dressing gown so that she seemed almost to shimmer, standing there.

'Won't go where?'

'To the reunion.'

'*What*?'

Anthony Bonham had recently read in a health magazine that molasses could halt baldness. He came marching crossly out of their bathroom, rubbing the sticky black mess into his hair. But even as he spoke he still stared at his hair in the mirror in the bedroom, turning his head from side to side looking for signs of success.

'Did you say you're *not* going?'

'Yes.'

'But this is ridiculous. You sent an RSVP; you said you'd go.' He sounded indignant, as if Pauline's manners left something to be desired and it reflected badly on him; she knew of course that he was indignant because he hated going to such things on his own.

'A great crowd of actors all talking about themselves in a hot stuffy room!' she said wryly. 'I shouldn't really think my absence will be noted.'

'I thought we were going together. After all it's where we met.' Anthony spoke grumpily, stalked back into the bathroom, still massaging. 'You ought to come. It'll be interesting to see everyone, see how they've done after all these years.'

She looked out to where the River Thames flowed past the bottom of their long garden; it would be another hot day in this endless, endless summer. 'See who you've done better than?' she asked.

In the bathroom mirror Anthony viewed himself again. 'There's that too of course, yes,' and Pauline Bonham, née O'Brien, once named the Most Promising Newcomer of the Year to the West End stage, gave a slight smile, looking at the river. Anthony Bonham of course was now more successful than almost everyone.

Anthony rubbed particularly hard with the molasses where his hair was disappearing at the front. 'I wonder who'll be there,' he said. And then suddenly thought, but did not say: *I wonder if Molly will come.*

Pauline regarded the holdall Anthony always brought home from Stratford-upon-Avon full of dirty socks and underpants. She thought, but did not say: *I suppose Molly will be there.*

'Do you suppose Terence Blue will come?' she said.

'Terence? Don't be ridiculous. He'll be in Hollywood swanning about.' Anthony stepped into the shower in irritation but did not turn on the water; he hated getting the taps sticky. He did not like to have to consider Terence Blue. *The only actor from the class of '59 who's more successful than me, became a bloody film star, lives in bloody Hollywood, the whole bloody lot.*

He wiped the molasses carefully off his fingers with a flannel and then turned on the water. Automatically he began to exercise his voice: MAHNAHLAH MAYNAYLAY MEENEELEE MAWNAWLAW he sang, and his voice echoed around the bathroom. And just once more the thought came to him: *I wonder if Molly will be there.*

His wife turned away impatiently at the sound of the voice exercises and went downstairs with the holdall of dirty washing.

Their children Viola and Benedict were still asleep of course; nothing would wake them on a Saturday morning till at least midday. Usually their bedroom doors were shut tight on their secrets but today all the windows and doors were open, trying to catch some other breeze. Benedict lay wrapped in a sheet, surrounded by computers, monitors, printers, and paper all over the floor. Viola's room was even more untidy, if that were possible: short skirts and jeans and bright dresses and infinitesimally small items of underwear lying everywhere, and every conceivable kind of make-up piled up on the dressing table. She slept on her stomach and her long dark hair spread across the pillows.

Pauline made a pot of coffee and unlocked the French windows that opened all along the house on to the garden. For a moment she drifted out on to the lawn, looking at the trees and the river, catching the fragrant scent of the roses. *I have measured out my life with coffee spoons*, she murmured conversationally to the bright morning

The telephone rang in the large kitchen.

It was their eldest daughter, Portia, and the voices of the two women crackled with restrained antagonism, as they almost always did.

'I want Daddy to get me two free tickets to *Othello* at Stratford on Tuesday night; I want to see it again and bring a friend.'

'Actors don't get free tickets Portia,' said Pauline, 'you know that.' Thinking: *you're a well-paid public relations consultant; you can afford to pay for theatre tickets.*

'I bet he gets them at cut price at least, he's a Star, the reviews say it's the greatest Iago ever.'

'Hello, hello, is it for me?' said Anthony's voice on the bedroom extension.

'Oh Daddy darling,' said Portia.

Pauline left them to it.

There was another mirror in the kitchen. Pauline stared at herself.

Everyone said she was beautiful, even now. Her short, dark hair framed her pale, oval face, her dark eyes gave nothing away, even though she was alone in the empty kitchen. She had long ago perfected the art of presenting her face as a beautiful mask that hid her heart.

The kitchen extension of the phone buzzed and she picked it up.

'Oh come on, come to the reunion Pauly,' said Anthony from the bedroom telephone. 'You know I hate going by myself.'

For a moment Pauline was silent. The aroma of fresh coffee filled the sunny kitchen. And then a swift, abrupt pain of memory, and of loss, caught at her heart so absolutely unexpectedly that she actually gasped.

Anthony, looking at his hair with such concentration in the bedroom mirror, did not notice. 'Will you come Pauly?' he said again.

Finally his wife said, 'It was all so long ago.'

'It'll be *interesting*,' Anthony insisted.

She stared out again across their long garden. 'No, I'm not coming, I need to be at the shop for a while and there's eight for dinner tonight. Try and remember we've got guests, don't get too tired and emotional at the reunion just because you've got a Saturday night off for once.' And then she added placatingly because she knew he really did hate arriving at things by himself, and because he was her husband, and because, of course, she loved him, 'Come and have your coffee darling.'

Anthony did not deign to answer. Hung up his telephone loudly.

Pauline Bonham stood quite still in the kitchen in her beautiful blue dressing gown. There was something odd about the way her eyes hooded for a moment as she stared at the river. Then she shook herself slightly, as if warding off a dream.

On Saturday mornings a street market was held quite near Molly McKenzie's big old Victorian house in Clapham; often she'd be woken by the sounds of vans unloading flowers or pumpkins or scented candles or cane furniture or mini-skirts. Once, as if she awoke and found herself on some urban farm, there had been the sound of hens and chickens squawking, brought along by a Jamaican with a hatchet; this stall had soon been closed down after complaints about blood and feathers. Molly walked through the Saturday market at her peril: *Louise* people would shout *Hey, hey Louise*. At first she had rather enjoyed it; later she could not bear the fact that she couldn't go anywhere unrecognised. She was not sure that the people who called at her knew she was a real person.

This Saturday morning, hearing the market sounds, Molly extricated herself expertly from Banjo's tight grasp. It was so *hot*, the sheets were damp, their bodies were damp. She had got quite adept at pulling herself out of his embrace without waking him, moving to the space on the other side of the bed, stretching her limbs, freeing herself. But she always left a hand or a foot just touching, so that she knew that he was there.

She opened her eyes now and, to her surprise, saw a ray of blazing sunlight falling through a gap in the curtains and across the brightly coloured duvet on the big double bed. She leant across to the clock on the bedside table and looked at the time. *God it was nearly ten o'clock*. Not that she really wanted to go to a bloody class reunion after all this time, what unemployed actress in her right mind would want to go anywhere where there'd be a lot of other actors whose first question was invariably, casually: Working darling? Still the same old question after thirty-six years. *Thirty-six years* since she'd arrived at Euston Station with two suitcases, carrying her life carefully in her hands.

There was a black and white photograph of her from that time: her brown, shining hair pulled back into a jaunty, bouncing ponytail; full skirts and flat ballerina shoes and lipstick. And a face that looked so hopefully out at the world, so eager and so interested, that Banjo sometimes, looking at her old photographs as he loved doing, used to kiss it. *Look at you in those funny clothes*, he would say. *I can see energy coming out of your ears. Of course you were going to be an actress*. She knew Banjo loved the old photographs because it was the only way he could share her past.

He had turned away from her now in the bed. Even though it was so hot, she leant into his strong, long back for a moment and he moved slightly in his sleep to fit into her embrace. His body was so comfortable, she wanted to stay here; she didn't want to go and meet a lot of other actors. Maybe they'd all have jobs. She moved closer against Banjo, she didn't want to think about this.

I made a mistake.

I was quite mad to ask to be written out of a crap telly soap where I was playing a well-paid glamorous part, thinking I'd get more serious work. What is 'serious' work? In my profession all work is serious. There is almost no work for women of my age. Men in their fifties are in their prime, women are old: end of story.

I made a mistake.

Banjo stirred. 'What time is it Moll?'

'After ten. I should get up, I've got this drama school reunion, what a bloody bore, I can't think why I agreed to go, it makes me feel quite nervous. I think I'll have a large vodka before I go.' She knew Banjo's body so well she could feel it smiling, it moved slightly as if a smile moved through it slowly.

'Be brave,' he said, 'you're probably the most well-known of them all – you've been a soap star, they'll all call out: *Louise, Louise*.'

'Thanks,' said Molly, 'an out-of-work soap star who no one knows is a real person, I'll make it a treble vodka.'

'Meet me back here this afternoon and we'll go to Leicester for that concert, okay?'

'Okay.'

'Is the sun shining again?'

'Yeah.'

He yawned, stretched and settled himself more comfortably. 'Will this summer ever end?'

'No,' she said, 'never never never.' And for a moment she lay her arm across his body. Across his warm, twenty-year-younger body, stroking his skin. 'And will I never work again?' she added wistfully after a moment.

But Banjo was asleep.

Reluctantly Molly left the comfort of their bed, nearly tripped over his saxophone in the corner, retrieved it as it slid slowly down the wall. She bounced down the long hall and down the stairs the way she always did, fifty jumps before she cleaned her teeth, she'd been doing that since she left drama school because she'd been told it started her body going at the beginning of a day better than any other activity, except sex. She put on some coffee, turned on the radio, threw open the kitchen windows that they always locked at night just to be on the safe side. The big house was filled with music, and with sunshine.

Who will be there? Will they all be working? Will I be the only one out of work? But she knew how unlikely that was. Most of them would be out of work probably, that's how it was for actors, the latest figures said eighty-one per cent of the members of her profession weren't working. *Oh shit what an awful profession it is.*

Under the shower she washed her now short blonde hair. Her firm body looked like that of someone much younger but Molly was not thinking about her body, she was thinking about the people she'd been a student with so many years ago.

Anthony and Pauline would be there perhaps. She turned her mind away from them deliberately, she did not want to think about Anthony and Pauline. Terence Blue? *Oh God poor Terence. I wonder if I'm the only person who's ever seen a Hollywood sex symbol cry?* Frances? Emmy Lou? Harry? And then her heart sank. Would Juliet Lyall deign to go to a drama school reunion? The one person she really dreaded meeting at theatrical gatherings was Juliet Lyall, because once they had been equals.

In 1962, in a big article in the *Evening Standard*, Molly McKenzie and Juliet Lyall had been singled out as two of ten young promising actresses expected to become the stars of the new generation. But Juliet Lyall's father was a film producer. Juliet Lyall had had such luck in the sixties: a leading role in a famous English film, *The Red Dress*, meant she had never from that moment looked back. Juliet Lyall was now starring in an award-winning stage production of *The Seagull* in the West End, and Molly McKenzie ex-TV-soap-star was out of work.

A father in the business was a huge bonus. Even a father was a bonus. Molly McKenzie didn't even know who her father was. Nor did her mother.

She stepped out of the shower, not noticing her body in the long mirror. She wrapped a big green towel around herself and went back to the kitchen, got herself a long glass of orange juice. Cheerful jazz piano filled the kitchen and bright sunshine poured in through the open windows on to the wooden table where a jug of sweet-peas and a bowl of peaches stood by the coffee. It was a beautiful day.

But oh I would love to be working again thought Molly McKenzie.

At 10.30 am Juliet Lyall's personal assistant knocked gently on the bedroom door, entered the room and quietly opened the curtains of the big windows that looked out on to a private Chelsea garden in the sunshine. She carried a tray which she put beside the bed. On the tray was a long glass of hot lemon and water, some fizzing vitamin C in another glass, a multi-vitamin pill, an oestrogen pill and a copy of *The Times*. And a flower from the garden, this morning a pink and white geranium flower from a plant that never stopped blooming no matter how long the summer went on. Juliet Lyall always insisted on a flower.

The personal assistant put on a CD of the Brahms violin concerto, not too loud, and left the room.

Juliet heard the opening bars of the concerto, opened her eyes. Sunshine again, she closed them quickly, when would this summer be over? She preferred a more gentle light. She felt for the telephone, punched in her agent's home number.

She noticed her body always felt stiff now when she first woke, something new, some further sign of age. *Where was Horton? Why wasn't he answering his phone at once?* She stretched carefully, holding the telephone. Saturday: the girl would be here to give her a massage before the matinée of *The Seagull*. But then she suddenly remembered: today was the day of the reunion and she'd promised to put in an appearance before the matinée, however brief, because, as one of its most illustrious graduates, she was on the London Academy of Drama's Council and it would look odd if she wasn't there.

Damn. The last thing she wanted was to mingle with a lot of ageing out-of-work actors. But it was part of the business, a necessity, it needn't take long.

'Hello?' Horton was eating his breakfast but Juliet didn't notice.

'Have you sent it?' Juliet wasted time on neither introductions nor preliminaries.

'Yes Juliet, it went last night, it'll be on his desk by now, his office is in his fabulous house up in the Hollywood Hills where I once had a martini and met Julia Roberts lucky me and I *know* he's flying back there tonight.'

'Horton I want that film, I want that part, you should've been able to arrange for me to see him today before he left.'

'I told you darling, Bud Martin's been incommunicado

for two days. Even his secretary couldn't get him, she says he's on a boat somewhere, that he does this, disappears. But we've done everything we can, the filming we did is marvellous, I saw it myself at five o'clock last night as soon as it came out of the lab, and the courier was waiting. Believe me, he'll see that piece of film and he'll want you. My LA partners will deal with it from that end, they've got instructions to contact Bud Martin later tomorrow. Just relax darling and we'll talk as soon as I hear.'

Juliet felt her whole body twanging with frustration. 'I want that film *so* badly,' she repeated tightly, wanting to scream at his leisurely tone. But she said only, 'Call me the minute you hear,' and put down the receiver. *He's my agent, he makes ten per cent of everything I earn, the least he could do is show a bit of initiative. Why doesn't he find the fucking boat?*

The concerto rose to a crescendo.

She sat up in her big bed, sipped the hot lemon juice to cleanse her system, took the vitamins to strengthen her stamina. And swallowed the oestrogen for – for what? Juliet frowned. For youth perhaps, that's what they said. She reached out for the magnifying mirror in the drawer beside the bed, put on her spectacles, stared at her face. Sometimes it seemed as if lines appeared overnight. She looked very carefully, very critically, at her eyes and at her mouth and at her skin. No, she still looked good, at least she would when she'd showered and let water run on her face for a while and done some exercises and had a massage. She knew very well that she still looked fantastic, that some actresses would give

years of their life for cheekbones like hers, high bones
that carved her face, that caught the light in the right
way, that looked wonderful both on the stage and in
front of a camera. She was lucky: one's bone structure
was luck, after all.

And when other luck had come her way she had
seized it with both hands. In an embrace of iron.

*As long as Terence Blue isn't at the reunion. But that's so
unlikely, he's in Hollywood surely, of course he won't be there.
The only thing in the world I simply could not bear would be
to see his face.*

Frances Kitson, red-headed and plump, lay on her sofa
making fanning motions half-heartedly and totally inef-
fectually with her padded bra. This article of clothing, if
worn, enhanced her already large bosom to mesmeric
proportions. Her yellow dress lay across the back of the
sofa and she was considering whether or not the padded
bra, useful for auditions for fat ladies, was quite the
thing for a drama school reunion. She had already put
on her rings, eight of them, a way of keeping her marital
status private; her rings at the moment were all she
wore. She always hoped that, naked, she looked like one
of those plump nudes in old paintings who lay on sofas
while little cupids held mirrors for them to look into;
she feared she probably looked like a beached whale.
She had lowered the blinds in her sitting-room but they
were rather ill-fitting and sun sneaked in, round the
sides, at the top: thin shafts of sunlight angled in across
her bare plump legs and on to the wall behind her where

an old photograph of her father doing a comic turn on Blackpool Pier hung in its wooden frame. *Oh, it is so hot again, why won't this summer* stop? *If it doesn't stop soon I will just have to kill myself and have done with it.*

The telephone rang beside the potted ferns. Frances sighed, sat up, picked up the receiver, still holding the padded bra. 'Good morning, Frances Kitson speaking.'

'Franny, it's me, look – I don't think I will go today, after all.'

'Oh Emmy we agreed, don't be silly! You never know who you might meet who might help you get work.' She regarded the padded bra again and added cheerfully, 'The one great thing about our business is you just *never know what's round the corner*.' She heard Emmy Lou sigh.

'All I want to do in the whole world is act. Get up on a stage and do my job. Why should it have anything to do with meeting the right people? Plumbers don't have to.'

'Oh Emmy!' said Frances, and her tone held both exasperation and love and Emmy Lou heard it.

'I know. I know, I slept badly that's all, feeling nervous about meeting people after thirty-six years, my face looks all tired and horrible, I've been staring at it for hours.'

'Now listen Em, since I was *forty* my face has looked horrible when I woke up! I no longer look at it first thing, I actually avert my eyes. I don't allow myself, or anyone else, to look at it until I've had a shower, had breakfast, rubbed in some moisturiser, put on a colour that suits me. Then without putting my glasses on I look in a long mirror from middle distance. I know I'm fat but from middle distance without spectacles, do you know, I actually look voluptuous and desirable.'

Emmy Lou started to laugh. 'What do you do if someone comes before you're ready? Like a lover or a telephone engineer?'

'Chance would be a fine thing,' said Frances wryly, sitting naked on her sofa. 'You know perfectly well I haven't had a lover for years and where I'm temping at British Telecom all the men are about fifteen and spotty. And laughingly talking of men – *where's Harry?* I've been phoning him since ten o'clock, we don't want to appear without any man at all do we, even if it's the queen of Kentish Town, but all I get is his answering machine, look I'll meet you at Victoria at twelve-thirty, and I'll keep ringing Harry on my mobile. At least there are some advantages working for British Telecom – I don't pay for my calls, don't tell anyone. Now what are you wearing?'

'My tracksuit; I've been jogging.'

'No no, to the reunion.'

'Oh.' Emmy Lou sounded uninterested. 'My suit?'

'No no, it's not that sort of formal thing, wear that blue dress, it makes you look pretty, and someone will see you and have a flash of inspiration and cast you in their new TV series and you'll win lots of awards and make pots of money and hire a PR man and become a Star Overnight in Hollywood where I'll join you as the next, slightly older, Rita Hayworth with my flaming auburn locks and my voluptuous and desirable figure and we'll have a swimming pool under a magnolia tree up on the Hollywood Hills and Terence Blue will come to tea.'

'Yes yes yes, OK OK,' said Emmy Lou but she was laughing. 'You don't think Terence Blue will be there today?'

'He might be: he was in London lately promoting his new film, he was in our class and it's a class reunion.'

'Well, I'll put my blue dress on in hope! See you soon.' Emmy Lou Brown was still smiling as she put the receiver of her white telephone down in her white flat, beside the large white bookcase that held almost every play in the English language. Automatically she glanced at herself in the mirror. Her face became serious and still. Bright sunlight shone in across the polished wooden floors and on to the white walls and on to Emmy Lou Brown herself but Emmy Lou did not see.

In the mirror she saw an actress.

And in the Dorchester Hotel the blonde-haired woman in the purple dress who none of them remembered, but who after today none of them would forget, stared at herself in the mirror also.

 # TWO

Pauline O'Brien Bonham, wife of the famous actor Anthony Bonham, had developed style.

She was rich now of course, and it showed, but only in a very stylish manner. Her clothes were Liz Clairbourne or Nicole Farhi or bought in Rome or New York where she went several times a year, but she wore only colours that suited her, rather muted colours, never colours that were there for the fashion. For some years now she had made sure that sleeves were at least three-quarter length, flattering, covering elbows that had begun to show her age. Her shoes were always Italian. Her dark hair was only ever touched by the top stylists or tinters at Vidal Sassoon. Even when she worked in the big garden, or in her antique shop, there was something elegant about her. The only mild eccentricity that didn't quite fit with all that elegance perhaps was that her Mercedes was pink and nobody could persuade her to change the colour.

And there was that other thing about her, that mask that hid her thoughts.

Still in her blue silk dressing gown, she sat with another cup of coffee under the old oak tree that grew beside their house, staring down at the green, smooth water at the bottom of the garden. Anthony had already sulkily stalked off, early, to pick up a taxi to take him to the reunion; Viola and Benedict were still asleep. Pauline's face was beautiful and blank, as always. But that sudden pain of memory had dislocated her, and her hand holding the coffee cup shook very slightly.

And her past insinuated itself into her thoughts, drifting there like smoke as she watched a long canal boat gliding into view along the river.

One night when she was eighteen (tall and gangling, with the air of a wary colt but already beautiful and, despite her father's disapproval, about to become a student at the London Academy of Drama) her mother, watching black and white television and drinking her third brandy and ginger ale, suddenly and quite involuntarily cried, 'My God it's your father Roger Popham at the back in that Persil advertisement. I thought he was in the circus in France!'

When Pauline turned to her in shock and disbelief, Mrs O'Brien said in amazement, 'Do you know, I think I'd actually forgotten!' Seeing her daughter's face, Mrs O'Brien poured herself her fourth brandy and ginger ale and reluctantly began to relate the story of Pauline's conception. 'Oh dear, I hope this isn't going to upset you,' she said, 'your father's not Ronnie, your father was a queer.'

Slowly, over many more brandies, it was revealed that Pauline was actually the daughter of a man called Roger Popham: a homosexual, an actor and a sometime employee of The Great Zelda Brothers' Circus.

In his thespian youth he had known Pauline's mother, a pretty young actress with a big smile, and just before the war, to the embarrassment of all concerned, he had sired Pauline while on tour with *The New Morality* at the Darlington Civic. Luckily for everybody Ronald O'Brien, the company manager, a very serious young man in his mid-twenties, believed himself to be in love with Pauline's mother who had recently won the Essex junior tap dancing competitions and who in *The New Morality* was playing the maid.

Ronald O'Brien married the already pregnant tap dancer when the company got to Hull.

His new wife understood on their wedding night (although she did not tell this part to her daughter) that, although part of him was unable to believe his luck that the pretty actress had become his, albeit in unconventional circumstances, he believed he was doing a very honourable thing and he would expect to receive due gratitude for the rest of his life.

The rest of the story Pauline of course knew.

Ronald O'Brien was called up to serve his country; his wife continued to tour theatres with her daughter under her arm, tap dancing still. But when he returned from the war to his wife and daughter Ronald O'Brien sternly put an end to theatrics, joined an insurance company; his wife tap danced no longer.

But Pauline had always remembered (or thought she

remembered but perhaps it was her mother's memories)
the smell of greasepaint and powder and used costumes,
and the warmth and the laughter and the tears, in backstage dressing rooms where lights shone round mirrors
and boys knocked on doors crying: *five minutes please
ladies and gentlemen five minutes.* She always knew she
would be an actress: through the dreary childhood years
dominated by the cold and puritanical Ronald O'Brien
some instinct in her heart told her that if she became an
actress she would find that laughter and that warmth
again.

When she suddenly understood that she was not the
daughter of Ronald O'Brien, insurance salesman, but of
a man who worked in a *circus* she felt as if a cold veil had
been pulled from her heart. The idea of her real father
became the most important thing in her life: she thought
of him flying through the world, the daring young man
on the flying trapeze; her mother's completely unexpected story was the most exciting thing that she'd ever
heard in her life. The fact that he was a *homosexual* –
Pauline knew nothing about homosexuals – was irrelevant. *He was very good-looking and he was very confused
and I thought I could help him* was all her mother would
ever say.

She insisted, against the express wishes of her mother,
who refused to help her, on trying to trace Roger
Popham but could only ascertain that he worked with
The Great Zelda Brothers' Circus somewhere in Europe.
His appearance in the background of the 1959 TV wash-
ing powder advertisement remained a mystery.

*

Pauline O'Brien became a drama student with Molly McKenzie, who became her best friend, and Juliet Lyall and Terence Blue and Emmy Lou Brown and Frances Kitson and Anthony Bonham and many others.

As soon as she walked into the small theatre attached to the old drama academy building, the smells and the memories came pouring back. They had make-up classes once a week in the small backstage dressing rooms and her mother gave her the old make-up box she used to take from theatre to theatre. When Pauline opened the box it was as if she opened a memory window. Their make-up teacher in 1959 still taught them to use the same base to catch the lights that her mother had used; a combination of Leichner sticks five and nine. The smell of the make-up sticks was as potent as ever as Pauline held them to her nose, breathed them in. And she began to laugh. It was as if laughter was tied up with the memories and the smells. Pauline O'Brien, and Frances Kitson whose father was a comedian, used to laugh together till tears ran down their cheeks, as if the profession and the make-up and their footsteps across the stage tickled them, entranced them. Because they both came from old-fashioned theatrical backgrounds it was as if they were stepping again into their childhood. They were already actresses.

Pauline told everybody at the Academy that her real father was a trapeze artist in a travelling circus in foreign climes, talked of him often, of joining the circus and flying on a trapeze too when she'd finished her training. Anthony Bonham had, like all the other students, found this fact romantic in the extreme, coming as he did from a banking background, but at that time he was involved with a Hollywood film star's rather lumpy daughter who was in the class also. But he remembered Pauline's exotic story, kept his eye on her.

Then finally, when Pauline O'Brien had left drama school and had become one of the new young actresses people noticed, playing the juvenile lead in a new West End play where memorably, just for a moment – her back to the audience – she had to take off her blouse and was revealed to be wearing nothing underneath, The Great Zelda Brothers' Circus came to Blackheath for a three-week season.

Pauline begged and begged her mother to go with her on a Sunday afternoon; finally, extremely reluctantly, Mrs O'Brien agreed as long as they didn't tell Ronald. It was September and there was a chill, crisp feeling in the air and the leaves in Greenwich Park were just turning colour and dropping on to the concrete paths up by the Observatory.

'This is probably a mistake,' said Mrs O'Brien for about the tenth time as they walked up the hill and Pauline caught the familiar scent of Tweed perfume and brandy, mixed. They walked with the chattering excited crowds towards the Big Top, children running, calling, looking back impatiently at their slow parents. The childhood smell of sawdust and animals and canvas engulfed them as they entered the huge tent and Pauline's heart now beat so fast she thought she would faint: *my father's circus my father's circus*, the words kept running round and round her head, *my father's circus*, as she stared up at the trapeze wires stretched above them across the high canvas roof. Drums rolled, white horses pranced, Pauline wanted her father to open the circus with the crack of a whip, to dance across the trapeze wires, to enter the lion's cage, to ride a one-wheeled bicycle.

'I'll poke you when he comes on, *if* he comes on,' said Mrs O'Brien crossly.

The ringmaster, the trapeze artists, the chimpanzees, the clowns all ran around the ring and still Pauline wasn't poked. An elephant sheered nervously on to a ramp, the lions were wheeled on in their cages, the lion-tamer – a woman – opened the cage door as the drums rolled. Trapezes swooped and rose in the heat and the excitement, children screamed and hid their faces and laughed and looked again.

'He's nowhere there,' said Mrs O'Brien, flatly, finally. In the middle of the horses' dance, white horses carrying red-dressed ladies and trotting through flaming hoops as the whip cracked on the sawdust, Pauline O'Brien began to cry.

Afterwards she dragged her mother, who had a headache, to the trailers at the back of the Big Top, pushing past little boys trying to catch sight of the elephants, finally stopping a woman in blue sequins and black tights at the door of a caravan.

'Excuse me,' said Pauline tremulously, 'do you know where I might find Roger Popham?'

The sequinned lady was a Russian and smiled at them in incomprehension but, seeing Pauline's beautiful tear-stained face, called to a small man nearby who was still partly in his clown costume and still made up. They had seen him riding a one-wheeled bicycle and falling flat on his face in the sawdust.

'Zarko, Zarko,' the woman called.

Zarko came up to the women and bowed, pulling at his bright green braces, his pink lips smiling politely through the huge red painted smile on his face. It looked very strange, close up.

' 'Ello ladeez, can I 'elp?'

'We're looking for Mr Roger Popham,' said Pauline desperately. 'We thought he would be here with the circus.'

The clown's polite, enquiring face changed almost at once. His own lips stopped smiling under the big red painted lips. He looked at the two women very carefully and then he said, 'Yes?' quite blankly, like a question, as if he didn't understand. A lion roared somewhere nearby and Pauline jumped slightly, bumping into the sequinned lady.

'Sorry,' she said miserably, 'sorry.' For a moment they all stood there silently.

Mrs O'Brien said, finally, 'An Englishman joined this circus after the war. He was . . . he needed to leave England and he joined The Great Zelda Brothers' Circus and I think he sometimes worked with the clown troupe and someone called Zarko and he loved the chim- panzees and I think he might have . . . used another name.'

Pauline remembered always how the light seemed to fade just at that moment, looking at her mother then, understanding that her mother knew more than she had told. Lights flickered in the dusk in the trailers, and in some of the houses across the heath. People were still streaming away down the hill, shadowy groups now; small boys looked wistfully for elephants still, there was the smell of animals; somewhere there was the smell of woodsmoke. Great patterns of cloud formed in the vast sky that darkened above Blackheath and again a lion roared, incongruous there, and yet not.

In the silence, just afterwards, the little clown said, 'You mean Popka.'

'Yes,' said Mrs O'Brien. Pauline stared at her mother.

'Well zen you know,' said Zarko. ' 'E iz of courze not 'ere. And 'e doz not want to see 'iz familee, none of you. They . . . shamed him.'

Mrs O'Brien looked surprised and half laughed despite herself. 'Well I suppose you could say he shamed them,' she said.

'Yes,' said the little clown, 'depending on you *point*. You view *point*.' He pronounced the word in the French way giving the sentence an exotic quality.

'Where is he then? Isn't he still with the circus?'

'Are you 'is familee? You are one of 'eez seesters I suppose?'

'No,' said Mrs O'Brien.

'Yes, yes,' said Pauline, 'we are part of his family, we *are*.'

' 'E doz not wish to see 'iz familee,' said the clown and his mouth was quite tight beneath the painted red smile as he walked away in the dusk. The sequinned woman went into her caravan and closed the door.

After a little while, Mrs O'Brien and her daughter Pauline turned away from the caravans and walked across the heath to a pub where Mrs O'Brien bought a large brandy for herself and a small one for her daughter.

'I expect he decided not to come back to England,' said Mrs O'Brien, sitting back at last, drinking her brandy with relief. 'With the circus, I mean. He might have thought it was dangerous still, and he was probably right – look at the Profumo case and Stephen Ward and that lot, it's still not safe for queers in England. Why should he go through all that again?'

Her daughter sat pale and silent, staring at nothing.

Mrs O'Brien sighed, sat forward in the wooden chair again and spoke quietly, first flicking her eyes round the pub. 'Listen Pauline. You wanted to go through with this, not me. I told you about him. I told you he was a queer. I didn't really want to tell you all the rest; you young people think sex is all love and stuff. Do you know anything about queers?'

'Of course I do.'

'Do you know anything *about* them?'

'Like what?' said Pauline defensively, thinking of Harry Donaldson from her class at the Academy. His classmates from the class of '59 whispered about him, thought he was probably a queer but they liked him, no one disliked him. 'I know one,' she said. 'I know all about that.'

Her mother sighed. 'Yes yes, and you think you're very open-minded, but I wonder if you know how things are for them really, it's not easy for them, not even now, and it certainly wasn't for Roger. It's illegal you know; you can go to jail. What I didn't tell you was soon after you were born he got arrested for soliciting. In a public lavatory. In Piccadilly Circus actually. It was horrible and sordid, put his cock through a hole or something, and it got in the papers and his family got to hear about it and there was a terrible to-do, his father had been made a Sir for something and as they couldn't hush it up they disowned him and wouldn't help and your father – I mean Ronnie, your stepfather if you want – he's a –' she searched for the right words '– a man who does what he thinks is right you know Pauly, even if he is disapproving with it. Anyway, he thought he should help Roger because Roger was your father, and so he found the bail for him. He borrowed the money. But Roger skipped the bail and went to Paris. We had a very difficult time for a while but . . .' Mrs O'Brien sighed. 'I don't blame him, not really. It was horrible and sordid and he would've had a terrible time in prison, poor chap, no I didn't blame him at all,' and she sat back in her seat again, exhausted by all the talk, her glass already almost empty. But she saw the white face of her illegitimate daughter Pauline turned away in pain and something else that might or might not have been disgust.

'Listen love, listen, he paid the money back finally. One day years later we get this parcel from France, just ordinary, through the post, and you know what it's full of? French francs – almost double the money he owed us for the bail. That's how we had those two French holidays when you were at school. And a long letter about the circus and about the clowns and how he was the one who could calm the chimpanzees and how he was sometimes allowed to fly on the trapeze and how he called himself not Roger Popham any more but Popka and about his friends in the circus and one was called – I remember because it was such a funny name – Zarko. Well, at least you met Zarko. He didn't want to know us, did he?' She emptied her glass quickly. 'So there you are. You wanted to have a romantic hero for a father and who was I to stop you?'

Still Pauline said nothing.

Mrs O'Brien added kindly, 'He was a kind man.'

'Did he ask about me?' said Pauline in a small voice, 'in the letter?'

'Well, I expect he did,' said Mrs O'Brien expansively, getting out her purse to buy another drink.

Very soon after this Sunday afternoon, Pauline was named as the Most Promising Newcomer in the West End Theatre for the Year 1964. Very soon after that Anthony Bonham, her first lover, made her pregnant. Unmarried pregnancies were still shameful; they had to try and hide it from her stepfather, so quickly got married. The play ran on in the West End, a huge success, but of course Pauline had to leave the job that had meant so much to her as soon as her pregnancy showed.

She never mentioned her father again.

She was now, over thirty years later, rich and elegant, and still very beautiful. The wary, gangly movement of her body had long ago developed into a cool stylish sophistication. She owned a thriving antique business in Chiswick and she enjoyed the work in a way; she still did the odd acting job though Anthony kept reminding her it wasn't necessary, they didn't need the money.

And she knew, because she had found out the hard way, about her husband's infidelities.

Over the years, if she felt her life had turned out differently from the way she had planned, no one ever knew. She perfected that art of hiding her feelings.

She wore her mask.

But the real reason she didn't go to the reunion of the class of '59 that day was because she didn't want to think about – but when she looked out across her garden in her blue dressing gown that Saturday morning had been so suddenly, piercingly reminded of – the days when she had found the laughter and the warmth again, when she told everybody her real father flew on a trapeze in a circus in another country, and life waited for her then, unbreakable.

She did not know that the reunion would change her life forever.

THREE

At the door of the old building, as they kissed, embracing awkwardly the way old lovers sometimes do, Molly McKenzie smelt that he'd been drinking too. She wondered if he could smell her vodka and pulled away, looked up at him, gave a little tinkling laugh.

'How well you look darling,' she said.

But what she saw was his expensively cut but thinning hair and the bags under his eyes and the lines on his face, the things time does.

Anthony Bonham smiled down at her, at her cleverly dyed blonde hair, the good figure she had kept, her exotic green dress. 'You look just the same Molly darling,' he said, remembering. His eyes flickered for a split second to where a taxi drew up beside them, flickered back to Molly again when some old grey-haired woman he didn't know got out.

'Just the same,' he said again, looking at Molly's face,

looking at her mouth, his eyes lingering there, remembering. Then he seemed to pull himself together. 'Let's go in and get it over with,' he said. 'Jesus it's hot, Jesus I need a drink,' and he took Molly's arm, whether to support her or comfort himself she could not tell, and they entered the building.

The grey-haired old woman, who was actually fifty-four, paid off the taxi, saw Anthony Bonham and Molly McKenzie disappear into the old building, stood alone on the pavement, staring up at the carved stone figures of comedy and tragedy over the doorway. She closed her eyes; she was so assailed by memory she almost fell. But she breathed deeply, as she had learned to do and then opened her eyes again. *London Academy of Drama 1897* was chiselled into the old stone. If she was fifty-four, so were all the others, more or less – slightly older in fact because she had been the youngest. But she had not dyed her hair nor had her teeth capped nor bought a house in Portugal or France. She had lived somewhere very different and just for a moment, remembering, she closed her eyes again at the weight of all the changes.

'*Nicky*? Oh my God, I'm sure it is, but I – it can't be – is it . . .?' and the voice wavered for a moment, unsure, ended the sentence on a nervous note, '. . . Nicky?'

The old lady opened her eyes and saw Juliet Lyall, one of England's most well-known, best loved, actresses. Standing there, pale, in the sunshine.

'It *is* you Nicky,' said Juliet, her voice shaking very slightly. 'My God – it *is* you.'

'Yes,' said the old woman after a slight pause. That unforgettable voice. 'It is me.' And just for a moment the two women stared at each other and between them something flickered, almost tangible on the air, something there in the midday sun on the shimmering hot pavement in the unseasonable London heatwave.

More taxis, more voices, more cries of greeting and recognition. Someone called Juliet's name.

'Juliet, Juliet, saw you in *The Seagull* you were wonderful darling.'

Juliet waved vaguely at the taxis, turned back.

'How – how are you Nicky?' she said uncertainly to the old woman.

'As you see me.'

'What I mean is . . .' Juliet's voice faltered again and then came out in a rush. 'Nicky why on earth are you *here*?'

'It's a reunion.' The voice that Juliet Lyall knew – had known – so well. Dark and smoky, like autumn. It had sat oddly, and memorably, on a young girl of seventeen.

'But . . . I never thought for one moment – I mean, I didn't expect . . .' Juliet's voice fell away.

'No,' said the old woman. 'No, I don't suppose you did.' She stared up again at the carved stone figures.

Voices called *Juliet, Juliet*. Juliet looked trapped. 'We'd better . . .'

'Yes,' said the old lady, and it was a sigh rather than a word. 'Let's go in and get it over with.'

'Oh Juliet's gone in, she could've waited, there's no point in her being grand with us.' Frances Kitson's make-up was a little heavy perhaps but immaculate, certainly not put on in a long mirror from middle distance; her yellow linen dress was cut to reveal her magnificent bosom although she had finally decided it wasn't necessary today to wear the padded bra and startle the people who used to know her. She caught at something on the dress with her manicured nails, careful not to let her rings snag the material and her auburn hair fell forward, shone in the sunshine.

Her best friend, Emmy Louise Brown, who had no bosom at all and was dressed in blue as instructed by Frances earlier, was made up in exactly that same immaculate way. But for Emmy Lou the make-up couldn't cover any longer the way her skin drooped slightly, the way her mouth turned down at the corners in disappointment, or despair.

'Why ever did we come?' said Emmy Lou in her blue dress as she too stared up at the carved stone figures. 'Back here after all these years – what's the point?'

'We agreed on the phone Em, you never know who you might meet,' said Frances firmly, 'we agreed Em. Oh look, oh look, for God's sake are my eyes deceiving me? Look it's *Terence*!' And Terence Blue, in his red con-vertible BMW, cruised slowly towards them.

'Terence,' they cried joyfully waving their arms, like gaily coloured birds on the pavement, '*Terence*!' And leant upon each other for a moment, giggling like the young girls they once were, like the young girls they were when they first knew Terence Blue.

The red car pulled up beside them, motor still run-ning, and Terence gave them his famous, wide film-star smile, his amazing eyes crinkled, he pushed at his grey-ing but thick and curly hair.

'It is actually being held here is it?' he called to them. 'I wasn't sure.'

'Well of course darling,' cried Frances, 'where else did you think?'

'I didn't know if the place was still standing!' he said, 'OK, I'll just go and park,' and Terence waved again and roared off round a corner into a side-street.

'He's still driving a red one I see,' said a voice dryly behind them. 'You know what they say about men who drive red convertibles. God my darlings isn't it hot, who'd believe it was the end of August! I phoned you Frances but you must've already left—'

'You said you'd phone at ten Harry,' interrupted Frances crossly. 'I've been talking to your answering machine all morning.'

'Yes I know darling, sorry, but I didn't get to bed till five.'

'You know we hate it when you're unreliable, Emmy Lou and I wanted to be escorted by you.'

'I am here after all to do that,' he said reasonably, 'even with a fierce and throbbing hangover of magister-ial proportions,' and Harry Donaldson gave both women such a woeful grimace that Frances and Emmy Lou both smiled at him and kissed him, Frances mutter-ing *unreliable old queen* into his ear.

'Oh what do we all *look* like after all these years!' cried Harry melodramatically, 'and in this *heat*.' He put out both his arms, exaggerated, theatrical. 'Come on my dar-lings, one arm each, The Three Stooges, let's get it over with,' and the three of them walked up the stone steps and into the building.

A short, rather overweight woman whose name was Izzy Fields arrived, perspiring slightly, on a bicycle. She locked it to the railings outside, ran up the steps taking off her safety helmet, thinking with pleasure of seeing everyone again. The helmet had pulled her short brown hair upwards and she looked like a middle-aged pixie.

Inside it was cooler and dark. Students passed, running up the stairs, calling, laughing, already perhaps sounding slightly exaggerated as out of the corner of their eyes they surveyed the old people coldly; their eyes lit up, however, as Terence Blue walked in the door.

'It's *Terence Blue*!' they whispered to each other.

'Up to the third floor, to the Music Room,' somebody said and the visitors, who had once owned these corridors, stepped meekly into the lift or began walking up the old winding staircase. They passed young people: with trainers or tapshoes slung round their necks, with books in their hands, wearing crinolines, wearing tights, wearing corsets – for nothing looked out of the ordinary here; young people, *young* people. Just beginning.

Emmy Lou Brown stared at two pretty, laughing girls on the second staircase who almost danced by, oblivious, trailing rather grubby Victorian petticoats.

'I could tell them a thing or two,' Emmy Lou said as she stared, turning, watching them running down the stairs. Harry, who knew her so well, nudged her in exasperation. But when he saw the odd expression on her face, a kind of envy, a kind of pity, he only said gently, 'They have to learn it themselves Em.'

'Emmy, Emmy!' a voice called. They looked over the bannisters and saw Izzy Fields running up the stairs carrying her yellow helmet, smiling at them all.

'Oh look it's dear old Izzy, she must've come on her bike,' they all said, and smiled too.

On the third floor, along a dark mahogany corridor from the stairs, there was a blackboard outside the Music Room on which someone had written WELCOME TO THE CLASS OF '59. There were a lot of them: there had been two new intakes each term during 1959. The room was already full of people wearing name-tags who laughed and talked very loudly. The tinkle of glasses and the tinkle of laughter was almost, after a while, indivisible. When Terence Blue made his entrance there was a slightly perceptible hush for a moment and then voices cried *Hello Terence, Hi Terence* and the noise rose again. Terence Blue smilingly waved away his name-tag because Terence Blue was the most famous of them all. He was a film star: his latest film, *Diversions*, a trendy sexy Hollywood thriller, was on in cinemas all over the world; he was rich, he was famous, he had made it, completely. He most certainly didn't need a name-tag pinned about his person.

Molly McKenzie, who still stood with Anthony Bonham, held a glass of wine. She wondered if the wine would mix with the large vodka she'd given herself courage with, fanned herself with the *List of Students* as she watched Terence Blue's entrance, and then said very quietly so that only Anthony could hear, yet her voice was wistful rather than flippant, 'Think of this Tony: that wonderful stud of our youth can't do it any more.'

Anthony looked at Molly in surprise, wondering if he'd understood her correctly but just at that moment he was accosted by someone whose name he couldn't remember.

'Hello *darling*,' he said heartily.

Molly drifted off to talk to somebody else, stretched for another glass of wine from the first year student who was acting, today at least (and probably many more days, thought Molly wryly), as a waitress.

Terence Blue saw Molly, came across, kissed her and she saw a look in his eyes – a question; wished she had not spoken like that to Anthony; kissed him back and then just for a moment rested her hand on his cheek. *It's all right darling, of course it is*. Almost at once he was dragged away.

But some drinks later Anthony Bonham came back looking for Molly, took her arm so that – he knew – his hand touched the side of her breast.

'What did you mean?' he said, and Molly knew what he was asking her, knew both things he was asking her.

'I was just joking,' she said, shrugging, moving away from him imperceptibly. But Anthony, who had once known her very well, looked at her carefully.

'No you weren't,' he said 'I know you Molly.' And Anthony Bonham, who had been jealous of Terence Blue for thirty-six years, smiled to himself with pleasure, to think that Terence Blue had problems.

And then he looked hard again at Molly. 'And I

wonder how you would know about it Ms McKenzie.' He moved his hand from under Molly's arm and brushed it now, as if accidently in the crowd, across her breast under the thin green silk dress. For a split second through the thin material they were aware of each other like electricity: he could feel the warmth of her breast, she could feel the warmth of his hand and quite suddenly her nipple hardened. She breathed in quickly, sharply, and then moved away at once. He swallowed suddenly. Molly saw it, knew it: memory and desire

'That dress is disgusting,' he said and tried to smile. And then he said very quietly, and his voice shook slightly, 'Could we go somewhere?'

Molly's eyes were unreadable. 'I have an appointment,' she said and she turned away. But then, somehow unable to stop herself, she added, even as, turning back, she saw again the lines under his eyes and his thinning hair, 'Call me some time, all the same. It's still the number you used to have engraved on your heart.'

Izzy Fields, the cyclist, of course saw Terence Blue's entrance too. Remembered the shining boy with the amazing eyes that all the girls fell in love with, including Izzy Fields who had never to this day forgotten that Terence had kissed her several times on these very Academy stairs one night when she was looking woebegone when the cast lists went up on the noticeboard and she was playing old ladies, as usual. *Cheer up Izzy you'll come into your own later in life, you'll see* he had said and he had kissed her and then, to her immense surprise, kissed her again, harder, meaning it. And because, in the hot, stuffy smoky Music Room that afternoon Izzy was watching him so closely, she saw two things that Molly McKenzie did not. She saw Terence Blue and Harry Donaldson greet each other: they simply put their arms around each other, stood there quite still for a moment in the crowded room, and then parted without saying a single word.

How odd thought Izzy and she felt tears prickling at the back of her eyes without quite knowing why.

And then a few minutes later she saw Terence coming face to face with the famous actress Juliet Lyall who was the talk of London for her performance in *The Seagull.*

She saw Terence and Juliet stop abruptly. And then they both gave an odd, cold, inclination of the head (as if to say: *I see you*) and passed on again, into the crowd.

What a shame, thought Izzy, *she was his girlfriend once, they were engaged even, it seems a shame they can't speak to each other, after all these years, at a nice reunion like this.*

The grey-haired old woman was unused to crowds, felt deeply disoriented to be in the old building again, slipped out of the Music Room. It had been such an effort to get this far; she must stay calm now. She walked along the dark corridor towards the staircase so that the noise drifted away behind her, so that the beating of her heart slowed a little. She came face to face unexpectedly with the Honours Board and looked quickly away, moved away even, then very slowly turned back again. Her eyes reluctantly found the date. And there it was, under the stage name she'd assumed at the Academy, not her real name:

The Henry Irving Award for Excellence
Awarded to the Best Student 1961: Nicola Abbott

She started slightly as two students came out of a class-
room carrying a clutch of painted masks, some weeping,
some smiling, some blank-faced, all the faces huddled
together in the students' arms.

'And he said – you know – we will find it much – you
know – harder, that we'll have to use our bodies much
more when we wear masks, that we are too used – you
know – to sort of relying on our faces, on our facial
expressions, that wearing masks will teach us control . . .'
The voices passed her, enthusiastic, young; on the stairs
a mask dropped, smiled upwards, was retrieved, disappeared with the students round the big bend in the
staircase.

'You chose Abbott as a surname so that you'd always
be at the top if a cast list was in alphabetical order.'

Nicky didn't turn, recognised Juliet Lyall's voice
again; Juliet had followed her down the dark corridor.
She answered carefully. 'I liked Budd Abbott and Lou
Costello, you remember.'

'But you didn't choose Costello,' said Juliet.

'No.' Still Nicky didn't turn. 'And Nicola, Nicky.
Nicky seems to be the name of such a young person,
doesn't it? Not someone who looks like me. When I
chose it instead of Mary I never considered I would be
old one day.'

Juliet said nothing, could not bear to answer, and after
a minute Nicky added in the smoky, broken voice, and
Juliet could not tell whether she was joking or serious,

'Weren't we lucky – in what other profession can people change their names with such extraordinary impunity?'

Still Juliet remained silent, simply unable to speak. And something else: some other, unexpected feeling lurked there, around her, beside her.

She was afraid.

There was silence except for the voices and the laughter at the other end of the long corridor. Finally Juliet said, 'Nicky – I'm sorry, I just don't know what to say, how to make proper conversation, it is so extraordinary to – to see you here.'

'Yes,' said Nicky, 'I expect it is.' Still she looked up at the Honours Board, the place with her name; she did not look at Juliet Lyall. All her strength was needed to remain where she was, to remain calm, not to run away. She held one hand with the other, to stop the trembling.

'Nicky – I can't stay long, I've got a matinée but – please – we've got to meet, we've got to talk, my God how could I possibly imagine you'd be at something like this, will you come to my house, or – I don't understand, are you living in London? I mean – could I come to see you? Could I Nicky?'

Then at last the grey-haired woman turned to face the beautiful woman of a certain age (she would be fifty-six, Nicky knew) who stood beside her: Juliet Lyall, one of the renowned and respected actresses of her generation.

'No,' said Nicky simply. And then she looked at Juliet with a small, strange smile on her face. 'Tell me Juliet,' she said, 'what would we talk about?'

And she walked away, further down the dark corridor.

Juliet Lyall remained, motionless, under the Honours Board. She was shaking.

A group of people spilled out of the Music Room laughing, saw Juliet, called *Juliet there you are Juliet darling saw you in* The Seagull *you were marvellous darling, simply marvellous,* and finally Juliet walked back towards the voices.

There was no sign of an old lady; like the smiling, crying and blank-faced masks she had disappeared.

The Academy principal, who had enthusiastically welcomed the class of '59 (though he was a keen, young, new administrator rather than a thespian, and not of their era), announced from the raised platform at the end of the room that he thought it would be a good idea if Terence Blue, their most illustrious graduate, said a few words. Several actors groaned quietly.

Terence, who had had several drinks, finished another one and then stepped up on to the platform. He smiled his famous smile at his audience and launched into a story about their youth. He charmed them into listening, even those who didn't want to: he had a sort of self-deprecating humour that made people smile back at him, despite themselves.

Standing near, listening, transfixed, was the woman in the purple dress who had anonymously phoned his answering machine from the Dorchester Hotel so early that morning. When he had arrived in the Music Room she had pulled at his arm and smiled and smiled and said in her little girl's voice *Remember me?*

Terence spoke easily, used to telling stories,

reminding them of their first day at the Academy in 1959 and making them laugh.

Then out of the corner of his eye he saw Nicola Abbott standing by the door, looking at him.

He was so utterly thrown he simply stopped speaking, and even as he stopped, the old woman was gone. So that Terence stood there, his mouth open, staring in amazement at an empty doorway.

He was a little drunk, certainly, but he had that immense charm and he was infinitely experienced at impromtu public speaking. He recovered, found his thread, brought his few words to a hasty conclusion.

Smiling his famous smile, he pushed his way through the people, constrained by colleagues wanting to say hello, not seeing the woman in the purple dress looking puzzled, not seeing the white face of Juliet Lyall; pushing past faster and faster smiling still, to get to the door. But there was nobody there along the dark corridor, nobody at all. He ran down the flights of stairs two at a time, stumbling and running down and down to the front door.

There was no old lady in the bright, sunny street; nobody.

'Terence my dear fellow, you're not *leaving*? You can't *leave*, you are our star turn.'

Terence Blue turned back from the sunshine, blinking into the dark foyer and into his mind came the words that had haunted him for over thirty years.

He doesn't know the meaning of love.

He looked like a man who had seen a ghost.

*

Molly McKenzie and Juliet Lyall inadvertently left the reunion together, early, Juliet to go to her matinée of *The Seagull*, Molly to meet her lover.

'You look good, Molly,' said Juliet quickly as they came down the old winding stairs. 'I like that green dress. How are you? Haven't seen you for ages. You're in a soap opera aren't you? That must be fun.' She felt so disoriented after talking to Nicky Abbott, then seeing Terence rush out of the Music Room, that she hardly knew what she was saying.

'I loved *The Seagull*,' said Molly not answering her directly. 'I was there on the first night.' They both blinked in surprise as they came through the dark foyer and out into the bright afternoon sunshine. Someone tooted, someone leaving, or arriving. They both waved, rather short-sightedly.

'Did you see Nicky Abbott?' said Molly. 'I didn't recognise her, not at first, she was so – so old I suppose I was thinking, though she was younger than any of us, of course. It was just such a . . . shock after all these years. And there seemed to be something wrong with her shoulder. But I heard her voice and knew it was her; I've never forgotten her voice.'

'Was she there? Really?' said Juliet. 'I didn't notice.' And in her mind, over and over, *Why was she there? Why was Nicky Abbott there?*

They walked along the pavement and the afternoon shimmered.

When they had left drama school Molly and Juliet had both, like Emmy Lou Brown and Izzy Fields and Pauline O'Brien and Frances Kitson, gone straight into repertory companies in the provinces: Liverpool, Manchester, Salisbury, Worthing, York, Ipswich, Birmingham, Newcastle, Edinburgh. They criss-crossed their country by train, knew the times of every late-night train in the timetable, *we could get jobs on the railways as speaking timetables*, Frances had said, *we know more about train times than the engine drivers*. Molly and Juliet had played good big leads. Sometimes they even played the same parts even though they were different types of actresses: once they had both played Juliet in different theatres at exactly the same time because *Romeo and Juliet* was on the school curriculum; they met on a train and compared notes.

They both did so well, both soon joined the big national companies, a kind of equal battle – until Juliet's film-producer father got his daughter the part in *The Red Dress*.

The battle was not equal, after all.

'Is soap opera fun?' Juliet continued, trying to make normal conversation as they walked along.

'No Juliet, it's not much fun,' said Molly. 'You have to work too fast for it to be fun,' and they slowed down at the corner. 'Do you know that for most TV jobs now you don't even rehearse? You don't even have a read-through. I've almost forgotten the joy of the work, the reason I started, that wonderful day after day concentration on a play, rehearsing a part, trying to make it work, and how I loved it. Nowadays all the young actors arrive with their part prepared, their performance ready, Thatcher's children desperate to succeed, well who can blame them, no time to try and fail for a day or

two. There's a kind of – I don't know . . .' Molly fumbled
for the right words '. . . a coarsening of the creative
spirit, of the thing we loved. Or so I find it,' she finished wistfully.

Juliet, who had had eight weeks' rehearsal with one of
the best directors in the country and a short provincial
tour before *The Seagull* opened in the West End to critical
judgement, appeared not to hear. She looked at her
watch. 'I think I'd better take a cab to the theatre, may I
give you a lift somewhere?'

Molly shook her head. 'No thanks, I've got my car.'

A taxi cruised by on the other side of the road. Juliet
hailed it, dodged the traffic, turned back and waved to
Molly, got in and gave the driver the name of the theatre
in Shaftsbury Avenue. She sat back in relief, breathing
deeply *in and out in and out*, calming her heart *in and out
in and out*. At last she felt her heart beating more slowly.
She had two shows to do: full houses, of course. She
would be fine.

But as the taxi inched through summer Saturday
shoppers in ridiculous shorts and flimsy tops, spilling
with their parcels on to the streets, she could not control
her thoughts. *After over thirty years why would she have
come back to the Academy? What did she want?* And her
heart, that depository of so many emotions both public
and private, gave another lurch of anxiety. They passed
a huge poster for Terence Blue's latest film, *Diversions*,
with Terence smiling out, and Juliet turned away
sharply.

At the theatre she stared briefly at the huge famous
photograph of herself outside, smiled at the stage

doorman, collected her mail, went quickly to her dressing room, the Number One dressing room. She locked
the door, turned on the fan, took off her dress, lay on the
floor as she always did, her feet on a wooden chair, a
book under her head. She breathed slowly in and out,
filling her lungs, her rib-cage, her abdomen and, as she
had been taught, her groin. *In and out in and out in and out*
she felt the air in her body, around her body. She calmed
her heart; she had to calm her heart. She prepared herself.

Under the shower she sang sounds that actors sing:
MAHNAHLAH MAYNAYLAY BIDIGA PITIKA
BIDIGA PITIKA. Out of the shower she sang on, using
her voice carefully, knowing how much to use, how
much to extend. She tried always to be early at the
theatre so she could have this preparation time and was
often already made up as younger actors ran up the
stairs almost late for the half-hour call. Soon her dresser
would knock at the door and the wig dresser would
bring in the wig, and actors would pop their heads
politely round the door and say good afternoon. In their
own dressing rooms they would moan about the heat,
exchange gossip and news, glad it was Saturday, off
tomorrow.

In front of her make-up mirror, Juliet breathed in
deeply again. She always went over the first lines of the
play, of any play she was in, as she put on her make-up.
It always calmed her, put her into the mood of the play.
She put cream on her face, removing the make-up from
the day, removing the day. Some of her first lines as the
actress Arkadina were from *Hamlet*:

'O Hamlet, speak no more,
Thou turn'st mine eyes into my very soul;
And there I see such black and grained spots
As will not leave their tinct.'

Saying the lines as she always did, she suddenly heard them differently. A shiver ran up her spine, pulled suddenly and sharply at her neck. She forced herself to breathe again, *in and out in and out in and out*, she must not think of Nicky Abbott now, *in and out*, she had seized her chance with both hands – that was all, *in and out in and out*. She automatically smiled very widely at herself in the mirror, combining the smile with a mouth exercise that stretched the lips. She breathed deeply again *in and out in and out in and out*. As for Terence Blue, she never thought of him, never never *never*.

And finally, in the Number One dressing room, as the Deputy Stage Manager at last called, 'Five minutes to the matinée performance, ladies and gentlemen, five minutes please,' as the sound of the audience chattering, excited, came over the tannoy; then finally, getting ready for a performance, all the anxieties and the outside fears dropped away. She loved her work more than anything else in the world. This was her place; this was her work: nothing else mattered.

She was an Actress.

By 3.30 pm, even though the invitation had said 12.30–2.30, the Music Room at the London Academy of Drama was still crowded, but the drink was just beginning to run out. Terence Blue still had a little group around him, seemed very drunk, seemed slightly manic even, as he retold stories about himself with Robert Shaw and Richard Burton and Albert Finney and Anthony Hopkins in Hollywood, *us Brits taking the piss* as he described it.

Anthony Bonham swayed away in disgust, at the same time managing to appropriate one of the last, half-empty, bottles of wine. He'd looked everywhere for Molly, he wanted to talk to her again, but she was nowhere to be seen. He sat down, rather more abruptly than he'd meant to, beside Harry Donaldson and Izzy Fields, who had parked themselves on the floor by a tall, open French window.

'Jesus it's just so fucking hot,' sighed Anthony, stretching out his long legs, 'give us your glass you little pervert, how are you? Haven't seen you since that TV series, what're you doing? Oh hi Izzy,' almost as an afterthought.

'Hello Anthony,' said Izzy, smiling warmly at him. She knelt up for a moment, craning her head around a corner to check that her bicycle was still chained to the railings, then settled back again on to the floor.

'Well luvvie,' said Harry, 'I've come out of *Les Mis* at last, hallelujah, never never again, not for all the money in the world, you can't hear that music every night for a year without going bonkers. And, strange as it may seem, I've got a lead in a new – ah – literary TV adaptation,' and Anthony and Izzy both laughed because it wasn't strange at all.

'Jane Austen or Charles Dickens or George Eliot?' asked Anthony, and Harry grinned. He had cornered the market almost in slightly roué British eccentrics of days gone by, *the Tory nostalgia market* he called it. Old ladies were always accosting him in the street.

'Thomas Hardy this time,' he said, 'but before that thank God I'm off to Morocco soon for a fortnight's holiday. What about yourself?'

'I'm at Stratford,' said Anthony, affronted.

'Oh God yes of course, good reviews, really good – I read them Tony, congratulations, you're playing Iago aren't you?'

'*And* Claudius,' said Anthony stiffly.

'Of course, Claudius, of course – I knew, I knew, it just slipped my mind. What's that new young chap like, playing Hamlet?'

'Middling,' said Anthony. 'He's got a lot to learn.'

'Ah,' said Harry, nodding wisely (thinking that playing Hamlet to Anthony's King might have its drawbacks for a young actor).

'No *voice*,' said Anthony. 'Young people coming into the business can't do it, they can't speak Standard English properly, they don't know how to use their voices in a big space; they mumble for telly and then they think they can do that on stage.'

'Ah,' said Harry.

'Still, no performance tonight, that's the joy of repertoire,' and Anthony let the remains of the bottle trickle down his throat. Then he stared at the empty bottle gloomily and gave a huge sigh. 'Do you notice the smell of this place?' he said, dissatisfied, perplexed. 'I've always heard that smells can distill memory somehow, in some subtle way, but when Molly and I walked in the door I swear that smell of furniture polish and cabbage hit me in the stomach like it was 1959 again and all the rest hadn't happened, nothing subtle about it. How utterly depressing.' He shook his head.

'The smell of your youth,' said Harry. 'We're the older generation now, it's hard to believe isn't it?'

'We are not old, we are in our prime,' said Anthony, 'only people who've been unhappy in their youth grab at old age the way you do, welcoming it.'

'I wasn't quite welcoming it,' said Harry wryly, 'just mentioning it. Anyway I'm a character actor, I've been old since I was young.'

'That's not the point. *We are not old!*' Anthony's face had become quite red. 'I'm playing Iago; Iago is not old.'

'In the terms of his time you could definitely call him menopausal,' said Harry mildly, 'worrying about where he's got in the world, jealous, feeling his life a failure, someone else getting the job he wanted, maybe even sexually . . . and of course, as for Claudius—'

'Shut up Harry,' said Anthony shortly. He looked away, felt for a new cigarette packet, fumbled with the cellophane. 'Why the fuck did we come?' He moved his body, turned, trying to feel some movement of air on his face from the open French window, looked out over the rooftops and the chimney pots that shimmered in the sweltering London afternoon.

Izzy, sitting beside them on the floor, looked bemused. 'But isn't it nice to see everyone, see how they've got on?'

Both Anthony and Harry looked at her almost guiltily. They'd forgotten she was there.

'It's nice to see *you* Izzy,' said Harry and even Anthony smiled for a moment.

'Yes it is Izzy,' he said, 'what are you doing? Are you working?'

Izzy smiled at them both, but not self-consciously.

'I do get by,' she said. 'I don't get the big jobs like the rest of you; I was never as good as you – no I wasn't,' as Harry seemed about to interrupt. 'I know I looked – sort of – middle-aged, even when I was young, and I wasn't nearly as good as someone like Emmy Lou, or Molly or Juliet, but I do work you know, I just seem to go from job to job. I'm understudying at the National now and playing small parts – and I love it, I feel privileged to be in this profession, I *love* my work, I do really.' She stopped, pink-cheeked.

Anthony and Harry smiled back at Izzy, it was impossible not to. But both of them were thinking that if they were doing what she was doing they would have committed suicide or become insurance salesmen long ago.

Anthony poked at the empty bottle as if to conjure more wine out of it and then rolled it along the floor. 'Do you know,' he said, 'I thought for a moment I saw Nicky Abbott, but when I looked again of course it wasn't her.'

The glass slipped from Harry Donaldson's hand. It didn't break, the remains of his wine dribbled across the floorboards.

'What is it Harry?' said Izzy.

But Harry only shook his head, felt for his handkerchief, dabbed at the spilt wine. 'Sorry,' he said shortly. He looked quickly around the crowded room. And then, recovering, though Izzy heard anger in his voice, he said,

'Nicky Abbott was the best actress I ever saw.'

'I always remember her voice,' said Izzy, 'all smoky and strange and dark.'

'I wonder whatever happened to her,' said Anthony. 'She made that one film, *Heartbreak*, that should have made her a star for life and then she just disappeared off the face of the earth.' He looked up just at that moment and saw Frances and Emmy Lou coming towards them. 'Oh dear,' he said, 'the menopause twins,' but dryly to Harry, knowing they were his best friends. 'Hi darlings,' he said aloud.

'They're your age exactly Tony,' said Harry.

'Who is?' said Frances, 'God isn't it hot!' She and Emmy Lou plonked themselves down on the floor by the big open window with the others. Frances' large bosom wobbled, then settled. 'God he is charm incarnate of course but he does go on, that Terence, what's the *matter* with him today? He's not just ordinarily drunk, he sounds as if he's on something – he's telling stories like a man possessed. He doesn't have to do that here, poor thing. He forgets we know him.' She stared across at Terence. 'Who's that blonde woman in that extraordinary purple dress hanging on to his arm, don't we know her from somewhere?'

'Oh my God,' said Emmy Lou, 'look – it's that one who couldn't act, with the little-girl voice, you know, that American who thought she was Judy Garland.'

Izzy followed her gaze. 'Oh that's Simone Taylor,' she said, 'yes, don't you remember she was in our class, she used to be in love with Terence, don't you remember? Don't you remember that time he wouldn't go with her to dinner to meet her parents who were over from New York and she lay down on the staircase and wept and banged on the bannister with her stiletto heel and screamed: I LOVE TERENCE, I LOVE TERENCE?'

Frances' infectious laugh echoed round the room. 'The one who used to sing Judy Garland songs kind of leaning on the piano? Is that her? Damn I haven't got my glasses.'

'That's her. She'd seen *The Wizard of Oz* and *Easter Parade* and *A Star is Born* far far too often,' said Emmy, grinning. 'Still, if she'd hung on in there maybe she could've become a gay icon!'

'Thanks,' said Harry dryly.

Even Anthony was laughing. 'Jesus wept,' he said, 'I remember her, Simone Taylor, she talked like Minnie Mouse.'

'Ssssh,' said Izzy Fields. 'She's now a Cosmetics Executive and lives in New York and is very rich and has two cadillacs.' The others turned to her in astonishment. 'Well, I've been talking to her,' said Izzy rather apologetically, 'well *she*'s been talking to *me* strictly speaking, we didn't discuss my illustrious career. She's fifty-six now, we had birthdays close together I remembered, but she still talks in a little-girl voice; it does sound a bit odd.' And then, because she was a charitable person, Izzy added, 'Very nice hair though, nicely cut and coloured.'

'She's kind of glued herself to Terence,' said Emmy Lou who had the best view through the groups of actors still gathered everywhere, 'like a purple limpet. But he's so drunk now I honestly don't think he's noticed.'

Harry stared across the room at Terence Blue.

It was years since they'd met. But there had been nothing they could say as they had greeted each other earlier, just for a moment caught in their past.

A plump actor stopped to say goodbye loudly, bent down to kiss Frances.

'Who's that?' said Anthony, when he'd finally gone.

'Billy Butler,' said Frances. 'He was in the term ahead of us. He played that animated daffodil for years in those cereal ads; he was telling me earlier he made enough from those adverts to buy a castle in Scotland!' and she began to laugh again. 'Where's Pauline?' she said to Anthony, wiping her eyes. 'She'd have enjoyed all this, she was the only person who could laugh as much as me.'

'Busy,' said Anthony. 'Not that she laughs much these days to my knowledge.'

'That's because she's married to you,' said Harry mildly. 'Has she been working?'

'What, as an actress? No, not much. She's got her antique shop; that keeps her busy.'

'Hmmmm,' said Emmy Lou and she and Frances exchanged glances. Once, long ago, it was Pauline who had been successful, not Anthony.

'Well you can all see her to your hearts' content next weekend,' said Anthony. 'It's the first garden party we've had for years and years. I hope you all got your invitations?'

The others all nodded and Izzy added, 'And I shall cycle.'

'You're quite mad Izzy,' said Anthony, and he lit

another cigarette. 'Viola begged us to have another one because she and all her friends are about to leave drama school and she thinks they all ought to get a chance to *network*, as she calls it, with the help of food and sunshine and wine. She instructed us to ask every casting director in London.'

'God,' said Emmy Lou, 'how can you and Pauline encourage your daughter to enter this profession? It's all about status and stars and exposure now, not talent and training – Princess Diana as Hamlet, mark my words.'

'I know, I know,' said Anthony, 'I *know*. But she wants to do it so much, how could we stop her? I can help her anyway: she'll *have* status – being my daughter will give her status. We all know perfectly well that casting directors look at children of famous actors before they look at other young hopefuls; they're as star-struck as anyone else although they deny it so vehemently,' and he loudly and slanderously recited a litany of youngsters with famous names and what he thought of them, including the young man playing Hamlet. 'And Viola's *good*. She's really good. I can help her. I know people.'

But they sighed, all of them, even for Viola's chances, and Anthony's cigarette smoke hung unmoving in the hot air. For a moment his eyes closed and his head suddenly fell on to his shoulder and then jerked up again. He looked surprised, and then looked at his watch.

'Jesus wept, look at the time,' he said. 'I suppose I ought to get back to Chiswick.' But he didn't move.

Izzy said, 'I've got a matinée at five. Only I don't go on stage till twenty to seven.'

'What play Izzy?' said Harry.

'*The Jew of Malta*. I play a short nun.' The others laughed and stretched and Harry rumpled Izzy's short hair.

Anthony stared into space, unfocused. 'Molly looked good, didn't she. I was surprised how – well actually how young she looked. She looks good, yeah. I hadn't seen her for ages, she looks – good.' And he nodded to himself.

'She does,' said Frances. But everybody was remembering his long, passionate affair with Molly McKenzie years and years ago, soon after he'd married Pauline.

Anthony suddenly pulled himself together. 'There's no wine left, none, not a single sodding drop, can't we get some more somewhere?'

'Maxi's!' cried Frances, 'let's go to Maxi's,' and Anthony cheered up greatly at the thought of the drinking club only five minutes' walk away.

'I'll just come for one drink,' he said.

'I've got to go to work,' sighed Izzy.

It wasn't far really, to the National Theatre by bicycle, and Izzy Fields enjoyed the way her head was clearing as she cycled, the way she made her own small breeze in the heat. She looked ridiculous in her yellow safety helmet, she knew that, but it couldn't be helped; she wanted to arrive at places in one piece. Almost at once she cycled past a huge poster for *Diversions*, Terence's latest film. There he was, the object of her youthful passion, smiling out, just as he'd smiled at her this afternoon at the reunion. The poster gave her immense pleasure: her friends' success gave her immense pleasure.

When she'd cycled down Shaftsbury Avenue earlier that day she had seen outside one of the theatres a wonderful huge award-winning photograph of Juliet Lyall as the actress Arkadina in *The Seagull* – her striking face smiling at her lover as her hand reached out behind her and caught the arm of her son. And on the buses the Royal Shakespeare Company's posters for *Othello* had Anthony Bonham's face, taut and angry, just behind the black and beautiful face of the actor playing Othello.

These were the friends of her youth: she'd known them before they were famous; she knew them, she'd studied with them and she was proud of them; they were the success stories of her profession.

Yet there were many more failures than successes; some people there today hadn't worked as actors for years. One man she'd spoken to, and not remembered, said he bred Alsatians for the Police Force.

But, and Izzy sighed as she pedalled, it was Emmy Lou Brown's bitter, turned-down mouth that bothered her most of all. Izzy had been in the repertory company in Salisbury with Emmy Lou in the sixties, shared digs with her, knew what a good actress she was, how hard she worked. Yet somehow success, or even security, had eluded Emmy, as if she'd wanted it too much to the exclusion of everything else: love, family, any other kind of joy. And yet it *shouldn't* have eluded her: Emmy was a better actress than many other much more successful ones. Izzy thought of Emmy Lou as a casualty of their profession, the cruel profession with the insecurities and terrors and dreams that nobody except actors had any idea about, this well-kept secret of despair.

She suddenly felt so depressed she got off her bike and went into a phone box, pulling a phone card out of her pocket. Her youngest son, Lysander, whom they hadn't planned but who brought them great pleasure, answered, his voice just breaking.

'Hello my love,' she said, 'all right?'

'Yep.'

'Daddy there?'

'Yep.' She heard him shouting 'DAD it's MUM.'

Peter came to the phone. 'Hello Izzy,' he said, 'how was it?'

'It was nice, yes, it was really interesting, seeing everybody again. But I just suddenly felt terribly glad you're a schoolteacher.'

'I'm not very glad at the moment,' he said. 'I'm marking exam papers and I've got toothache in *two* teeth.'

'Put cloves on them,' she said.

'Wouldn't go down well with the Education Board,' he said.

'Ha ha,' said Izzy. 'See you tonight.'

'Is that all?'

'Yep.'

'OK – bye.'

'Bye.' She put down the receiver and got on her bike again. Not quite like being married to Terence Blue. She cycled on but Emmy Lou was still on her mind.

There had been a boy at Salisbury Izzy remembered, in stage management, a handsome dark-haired boy with long eyelashes who had been very very keen on Emmy

Lou, used to watch her different performances from the wings, fascinated. In those days the young actors in the companies were contracted for months and played different parts every fortnight. Emmy Lou had played first Hedda Gabler, then Viola, then made the audience laugh when she played Mae West, then terrified them when she played in a thriller: fortnight after fortnight of good, true, lead performances, learning her trade, practising her craft.

Izzy had learnt her trade too. What she had learnt was that she would never be an actress like Emmy Lou, she wasn't good enough.

But when Izzy (already in love with a shy schoolteacher called Peter, already thinking tremulously of marriage, children, a future) asked Emmy Lou what she thought about the dark-haired boy Emmy had looked impatient. *Of course he's nice Izzy but of course I can't get seriously involved with anyone.* And she had bent over the next play to be learnt.

Izzy, whose heart fluttered with joy and longing when she kissed Peter in dark corners in Salisbury in the night, couldn't understand Emmy Lou. *Because I'm an actress*, said Emmy simply, *and that is all that is important to me. There will be time enough for other things later on.*

But they were already twenty-four, Izzy had thought. *When would later on be?*

An impatient lorry-driver hooted at her at a corner along the Strand. She did what she always did: smiled and rang her bell, a plump middle-aged helmeted lady on a bicycle.

And another deeper, more disturbing thought

haunted her sometimes still: had she fallen in love with Peter so easily, so quickly, *because* she had discovered she would never be the actress she'd once hoped she would be?

It was that kind of profession: it sucked you in, made you hope and dream, then rewarded you with nightmares and jealousies and insecurities. And even if you were really talented it let you down because there were no rules, no exams to tell you that you had passed, that you were qualified – only luck, and how you looked, and who you knew, and where you happened to be.

And most of the time you were frightened. Frightened when you were working that it would all go wrong; frightened when you weren't working that you would never work again. Because this was the most over-crowded profession in the world and no one not in the profession, no one not an actor themselves, really understood the day to day lives and the *waste* of the people who had stood speaking too loudly in the smoky music room, the class of '59.

The River Thames sparkled in the bright afternoon sunshine as Izzy cycled up to Waterloo Bridge. She had expected only to enjoy the reunion; somehow it had thrown her, unsettled her. She got off her bike, stared down the river for a moment, at St Paul's Cathedral, hazy in the distance. It was true what she had said to Anthony and Harry at the reunion: despite everything, she loved her profession. She now, at Britain's National Theatre, sat in on some of the most prestigious rehearsals in the world, always playing a small part, or understudying a couple of the other actresses. And she saw how it was: even in this famous company there were good actors and bad actors. And among those good and bad actors there were the usual Show Business Luvvies as members of her profession had begun to be dismissively called; there were the celebrity appearances and chat shows and scandals in the newspapers.

And sometimes it was the people in the headlines that got the work, not the people who could act.

It was a bit like the Royal Family, mused Izzy. Her profession that had once been so admired had become so unpopular. At the last film and television awards one of the papers instead of praising any actor for a good performance headlined their report: LUVVIES, EGOS ABLAZE.

She got on her bike again to cycle over the bridge but she wasn't concentrating. She wobbled dangerously and a taxi hooted angrily. Automatically she smiled and rang her bell. The taxi-driver gave her two fingers and she calmly gave him two fingers back. The taxi-driver looked shocked.

The real magic, the magic of acting, had nothing to do with luvvies and headlines in the newspapers. The real magic came when something sparked suddenly between director and actor, between actor and actor, between actor and writer: some absolute meeting of minds, some instinct, some miraculous energy; almost always the result, though, of hard, hard work.

And the real, *real* magic came when that was transmitted, as if through a kind of electricity, to the audience. Izzy Fields had seen Emmy Lou Brown do that.

She sighed, got off her bicycle again, chained it to the

side of the bridge, pulling at her blouse that stuck to her back in the heat. Then she plodded down the concrete steps to the ugly concrete South Bank complex and the stage door of the National Theatre and, pulling off her safety helmet, went in through that door: part of the profession that she admired, and respected and loved.

FOUR

All the papers said it was the hottest summer for nearly twenty years. That Saturday afternoon the temperature rose to thirty-five degrees.

The man who owned the discreet boat moored on a little-known tributary of the Thames made a great deal of money from rich Americans. The name of the boat was *Rose II* but the rich Americans, passing the information about the boat amongst themselves, called it *The Little Love Boat*.

Bud Martin, the Oscar-winning American film director, and Waylon Jones, a less successful American television director, had both been working in London. Yesterday they had hired the discreet boat for two days and would have one more meal on board later before Bud flew back from London to Los Angeles that evening. They had both brought young girls along: the girls, tanned and lithe and, of course, beautiful, lay on the deck in their bikinis and dark glasses in the hot afternoon sunshine.

The men had not seen each other for many years. They had come across each other in a restaurant in London; had spent most of yesterday, when they arrived on board, locked in the cabins with the large beds and the mirrors on the ceilings and the girls. Now the two men sat in the shade on the other side of the deck from the girls, talked, drank chilled white burgundy; the girls were out of earshot. The boat moved gently in the water, sometimes pulled a little against a rope; this was a secret part of the river: only long, dry grass almost as far as the eye could see. A waiter stood at the stern of the boat, staring at the water.

The men talked of Harvard where they'd first met, and their youth, as well as business; each had noticed the other was going bald. They stretched their brown Californian legs out in front of them, looked across sometimes at the young girls, lying there. They were both the same age: sixty-one.

'Had dinner with Joseph Wain this week,' said Bud Martin. 'Remember him?'

'One of the Heads of British Commercial Television, right?'

'Yeah. Spent some time at CBS, got a lot of British programmes shown in America in the eighties.'

'Joseph Wain? Have I met him?' And then Waylon laughed suddenly. 'The one with the hair?'

Bud leaned back and stretched. 'Yeah that's him. *Surprised* hair I remember the office girls in CBS used to call it. He's cut it off now, looks much like the rest of us.'

'What's he doing?'

'Says he's working on the most exciting television

project he's ever come across. He was a bit cagey, wouldn't tell me too much about it except to say it's international.'

'What, pre-sold to the States?'

'No, I think he was talking much bigger. Pre-sold to the world.'

'What, before it's made?'

'He says.'

'Lucky motherfucker.'

'He says it's the first time he's had people begging to *give* money.'

'Jesus, who's in it? Princess Diana?'

'He said he was hoping for Nelson Mandela.'

'*What?*'

'As himself. It's something big all right.'

'Jesus. Well I hope he's not working with the British fuckwits I'm having to work with.'

'What, your Scottish bride murder thing?'

'Yeah. Ah – the Brits are so *picky*. Just because it's based on a true story. I keep telling them – forget the true story, make them all beautiful people, but they talk about the sensibilities of the people involved, all that crap. What makes them think a murder in Scotland is different from a murder in –' he waved his arm about indiscriminately '– Wyoming? Only the accent is different. Makes me wanna regurgitate, the way they talk, this is show business not life and people wanna see beautiful people not dandruffed losers,' and Waylon leant away from the air to light a cigar, pulled on it, puffed on it till it was alight. Cigar smoke spiralled upwards. 'Finished casting your movie?'

Bud Martin refilled their glasses from the wine in the ice-bucket, signalled the waiter for another bottle. 'Except for one part,' he said. 'I got everybody I wanted –' he mentioned an old distinguished English actor he'd been in London to persuade to work for him, and several American stars, '– but I still have to find an actress in her mid-fifties.'

'Jesus plenty of them around,' said Waylon, 'all panting for work.'

'This has to be someone who still looks good, and still . . .' and he stared at the wine in his glass for a moment, '. . . wants it. Sex. I'm having real trouble finding exactly what I need.'

'I'd say they'd be fucking grateful to *get* it, in their mid-fifties,' and Waylon laughed.

Bud Martin grunted. 'Plenty of actresses available of course, I've seen literally hundreds, I saw someone here who might do and I've got at least another fifty lined up for me to see this coming week when I get home – but really I want . . .' and he sighed '. . . one of those wonderful women. Barbara Stanwyck.'

Waylon puffed on his cigar. 'They don't make them like that any more,' he said. 'What's it about?'

'Well the main plot's the usual stuff,' and Bud stretched his legs out in front of him again, 'power, money, corruption. But the sub-plot's something new.' He turned his head, looked at the long dry grass reaching back as far as the eye could see along the side of the river. A butterfly, orange-winged, fluttered there. And then he said, 'Age and desire.'

Waylon looked at him. 'Come *on* Bud, what's new

about that? That's not new, there's been a hundred films about that: *Limelight, Gigi, Pygmalion, The Misfits, Lolita* – and every time Humphrey Bogart fucked Lauren Bacall in fact . . .'

'In women Waylon,' drawled Bud Martin. 'Age and desire in *women*.'

'Jesus,' said Waylon Jones. 'Why?'

'Whaddya mean *why*?'

'Why would anyone do a film about that?'

'That's the story.'

'Well fuck me that's the most uncommercial subject I ever heard: sex and old women. You've got to be joking.' He looked across at the two young bodies lying in the sunshine.

'Ageing women,' Bud Martin corrected him mildly.

'Yeah, maybe. Great script though.'

'Sounds like a load of laughs to me!' And Waylon did laugh, reached out for the new bottle of white burgundy. 'So why don't you change it a bit?'

'Like what?'

'Make it a *young* woman.'

'But age is the point.'

'Well make it an older man then.'

Bud shrugged. 'Like I say, that's the story.'

'It'll be a dog,' said Waylon Jones, 'I'm telling you now.' He poured more wine. 'Wanna eat?'

But Bud Martin stood up, tall and impressive in the sunshine. 'Sophie!' he called, emptying his glass. He looked at his watch. 'In an hour I guess,' he said to Waylon, as Sophie came towards him in her dark glasses and her bikini. He put an arm out to her without speaking and they disappeared again into one of the cabins.

Waylon Jones remained sitting by himself in the shade, puffing on his cigar. He looked across at the other girl, lying there on the deck in her bikini. She had undone the top, so as not to get marks across her back.

Age and desire in women. What kind of a fucking subject was *that* for a movie? He stared again at the young girl lying in the sunshine, she turned her head and caught his eye. But he looked away, poured himself another glass of wine. He remained sitting there, on the deck of *The Little Love Boat.*

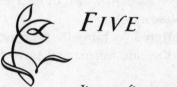 # FIVE

It was after seven o'clock when they finally tottered out on to the pavement of the side-street where the tiny club, Maxi's Drinking Emporium, was housed in a basement. They hailed taxis and called loud goodbyes; the city pigeons, disturbed, flapped off the windowsills of the old brick buildings in the evening sunshine, flew upwards.

'See you at the garden party, all of you,' cried Anthony, as he staggered towards the first taxi; Frances and Emmy Lou took the second one. Harry said he would walk. Their over-loud voices called to each other until the side-street was empty. Then the city pigeons flapped back to the grimy windowsills, cooing and whirring in the hot, gritty air.

Harry Donaldson breathed deeply as he walked, shook his head, tried to clear it, but such small gestures were useless, he'd need several strong black coffees before he talked to anyone else.

Especially before he talked to Michael.

It was his turn tonight to be with Michael, his turn to relieve the rota of friends who looked after a man who was dying. Michael would be querulous and difficult which was his right. And the same old worry nagged at Harry as he walked into a café and ordered a large espresso: was he losing weight? Did he feel as well as he should? It would surely be best to know: he couldn't put off his own test much longer. A grown man in his late fifties behaving like an adolescent.

'But I feel fine,' he muttered to himself. Then he caught sight of himself in the café mirror and turned away.

At the tube station Frances Kitson, pulling at her yellow dress that had seemed to get caught round her large bottom, had waved goodbye to Emmy Lou Brown; the taxi, caught in the Saturday traffic, allowed her to watch as Emmy Lou, her back dispirited somehow, disappeared downwards, rather unsteadily, underground.

Her taxi passed Terence Blue's red BMW, and Frances waved but they didn't see her. *The reunion must've dribbled on for hours*, she thought to herself. Sitting next to Terence in the front seat in her purple dress was Simone Taylor, who used to be crazy about him and banged her shoe on the bannisters and sang Judy Garland songs leaning on a piano.

Twice, as the taxi slowly made its way through the traffic to Shepherds Bush, Frances saw huge posters for *Diversions*: Terence's face smiled out, shining in the evening sunshine.

When she arrived at her mother's place she had a pounding headache. *All my own fault.* She rang the bell, stared at the still blue sky and wished with all her heart that it would rain. She hated this heat, she was too fat, it made her sweat too much, her hair stuck to her forehead; the heat didn't suit her. She knew it was so unusual for London, this heatwave going on and on even though summer was nearly over; people couldn't deal with it, kept looking for rain and arguing about privatised water. Finally her mother's voice crackled on the doorphone.

'It's me Mum,' said Frances and her mother pressed the buzzer to unlock the communal front door. Frances was glad to get into the cool, dark corridor; walked along to the door of her mother's ground-floor flat. Her mother would have prepared, slowly and painfully because of her arthritis, what she usually prepared when she was expecting Frances: cold chicken and boiled potatoes and some lettuce.

'Hello dear,' said Mrs Kitson, opening her door, kissing her daughter. 'Had a nice time? Where've you been? Sit down dear, put your feet up, no I don't want any help, the vicar's been here again, I've told him it's no use, my soul's my own and God understands me and I'm not leaving my money to the church, nothing against you Father, I call him Father though it's probably wrong, he's a Baptist isn't he? Nothing against you Father, I said, but I think there's a lot of hypocrites in your business, there's lots of stories of young vicars with young girls and old vicars trying to talk old ladies round, same as doctors I said to him, we all know that doctors are after old ladies' money – and probably *dentists*.' (She gave the word special, loud emphasis to attract Frances' atten-tion, had never liked Frances' ex-husband.) 'It's in the paper every day . . .'

Frances smiled at her mother, let her ramble on, drank a long glass of foul-tasting tap-water, sat back in front of the quiz show on the telly, waited gratefully for cold chicken and boiled potatoes and lettuce, twirled some of her rings round her fingers.

She thought about the people she had seen again, wished Pauline had come to the reunion with Anthony. She and Pauline had understood drama school better than the others, they'd both come from theatrical fami-lies, had theatrical memories. Frances' father, now dead, had been a not-very-successful music hall comedian; he told stories, sang songs, and juggled. He'd occasionally taken his family with him on tour: she had memories of Christmas pantomimes and summer holidays on Blackpool pier; had been given her first taste for the theatre as she sat in his dressing room staring at herself in the mirrors with the lights around them, breathing in the smell of the make-up and the costumes and the paraffin heaters. Occasionally she'd even sung with her father in front of an audience, a rather plump little girl singing *with a gu-un, with a gu-un, no you can't get a man with a gun*, in a lace dress. Her father talked non-stop on stage and hardly ever talked at home; her mother, with three children and not enough money, had compensated by stopping talking only to breathe.

But tonight her daughter was glad to hear the familiar voice going on and on. Frances was of the generation who had been made to feel it was a matter of shame not to have a date on a Saturday night. For a long time now, she had been grateful that she had the excuse of her mother.

Anthony Bonham fell fast asleep as the taxi drove to Chiswick, so that when he arrived at his house he felt bad-tempered and disoriented and his headache was worse. It was nearly eight o'clock and he knew Pauline would be angry; maybe the guests had even arrived. He shook his head trying to remind himself who was coming, was it pleasure or duty, he couldn't remember. As he fumbled for his door key his younger daughter opened the door from the other side.

'Oh God,' she said, seeing him.

'Well thank you Viola. '

'You stink,' she said, 'of booze.'

'I've been to a class reunion.'

Viola looked at him pityingly. 'When I'm old and I have a class reunion with my colleagues,' she said, 'I'm sure I won't come home looking and smelling like you do.'

This conversation had gone on in the doorway, Anthony still standing on his own front steps. Viola stepped aside to let her father in and, by some miscalculation, as he stepped across the threshold he tripped and fell into the hall. His wife was just walking down the beige-carpeted stairs, pulling at an earring and smoothing down her skirt, so saw her husband lying at her feet. She bent right down to him and the voice he knew so well said quite loudly in his ear:

'Ah! may'st thou ever be what now thou art,
Nor unbeseem the promise of thy spring,
As fair in form, as warm yet pure of heart,
Love's image upon earth, without his wing . . .'

and as she said *without his wing* she kicked his leg with one of her high-heeled shoes.

'The guests will be here in about eight and a half minutes Anthony,' said Pauline.

Viola called, *'Goodbye, Mum, good luck,'* and her young laughter echoed back up from the front path where all the roses were still in bloom. But what she was thinking was: it is *real* style to quote Byron to your husband as he lies drunk on your front doorstep eight and a half minutes before the guests are to arrive for dinner.

Molly McKenzie stood in a small club in Leicester listening to another new group that Banjo had discovered. This week it was The Pelicans. She'd got good at it, she often liked the groups though she found it hard to see a connecting link to their music. How strange the reunion had been. How uncertain Terence Blue had looked for a moment when he saw her. How odd and slightly disorienting it had been to see Anthony again after so long; that sudden intake of breath as he'd stood too close, his hand brushing her breast. She shook her head slightly, to clear the memory away.

Banjo stood with his arm resting on her shoulder and she felt his hip tucked in against hers; his eyes were focused on the stage as always, or as focused as they could be when he'd had a joint or two, and he seemed to be having a lot lately. Molly always found his enthusiasm for new bands, when he had one of his own, endearing. But tonight her head ached in the hot smoky crowded hall and the sweet smell of the dope made her feel sick: she hadn't really wanted to make the long drive and she shouldn't drink at lunchtime, reunion or not, she was too old.

But she couldn't say that, she couldn't admit that.

Once she'd said to Banjo: I'm not going to drink or smoke, for a month. After five days, sitting in a café with his beer while Molly drank mineral water, Banjo had said so gloomily, *it's like going out with a Christian well not that I've got anything against Christians*, that she had laughed and ordered a bottle of wine.

Be Mine
In this groove
Be Mine

sang The Pelicans. The words were often such crap. Banjo told her the words weren't important, she didn't understand. He was right then, she didn't.

She looked up at his face, his dear face that she loved so much.

His dear, twenty-year-younger face.

She'd got over the embarrassment years ago, he had never seemed embarrassed so in the end why should she? Years ago he'd been doing the music for a show she was in; she hadn't expected to love him: he was a kid. She admired his music, she might have a quick fling with him, but he was a kid. His name was actually Edward, but everybody called him Banjo, even his Granny, for some long-forgotten musical reason lost in his past. *I think it might be because I called a violin a banjo when I was about three*, he told her once, *but everybody's forgotten exactly*. But as the quick fling became longer she began to observe: many of the men of Banjo's age were gentler, less aggressive than the men she knew of her own age; they had different priorities, didn't seem to feel that they must achieve in the way men she knew did. She saw that they could talk about feelings without getting embarrassed, saw that in his flat he cooked and cleaned and polished things and that he actually enjoyed it, saw that many of his male friends were also domestic in a way that would be simply unthinkable to men she had known before. Perhaps it was only Banjo's friends, the men she met through him, but she thought it augured well for the next generation of women, these men who would share; some girls would be lucky. But the age difference meant she would be careful not to love him. The press would make a meal of it.

Then one day she saw Banjo kissing a white carpet.

He had bought it for the flat he was living in at the time and he was so pleased with it that he'd lain down on it and kissed it. And she had decided that it was such an eccentric and somehow curiously endearing thing to do that age had nothing to do with it: she loved him because he was loving. And now she could not imagine, ever, caring for anyone else like this: this wasn't immoderate passion or passing foolishness or love at first sight or even sex (although of course she realised that's what everyone thought it was: a woman of a certain age with a toyboy). The press did indeed make a meal of it for a few days until something more interesting came up: LOUISE LOVES TOYBOY the headlines screamed when they'd been photographed coming out of a trendy restaurant, kissing. (As if Molly McKenzie herself did not exist, only her soap opera character.) But she and Banjo had learnt to live with it over the years and seldom went to trendy restaurants any more.

This was the man she loved, the man who made her happy, the man who made her laugh, the man who gazed in amazement at her school photographs that seemed to him to be from a different era: *look at you there with plaits and that funny little schoolbag*, the man she sat and watched TV with on cold rainy evenings and read Sunday papers with and shared bills with and shared thoughts with and went on holiday with and planned Christmas with and, above all, the man who had held her together when her mother finally had committed suicide after all. This was, and she knew it (and it had been going on for over eight years now) the man she had loved most in her life.

So she went on listening to The Pelicans in Leicester on a hot Saturday night, as her head ached and the music blared and Banjo's arm rested there, around her shoulders.

Emmy Lou Brown lived in a very small flat in Finsbury Park that she'd bought outright when her parents died. She was the only child of elderly parents who had lived in Bath, where her father was an architect, but who had often taken her to the theatre in Bristol and London when she was a child. They were already in their sixties when she went to drama school and had both died at seventy: first her father, her mother two years later. She was lucky to have the flat, she knew, and the money they had left her. What if she still lived in rented accommodation, what would have happened to her?

She had felt sick on the early evening tube: the sharp smell of aftershave and cheap perfume wafted through the half-empty carriage, the smell of Saturday night people, going somewhere. But her date was Saturday night in a small flat in Finsbury Park that was entirely white: white walls, white curtains, white furniture, a white telephone. There was only one picture on the wall: a copy of Joshua Reynolds' painting of the eighteenth-century actress Sarah Siddons entitled *The Tragic Muse* which Emmy had owned since she was a teenager and had heard that the ghost of Sarah Siddons stalked the corridors of the Theatre Royal in Bristol. And had first conceived a longing to be an actress herself. The white television which she always put on as soon as she walked into her flat immediately blared out a quiz show, flashed the lottery numbers across the bottom of the screen.

'I'll have an egg in front of the telly,' said Emmy Lou to the empty kitchen. But before she reached the fridge she began to weep. First tears just arriving unannounced on her cheeks, then big racking sobs.

'I must be drunk,' she said to the kitchen between sobs. 'I shouldn't drink like that on an empty stomach.'

Later she had an egg in front of the television set, sitting next to the large white bookcase that held almost every play in the English language.

Later, in bed, lying under the white crocheted bedcover her mother had made for her when she first left home, she finally reached for the bag in one of the drawers. And the little bottle. First she put in the batteries. Then she opened the bottle and opened her legs, smoothing herself with the oil. Then she turned on the motor and pushed the long object inside her; pushing it, feeling it vibrate against her, she moved with it almost immediately.

'Yes,' she whispered alone in her small flat in Finsbury Park, 'yes, yes.'

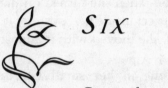 # SIX

Guests do not, of course, do their own laundry at the Dorchester Hotel in London, turning on the big chrome taps, leaning across the marble tiles and filling the huge bath to the top with water, but the smell of the sheets and the stains on them made her vomit and she kept thinking she could smell garlic, somewhere there, in the room, mixed with the smell of spilt whisky.

The maid, summoned late on Sunday afternoon, had been surprised to discover the sheets from the huge four-poster bed in the bath where Simone Taylor had thrown them after she had bathed and bathed herself, trying to wash away fear and pain and thoughts, scrubbing hopelessly at the violent bruises on her breasts that looked like red and purple burns. That she was also washing away evidence in the bath did not occur to her, perhaps.

The maid took away the sheets, made up the bed with fresh crisp ones. Then she saw something odd. A beautiful purple dress was protruding from the waste-paper bin, partly lying across the marble floor. The maid hesitated. Perhaps it had fallen there by mistake. She would look again tomorrow. She closed the door quietly.

Terence Blue smelt of Dior and Calvin Klein. And the whisky of course.

Simone Taylor knew about smells, and scents, and fragrances: that was her job. She travelled for her company all over the world. But, like Bianca Jagger who had left the glamorous world of pop music and become a roving troubleshooter in South America, Simone Taylor carried her past around in her passport. It was not a famous surname that Simone Taylor still kept, but the old, old words that reminded her of her lost dreams: *Occupation – Actress.*

There, in the room, beside the potted orchids and the lacquered cupboards and the dark mahogany wood panelling – holding herself, her arms around herself – she tried to stop shaking, but the shaking came from her stomach and she could not.

This could not have happened.

This was not how it was meant to end, her dream. And fear clutched at her: he had warned her she must never tell.

Sometimes she held her hands over her breasts, as if to protect them still; sometimes she thought she could smell garlic, there in the room again. The faint, muffled sound of the Sunday afternoon traffic from Park Lane sounded like an ominous earthquake gathering in the distance; far away the Serpentine glittered dangerously

in the hot hot sunshine. Simone Taylor shook uncontrol-
lably, wept, reconstructed the night, deconstructed it,
built it up again, tears falling on her jacket.

She could not bear it, she would not be able to bear it.

And then, finally, she watched in a haze of pain and
fear and dreams as her own arm stretched out to the
telephone beside her. Clear and yet not clear about what
she was doing, she very slowly lifted the receiver.

In the high, childlike voice that sat oddly on a woman
of fifty-six she called the police.

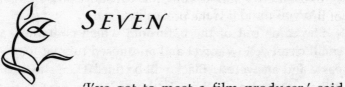

SEVEN

'I've got to meet a film producer,' said Molly McKenzie, kissing Banjo's tousled hair. He reached up from the bed, half-asleep, kissed her.

'Good luck darling,' he said and fell asleep again.

Contrary to popular myth, a lot of film producers these days weren't fat, Molly found; many didn't even smoke cigars. Even the one who had tried to seduce her in a small flat off Wardour Street soon after she left the Drama Academy wasn't fat. But he had smoked expensive cigars and to this day she remembered the faint smell of a cigar mixed with an aftershave called *Brut* and the pristine coldness of the place he had called his London Office. She had maintained a stony silence during the seduction attempt and laughed a lot with her friends afterwards at the thought of how much trouble she'd taken to dress.

She was being interviewed – she had thought, in those long-off innocent days – for a part in a new film; it would be her first film. She had washed her hair and spent hours on her make-up, and had discarded at least three dresses before settling on the green one with the wide belt and the taffeta underskirt; she brushed her long, dark hair a hundred times before pulling it into a ponytail. When she got there the cigar-smoking, aftershave-scented Producer, all alone, had offered her a drink and she'd asked for tea. He'd looked slightly disconcerted, rummaged about in the small clean kitchen.

'Do you mind it black?' he called finally.

She came out of the bathroom which contained a small clean yellow towel and an unused tube of toothpaste and answered, 'Black will be fine.' Then she said, 'What's that strange thing in the bathroom next to the toilet?'

The producer again had looked, she remembered, slightly disconcerted. 'Well,' he said, patting the sofa for her to sit beside him, 'that's to wash your pussy.'

'Oh.' Molly was very surprised. 'I never saw one before, how peculiar, doesn't it hate getting wet?' The Producer now looked definitely uneasy.

'Where is it?' she had asked finally, looking around for a cat.

When she told this part of the story to her friends they accused her of making it up, but she wasn't. She'd had a rackety and neurotic upbringing in Manchester before going to the Drama Academy but the use of the word 'pussy' for anything other than a cat was new to her.

The Producer had made spasmodic lunges at her for the next half-hour pushing against the taffeta petticoat but his heart, after that, wasn't really in it, especially when she'd stared at him sulkily when he put his old hand on her young breast. She didn't get the part, if there was a part, but remembered always the smell of the cigar and the aftershave and the way it seemed to linger in her hair long after she'd left Wardour Street.

Since that time she'd met many producers and had learnt that often they were neither fat, nor smoked cigars – she'd had affairs with one or two. Lately they were often from Oxford or Cambridge or Edinburgh and were, more and more often, somewhat younger than she was.

On this sunny Monday morning after the drama school reunion she'd been called into an office in Soho to see about a cameo role in a TV film based on the true story of a murder of a young bride in Scotland.

'A *cameo role*,' she groaned to her agent. 'God I came out of the series to do proper acting!'

'I know darling,' said her agent, 'but I did warn you, and you know the situation as well as I do, work in your age group is scarce; everybody thinks of you as Louise still, and anyway nobody's interested in middle-aged women.'

'Wives and mothers, wives and mothers, I know I know, but why, why, when *middle-aged men are in their prime*?' But it was a rhetorical question and both of them knew it.

'Why do we have to go over this Molly? You made the choice against my advice; this is how it is.' The crisp voice crisped impatiently down the telephone line. 'Glenda Jackson's become an MP, Joan Collins started writing novels when she saw her first grey hair, and every single actress who has survived this long is available.'

Molly's agent, Anastasia Adams (Ltd), was a middle-aged woman herself, and had recently very cruelly, but realistically, divested herself of four other middle-aged actresses on her books, keeping only Molly (who had been a TV star, at least) and a very fat actress who got an enormous amount of work doing voice-overs for adverts, made ninety-five thousand pounds gross in the last financial year, and spent a good part of her time in Ibiza.

So Molly washed her now short blonde hair, discarded several outfits before settling on the right one and arrived at the producer's office on time, as she always did. The producers may be late, but the class of fifty-nine had been well-trained.

'This is Waylon Jones, the director,' the young and very English producer said to Molly, after she'd waited almost half an hour, and a grey-haired balding man nodded to her without speaking.

'The reason we've asked to see you,' continued the producer, 'is that we're doing a film about that young Scottish bride who was killed on her wedding day in the eighties by her husband's brother who was also in love with her and had wanted to marry her – I expect you remember the case – and we're interested in you playing the young bride's aunt.' Molly waited politely, put an interested look on her face.

'We want her to be a very attractive aunt,' said the producer. 'In fact, we're making the parts of the parents and the aunt very attractive. Someone like you,' he added somewhat, Molly thought, oleaginously, but she smiled at him, dutifully accepting the compliment.

The balding director took a cigar out of his pocket, lit it slowly, puffing and huffing, looking at her. 'Are you interested?' he said, and she heard he was an American. 'I've seen you somewhere.'

The casting director, also a middle-aged woman, who sat on the other side of the desk with the men, looked embarrassed. 'Molly's a very well-known actress,' she said hurriedly, 'she's worked in the biggest theatre companies, she's played leads in many TV series,' but the director silenced her with his hand, not looking at her.

'We want the aunt to be attractive,' he reiterated, as if aunts were, on the whole, not; as if the word itself – *aunt* – had a fusty, musty quality to it, in this room.

'Have you got photographs of the aunt, of the parents?' asked Molly. 'What did they look like?'

'Oh God that's immaterial,' said the director, 'we just wanna make them attractive.' He stared at her in silence. The smoke from the cigar filled the small room, the casting director coughed quietly.

'I'm so sorry we couldn't send you a script,' said the producer, 'but we explained to all the agents, it's still being written; we hope to have copies here from America next week.' Molly wondered, but not aloud, why it was being written in America if it happened in Scotland.

'But anyway,' continued the producer, 'the bride was killed while she was changing into her going-away outfit with her bridesmaid. The brother – the murderer – came in and kissed her and then stuck a carving knife in her, saying if he couldn't have her nobody would – very dramatic stuff. '

'And where was the aunt at the time?' said Molly very politely and she saw the casting director bite her lip; whether it was to stop herself from coughing or laughing or crying, Molly could not be sure.

'In our story the aunt, at that moment, is tying a tin can on the exhaust pipe of the bridal car,' said Waylon Jones. 'Hey, we must think of a name for her,' he said to the producer.

'Ah,' said Molly.

She stood up, very gently, gracefully and with charm. This was something she'd learnt long ago at the Academy, where she'd been taught never to outstay her welcome in an interview; latterly the grace and charm came in handy in protecting her own self-esteem.

'Thank you so much for seeing me,' she said. 'It sounds fascinating and I look forward to perhaps seeing the script when the aunt has a name.' And she smiled at the three of them. They would never have known she had not worked for five months. The casting director came out of the room with her.

'Thanks for coming Molly,' she said, 'thanks so much. Sorry if it was a bit, you know, well you know what Americans are like. Oh hello Evie, thanks so much for coming in.' For waiting outside the door was Evie Thompson, another actress who'd played lots of television leads in her time. Evie and Molly saw one another, raised eyebrows and only smiled. They realised they were both up for the same small role along with,

probably, most actresses of their age in London. Evie
Thompson's newly washed brown hair, cleverly high-
lighted with auburn streaks to hide the grey, shone in
the light that slanted in from the Soho street as she stood
up to follow the casting director into the cigar-smoky
room; Molly went out into the muggy morning.

People in the street looked at her as they passed,
recognised at once that she was an actress from that TV
series, some called out a cheery greeting. As usual it was
mostly the name of her television character: *Louise . . . hey
Louise!* She smiled and sometimes waved an acknowledgement and kept walking on briskly, thinking her
thoughts. She hated it but she was used to it. The people
didn't guess, as she swung along the street, that she was
in her mid-fifties and hadn't worked for five months,
the longest period of unemployment she had ever had,
that she had begun to despair, to think that this time she
would never work again. Nobody would know that this
was the pattern of Molly McKenzie's life as she swung
along the street in the sunshine. It was only midday,
Banjo was probably still in bed; she could go back. She
knew he would be glad, would hold out his arms, pull
her down into the warm bed and the tangled sheets
where they had made love only a few hours before.

'I love you,' he would say.

But something about the waste of yet another day disturbed her, deterred her. She went down to the Berwick
Street market and bought the fruit and vegetables for
the week. It was on the corner of Broadwick Street,
loaded down with tomatoes and lettuce and potatoes
and peaches and beans, that she saw the huge headline

on the billboard for the *Evening Standard*: FAMOUS
FILM STAR: RAPE CHARGE. She walked over to the
paper shop and saw Terence Blue's face smiling up at
her from the front page of the early edition.

She was so surprised that vegetables slipped from
under her arm; beans lay on Broadwick Street, shining
green on the dirty pavement and a peach rolled into the
gutter. She knelt down among passing people, gathered
the beans together, discarded the peach that had landed
on a dog turd, managed to stuff everything else into her
bag. She felt for some change, bought a newspaper,
stood on the street corner and read in disbelief that
Terence Blue, the film star, had been accused of raping
an unnamed woman in a room in the Dorchester Hotel
in Park Lane on the Saturday night of the London
Academy of Drama reunion. *'But that can't be true'* said
Molly to the midday passers-by. *'I know it can't.'*

She hailed a taxi.

At home, Banjo had gone; his saxophone had gone.
The bed was unmade. He'd left a note, the way he sometimes did.

I love you I love you I love you, it said.

Once, in the beginning, they would say, because there
was plenty of time, because they lived for the day,
because it was merely a joke, a lovers' ditty: *I love you I
love you I love you will you marry me* but now, eight years
later, somehow the subject of marriage was never mentioned.

Molly dumped the fruit and vegetables on the kitchen
table, smoothed Banjo's note with her hands, looked
again at the bald account of the accusation of rape in the

newspaper and the large smiling picture of Terence Blue, famous film star in his prime. She thought for a while. She remembered what she'd said, and regretted saying, to Anthony Bonham as they stood at the reunion together: *he can't do it any more,* she had said.

Terence Blue. She owed more than anybody knew to Terence Blue. First she and Terence had kissed at student parties; he was the first person to put his tongue in her mouth, the first person to put his hand on her breast and then, one night, long, long ago in her room in a boarding house in Hammersmith (when the landlady had gone to see her sick sister in Derby), Terence Blue had, as the saying goes, taken her virginity; carefully, with a condom from his pocket so that she wouldn't get pregnant. Not for a moment did either of them think it was True Love but Molly felt extremely grateful for the gentle and unfumbling experience on the floor by the gas heater, for the genuine enthusiasm Terence obviously felt for her body so that sex seemed after all a good thing, not something to be ashamed of. Not the ugly thing from her childhood: the visiting men, the sounds from her mother's bedroom. *I thought it was dirty,* she had said wonderingly to Terence, *I thought it was something horrible. I didn't know it was like this,* and in front of the gas heater she told Terence things she had never told anybody else about her life when she was young. There was something almost simple about Terence Blue. She couldn't possibly have thought herself in love with him, but he had held her hand and listened to her, and the experience with him had allowed her to know that sex could be a good thing not a bad thing and so had changed her life. He had become a huge star now and their lives didn't cross so often but – and she stared again at the stark, unpleasant newspaper headlines – she owed him friendship.

She wondered if Anthony would remember what she'd said at the reunion. She stood undecided for a moment and then, almost not considering what she was doing, picked up the phone.

Not only had Pauline Bonham become stylish.

She also knew perfectly well of her husband's infidelities; in particular she knew very well indeed about his first and passionate affair with Molly McKenzie.

Molly McKenzie who had once been her best friend.

Molly McKenzie who had shared her tights and her books and her bone voice prop and her practice skirt and her dreams and her secrets, in the class of '59.

On their very first day at the Academy Molly, newly arrived from Manchester, and Pauline, who had just found out that her real father was in the circus, sat next to each other while the stern patrician principal warned them what a difficult profession they had chosen.

'I am warning you now it will be very very hard,' he had said, 'especially for the women,' and Molly and Pauline with the insouciance and confidence of youth turned to each other at exactly the same moment and grinned. *Not for us, it won't be difficult for us* they had seemed to say to each other and, instinctively, Molly had put her hand on Pauline's arm. Pauline, not a physically instinctive person at all, had despite herself put her hand over Molly's. They were friends from that moment. They were the same age but had different qualities. Molly was more sexy although she didn't know it, and more emotional just below the surface. Pauline's tall, gawky beauty enchanted her tutors but they saw there was something else there: already a kind of contained quality, only betrayed when she was afflicted with her new laughter. And so the parts they played were always imbued with these qualities of their person, of their psyche.

Once three of the students, Juliet Lyall, Molly McKenzie and Pauline O'Brien, shared the role of Viola in *Twelfth Night* in a class production. In the students' work the tutors saw at once that each Viola was stamped with their late teenage persona: Molly's was direct and inadvertently sexy and somehow made them want to cry; Pauline, the beautiful one, was wittier – even her occasional ungainly movements charmed them and made them laugh, yet she held something back. Juliet Lyall's was the most complex of the three: perhaps the least engaging, hers was nevertheless the most confident, the largest; her remarkable face with its extraordinary angular bones stuck in the memory and she emanated a powerful determination that seemed to be made of cold steel. You didn't forget Juliet Lyall.

In the staffroom the tutors murmured together about the qualities and talent of their pupils.

Of course none of the students understood what they showed, at the time. But already the basis of their acting was formed, in a way. Many of them thought, years later, about how hard it had been and how destructive to some: all their joys and fears and learning and growing up were compounded by the fact that they had to *publicly present* what they learned about themselves, on stage. They had to be aware of how they sounded, how they moved, how they looked, so that their knowledge of some aspects of themselves was extended in a different way from many people's.

Once when they were sharing fish and chips out of a newspaper one evening, walking along to the bus stop after classes, Pauline had said, 'Molly, don't you think we'll seem dumb when we're older; shouldn't we be reading more, studying more?'

'Oh Pauly, we read all the time! Look at us: Chekhov, Shakespeare, Goldsmith, Tennessee Williams, Euripides, George Bernard Shaw, John Osborne, we never *stop* reading.' Molly waved a chip in the evening air before she ate it. 'And also, we're learning about *ourselves*—' but then Molly stopped. 'No. No, maybe that's not right. I'm not absolutely certain—'

'What?' said Pauline, screwing up the newspaper, wiping her hands on it but stopping in the street also, looking at her best friend.

Molly stood still, grappling intuitively with something she didn't yet understand. 'I'm not certain Pauly,' she said slowly, 'that acting is how we find out about – about how our hearts work.'

Afterwards, after Pauline found out about Anthony and Molly, after that time of tears and treachery and pain, the two women still inadvertently met: at work, at first nights, or socially like at the Bonham's garden parties to

which all the members of the old class were always automatically invited. Once when Viola was a little girl she'd
played Molly's daughter in a TV series and in those days
had called her Auntie Moll. So they had met, these old
friends, every now and then, and they talked and smiled
politely. And between them, always unspoken: this
betrayal, which lay like a knife that sometimes twisted
still, in a corner of Pauline's soul.

But she wore a mask, that hid her heart.

She was extremely thrown nevertheless when the
phone rang on the summer Monday afternoon so many
years later and it was Molly.

'Pauline, it's Molly, I know this is a bit of a surprise,
oh dear,' and she gave a little nervous half-laugh, 'I've
sort of had a shock I – I think I was phoning Anthony
but, Pauline, you're probably more sensible and more
use, have you seen today's *Standard* yet?'

'No. What?' *Why is Molly phoning me after all these
years? What can have happened?* Visions of Anthony,
falling on his face on the Royal Shakespeare Company
stage, drunk or dead.

'You remember Terence Blue?'

'What a silly question.' Pauline had also kissed
Terence Blue many times while at drama school but had
not approved of Molly's loss of virginity to him: Pauline
had believed that love and sex and marriage were forever. Molly knew that.

'He's been charged with rape.'

'Good God!'

'It seems to have been after the reunion – well they
mention the reunion in the paper – maybe it was

someone *at* the reunion if you can believe such a thing.
Anyway why didn't you come Pauly, on Saturday?'
Pauly.

'We had a dinner party.'

'Oh. Shame, it was interesting. Anyway it happened
after that apparently and so the reunion is splashed all
over the papers. But the thing is – I don't think it can
have happened. And I said something to Anthony.'
Molly sounded muddled. 'Oh God, look are you doing
anything? Could I come over? I don't quite know how to
proceed, I need to talk to someone urgently I think, and
Banjo's not here. Maybe I should go to the police but I
really need advice and I let slip something to Anthony
on Saturday that he might remember.'

'I expect he was too drunk.'

'No, this was before, just at the beginning, when we
were all arriving.'

'He's gone back to Stratford; ring him there if you
want him.'

'Oh.' Molly paused, hearing the polite chill in
Pauline's voice. 'I don't know what to do,' she said. And
in a sudden very complicated mixture of motivations
and desires Molly suddenly wanted to talk not to
Anthony Bonham but to his wife, Pauline O'Brien
Bonham, her old friend. Wanted to talk to her after all
those years, wanted to talk to her so that the nonsense
with Anthony at the reunion – that sudden intake of
breath and memory – could be *eradicated*. As if it did not
happen. 'Pauly can I come?' she said.

Pauline heard a kind of longing in Molly's voice.

And Pauline Bonham stared at herself in the mirror,

there in her own hall, at the bottom of the stairs where her husband had fallen on Saturday evening. He'd probably been drinking with Molly all afternoon. Did she care? But *Terence Blue*, the golden boy who had kissed them all – out of kindness sometimes – involved in a rape case?

'Pauly?' Molly guessed some of the thoughts at least.

'Sure, if you think I can help, though I don't see how. Come over after four, I've got to go down to the shop for a while.'

'See you then,' said Molly.

Pauline put down the receiver but remained motionless by the telephone. She did not like these jolts to her heart: Molly visiting, Terence Blue, the days when she was young. She caught at a memory of herself, in a corridor after a voice class, telling Terence Blue she would probably become a trapeze artist. 'I don't have to run away to the circus like other people Terence,' she had said. 'My father wants me to join him in Paris.' Terence Blue had smiled his incredibly beautiful smile and put an arm around her shoulder.

'Come for a drink with me Pauly,' he had said.

Pauline Bonham quickly phoned a colleague and made a very large profit selling a Wellington chest.

Izzy Fields had also seen the *Evening Standard*. She did not believe the headline for one moment and almost wept as she cycled from Tufnell Park to the National Theatre.

Yet another media circus, she thought angrily, *yet*

another attack on the luvvies. Izzy had recently read a newspaper article entitled 'The Perils of Show Business' that counted how many actors had gone mad and she had thought, smiling grimly to herself, *and that's only the ones they know about.* She had taken to counting the number of derogatory stories that appeared in the newspapers about actors. But most stories weren't about acting at all: the love lives of soap stars, an actor running away from a play in the West End, grand divorce announcements to the press as if actors thought they were royalty, Hugh Grant on Sunset Boulevard – drugs, sex and rock and roll, not acting.

She parked her bicycle as usual on Waterloo Bridge. She had talked to the actresses in her dressing room about the reunion; they would not have forgotten. She took off her helmet, walked slowly down the concrete steps and entered through the stage door of the National Theatre. She skimmed the noticeboards, checked that the people she was understudying had arrived: *Hello darling, OK? See you later.* She got to the dressing room first, sat down and began to work carefully on a tapestry cushion cover. At first, when she began understudying, she had tried to read, tried to teach herself Spanish even, in these long, long spells in dressing rooms. But she had learnt many years ago that that kind of concentration was not possible, that one's ear was always half-tuned to the performance coming through the tannoy. She now made lots and lots of cushion covers and had begun to sell them, in a small craft shop in Archway. She would appear only in Act III this afternoon, no point in putting on the corset yet.

The two other actresses burst into the dressing room talking about Terence Blue, almost gasping with the thrill of such a drama in their already dramatic profession; first Hugh Grant and now *this*! One of them, clutching the *Evening Standard*, looked excitedly at Izzy.

'You were *there* on Saturday Izzy, weren't you.'

'Yes.' Izzy bent over her cushion cover with great concentration.

'*God*! You said he was there didn't you?'

'Yes.' Izzy plied her needle.

'Did you – talk to him?'

'Yes I did actually. I know him quite well. We were in the same class at drama school, and we both had religious problems.'

'Religious?'

'Yes.'

'You and *Terence Blue*?'

'Yes.'

'What do you *mean*?'

'We both came from religious families. We knew what it was like.'

The calls came over the tannoy, the girls threw on their costumes, still chattering excitedly and looking at Izzy with new interest. They were young and doing their understudying and playing their small parts in the big company as their first job, seeing it as the first step on a shining upwardly reaching ladder; Izzy knew they looked at her as a middle-aged failure coming down.

'Izzy?'

'Yes?'

'Did he ever try to rape you?'

'No.'

They looked disappointed and would have continued the conversation but were called on stage as nineteenth-century prostitutes.

Izzy Fields stared at the newspaper headline miserably after they had gone.

Nicola Abbot, who long ago named herself after Bud Abbott not Lou Costello, sitting in the one tall chair, looked at the big headline on the front page of the newspaper, stared at the photograph of Terence Blue for a long time. Her face was completely expressionless, still. She read the article twice. She knew it couldn't be true: Terence wasn't like that. Then she carefully took the front page from the rest of the paper and tore it: in half; in half again; in half again; in half again. Then she sat, quite still with the pieces of newsprint on her lap, in the one tall chair.

He had seen her.

He would come.

She had to see him.

When she saw a small article about the London Academy of Drama reunion in a newspaper, she had decided to go. She had to see him, that was all she knew. She had to catch the train and a taxi, events that filled her with trepidation, but she did them; she knew perfectly well how to do them after all.

This was living in the community. They said she was well enough to live in the community. They were pleased she had her own house, that they would not have to find her alternative accommodation. They brought her on a minibus.

When she arrived at the house, when she saw it again, she had stood quite still while they unpacked her belongings. And then she dutifully walked in through the door with the community psychiatric nurse. Someone had arranged for the house to be cleaned.

'How nice,' they said.

She did not tell them the house made all the memories come back.

A telephone rang and rang in the empty hall.

Molly McKenzie parked her car, admired the roses in front of the Bonhams' house, envied again the way the back of the property ran down to the river. On her mantelpiece at home was her invitation to the garden party that Pauline and Anthony Bonham used to hold every summer to which Molly – not, of course, as Anthony's ex-mistress but as one of the class of '59 – had always been politely invited. They hadn't had one for years and years but in the early eighties in that beautiful river-bordered garden, loud voices had called to each other across the lawn in the sunshine: *Darling, how lovely to see you again darling . . .* this was indeed exactly the sort of conversation Molly and Pauline usually had with each other, exuding bonhomie, excluding, any longer, intimacy.

So when Molly rang the doorbell and Pauline opened the door they kissed, twice, French fashion and Pauline said briskly, 'We'll have some tea on the lawn, such a lovely day,' and in a moment they were poised on deckchairs in the sunshine with Earl Grey tea and ginger biscuits. They exchanged pleasantries about the weather, 'Just a tiny bit cooler today I think,' the acting world and their colleagues, 'Have you seen Juliet Lyall in *The Seagull*?' 'Yes, good performance just her part of course, wasn't so keen on the men in it though. Are you working?' 'Oh up for a couple of things you know the way it is.' All the usual chit-chat that amounted to their world, more or less, both of them tense, neither of them quite able to run down the conversation and leave a pause.

But Molly was thinking *Pauline looks* terrific. *What has happened?* and then as they chattered on brightly she thought *oh my God I think she's had a little* facelift; *Pauly's had a facelift*. Quickly she went on talking.

'Did Anthony tell you about Nicky Abbott, that she was at the reunion?'

Pauline looked at Molly in surprise. 'Nicky Abbott? No he didn't, God where has she been all these years? She disappeared into thin air, what did she look like?'

'She looked like an old woman.'

'Nicky Abbott an old woman? What do you mean?'

'Well, she looked like what all of us would look like if we weren't actresses I suppose and didn't dye our hair and wear lots of make-up and have expensive dentistry and take HRT and wear clever clothes.' She did not like to mention plastic surgery.

'Did you talk to her?'

'I didn't recognise her at first and then I heard her speaking – remember her voice?'

'Of course.'

'And then I turned to speak to her and she was – just gone.'

'How bizarre.' Pauline sipped at her tea. 'Whatever happened to her all those years ago do you think? I never knew someone to disappear the way she did, the brightest and the best and that one film, the one that everybody was crazy about – what was it called? *Heartbreak*. And then phhitt – gone.'

'Well there she was again on Saturday,' said Molly.

'How strange,' said Pauline.

And at last they sat in silence for a moment.

'You look so – terrific Pauly,' said Molly quietly.

'Thank you,' said Pauline, putting on some large sunglasses. She said nothing more. The sun sparkled on the river and the silence between the two women lengthened.

'What do you think I should do about Terence?' said Molly finally.

'Like what?'

'I feel I ought to help him. I'm sure he didn't do it.'

Pauline regarded Molly from behind the large glasses.

'What were you thinking of doing? But yes, I can't imagine Terry raping anybody, I mean *who* at the reunion? He'd had them all years ago!'

'God knows.' Molly thought for a moment. 'Well – I left early but when I left he had that – what was her name now? – Simone – Simone Taylor, dressed in purple, hanging on to his every word. My God, do you remember her, poor old Simone Taylor who couldn't act?'

Pauline thought for a moment. 'American, draped across the piano singing old Judy Garland songs, "Over The Rainbow" or something? Yes, terrible actress.'

'Birds fly over the rainbow why then oh why can't I,' Molly intoned, 'yeah that's her, yes, *terrible* actress, she was there on Saturday.'

'She used to be crazy about Terence didn't she, talked like a little girl. What happened to her? I've never heard of her since we left the Academy, she can't be an actress surely?'

'Someone told me she became a Cosmetics Executive.'

'A what?'

'She's a Cosmetics Executive in New York,' repeated Molly. 'Max Factor or Poison or something, she apparently kept telling anybody at the reunion who would listen that she had two cadillacs, maybe to make up for having dropped out of the profession.'

'Two cadillacs is worth our profession any day,' said Pauline dryly.

'Oh come on Pauly, you know how it is, anyone who gives up feels a failure. There's something wrong with the whole lot of us, the wanting to do it in the first place, wanting attention, wanting applause, compensating for our childhoods, forcing the audience to become our parents and give us praise—'

'Oh come off it—'

'It's true, *they fuck you up your mum and dad* and then we become actors. I didn't even have a dad and that fucked me up just the same. And I remember you and your real father and how you were going to run away to the circus and find him, escape from your stepfather.'

Pauline looked away at once, down to the river, said nothing.

'Well I believe that's how it goes anyway,' said Molly, 'to me Cosmetic Cadillacs can only be a booby prize, someone should write a book about actors' childhoods it would make interesting reading. I've decided most of us are damaged in some way and that's *why* we become actors, but anyway, listen, about Terence, there's something odd about all this and Terence will so hate me for – for betraying a confidence, but – well – oh God I'll have to discuss it with someone now and . . .' She paused for a moment. 'Oh Pauly, you know Terence, how he kissed us all, how I lost my virginity and ran and told you, and how you – how you said sex must be forever?'

'I remember,' said Pauline shortly. She stared at the river.

Molly took a deep breath. 'Listen to me Pauly, listen, Terence and I were at a sort of cocktail party gala at the Ritz a few weeks ago, for World Hunger – I know, at the *Ritz*, isn't it silly,' as Pauline snorted, 'but it raises millions apparently. Anyway, Terence gave a speech, I had to give some awards, it was supposed to be Princess Alexandra but she was ill, I got roped in somehow at the last minute, horrible it was, people kept saying, *You're a soap star; where's the princess?* Anyway, Terence and I escaped and went and had dinner; we'd worked together on a film last year and we were reminiscing about that and drinking rather heavily, especially Terence, and Banjo was away with his band so it turned into rather a long evening. In the end I offered to drive him home, he wasn't in any fit state to drive his car, and he's not supposed to drive, he's been banned – anyway I parked the car outside his house and just as I handed him the keys he – well I suddenly saw that he was . . .' Molly paused for a moment. 'I know this sounds ridiculous but he was crying.'

'Terence *cried*?'

'I know I know, but he did, and he asked me to come in with him, into his house, he's got a beautiful house in Hampstead—'

'Yes, we went there a lot when he was married to Elvira, she's Benedict's godmother of course—'

'Well I went in and — God it was ridiculous – he didn't start kissing me or anything but he – he put his arms around me and – kind of leant on me and I – God I was stupid, how could I have been so crass – I misunderstood and I said, "Oh come on Terence we've done all this in my boarding house remember? We've known each other too long to do this and I love my young man." Or I said something like that and then he said, *"No, no, I wasn't meaning that,"* and it sort of came out that he'd really just been wanting a cuddle and – that he was – well, that he was –' and Molly looked embarrassed as she said the word rather quietly '– impotent.'

Pauline inadvertently let out an unbelieving hoot of laughter, quite unlike her. 'Sorry,' she said spilling some of her tea on the lawn, 'it's just so – unlikely. *Terence*?!!!!'

'I *know*, I know.'

'You didn't believe him?'

'But I did.'

'But we all know what he was like, he can't have lost

it, he was part of our learning experience.' And Pauline, recovering, shook her head in a kind of amused disbelief, leant back in the deckchair in the sunshine. Neither of them spoke for a moment.

Then Pauline said, considering, 'Well, I remember when I was about sixteen hearing that men could only have so many goes at sex and that was it. I think it was to put young boys off wanking. Perhaps Terence used up all his goes. Although I'd find it hard to believe.'

'I believed him Pauly.'

'I've noticed these days he does a lot of macho carry-on, you know those moody photographs against brick walls in South London wearing a leather jacket with a bottle in his hand, like a middle-aged James Dean?'

'Yeah I know, I've noticed. I think they were stills for that new film of his, *Diversions*. Nice actually, weren't they?' And they both laughed, and the afternoon softened, there on the lawn

'But – why would he have told you Moll? It's not something you'd expect him to go round talking about is it, not Terence, even in his cups.'

'I know.' Molly paused, uncertain. Not even Pauline knew how she felt about Terence, what he had done for her. 'I had the feeling – oh – that it just slipped out in a kind of desperation, that he didn't *mean* to tell me at all. I – I think he's always known that I was – grateful to him.'

'Grateful?'

'Pauly . . . oh . . . there were tough goings-on in my house when I was a kid, you know that.' Molly's eyes clouded over briefly for a moment. 'I could've been put off sex forever. But – in some way it was thanks to Terence that I wasn't. I can't exactly explain.' Nor could she speak to Pauline of all people about sex, as they skirted around the pain of the past. She went on quickly: 'We sat in that marvellous living room he's got in Hampstead, all those original paintings and soft sofas—'

'Yes I know that house, it's beautiful,' said Pauline.

'And I asked him, what did he know about it – impotence – how did it happen, if he knew why it had happened to him and he seemed as if he might tell me and then he just sort of stopped and said, "Oh it's something from a long time ago, it's too hard to explain." And I did give him a cuddle, he seemed so sad. I just kind of held him, I just held him in my arms. And after a while he said – oh God it was sort of pathetic – that he hadn't wanted to go to a doctor, that – that he'd gone to some library and looked up the word but it hardly existed, it was only a small item under **i** in medical encyclopedias. And that there didn't seem to be any books about it and twice people came up and asked for his autograph. His face was so sad, telling me all this and he sounded so – incompetent. One always thinks film stars will have people to *do* things for them. I felt like crying myself. This was the man of our youth, who – oh you know.'

Pauline nodded. 'I know,' she said.

'And I tried to say all the right things: probably just a stage, don't worry about it, surely you should see your doctor, isn't it maybe a sign of diabetes? Or perhaps there is some counselling that would help? I realised I didn't know anything about the subject at all really. And he said he disliked all doctors intensely and how could he go to any doctor about such a thing when he was a sex symbol! It made me wonder afterwards though if that's why Elvira Pugh left him. I did like her, he was lucky to have her compared to his other appalling show-biz wives.'

'No,' said Pauline, 'Elvira is Benedict's godmother, we see her a lot, and Elvira left him because he was having such a public affair with the appalling Iona Spring. Elvira said that as he hadn't even embarked on marriage till he was forty and Elvira was already his second wife she felt he should have tried harder. She walked out.'

'Remember his first wife?' and both women grinned at exactly the same time. 'And how surprised we all were that he'd taken the plunge at last at *forty*? Six months with Big Bosomed Betty Bailey. Remember that early TV series she was in, what was it called? *Tempest* or *Stormbound* or something, lots of heaving bosom through a flimsy dress in the rain, quite daring for TV in those days but God she was boring, Elvira must have seemed like a breath of fresh air, a crime writer instead of an actress. Foolish Terence Blue, to lose Elvira.'

'He was only following the correct procedure for a sex symbol,' said Pauline dryly, 'leaving a woman of his own age, he was fifty wasn't he, and so was Elvira, to marry a girl of eighteen. For all we know his agent told him to do it to boost his image, foster the myth of his sexiness.' She leant back in the deckchair, stretched slightly. 'Well, that's the correct procedure for ageing men of course – a young lover. Women who try it only get laughed at.'

Molly started as if she'd been hit, looked sharply at Pauline. Pauline's eyes were hidden by her sunglasses. Something there still, in the air, in the sunny garden.

'Anyway,' Molly said rather coolly after a moment, 'the point is I very foolishly said something about this to Anthony at the reunion, I mean I just said something silly like Terence couldn't do it any more, just a throw-away really because we all know Terence used to be the Academy stud. I felt ashamed after I'd said it, wished I hadn't. Terence genuinely liked women and I think I was lucky – lots of us were lucky – to have our first sexual experiences with someone like that rather than – well – some slob or someone who didn't know what they were doing. You had some good times with him too Pauly, I remember, you must have some nice feelings about him still.'

Pauline said nothing, stared at the river.

'And I thought Anthony might have remembered what I said on Saturday and that if I – if I explained it to him he might be able to – I mean Anthony might be able to do something sensible, talk to someone. I mean we've known Terence all our lives practically,' Molly finished lamely.

Pauline shrugged. 'Anthony's at Stratford. I told you on the phone. You'll find him there.'

Molly ignored the chill in Pauline's tone. She rummaged in her bag for the *Evening Standard*, thrust it at Pauline: FAMOUS FILM STAR: RAPE CHARGE and Terence's familiar, smiling face.

'Look Pauly, we knew him when he was a kid, when we were all kids, he's part of our past, and we know very well the sort of person he is. Shouldn't one do something?'

But Pauline only shrugged, looked briefly at the story. 'People change,' she said and the newspaper fell on to the grass. Terence Blue smiled upwards.

Neither of them said anything more. Still Pauline's eyes were hidden by her sunglasses. A boat came into view, slowly and quietly moving along the river, a green boat decorated with brightly painted flowers. They saw its name: *Mary Malone*.

Finally Molly said, 'You don't like me still Pauly, do you.' It was a statement not a question and it hung there between them in the hot Chiswick afternoon.

Pauline said nothing for a while, brushed at a wasp impatiently with her hand, watched the boat. When it had quite disappeared from view she gave herself an imperceptible shake then, still staring at the river through her dark glasses, said to Molly, 'I don't like what you did to me.'

In spite of herself, in spite of the fact that she had begun this conversation, Molly blushed.

'I know,' she said. 'I don't like it myself.' After a moment she added, 'I thought I loved him. I suppose I did love him sort of.'

'You didn't have any right to love him when I was stuck home with Portia only eight months old and I couldn't work and he was out working and fucking other actresses. At least it didn't need to be my best friend.' Pauline's voice was crisp but Molly heard the pain.

'I know. It's not the sort of thing I'd do now. He didn't love me of course, I was just fooling myself. I regret it terribly.'

Neither of them thought it was in the least odd that they were discussing something that had happened so long ago, almost thirty years ago.

Pauline looked at Molly, and at last took off her sunglasses. 'Do you regret it for yourself or for me?' she said coldly.

How smooth her face is, thought Molly, *it doesn't give anything away. Once I would have been able to tell what she was thinking just by looking at her. Only her voice betrays her now.*

'I didn't even think of you,' she answered truthfully, finally. And she looked down at her ringless hands. 'I did think I loved him. I believed he loved me, I thought we'd . . .' she stumbled '. . . just go on, working together, living like that . . .'

'Oh did you? And what did you think would happen to me and Portia?'

'I didn't think about it Pauly, I was very immature, I lived for the day, I know it sounds weird but I don't think I had any conception of "the future". I was stupid. And, like I say, I'm ashamed, I've had cause to regret it often.' And then Molly was suddenly silent. She thought of the nights, and the train station, and the tears. And the joy. The joy of playing opposite Anthony on stage in play after play in two-weekly rep: *Private Lives, Peer Gynt, Macbeth, Cat on a Hot Tin Roof,* the hard, hard work, the long hours, the intensity, the false but strong passion of their lives. And on Sundays Anthony went home to his family.

Finally Molly shrugged. 'That's how we lived: affairs and romance and work and immaturity.'

'That's not how I lived.'

'I know.'

'We were friends. You were my best friend.'

'I know. And I know he had no intention of leaving you and Portia, ever, for a moment. He was just playing. It was all the thrill of the moment, nothing was substantial or real.'

Then again Molly was silent. It had been something more than that and she didn't want to say so.

As Pauline had discovered at the time, Molly and Anthony had actually shared digs in the end: going to rehearsal together in the morning, learning lines together, coming home late after the evening's performance together, clinging together on his narrow bed because hers squeaked horribly, in a house in suburban Birmingham. And discovering a sexual compatibility that both thrilled and alarmed them, *that somehow became part of the way they worked together on stage.*

It was *that* that had held them.

It was that that had flared up that moment at the reunion when he'd brushed his hand against her breast.

How could a flat in Vauxhall and a wife and a young baby one day a week seem real when such heightened life was being lived the other six? How could they possibly have recognised reality, if it only appeared on Sundays? On most Sundays Anthony had gone home to his other life. And Molly, not wanting ever to go home to Manchester where her mother still lived her bitter, drawn-out days, stayed in Birmingham, her digs her only home. For Molly Sundays were long, exhausted, blue-tinged days doing their washing, learning lines, wandering the streets of Birmingham. Once the land-lady had taken something that looked like a beanbag out of a drawer in the dining-room dresser, showed it to Molly, put it in her hand. *I have cancer*, she had said, *this is my false breast.*

Molly shivered in the hot afternoon by the river, tried to push it all away.

'We had to get married,' said Pauline, staring at the old oak tree that grew beside the house, 'I suppose you knew that?'

'Of course I did,' said Molly.

'Doesn't it sound fatuous and old-fashioned now, "had to get married". My mother cried in a most unlikely manner considering that she was pregnant by someone else when she got married. And all we could think of was hiding it from my stepfather. And I always remember overhearing my uncle say – because of course everybody found out in the end – "the girl got herself pregnant", as if I did it all by myself.' She laughed shortly. 'However we had a white wedding.'

'I was there,' protested Molly. 'That was when I knew you Pauly.'

'Oh – yes. I'd forgotten.' Pauline looked up suddenly and gave Molly a half-friendly smile. 'You gave us a bedspread which I chose at Selfridges. It was green, your favourite colour.' This was the first time the two had spoken openly together since those days. Then Pauline sighed, leant back in the deckchair, closed her eyes. And then, not knowing she was going to say such a thing after thirty years of not saying anything at all, she suddenly said, 'It messed up my whole career of course.'

'I know Pauly, I know it did.'

Pauline suddenly sat up and said very fiercely, very strongly, 'I was better than Anthony.'

'I know,' said Molly.

'God I miss it.' Pauline's face was suddenly alive: taut, tense. 'Actors do get better, the more often they work, and Anthony has worked and worked and worked and got better and better and better while I seem to have stood still, that's the irony of it all.'

'I know. But you still work sometimes.'

'Not much. Less and less. It was as if I – missed my time. There's always a time, and you have to catch it.'

'Except that if you're our age and you're a woman,' said Molly, 'there's nothing much to catch any more. Look at Anthony and Terence and Harry Donaldson and all the other men in their fifties – in their prime – playing wonderful leads. But we're considered *old*.'

Pauline sat back in the deckchair, but the tension was still there in her face. 'I know. I know. At least I can be an old antiques dealer.'

'What happened to the old days?' said Molly wistfully. 'Think of Bette Davis and Katharine Hepburn and Joan Crawford, they didn't have to become MPs or retire gracefully, they were valued, films were built round them, even as they got older, so of course they still looked good.'

Pauline nodded. 'Barbara Stanwyck,' she added.

'Last year,' Molly went on, 'last year I was invited to

attend a workshop of actresses, and we worked on *Hamlet*, just for fun, just to see how it would be. I played Claudius – not boring old middle-aged Gertrude which I've played twice but Claudius, powerful middle-aged Claudius – and the thrill, oh God, I can't tell you the thrill of all that wonderful, powerful poetry coming out of my mouth.'

'But of course,' said Pauline:

> 'There's something in his soul
> O'er which his melancholy sits on brood;
> And, I do doubt, the hatch and the disclose
> Will be some danger; which for to prevent,
> I have in quick determination
> Thus set it down: he shall with speed to
>   England . . .'

Molly looked at her in great surprise. 'How do you know it?'

'But my dear I know Claudius and I know Iago and I know Benedict and I know Macbeth,' said Pauline dryly. 'I know all the wonderful parts. Who do you think hears Anthony's lines?'

'Oh Jesus!' said Molly and impulsively she leant over and touched Pauline on the arm and Pauline closed her hand over Molly's, as she had done so long ago.

For just a moment the two old friends sat very still in the sunny garden. Then Pauline took her hand away, leant back.

'Well – Anthony's succeeded; my career's more or less over now. And anyway I understood all this long ago – I became a realist and stopped hoping. I saw what it is for women, how destructive except for the lucky few. And even destructive for the lucky few, look at Juliet Lyall, a walking disaster if ever I saw one – those watchful eyes and that funny marriage to that weird stockbroker who's always abroad and no children.'

'Not everyone wants children,' said Molly.

'So I found other things. I make a lot of money from my antique shop you know. And the children have given me lots and lots of joy, after all.'

But suddenly Molly shivered again, as if she were ill; suddenly remembered one grey, cold November afternoon visiting Pauline in Vauxhall, out of work. How they'd gone to do some shopping, in their shabby coats and the baby Portia in a second-hand pram; how they'd passed the school crossing, the lollipop lady, all the mothers in the drizzling rain, waiting for school to come out as it grew winter dark, standing there. Like Molly's mother used to stand, waiting. And suddenly a feeling of such depression as she'd never felt in her life had shaken Molly and she had stared at her best friend, pushing the pram. *Never, never never this, for me* Molly had vowed to herself, *never never never never never never never* as she and Pauline and the baby in the pram moved on in the grey afternoon, past the mothers, past Woolworth's, past the vegetables spilling on to the pavement from the Indian shop, past the people standing at bus stops in the rain.

From that grey afternoon on Molly was sure: only her work as an actress was real, she would never be trapped like Pauline. It was almost as if (she suddenly thought now) it was *because* of her best friend Pauline that she had made her choices, as if Pauline's life had shaped Molly's. She arranged, almost at once then because it was 1966 and it was easy at last, to go on the Pill. It was soon after that she had got the contract for Birmingham. It was only natural that she and Anthony, graduates together, playing leads together now, would gravitate towards each other: within a week their tumultuous affair had already begun.

'I'd better go,' said Molly, standing up abruptly, and the warmth of the afternoon was broken.

Pauline peered up at her from her deckchair, squinting against the sun. 'And what about Terence?'

Molly shook herself slightly, remembered why she'd come. The newspaper lay forgotten on the grass.

'Do you think Anthony should talk to him?'

'Certainly not! Men don't talk about those things and anyway he's jealous of Terence, he'd do no good at all.'

Molly thought for a moment. 'Do you think I should do anything?'

'Like what?'

'Tell someone that there must be some mistake, go to the police perhaps?'

'Perhaps he got better suddenly. Perhaps that's what impotence does. Perhaps he wanted to – try himself out again. Rape's about power not sex anyway, that's what they say, perhaps he just suddenly wanted to try himself out.'

'Perhaps,' said Molly doubtfully.

Pauline said, 'If it comes to court maybe you could be called as a witness. Maybe you'd better offer, get in touch with his lawyers, if you really think it's any of your business. You could stand up in the witness box and tell your story – you'd be such a star! I mean just think of the headlines in the *Sun*: ACTRESS AND IMPOTENT FILM STAR IN COURTROOM DRAMA.'

And then suddenly Pauline began to laugh. She laughed and laughed in the sunshine. Molly looked bemused and Pauline looked up at her, shook her head apologetically, searched for a handkerchief in her pocket, tears in her eyes. And Molly thought: *this is how she used to be, she and Frances laughing as if they couldn't stop, this is how she was when she was young, she was so happy then.* Then she thought again of the grey afternoon and the children and the mothers.

Finally Pauline, still laughing, managed to say something.

'Sorry, sorry, it's just – well think of it, poor old Terence, he's caught in a cleft stick,' and Pauline began to cough, trying to talk but laughing at the same time, 'he's damned if he did it of course. But how can someone whose *whole career* has been built on sexual charisma admit in public that he's . . .' finally she got the word out '. . . *impotent*! Whether you wanted to be a witness for him or not – he just wouldn't do it – how could he!'

Just then the door into the garden slammed and her second daughter, Viola, ran down the grass towards them.

'Hello Auntie Moll,' she called in surprise, smiling and running, teasing Molly, knowing she didn't like to be called Auntie, 'it's ages and ages since you've been,' and she kissed her, not the way of the actresses on both cheeks, but with a warm hug. 'Hello Mum, anything to eat before I go out? I've only got an hour, look Mum I've got you a new very red lipstick like everyone's wearing now, you should try it.'

'Darling that's really not my colour,' protested Pauline, pulling herself together at last.

'Yes it *is*,' said Viola, 'I keep telling you it's all the rage now, red lipstick, you just have to *try* it.' And then she looked curiously at her mother. 'You look as if you've been laughing till you cried,' she said, surprised. 'What have you been laughing at?'

Pauline got up from her deckchair, linked her arm with Viola's and all three walked up the lawn to the house. Her face had resumed its usual calm look.

'The vagaries of this profession you're joining,' she said, putting the lipstick in her pocket, 'and yes there is food, I've made a chicken and melon salad,' and then, like a truce, to Molly, 'stay if you like.'

But Molly missed the gesture, was still cold, in spite of the hug from Viola, in spite of the day; something.

'I have to go,' she said, 'Banjo'll be home. You look lovely Viola,' and she rummaged in her bag, 'I hoped I'd see you,' and out of her bag she brought what she'd been bringing for Viola since she was a little girl and had played Molly's daughter in the TV series: the special butterscotch Viola loved. Molly had stopped for it at the special shop on her way to Chiswick.

'Oh Moll!' cried Viola, like a child. 'Oh no one's found this for me for years, you're the only one that still remembers, thank you,' and she kissed Molly again.

'I like your hair long like that darling,' said Molly to Viola. 'See you at the garden party and we'll have a good long gossip then.' She felt in her bag again for her car keys. 'Thanks for the talk Pauly. I expect it was foolish to think it was anything to do with me,' and she waved quickly, and was gone past the roses to the avenue. She looked back once, just as she got into her car: Pauline and Viola were still arm in arm, their heads close together, looking towards the river.

Driving back to Clapham in her beloved Citroën she played jazz loudly, blocking out thoughts of Pauline, Anthony, Portia, Viola, Terence Blue; if music was loud enough, she had found many years ago, she could make herself think of nothing. Only the bleak memory hovered there, behind the saxophone, of the rainy depressed afternoon and the school pedestrian crossing and the mothers and Pauline with the pram. *I couldn't have had a life like that*, she thought, *I would have turned into my mother*.

But as she turned at last towards Clapham, as her arm lay across the open window and as the jazz soared upwards in the warm evening, it wasn't Pauline or Anthony or Viola who still stayed in her mind. It was Banjo. She knew that what she had chosen for her life was not necessarily what he had chosen for his.

She changed her route, took another turning, went to the gym for an hour.

When she let herself into the flat she found Banjo lying on the sofa in front of the telly smoking a joint. But he'd found her shopping. From the kitchen came the tantalising sweet smell of a vegetable curry, cooking slowly on the top of the stove: garlic, coriander, turmeric, cloves. He smiled up at her with unfocused eyes, still lying on the sofa, held open his arms, and Molly went into them: enclosed, surrounded, safe.

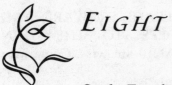

EIGHT

On the Tuesday morning after the reunion Frances Kitson put her padded bra into the bottom of her handbag. She liked to be prepared. She had been called in to an office in Greek Street for an interview for a television commercial for an insurance company. She found a room full of actresses of about her age, including Emmy Lou Brown. Some were plump, like Frances. Some were thin, like Emmy Lou. The actresses sighed, called to each other across the room, rolled their eyes, pretended it wasn't important: it was money of course, but it wasn't art. But Frances had done several adverts, had learnt something. When Emmy Lou began to whisper about Terence Blue she said firmly, 'We'll have coffee at Pritzi's afterwards,' sat in a corner of the chattering room with the three lines of the script marked **Plump Woman** and looked at them carefully.

A THIN MIDDLE-AGED WOMAN AND A PLUMP

MIDDLE-AGED WOMAN ARE EATING ICE-CREAM SUNDAES IN A RESTAURANT.

PLUMP WOMAN: How do you protect your assets?

THIN WOMAN: My husband does that for me. How do you protect yours?

PLUMP WOMAN: I prefer to protect my assets myself. I have learnt how to do it.

THIN WOMAN: How?

PLUMP WOMAN: (SHE LEANS FORWARD AND WHISPERS TO THE THIN WOMAN) I am wise. Come with me.

THEY ARE NEXT SEEN OUTSIDE A TALL IMPOSING EDIFICE VIEWED FROM BELOW. IT TOWERS UPWARDS AND HAS 'WISE INSURANCE' ON THE FRONT.

Frances excused herself to the secretary who was boredly taking Polaroid photographs of each middle-aged actress who arrived. She found a toilet down a corridor, locked the door. Out of her handbag she took the padded bra: she was fairly sure from long, long experience that she knew how their minds worked when they talked about *assets*, and *imposing edifices towering upwards*. Quickly and expertly she took off the bra she was wearing and put on the stuffed one. With the right wriggles and lifts her large bosom expanded considerably. She looked in the small dirty mirror, adjusted her low-cut dress, quickly combed her auburn hair that she always hoped people would describe as flaming red, and returned to the office. Back in her corner she learnt the three lines quickly. All around her she heard the voices . . . *darling such rubbish . . . I don't do advertisements usually of course . . . what about Terence Blue* . . . and the ubiquitous, anxious, casually posed question . . . *are you working?*

When she was called into the small studio she was confronted by a woman casting director, a male director dressed in a purple silk shirt, and a male video technician with a camera. A TV screen was disconcertingly placed so that she couldn't help seeing half of herself.

The casting director, plumper even than Frances, was looking feverishly at some papers on her knee, didn't seem to notice Frances' arrival, so she was not introduced.

'Look at the camera,' said the director without any greeting or polite preliminaries, 'give your name and your agent's name.'

Frances complied.

'Turn your right profile towards the camera.'

Frances complied.

'Turn your left profile towards the camera.'

Frances complied.

'Read the lines of the fat one in the script, read straight to camera.'

Frances complied, the casting director looked up from her papers, smiled, harassed, at Frances, read the thin part.

'Thank you.' The director dismissed her.

'Just a minute.' A disembodied voice from the

darkness behind her where she knew the clients' repre-
sentatives would be sitting looking at a TV screen. Quite
clearly she heard in slightly accented English '. . . the
right kind of figure. Tell her to breathe.'

The director came back. 'Look at the camera straight
on,' he said, 'and breathe in and out a few times.'

Frances complied: she leant forward for a moment
and then, pointing her enlarged bosom straight towards
the camera like a weapon, she breathed and said, 'My
name is Frances Kitson and I am – an actress.' She smiled
very slightly.

'Thank you,' said the voice with the accent from the
back.

Frances left the room.

She waited for Emmy Lou at Pritzi's, bought the early
edition of the *Evening Standard*. BLUE RAPE LATEST
screamed the headline. He had been remanded on bail
on his own surety of £50,000 providing he surrendered
his passport.

'Jesus bloody Christ,' said Emmy Lou, entering
Pritzi's looking sweaty and harassed. 'How can they
treat us like that, it's so insulting, I felt like a burglar
being photographed, not good-morning even, just *"left
profile right profile straight ahead"*, bastards.'

Frances only said, 'I bought you a coffee, just tell them
what you want,' and Emmy Lou smiled gratefully,
dumped her bag, went to the counter where the cappuccino machine whizzed and steamed.

They dismissed the advert from their conversation,
and Emmy Lou laughed when she noticed Frances'
stuffed bra (*how good she can look when she laughs*, thought

Frances). Soon they were poring over the *Standard* and the fuzzy black and white photo of Terence going into the court the previous day, looking away from the camera.

'What an extraordinary thing,' said Frances. 'How could he be so stupid, perhaps he was drunk, well he's often drunk, he was very drunk when we left the reunion – I thought he was actually behaving very oddly, I said, didn't I? Sort of manic, more than drunk.' And suddenly she remembered. 'I saw him, I saw him driving *Simone Taylor*, they passed my taxi just after you got out, I'd forgotten.'

'Simone Taylor! He'd hardly have had to rape *her*.'

'No, course not, she'd rape him. But . . .' she paused, puzzled, '. . . it doesn't sound like him does it.'

'You know that time I played his Lady Macbeth, whoops –' she knew it was bad luck to mention Macbeth, but only inside a theatre, a coffee bar shouldn't matter '– in our last term and everyone said how brilliant I was?'

'You were brilliant, it was an extraordinary performance.'

'Well the reason I was so good,' said Emmy Lou, 'was that I was so besotted by him that I actually wanted him to be King – King of Scotland, England, the world, Mars – anything; he used to kiss me backstage every night!' They both laughed over their cappuccinos.

'Oh poor Terence we shouldn't laugh, poor guy, what a drip I was.' She stared down at more photographs and at the story of the Reunion (which had now reached the status of a capital letter) rehashed again.

It is believed that Juliet Lyall (56), who stars in the hit production of *The Seagull* in the West End, was also present at the London Academy of Drama Reunion, as was Anthony Bonham, at present playing Iago in *Othello* at Stratford-upon-Avon. Ms Lyall was today unavailable for comment. It is understood that Mr Blue's third ex-wife, the film actress Iona Spring (25), from whom he was recently divorced, has been contacted in Los Angeles.

'That appalling Iona Spring'll be glad of the publicity,' said Frances, re-reading the list of Terence's films and his three wives' brief biographies:

> Betty Bailey, actress.
> Elvira Pugh, crime-writer.
> Iona Spring, actress.

'She believes publicity is everything. God he was so peculiar on Saturday, all that endless chat about the British Mafia In Hollywood as he calls it. Who gives a damn?' She looked at her watch. 'Come on, let's go to the movies, you said you wanted to see *The Piano* again, it's on down the road and the early show is cheaper.'

And they left the café and the noisy cappuccino machine and wandered in the sunshine down Greek Street to the cinema, still chatting: two actresses, resting.

'You'd only miss one performance of *The Seagull*, next

Monday night, they're happy to let your understudy go on once.' Juliet Lyall was also drinking coffee, but in her agent's office, poised elegantly on the cream sofa, under a large ageing but beautiful photograph of Vivien Leigh as Scarlett O'Hara.

Her agent, Horton, sat in front of a computer and a telephone and a fax on his assistant's desk and was using them all. 'It worked, you did it! This is a fantastic chance, fantastic, it'll up your status absolutely, it's what we've been waiting for for years. Female lead in a huge American movie, fantastic chance, fantastic. You'll fly first class of course, you can travel on a day flight on Sunday, meet the director in Hollywood on Monday morning, leave again early evening, back here 6 am Tuesday, sleep all day, back at the theatre Tuesday night. It's imperative darling, that you go, and *The Seagull* producers'll use it for publicity.'

'They won't give me one more night off?'

'I don't think you should ask for it. People ask for their money back if you don't appear.'

Juliet sighed but Horton did not give her even a moment. 'You are a business Juliet and this is a chance in a million. Plenty of time for you to get tired when you're not working.'

'Don't tell me that,' she said tightly. 'I know.'

'Right,' and he punched the phone, pushed a paper through the fax machine, opened the door for a moment to the outer office to call something. Doors slammed, voices called, phones rang out of time with each other. 'It's a fantastic part,' he said, 'and not quite like anything you've ever done before. The script arrived at your house last night, did it? I had a look first of course, fantastic part, very unusual.'

'I know,' said Juliet. A small flicker of anxiety just at the corner of her mind, pushed away, gone.

'I'm sure it's no more than a formality if you get on well,' said Horton, returning now to his own large leather-embossed desk 'they wouldn't get you to fly across the world on a whim. Bud Martin had seen *The Seagull* as you'd heard, so of course when the tape was waiting for him when he got back to Los Angeles he looked at it immediately, was very impressed. It was a clever idea of yours Juliet, to film that stuff and send the tape so quickly. And of course he'd seen you in New York too.' He sat back, pulled at his chin for a moment. 'He's not an easy man of course.'

'The director?'

'Mmmmm.' Horton's face was unreadable.

'I'm not an easy woman.'

'No,' said Horton, 'that is true.' For a moment he wondered whether to say more.

It is said there are no secrets in Hollywood. But it was a fairly well-kept secret that the American director, Bud Martin, would do *anything* to get the performance he wanted; Juliet Lyall would certainly not know that. The reason the secret was well-kept was because Bud Martin knew too much about some of the actors he'd worked with for them to want to talk about it. Ever. One of Horton's clients had had a nervous breakdown after making a film with him; that had been expensive, in more ways than one.

Horton looked at the self-confident, mature, but still

beautiful woman sitting elegantly across the room. She was valuable property. And, as he knew so well, she was tough. You had to be made of a toughness beyond the comprehension of ordinary people to get where she had got.

'Don't underestimate Bud Martin,' was all he finally said and he picked up the phone to dial Los Angeles. 'It would be a great great coup darling getting the part from all those American actresses, top billing, lots of publicity, and real proper money, not stage money and not English money either – real money, American money – hello *Art*, Art it's Horton, she'll be on the plane . . .'

Juliet smiled slightly, put down her coffee cup and lit a cigarette, one of the four she allowed herself each day, half listening to Horton confirming the arrangements. Everyone had known Bud Martin was casting but he'd said he wanted an *American* woman. Juliet had decided to try and persuade him otherwise; there were too few leads in movies for women in their fifties. It was Horton who had set up the filming: employed a director, a make-up artist and a crew, and couriered the video to Bud Martin's home in Hollywood, getting his American partner on to the job. But it was Juliet's idea when she had heard Bud Martin had been in the audience last week, Juliet's insistence that they make a tape of her looking completely different from the part in *The Seagull*. Juliet wanted to be a bigger star than she was already. Juliet always had energy, plans, ambition.

The script that had arrived from Los Angeles last night came back into her mind and she frowned. Of course she could do it. She was an actress after all.

'Terence Blue?' said Horton, on the telephone. 'God I suppose it's all round Hollywood, I mean *rape* of all the stupid things, what a clown, better to be caught with your pants down in Sunset Boulevard any day . . . yeah yeah Hugh Grant's now a waxwork in Madame Tussauds! . . . Terence Blue? . . . no no no, bail . . . God knows what the fuck this will do to his career . . . *Diversions* is on here now . . . wonderfully . . . yeah . . . mmmm, mmmmmmmm, well you know better than me how all that new right-wing Christian politics is working there . . . in the studio? hhhmmmm . . . well he's not my client thank God . . . yeah . . . next thing I suppose they'll make a film of his life – plenty of stuff there I should think if they nose around, yeah someone's probably snapped up the rights already, hah! Michael Jackson probably! . . . hmmmmmmmmm . . .' The conversation went on but Horton was somewhat surprised to see that Juliet Lyall had got up abruptly from the cream sofa under the photograph of Vivien Leigh and left the office.

'Darling?' he called, but she was gone.

NINE

Harry Donaldson decided to do everything on Wednesday, to settle things before he went to Morocco, quite aware of the irony of making these two particular arrangements on the same day: one cancelled out the other, so to speak.

He didn't tell Frances or Emmy Lou, his friends. He dressed in a good grey suit, put on what was for him a respectable tie even though it was hot again. In his newsagent *Good morning Mr Donaldson, started your new series yet . . . no not yet Ravi, another few weeks before I start* he avoided the headlines on the tabloids about Terence Blue, he actually averted his eyes from the photographs and the headlines about Terence's court appearance which were on the front page for the third day running.

He picked up the *Independent*, walked briskly to the part of the big hospital where he'd made an appointment. Simply unable to think coherently about what he was doing, he could only presume it was an act of great cowardice to come here, where the brickwork crumbled and people in plaster-casts jostled pregnant women down long corridors where the walls were painted pale, depressing green. Here you waited a week for the results; there were plenty of private clinics where you could get an answer the same day. *I have waited fifty-eight years*, Harry told himself, *I am going to wait another week*. So many young men in the second-floor waiting room. Some alone, some with friends: a pale unsmiling group sitting with notices about the Patient's Charter on the walls above their heads. Tension everywhere in the air. He thought of Michael.

His name was called by a nurse who looked harassed. A weary-looking Indian doctor talked to him briefly, told him to roll up his sleeve. He watched the needle go in, saw his red – almost black – blood fill a small test tube, red-black blood, healthy-looking enough, but what secrets did it contain? He was told to come back in a week, the appointment was made, he turned to go and then looked back at his blood once more as it disappeared on a tray with other test tubes into a small lift in the side of the wall and the doors closed. He felt a sudden sense of panic: how could they be *sure* whose blood was whose, there must be hundreds of mistakes, people being given wrong information, their lives changing forever.

He caught a bus, tried to read the newspaper but could not concentrate. As the bus slowed down by the roundabout he suddenly jumped off, then walked towards the cemetery. At the big iron gates he took off his jacket and slowed his pace, but not too much, walked to the area he knew best. The Council had cut back, he presumed, on caring for this place; many of the graves were cracked and crumbling and grass grew straggly and trampled, uncut: no Corpse's Charter, obviously. He always noticed, up towards the back of the cemetery, the same old headstone, half-broken, which nevertheless clearly said:

JOHN ANGUS TRADE
1868–1931
always remembered

'Always remembered by me John Angus Trade,' he said aloud. Someone of course had tried to obliterate the G.

A woman was passing with a small corgi like the Queen's. She averted her eyes as she passed Harry, walked a little faster, she believed she had seen a madman talking to a broken gravestone.

As Harry came to the quieter part of the cemetery where the trees were, he felt his heart beat. He was older now, no longer to be picked, as he once was, for his body. But you never knew: that was part of the excitement. A young man in shorts and trainers passed him, glanced, looked away, walked on. Further back a man in jeans read a tombstone casually, not loitering exactly. Harry slowed his walk slightly, felt his heart beating faster, held the *Independent* in his hand, caught the eye of the man in jeans, held it, held it, slowed, waited. The man in jeans gave a trace of a smile; Harry turned across the grass towards an old statue of some kind and the man in jeans followed. When he came up to the side of the statue Harry had already undone his trousers, waited, penis erect. The unknown man quickly undid the zip in his jeans, held his own swollen penis, knelt before Harry; Harry leant against the side of the statue, partly concealed by it from the rest of the area, pulled the man's head towards him, felt the lips grasp him, suck him, pull him, felt himself arch over the statue thrust himself at the mouth, felt himself coming, surging but holding his cry in, even now aware he was in a public place, part of the excitement. No other sound, only breathing, and somewhere a child called. The man had already pulled his mouth away, gave a sort of whispered groan, stood up, pulled up his jeans. Not a word had been exchanged, Harry had hardly seen his face, was still holding the newspaper in his hand. As the man walked away he looked back and just for a moment they exchanged a brief acknowledgement: a raised eyebrow, half a smile. Harry had a tissue in his pocket, folded it neatly after he'd used it, zipped up his trousers, picked up his jacket, walked back along the cemetery path, past John Angus Trade, out on to the afternoon-busy street, people hurrying past.

On the tube he read the *Independent*, his eye only running quickly again over the Terence Blue story which even in this newspaper was still on the front page. He thought for a moment of Nicky Abbott who had become a grey-haired old woman, and Juliet Lyall who had become one of the most admired English actresses of her generation. He wondered what they were thinking as they read the headlines. Angrily he made himself read the cricket scores. Then in his mind he saw the tray of test tubes of blood disappearing into a hole in the wall, and the doors closing.

In about twenty minutes the tube was running overground, past suburban houses, joined together row upon row in the sunshine. He looked again at the address he had in his trouser pocket as he got out of the train: Copperfield Hall, Acacia Avenue. The tube station had flowers growing in a flower bed on the platform and the ticket collector, in shirt sleeves, was bent over some fuchsia bushes pulling at small weeds. He waved Harry past with his hoe. Harry walked quite slowly, feeling the hot sun on his face, looking at people's gardens, noting that there was even a butcher's shop on the corner; not many butcher's shops left in the world, his father would have been pleased.

Copperfield Hall stood stolidly at the bottom end of Acacia Avenue, a turret pointing skywards, rose bushes, an oak tree beside the wide iron gates. Like cemetery gates. He put on his jacket.

Then he rang the bell and waited. He had made an appointment; he had decided.

The woman who opened the door was younger than him and rather pretty, and that gave him a surprise, cheered him slightly.

'Good afternoon,' he said, 'my name is Harry Donaldson, I have an appointment to see Mrs Beale.'

'I am Mrs Beale, Mr Donaldson,' she said. 'Come in.'

First he noticed a smell of disinfectant mixed with another, slightly sour, smell, then he noticed the red carpet, then he noticed all the pictures on the walls. There was a huge painting of the famous old actor

Beerbohm Tree in the entrance hall. He stared at the the-
atricality of it, all strange lights and vapours and
gestures to the heavens.

'Macbeth,' said Mrs Beale. 'We have lots of pictures,
people often leave them to us in their wills, we even
have some of the pictures Garrick owned. And see this,
this picture of a girl, Ellen Terry painted that. Come into
the lounge here and have a seat.'

But Harry stared back for a moment at the painting of
Macbeth.

'It's very – Victorian, isn't it?' said Mrs Beale, smiling.

'Very. I didn't know Beerbohm Tree played any of
the big Shakespearian tragedies, I thought it was more
Falstaff and Malvolio and Bottom.'

'He was very keen to try,' said Mrs Beale, 'but he had
a slight German accent you know, he was actually born
in Germany. He gave his Othello, terrible apparently. I
expect you know he built Her Majesty's Theatre in the
Haymarket so I suppose he could play whatever he
chose, and like most actors didn't always make the right
choices.'

'How do you know all that?' asked Harry curiously.

'My grandfather was an actor, and was in his company at Her Majesty's for some time. I was brought up
on actors' tales.'

'Have you ever acted yourself?'

'Heavens no, never. I saw what it did to my father,
being the child of an actor. But I –' she swept her hand
rather theatrically around the reception area '– I keep
my hand in, as it were, come and sit down.'

In the lounge two old ladies sat in armchairs with

covers on them; one was asleep with her mouth open, the other stared fixedly at the television set, which was off. A jaunty upright piano stood in one corner of the room with old sheet music piled on the top and Harry couldn't help himself, ran his fingers over the keys. The old lady watching the blank screen of the television turned to Harry and smiled at him very sweetly, then turned back to the television. Mrs Beale led Harry to some hard-backed chairs by the window.

'We have some great sing-songs,' she said, 'you'd be surprised how old people remember words of songs even when they forget other things. And how good some of their voices are still.' She looked at him for a moment and motioned him to sit down. 'Well, Mr Donaldson?'

Harry cleared his throat, found he felt slightly nervous, as if he was at an audition. 'I suppose you think this is premature?' he said. 'I'm not sixty yet.'

'Not at all.'

'I don't have—' Harry paused, stared out. There was a small pond in the garden, but it was fenced around by a trellis. Another old woman moved into view walking with a zimmer frame. *Oh God*, thought Harry, *what the fuck am I doing here?*

But he forced himself to continue. 'I don't have any family,' he said. 'And I've suddenly realised lately that I haven't ever really thought about – my future. I don't want to be suddenly old or ill and have made no – provision.'

Outside in the garden the woman moved infinitely slowly past the pond.

'Until lately I hadn't ever thought of being old, being ill, not working. I hadn't ever thought of – what might happen to me, how I might end up. At least I should know what my options are.'

'You've never been married?'

'No.'

'No children?'

'No.'

'What about your immediate family?'

'My parents are dead. I have a sister in Kenya. We exchange Christmas cards.'

'And what made you suddenly think now, of your future?'

Harold sighed very slightly. 'My past, I suppose,' he said. Mrs Beale looked at him shrewdly.

'Of course we do have medical care, and doctors are attached to Copperfield Hall. But this isn't a hospital or –' she paused for a split second '– or a hospice.'

'I understand,' said Harry. He understood. She had recognised that he was gay.

'Well I think you're very sensible in that case,' said Mrs Beale, 'to think about your future. Acting is such a precarious profession, one can never tell how things will end up and of course for some reason there seems to be a disproportionate amount of single people in your profession. Long ago a group of actors decided that old people's homes exclusively for actors might take some of the insecurity away from – unattached people. People here are the ones who aren't actually ill but really can't look after themselves any more, they're mostly in their seventies or older, but occasionally . . .

we have one lady here – you probably remember Alice Little?'

'Alice Little? Oh, of course I do, I've even worked with her when I was younger. But – she can't be old, she must be in her early sixties, no more.'

'Very late sixties actually,' said Mrs Beale smiling a little, 'she lied about her age of course. She has Alzheimer's.'

Harry saw in his mind Alice Little: tap dancing, shaking her curls.

'I'm sorry,' he said.

'She should be in a hospital really, she gets very disturbed sometimes and we'll have to move her soon but – I remember her dancing at the Adelphi when I was a little girl, and – I feel fond of her, silly really.'

Just then there was a cry, a cry of such distress that Harry stood up, alarmed.

'It's all right,' said Mrs Beale but she too got up. 'I'll be back in a moment.' The crying, the calling, continued; Harry at first thought he couldn't make out any words, and yet at the same time he could: *Mummy*, the voice called, *Mummy Mummy Mummy*. The idea of an old old lady calling for her mother like a child so disturbed him that he turned quickly, knocking over his chair. The woman who had been asleep in the lounge began to shout.

'Shut up!' she shouted. 'Shut up shut up shut up!' Harry saw that the second woman still stared intently at the empty television screen.

'Sorry,' he said anxiously. He picked up the chair, looked out of the window, rattled some change in his pocket. Two women in pink overalls, obviously nurses or nursing aides, strolled past outside, both smoking, both laughing uproariously at some shared joke. The old lady with the zimmer frame stood motionless now beside the pond.

Mrs Beale came back. 'Sorry about that,' she said. 'That's Alice Little. She gets upset. I know we'll have to move her from here soon.' *Mummy*, called the voice, but softer.

'Perhaps you'd like to ask me some questions?' said Mrs Beale.

What am I doing here? thought Harry. *I'm not going to be old anyway.*

They discussed the home, the facilities, the cost, the medical care. The sun shone outside on the pond with the trellis around it and on the motionless old lady beside it. An elderly man wandered rather aimlessly into the lounge, saw Mrs Beale and Harry and came over to them at once.

'Good afternoon my dear,' he said to Mrs Beale, 'lovely day.' He looked expectantly at the visitor, someone new to talk to.

Harry's jaw dropped. 'Good God!' he said and his voice caught in his throat. He stood up quickly.

Mrs Beale laughed. 'If I had fifty pence,' she said, 'for every time someone has walked in here and said Good God because they met someone they'd worked with I could retire to Florida. Well – actors always know each other, don't they!'

The old man stood there for a moment, quite still. And then he said courteously to Harry, 'My name is

Roger Popham. Have we worked together perhaps? You must forgive me, I forget things, it's one of the disadvantages of getting old.'

'Oh yes!' said Mrs Beale. 'You remember what you want to remember Roger Popham, I know you!'

Harry recovered almost immediately. 'I think we must have met somewhere,' he said. 'But years and years and years ago. Harry Donaldson.' And the two men shook hands politely, but Harry's hand was shaking.

'Well Roger,' and Mrs Beale stood up again, 'perhaps you'd like to show Mr Donaldson around, he's interested in Copperfield Hall, tell him about the place, tell him what ogres we are.'

The old man nodded, politely held Mrs Beale's chair away from her. 'Delighted, delighted,' he said smiling at her. 'There will be no ogre stories from me however. We are very lucky here,' he said to Harry, 'as you will see for yourself when I escort you around these hallowed halls. Though I must say you look like a very young man to me, hardly yet in the need of the services of our esteemed Mrs Beale and her staff.'

Mrs Beale laughed again. 'He always talks like that,' she said to Harry, 'it's all that Shakespeare he used to do,' and Harry saw how fond she was of him. 'I'll see you before you go Mr Donaldson,' she said and she bustled away.

'I have done very little Shakespeare actually,' said the old man, 'but when I was young we all talked like this, that's what actors sounded like in those days! Sometimes I quote a bit of *Romeo and Juliet* to her just to keep her happy,' and his eyes twinkled mischievously. 'Blame Noël Coward and Johnny Gielgud.'

'Did you work with them?' They wandered out into the hall and up some stairs.

'Oh I knew Noël slightly, as did all the pretty young men of my time. Now here the bedrooms begin, they are small but perfectly formed as you will see.'

For half an hour the two men wandered slowly round Copperfield Hall, looked in rooms, talked about toilets, finally sat in the garden drinking tea which had been brought round on a trolley. Not once had the old man acknowledged that he recognised Harry and Harry realised it was very likely he had forgotten. But Harry knew this man.

With their teacups from the trolley they sat in the warm garden and the old man talked about a life that had been. Harry, unsettled, nevertheless sat back in the garden chair, felt the sun on his face, let the old man talk on which he so obviously enjoyed doing. He shook his head once more at yet another name mentioned. 'George Thomas, you must remember him at the old Gaiety Theatre?'

'I'm afraid I don't,' said Harry politely, or occasionally, 'yes I think I've heard that name.' Roger Popham was talking of people who worked in the theatre almost before Harry was born. Very occasionally he could say, 'Yes of course I've heard of him,' and once even, 'Oh yes, Algie Twod, I worked with him in my very first musical, I remember wondering if that could possibly be his real name.' He felt there was something infinitely sad about all the unknown names: *so much for fame*, he thought.

And all the time, in his mind, he saw the piece of waste ground in York, remembered the taste of blood on his lips. And then, like an odd flick of a switch, he saw the blood in the test tube.

'All these names,' said Roger suddenly, 'well of course you won't know most of them, it's foolish of me, I lived abroad for much of my life you see, that's why the people I talk about are from long ago. Anyway I was never a well-known actor dear boy, well, I wasn't good enough. Pretty face, that was all. I only ever worked here occasionally, I'd come back for a while now and then but I always felt . . .' the old man paused '. . . uneasy here. I was happier in the circus.'

Harry looked at him in astonishment. 'You worked in a circus?'

'For many years I did, yes, you'd be surprised how many actors ended up doing something like that, we travelled around France and other countries in Europe. I sometimes worked as a clown, I worked with the chimpanzees, I even, if you can believe it looking at me now, did a little trapeze work, just the simple stuff, you know?'

Harry looked again at the old man, at his thin body, that looked somehow fragile now. 'I wonder why it is that the circus always seems so romantic,' he said, 'the kind of place you want to run away to and change your life.'

'I did just that,' murmured Roger Popham.

'We had a girl in our class at drama school whose father worked in a circus. We thought it was the most exciting thing in the world.'

'Which circus was that?'

'Oh heavens, I've no idea, I'm talking more than thirty years ago. And she – what happened now? – I think he disappeared or she lost touch with him or something. But I remember she made him sound so glamorous, we were all so envious. My father was a butcher in Falkirk, which couldn't compete at all!'

The old man nodded. 'And it's all true in a way, it was a wonderful world, the circus, for someone like me anyway. It was like having a family. Occasionally I came back here, tried to make a go of things, tiny parts in TV when it started, tatty tours – that sort of thing. But I always found I missed the circus, went back again. They always took me back.' He paused to blow his nose. Harry saw his watery eyes and the red veins on his cheeks, but he also saw the fine high cheekbones and the full head of white, white hair.

'But when I was too old, well – then I had to come back for good.' And he sighed very deeply. 'You can't be old in foreign countries.' Laboriously he put his handkerchief back in his pocket.

'But I miss the life – the circus was my family I suppose – well that's what theatre is isn't it? Like the circus, all that working together, all that packing up together and travelling late at night together after the audience is gone, all the cases and the scenery piled up on the station platforms at midnight, do you still do that young man, last train to Edinburgh via York, that sort of thing?'

Via York.

But the old man was sitting back in his chair and his eyes were closed.

Harry said carefully, 'You must be talking about a very long time ago. I don't think British Rail runs trains that late any more, people are always rushing about in cars, someone else does the scenery these days.'

The old man nodded slowly. 'I expect it's all very different now,' he said.

Harry glanced at his watch. His turn with Michael tonight. It was almost six o'clock, birds were coming to settle and squabble in the trees around the garden.

Almost reluctantly he stood up. 'I have to go,' he said, 'but it's been good to talk to you Roger. Perhaps we'll meet again.'

'Oh I don't expect we shall,' said the old man, getting up very stiffly from the garden chair, grateful for a moment for Harry's arm. 'By the time you're old enough to come here dear boy I expect I will have gone to that Great Stage Show in the Sky. You have no idea how young you seem to me. But I'm extremely glad to have had the pleasure of your company and I do hope I haven't bored you rigid. '

'Not at all, not at all,' Harry said. *I think he remembers me. Yet why should he remember me? It was all so long ago. Would I even remember the one from the cemetery this morning if he came to my door?* But finally he added because he had to, 'I'm – I'm so very grateful to you, Roger.'

'Yes,' said the old man and for a moment he looked at Harry. Then he said, 'Don't think of old age before it comes to you Harry. You shouldn't be thinking of it yet, you're too young. And you know dear boy, I think anyway that a certain kind of queer like I am, and like you are, is used to being alone. That's after all how it often was, wasn't it?'

Harry looked startled, felt something, a blush almost, some expression he couldn't hide in his own face. But the old man had moved ahead, gone into the lounge again to find Mrs Beale.

When Harry got back to his flat, there was a message from Juliet Lyall on his answering machine.

As soon as he heard her voice, which he recognised at once, he switched off the machine, lit a cigarette. They had bumped into each other, of course, at the reunion. *Hello Harry*, Juliet had said, *Hello Juliet*, said Harry. That was all. Just the sound now of her voice in his study disturbed him. *Yet it was more than thirty years ago.*

Finally he turned the machine on again. Juliet wasted no time on preliminaries.

'Harry it's Juliet could you call me as soon as you get this message either at home or at the theatre?' She left two numbers.

The answering machine ran on; two more messages.

Michael: 'Where are you Harry I need you, you know it's your turn tonight.'

His agent: 'Ring me darling about a costume fitting before you go to Morocco.'

Harry did not ring anybody. He was due to take over with Michael at nine, he was on all night again. He sat on the first-floor balcony of his small house in Kentish Town which overlooked communal gardens. A beautiful warm evening and yet somehow you knew it was the end of summer now, the light was different. *Where is the test tube of blood now, this minute, is it sitting in some corner of the hospital, waiting quietly with its secrets in the dark?*

Children called to one another; a group of them were playing with something that looked like a surfboard, incongruous in this urban garden so far from any sea. They were sliding along the grass, pushing each other, laughing.

One night long, long ago in York, when he was in the repertory company there, just before he took Juliet Lyall to Brighton, Harry Donaldson had been beaten up on some waste ground near the railway station. He was wandering there that night, late after a performance, because he knew homosexuals came there and he knew he was a homosexual but he didn't know what to do about it. *I wanted to meet someone, I was twenty-four and I was unformed and I was desperate.* He thought the man in the park was giving him a signal, he approached him and – he blushed even now to think of it – he'd put out his hand to touch the young man's cock. The young man shouted out QUEER QUEER and two others had appeared from nowhere and had set upon Harry, kicking him, kicking him especially in his genitals but another man had also appeared suddenly with a stick and had hit out at the young men and told them the police were on their way. One more kick in the face and the young men fled and Harry lay there on the ground, weeping and bleeding, curled up in a ball.

The man with the stick had knelt down. It's all right dear boy, he had said, it's all right, and he had given him his handkerchief.

I wish I was dead, Harry had said.

No no, said the older man.

After a while Harry stopped crying, wiped the blood from his nose.

Where do you live? said the stranger. Can you get home all right?

I'm an actor at the theatre, said Harry, I live in digs just near there.

Good heavens I'm an actor too, I'm just waiting for the train connection to Edinburgh, I'm on a tatty tour, round the number two theatres, terrible play, terrible part, what are you playing?

Snug the Joiner, Harry sniffed into the handkerchief, *A Midsummer Night's Dream*.

Ah, nice part.

I'm rubbish, said Harry, I'm just rubbish, all I am is rubbish, and he began again to cry.

Dear boy, said the older man gently, I'm sure you're not. But let me give you some advice. Find out about yourself, but not on pieces of waste ground like this. There will be others like you in the Company, there always are, look carefully and you'll find them. But don't come here again. Not until you're surer of what you're doing. It's too dangerous in this country. And he got up. Harry saw him dust the dirt off his big winter coat and then *finish doing his trousers*. And in that second Harry understood: the man had been here to try to meet someone too. The lights from the railway station shone there, not so far away.

I must hurry to catch my train, the older man had said, get home quickly now, and he waved and turned away. But Harry called out after him.

What is your name? he had cried out in a kind of despair.

And the man, good-looking, in his late forties perhaps, had turned back for a moment. *Some people call me Popka*, he had said.

It began to get dark in Kentish Town but still Harry Donaldson sat staring at nothing as the light faded.

TEN

Frances Kitson, too, had noticed the change in the light. It was less than a week since the reunion, yet the heavy feeling in the air had changed. Summer would soon be over at last. She smiled to herself and hummed, enjoyed the small morning breeze drifting in through her open window. She had work.

The coming autumn was always a better time for her profession: the work suddenly appeared, new TV series seemed to be cast, repertory companies planned their next year's season. But best of all Frances had got the part of the plump lady in the television commercial for the Wise Insurance Company which meant she would earn some money; she and her agent worked out that she'd make at least £8,000 and a great deal more if the advert was very successful. It was a big campaign that the insurance company was planning. She patted her padded bra fondly as she washed it by hand in the bathroom basin.

But Emmy Lou hadn't got the thin part and Frances

sighed for her friend. Emmy Lou was such a good actress – much better than Frances, better at her job than most of them. But over the years most of them had realised: often it wasn't just about talent, it was about energy, and it was about fierce ambition and it was about who you knew. And even after all that, so much of the time it was just about luck.

'I just feel so – hopeless. I feel I can't go on any longer like this.' Emmy Lou's voice on the phone was bleak. 'All I want in the whole world is to work.'

'Em, this is our life, it's like this.'

'It's like this for some of us. It's like this for me.'

'Shall we go to the movies again?'

'Thanks Fran, not today. Glad about your advert.' And Emmy Lou hung up, picked up her keys, went out into the corridor. There was a lift in her block but she ran down the stairs, picked up her mail from her pigeon-hole on the ground floor. Brown envelopes and charity brochures. She stuffed everything back into her pigeon hole, went out into the Finsbury Park morning, not noticing the sunshine. She walked quickly along the street. Outside the newsagent she saw that Terence Blue was still on the front page, but smaller because there were developments in Bosnia. Interviews with all three of his ex-wives were promised on Sunday.

She made for the park, walked quickly, hoping that somehow exercise would push some of those endorphins into her blood, somehow make her feel less angry at the thought of the unfairness of her life. She knew she was a good actress, she had held on to that knowledge fiercely for years. But she hadn't made it and now it was too late because, and it terrified her to think of this thought, *now even success couldn't make up for the waste of the years.* Over and over again in her mind the words of an actress who had committed suicide echoed: *If you make acting all your world, it will let you down.* Faster and faster she walked, past the children's playground, past the full-blown roses, past mothers with prams, past the dry leaves lying on the paths.

Walking out her life, on a Thursday morning.

'Darling they want you to play Harriet Richards. They're sending you a script.'

'Who am I to play?'

'Harriet Richards. The aunt.'

'Oh she's got a name now, good!'

'Quite good money if you like it. They say the role has developed since Monday, and may develop further.'

Molly laughed. 'Who knows what it'll be then in a week's time,' she said. 'I might turn out to be the murderer after all.' She had taken her agent's phone call still in bed, still wrapped around Banjo who often slept till noon whether he'd had a gig the night before or not. She put down the phone, curled herself again round his back.

'Good?' he mumbled.

'A job,' she said. 'A bloody job at last. '

He turned at once, put his hand between her legs, kissed her hair.

'Good,' he said, as he fell asleep again.

•

Although they hadn't had one for so long Pauline had always liked planning the garden party, she liked arranging it all: the invitations, the food, the wine, the garden. They'd stopped them for some time, not for financial reasons, although like everybody else they'd felt the recession, but because in the summer Pauline and her two younger children had started going to France for long periods so that the children's French could really improve. Sometimes even Portia came in her designer leisurewear, taking brief time off from her public relations job (*actually it's called corporate communications now, my work*, she would say to her mother's friends), but she and her mother snapped at each other, old battles unresolved.

'Please, please, please, *please*,' Viola had begged them months ago, 'won't you have a garden party again when our last term starts in the first week in September; you haven't had one for years and years. Don't you want to see all your old friends again? And it's so important for all my classmates to meet people in the profession, we'll be on our last lap at the school. We all know nepotism rules, it's all right for me, I've got you two and know lots of people but some of them know nobody and it would be so important for them, there's only ten in my class now, please please *please!*'

'I hope you don't expect me to be there if you have it,' Benedict had said gruffly when they first talked about it, sprawling at the kitchen table with his maths homework, long legs reaching almost to the door.

'I would expect you to be there young man,' said Anthony, 'a seventeen-year-old should have some social graces.'

'He's got social graces,' protested Pauline, 'he just finds actors boring because they're not computers, in fact knowing actors all his life probably sent him screaming into computers.'

Finally it had been agreed; Viola had whooped with delight and kissed her father, and Benedict had finally been persuaded that it could hardly proceed if he wasn't there pouring wine, as he had done with great enjoyment every year when he was a little boy.

Now Pauline read out the order to their wine merchants on the telephone, confirmed it should be delivered tomorrow, Friday.

'Didn't you know Terence Blue?' said the vintner, who used to take great personal interest in the Bonhams' garden parties, often contriving to be there on the day with the excuse of an extra order, extra glasses, something.

'He was in my class at drama school, years and years ago.'

'And often at your garden parties. So pleased you're having one again.'

'That's right, yes.' She realised with a start that Terence would have received an invitation to this one. *But he wouldn't come, surely.*

'Terrible business, terrible,' and she could already hear the prurience in his voice.

Viola flew into the kitchen, mimed to her mother that she was going to a party that night (waggled her hips, took a drink of champagne, kissed a fellow thespian, smoked a joint, danced a tango) and was gone.

The voice on the telephone was still discussing the terrible business of Terence Blue. 'Right, yes it is terrible, thanks Mr Cooper, see you tomorrow,' and Pauline hung up still smiling at Viola's performance. Viola had only ever wanted to be an actress; both Pauline and Anthony had tried to dissuade her, talked to her about the difficulties of being a woman in the profession, and the heartache. Pointed out how successful Portia had been in a different sphere. But Viola could not be dissuaded: *I'll be luckier even than you were Dad*, she had said, *my drama school's not stuffy and unrealistic like yours was. They teach us to be strong in adversity. And after all: nepotism rules OK!*

So Pauline smiled to herself as she went out into the garden to trim the edges of the lawn, clip the hedges. She had once been like Viola. Viola would make her own decisions. And she had made very sure that Viola knew everything about birth control and condoms.

And hopefully, she found herself thinking wistfully, Viola would put her career before anything else in the world.

Juliet Lyall stared again at the silent telephone. Then she surveyed her face in the mirror.

She shouldn't have fought for this film perhaps. She did not read the script a second time. She was not sleeping, had had to resort to more sleeping pills that left her looking puffy and jaded in the mornings. She would not go out until she had done hours of exercise; stood for a long time under the shower till her face had somehow miraculously righted itself.

And on Sunday she was to fly to Los Angeles for a meeting.

She scanned every newspaper, saw how Terence Blue's life was pulled apart and examined, half-truths and outright lies mingling with the facts of his life up until the day of the reunion and its bizarre conclusion and she heard again Horton's voice on the telephone to Los Angeles *I suppose they'll make a film of his life . . . Michael Jackson probably . . . plenty of stuff there . . . if they nose around . . .*

Horton arranged the plane tickets, biked scripts to her that he felt she should read, turned down the more ridiculous offers that came her way most days, fielded the press who clamoured for some more interesting statement from her about Terence Blue rather than the bland one about her shock and distress for a respected colleague that the agency had finally put out late yesterday. She and Anthony were the most famous of the class of '59 after Terence: most newspapers were managing to make the innocuous lunch-time drama school reunion sound like a bacchanalian orgy of luvvies that somehow Terence and Juliet and Anthony had personally organised.

Juliet Lyall, one of the most well-known English actresses of her generation, sat alone in her house in Cheyne Walk and waited in vain for Harry Donaldson, who had been with her in the class of '59 to return her call.

Harry, who knew everything.

Putting on his make-up, in his dressing room in Stratford-upon-Avon, Anthony Bonham thought about Molly, and how it had been, so long ago.

She wants me again, he said to himself, *I'm sure she*

wants me, and she looks terrific for her age, not like any of these silly young things. He quite bitterly realised that younger actresses who interested him were, some of them, the same age as his daughter Viola and the thought discomforted him and he felt sour and old, wondered if he had bad breath, used mouthwash and dental floss. He was still a catch, of course, because he was one of the leading actors in the company; he could have had, had indeed had, affairs with several of them. He would buy them little gifts and take them to restaurants outside Stratford where discreet waiters knew him and put him in quiet corners. Occasionally one of the young actresses had got too serious, even caused scenes, and these things had begun to tire him. He would stop that silly business. He assumed it was a sign of a new maturity and he pulled his shoulders back, felt strong and wise. But Molly was his age, and sensible, they had known each other for more than thirty years, loved each other in fact, all that time ago in Birmingham. A quiet affair with Molly, that would be calmer. He hadn't really thought about her much for some years, but he found that when he did think about her now, as he had continually since the reunion, that actually, calmness was far from what he felt. Her mouth. He remembered her mouth. He knew she was sometimes knocking around with a young musician, had brought him once to one of the garden parties years ago. *But she must want me still – something happened there between us at the reunion; I know it did.* He decided to write her a charming note and courier it to her, saying he was looking forward to seeing her at the garden party, but intimating more, that would please her.

Anthony Bonham was frightened of getting old.

He wanted his youth back and Molly reminded him of his youth.

He wanted Molly.

The telephone rang in his dressing room. It was one of the most powerful men in the business.

'Tony it's Joseph Wain. I've got a fantastic project. I want to arrange to meet you tomorrow to talk about it even before I talk to your agent.'

The tannoy in the dressing room called fifteen minutes as he put the phone down. His heart had leapt as it always did at the thought of something new. *A fantastic project* – Joseph Wain was not the kind of man who used words like that lightly. He looked in the mirror, and automatically hummed. So that his lips vibrated and his whole head became an echo chamber for his voice.

Nicky Abbott lived, now, by the sea. Long ago, when she was briefly one of the most famous and glittering young actresses in England, when anything seemed possible and her star shone, she and her new husband had bought a house in Brighton.

Laurence Olivier had suggested it while in some theatre green room where a lot of actors sat together. *Dear people it is an actors' haven, and breathing the sea into our lungs is good for us all. And what's more,* he rolled his rrrs and ended in a declamatory tone known to half the British public from his film of *Henry V, I've arranged kippers for breakfast on the early morning train to London.*

Nicky Abbott's house had been let for years, had

grown shabby as successive tenants had passed through. One lot had painted the kitchen and bathroom walls orange. Nicky, now, very slowly, was redecorating her house.

'How are you Nicky?' said the social worker. 'Managing all right are we?'

'I think I'm managing,' said Nicky in the dark, smoky voice.

'Using the supermarket and the library all right? Managing the money?'

'I've always known how to do that,' said Nicky. She had done the shopping since she was eleven, when her mother first became ill. She was the one who'd actually arranged to buy this house in Brighton because the man she was to marry was away working. It was silly to think people would forget such skills just because, when they came back, everything cost more and there was decimalisation. She wasn't a fool.

'How do you feel Nicky?' said the community psychiatric nurse.

'I feel all right.'

'Taking your medication?'

'Yes.'

But it wasn't true. She had stopped.

She didn't say that, even with medication, being in the house had brought the memories back, sharp and clear. The things she had been cured of.

She didn't say that she knew Terence Blue would come.

Neighbours didn't know who this grey-haired woman was, they were new, they saw her sometimes up ladders, sometimes staring down at the sea, smoking a cigarette. These old and beautiful Georgian houses were in a crescent that encircled grass, away from where most of the tourists trampled as they poured out of the railway station and down to the sea-front and the fish and chip shops.

Sometimes the neighbours saw that she seemed to stare oddly at the grass, as if puzzling about something.

In this crescent the sun shone in through long windows across wooden tables and comfortable chairs; in the evening tasteful lampshades reflected light on to people who had money. The grey-haired woman, the neighbours saw, painted her walls and window-frames very slowly, very meticulously, but had very little furniture yet in her front room. Just one wing-backed chair that they could see. One or two of them had been told her name: Nicola Abbott; one man thought he vaguely knew the name, couldn't quite put a finger on it.

Nicky Abbott painted, very slowly, the house of her dreams.

She knew that he would come.

Back in her large penthouse that overlooked Central Park in New York where the doors were only opened by combination codes and where security guards were always on duty downstairs, a woman woke in the night, screaming out before she realised where she was. It was the smell that haunted her: not of Dior and Calvin Klein but of garlic, and stale sweat, and the smell of the sheets. And the whisky.

And at the end of that week, one week after the reunion, Simone Taylor, who used to lean on the piano and sing Judy Garland songs and who lived in a country where giving confessional interviews was really part of the show business to which she had always dreamt of belonging, gave an interview to the *New York Post*. Her business colleagues in New York read her interview with utter amazement. They became deeply embarrassed at her revelations, didn't know what to say to her, cleared their throats anxiously when she came into a room, began treating her like an ageing, fragile doll.

When her husband, a Wall Street banker, left her for a younger woman after twenty years of childless marriage, Simone Taylor was given anti-depressants. And it was to Terence Blue, her old obsession, that she turned for solace. In her mind.

She was a very clever businesswoman.

Competitors were fooled by the little-girl voice, didn't take her seriously, next thing they knew they had been subject to a takeover bid and no longer had a company. Her business colleagues found her energy exhausting, and her little-girl voice extremely irritating; they nevertheless admired her business acumen and were sometimes rather afraid of her. There was something almost demonic about the way she took over company after company, especially after her divorce. She had many important contacts and many important acquaintances.

But no close friends, who might have said to her: *What are you doing Simone?*

STAR'S RAPE VICTIM SPEAKS the headline ran. The information could not, for legal reasons, be republished in England where a rape victim's anonymity is protected by the law. But within the gossipy world of show business, and especially among the group of survivors of the class of '59, within twenty-four hours it was common knowledge that it was Simone Taylor, Cosmetic Executive, who was accusing Terence Blue of rape.

As the sharp pain in her vagina became a dull ache, as the bruises slowly faded on her breasts, she stared at herself in the mirror and whispered to herself, in the little-girl voice, not *What am I doing?* But what she had said in the Press interview: *I am doing this for all women.*

She thought of Terence Blue and the way he had kissed her.

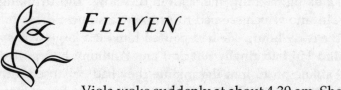

ELEVEN

Viola woke suddenly at about 4.30 am. She thought she heard rain. But it was only the Thames, stirring for a moment in the darkness, and Viola threw her duvet aside, too excited to go back to sleep. Then drifted off again, lying on her back and snoring slightly, dreaming of Fame.

The Sunday of the garden party at the Bonhams' house dawned sunny, just a little crispness in the air at first to show it was September in England. From early morning, small boats and long boats chugged along the Thames at the bottom of the garden, people looked up as they passed, at the tables and the glasses laid out on the lawn. Viola waved to a small boy who was trying to get her attention by leaning over the side of a canal boat calling out 'bugger bugger'.

The Bonhams had hired the Chinese boyfriend of an actor who had Aids to make the food, to show that they were not ignorant or prejudiced about a subject that was so rife in their profession; he'd spent all yesterday in their kitchen preparing. When Anthony had arrived back from Stratford-upon-Avon at 2 am, having driven home after a few drinks with a young actress understudy who lived in Hammersmith who had kissed him rather lingeringly as she got out of the car, he had found the young Chinese man, Ho, still in the kitchen preparing duck. Pauline was sitting at the kitchen table smoking, a thing she seldom did now, and drinking Cinzano which seemed to Anthony a strange drink for the early hours. He had poured himself a large whisky and Ho had finally left at 3 am. Anthony had pulled Pauline on to him the minute they had collapsed into bed. He pushed his finger into her anus as he thrust himself up into her, stroked her clitoris with rapid precision as she strained back. And he briefly contemplated (as she moaned very quietly just after he came) how good it was, after all, to be married to someone whose body you knew so well.

'I'm so glad it's sunny,' crowed Viola. 'See Mum, it was all right to wait, it's a lovely lovely day, did you see that little boy shouting BUGGER at me, little bugger, his parents were cracking champagne at the front of the boat. He'll grow up to be an actor, I bet you a thousand pounds.' Viola had, some years ago, decided that anyone she saw behaving badly would grow up to be an actor, like her father.

'We did invite Angela Dee didn't we?' called Anthony, slightly hungover by the French windows.

'Yes, yes, I checked all the casting directors,' whooped Viola, 'you asked all the casting directors who'd ever employed you from that list in your study and a whole lot of the new young ones as well.'

'Don't shout,' said Anthony.

Pauline put more glasses on the tables on the flat part of the lawn at the top of the garden before it sloped down to the river. The voice of Tom Waits echoed soulfully and almost but not quite out of tune from the sitting room, where the Sunday papers, already rumpled by Anthony, lay on one of the sofas.

'Look at this crap,' he called, waving one of the papers at them on the lawn, 'the appalling Iona Spring has revealed to the world that Terence liked her to wear no knickers. Do we need to know this? I ask myself, and even Elvira is featured, in her spectacles.'

Exotic smells wafted from the kitchen where Ho had begun cooking in earnest, helped now by two Chinese women he'd brought with him at 9 am. Benedict appeared, yawning.

'Any breakfast?'

'Have you had a shower?'

'Yeah, yeah.'

'What are you going to wear?'

'This.'

'Over my dead body,' said Anthony.

'Go and get some Weetabix,' called Pauline.

'*Weetabix*?' queried Benedict in disgust.

'Weetabix,' said Pauline firmly. Benedict wandered off but Pauline saw him look carefully at himself in the long mirror by the French windows.

'And don't forget,' she called after him, 'to check that the Smartie machine still works, I've put it down by the river.' Benedict had invented a little machine that dispensed Smarties when buttons were pressed in a certain order, to entertain visiting children (and to introduce them, he said, to computer basics). Some of the actors of Anthony's generation were on their second or even third families and brought their latest offspring to such occasions, with their young, young wives.

Pauline's mother, the ex tap-dance champion, frail now and a widow but who wouldn't miss a garden party while she could stand upright – an event less and less likely by three in the afternoon, had already arrived and had already had a drink with Anthony. Rather unsteadily she laid piles of plates, and forks wrapped in serviettes. She used one hand, holding her glass rather gaily in the air with the other. She and Viola were discussing a Hollywood movie about the life of George Sanders which had recently been on the television. *I knew him y'know Vi*, Mrs O'Brien was saying, *I did the foxtrot with him once in the Café Royale*. She was just giving a little foxtrot demonstration along the carpet when the doorbell rang.

'Jesus, it's only quarter to twelve,' groaned Anthony, 'people aren't supposed to arrive till half past, Benedict go and change that T-shirt *at once*,' and he walked to the front door.

They all heard Anthony's surprised voice because the Tom Waits CD had just come to end.

'*Iona*! Iona, come in darling, come in, what a surprise!'

'Heavens,' whispered Pauline to the others, 'it's the

appalling Iona Spring, how on earth did she get here? She lives in Hollywood. Thank *God* Elvira's at a crime-writers' conference!'

Iona Spring, the third ex-wife of Terence Blue, wafted into the sitting room of the Bonham's house trailing clouds of Guerlain and sighing. Benedict, coming down the stairs with an almost identical T-shirt on, gave an audible gasp as he caught sight of her.

'Darling!' cried Iona Spring to Pauline, '*was* it all right to come?'

'Of course Iona,' said Pauline pleasantly. They kissed, more or less, on both cheeks. Iona did not take off her dark glasses

'I just hope the press don't follow me here, I'm having such a *dreadful* time with them. I knew it was the garden party because I saw Terence's invitation on the mantelpiece in the Hampstead house, I still have a key, I only arrived yesterday. Terence wasn't there of course, I expect he's in his house in Suffolk, well I mean where does one *go* actually when one is remanded on bail for rape?'

'Have you spoken to him?'

'Oh we don't speak darling, not since we split up.'

'But you went to his house?'

'D'you know darling I left some exquisite shoes there when I moved out, so I thought I'd pick them up.'

Just for a second, just when she said *I thought I'd pick them up*, Iona's South-London accent broke through. 'Do you know the press were *camping* in his front garden, I suppose they urinate on the roses.' She shuddered slightly. Then she turned to Anthony and in the sweetest

Received Pronunciation said to him, 'Darling is there just a little champagne with perhaps mostly orange juice?'

'Come and sit outside Iona,' said Pauline, 'and Anthony will bring you a beautiful Buck's Fizz.'

'Is there *just* a little shady bit?'

'There's just a little shady bit, under our beautiful oak tree, you will look a picture.'

'Don't mean to make a fuss darling but I'm in the middle of filming and I must be careful. Oh – Elvira won't be here will she?' She dimpled prettily.

'No,' said Pauline rather shortly.

'Does she hate me still for taking Terry away from her?'

'Elvira never hated you Iona,' said Pauline. 'She is very happily married now to a very very rich farmer who is a friend of the Queen.'

'Oh,' said Iona.

'Why ever are you here in London, Iona?' said Anthony, bringing champagne and orange juice, settling Iona under the oak tree. 'Not that it isn't lovely to see you,' he added hurriedly. Viola hung behind, tongue-tied for once in the presence of a film star; Mrs O'Brien was also speechless and Benedict had only just moved from the staircase, his mouth still open in a kind of O of admiration as he walked automatically towards the CD player.

Iona shrugged, accepting the drink. 'One of the Sunday papers paid for me to fly over, I had lunch with the editor as soon as I arrived yesterday, they wanted me to spill the Terence Blue Beans, you can read it all today if you want to, paid me loadsa money. Of course you know that Cosmetic Executive has talked to the American newspapers but that can't be printed here so they need people like me to tell my story.' She gave a little smile, waved her hand vaguely in the air.

Pauline looked shocked. Iona had been a model, an eighteen-year-old not very well-known model, when she married the very very famous Terence Blue, after he'd left (*been pushed darling*, said Elvira) fifty-year-old Elvira Pugh. Now Iona Spring was a film star in Hollywood.

Pauline knew very well that the acting profession was littered with women whose careers had sky-rocketed when they married, or had a child by, or at least had a well-publicised affair with, a man whose power in the profession could give them work. Several actresses working in the big London companies would be here this afternoon whose careers had flourished due to these well-timed personal moves. It didn't mean they couldn't act: often they were very good actresses which is how they came to the attention of the men in power in the first place; but there were plenty of good actresses. These ones simply leapfrogged ahead in the game. Viola would, at least in the beginning, leapfrog over her class-mates because her father was Anthony Bonham, a leading English actor, and her mother had been very well-known in her time. Pauline felt grateful that Viola at least had that start, knowing many people in the busi-ness. Iona Spring's rise in Hollywood had been spectacular because she wasn't an actress at all when she married Terence; the least she could have done in grati-tude, Pauline thought now, was keep her mouth shut.

Last night, when Anthony had come home, she hadn't mentioned Molly's visit earlier in the week and their talk of Terence. But she suddenly wondered what Iona had actually said to the Sunday papers, hoped it wasn't to do with Terence's sexual prowess

'Why ever would you want to talk to the press about him when he's in such trouble?' she said to Iona, more angrily than she meant to.

'Any publicity is good publicity, and we always need publicity, you should know that,' said Iona sharply, the South-London accent quite clear again and for a moment her mouth shut tightly, like a trap.

'Jesus I don't know why there's all this fuss,' said Anthony crossly, 'it's only a rape.'

'What do you mean *it's only a rape*?' said Viola angrily. 'Don't talk like that Dad.'

Madonna suddenly sang loudly *like a virgin* from the sitting room and Benedict sauntered through the French windows.

'I only meant darling,' said Anthony to Viola, 'it's not murder, nobody's died, nobody in the profession knows Simone Taylor except us who were in the same class and know what a hopeless actress she always was, I'm surprised at all the fuss.'

'You mean it doesn't matter if she was raped because she can't act?'

'No Viola, I *don't* mean that. I just mean it seems to be dominating the newspapers out of all proportion to its importance.'

'It's a crime, for God's sake, and he's famous!' said Viola. 'He's one of the most famous men in the world, his films are known everywhere. It's as if – Prince Charles raped somebody.'

'My God, I wouldn't put it like that,' said Anthony, exceedingly put out. As long as Terence stayed in Hollywood and didn't move in on his English patch, Anthony could feel he was the Star of the class of '59. 'One of the most famous men in the world, bloody old Terence?'

'Bloody old Terence.'

'Who can't act, we all know he can't act *really*, we were at drama school with him!'

'He can act on film,' said Iona yawning prettily in the sunshine. 'Oh my darlings they love him in Hollywood, his agent's going spare, the producers of the movie he's supposed to be starting are going spare. I was very careful what I said to the press, I'm not –' and for a second she looked up at Pauline shrewdly through her large sunglasses '– a fool you know. On the other hand I don't want my career to go down the drain even if his does, I gave them lots of tits and bum stuff but I said I had loved him dearly and I couldn't imagine him raping anybody but I left him because I wanted to have children. And, as Elvira knows too, he didn't.'

'And are you having them now?' enquired Pauline.

'There's plenty of time,' said Iona sweetly, 'for me.' But she looked suddenly sulky and fiddled with her glass, looking down. She knew very well it would have been better for her career to stay married to Terence: she was already finding it harder as only one of his ex-wives, couldn't get quite the same attention, and she was twenty-six now, that was old in Hollywood. No one knew it was Terence who had forced her to go, who suddenly in the spring wouldn't sleep with her any more, had divorced her in Reno before she'd even had time to get used to the idea.

'Will it?' said Mrs O'Brien anxiously, speaking at last but already slurring her words very slightly.

'Will it what?' said Iona, looking up at Mrs O'Brien in slight puzzlement.

'Go down the drain, his career?' said Mrs O'Brien.

'Depends,' said Iona, taking a compact out of her handbag, staring at herself, still with the dark glasses on, then putting on more lipstick, moving her lips against each other, looking at herself from both sides. The family, all intimately connected to show business and quite used to seeing make-up being applied, nevertheless all stared. Then Pauline smiled like a hostess.

'Oh sorry Iona,' she said, 'you don't really know our family do you, perhaps you might have met the children years ago but – well they're grown up now,' and she introduced everybody to Iona, whose eyes rested speculatively on Benedict. The doorbell rang.

The doorbell didn't stop ringing from then on, even though the door was open; people seemed to want to announce themselves by ringing the bell loudly and long, *I'm here I'm here*. The guests arrived thick and fast, crowding in at the door group after group, thronging in the hall, spilling out into the garden, noisily greeting the Bonhams and each other. They held out glasses and accepted drinks. Anthony stood in the hallway, greeting people warmly, kissing them, making himself as charming as he knew very well he could. He was peeved to notice that Molly had brought her young musician, but smiled knowingly down at her when she kissed him on the cheek and thanked him for his note. He saw that she was dragged away almost at once by Viola; the two of them sat together on a corner of the lawn, heads together, laughing. It made him feel slightly odd.

Pauline also watched Molly, and felt, suddenly, some odd constriction in her heart. *Oh God I missed her*, she thought. *Perhaps we will be friends again after all.* She put on her big dark glasses suddenly so that nobody would see the sudden softening in her eyes.

Frances and Emmy Lou and Harry had, after conferring with Pauline yesterday, brought Michael. He was thin and gaunt, had no hair now. Michael had been, for a while, one of Harry's live-in lovers, a beautiful boy of seventeen when Harry was already over thirty. He'd been a dancer in the first production of *Cats*; when he'd got too old to dance he'd become an under-manager in the linen department of one of the big London department stores. He was dying of Aids.

'Hello Michael,' said Anthony warmly, 'good to see you old son,' and Pauline kissed him, took his arm, walked with him, very slowly, into the garden.

The female host of a chat-show, whom everyone disliked intensely, arrived with her new lover. Anthony smiled and kissed her and said how pleased he was that she was able to come (and Pauline observed how put out she was to see Iona Spring sitting under the oak tree). But the chat-show hostess was soon surrounded by her own coterie: people hoping to be asked to appear on her programme.

Izzy Fields tripped in behind them with her school-teacher husband and her youngest son, Lysander, and her safety helmet.

'Bet you didn't come on your bike all the way to Chiswick from Tufnell Park,' someone called cheerily to Izzy, and she surprised them all by calling back, 'Yes I did. Peter came on later with Lysander. It was absolutely lovely cycling along the tow path at Hammersmith, I so enjoyed it.' People shook their heads in wonderment, guiltily lit another cigarette; Izzy Fields was a character, she must be nearly sixty, surely.

The garden was soon full of people holding glasses and talking loudly, seeing who they could see, the atmosphere heightened even further as one by one people realised that *Iona Spring* was sitting under the oak tree in dark glasses drinking champagne and orange juice. Many of the visitors didn't actually know her, only recognised her, whispered to each other, *that's his third wife* while young children ran down the lawn to Benedict's Smartie computer and the river. A well-known television director who suffered from asthma was surrounded by younger women because he was casting a new series about beauty contests. Directors from the National Theatre and the Royal Shakespeare Company stood in the sunshine, earnest men huddled together with the ones with whom they were on speaking terms; actors crowded around them. And, in one corner of the garden, another group of directors laughed together, the new power: the women.

There seemed to be two topics of conversation: the main one of course was work, who was doing what, who had seen what, plans, intrigues, gossip, but most people also looked at Iona Spring out of the corner of their eye and speculated about Terence Blue.

Benedict served drinks as people's glasses emptied – his job. Now and then he flicked his long floppy hair out of his eyes with a shake of his head like a nervous horse, gangling and beautiful as his mother had been. Iona Spring called to him as he passed.

Pauline watched all the networking – it was called 'networking' (though she knew there were other, more unkind words for it) – going on all over her garden. The young ones from Viola's class – the boys cocky and nervous, the girls excited and shy – were the most blatant but somehow the most endearing.

'Excuse me,' she heard one of them, Zac, a handsome dark-haired boy, say to Anne Schwartz, a powerful casting director in film and television who swayed slightly drunkenly in the sunshine. 'Excuse me Miss Schwartz, I'm Zachary O'Shaunessy – no it is my real name –' as he saw her smile disbelievingly '– I'm a classmate at drama school with Viola, you know Anthony Bonham's daughter, I'm playing Coriolanus at the end-of-term show, would you come?' Pauline saw the casting director's eyes first look appraisingly at Zac, then glaze over at the very thought of a student production of Coriolanus. But then they focused again on Zac's very presentable exterior.

'Hello Zachary,' said Anne Schwartz, and she smiled into his very young face. 'Would you mind getting me another drink?'

Pauline turned away from Zac's progress to see a

group of men huddled together in one corner of the garden, by the rose bushes: she saw the Director of the National Theatre and the Chairman of Channel Four in the group, among others. They were surrounding a slightly taller man who seemed to have engaged all their attentions and as she watched, she suddenly recognised him, *my God it's Joey*. Most unusually for her, her mouth literally dropped open in surprise.

Just at that moment the taller man looked across at where she was standing. She saw him excuse himself from the group, and then come across the lawn with the long, lolloping stride she remembered. *My God it's Joey*.

The most powerful television executive in Britain stopped in front of her. He didn't kiss her, or even put out his hand.

'Hello Pauline,' said Joseph Wain.

'Hello Joey,' she said.

She hadn't seen him for years and years. She'd known Joseph Wain in her West-End, blouse-removing days when he'd worked in the production office of the company that had put that play on.

Everybody remembered Joseph Wain because of his hair. Due to some quirk of fate, or genes, it grew upwards only, so that he looked like Struwwelpeter in the old admonitory German children's stories, or like a comic-book version of somebody having an electric shock. In the sixties when Pauline knew him it just made him look surprised all the time. In the seventies his career was meteoric and that may have been partly due to the fact that, to the trend-setting media world, as well as being a whizz kid he looked like a punk in a suit. He was one of the few television executives who occasionally appeared in front of a camera, as well as behind it, his hair his mark, the thing people remembered. In the eighties and nineties his hair had suddenly turned white, growing upwards still. Once, long ago, by the ticket window at Leicester Square tube station, he'd told Pauline he loved her. *I love you because* – he had hesitated – *I see that kind of veneer of style that you've perfected so cleverly but Pauly I know your heart's underneath. And I love you because I think it's . . . endearing, that thing about wanting to fly like this father that I don't believe you've ever met.* Pauline, at the tube station, was deeply shocked, as if he could see the inside of her head. She had quickly laughed.

Don't be silly Joey, she had said, I'm in love with Anthony Bonham, you know that.

I know I know, young Joseph Wain had said. And had added slowly: I just wanted to tell you, because I'm getting married on Thursday.

And just for a moment she had thought, almost subconsciously: *oh*. Somehow she *minded*. And then she had quickly shaken the surprising thought away and said: Congratulations Joey.

She briefly remembered this odd, old exchange as she smiled up at him.

'Oh it's so good to see you Joey,' she said. 'I haven't seen you for ages, you look terrific.' And she looked at him again. His face looked young still, and his eyes were alive and beautiful still, although his hair was white. 'But there's something different about your hair.'

'I cut it really short at last,' he said, 'it's slightly less alarming for my old age.'

Pauline smiled. 'Well, even elderly I *would* have invited you,' she said, 'but it's years and years since I've seen you . . .'

He laughed. 'Anthony suggested I come, I had a meeting with him on Friday as you know.'

Pauline didn't know, but smiled again. And then, without quite knowing she was going to do it, she reached up and touched his short, white, springy hair, an odd, unusual gesture for her. 'It feels nice,' she said shyly and he smiled at her and did not move. For just a moment they stood together that way and then, feeling she was blushing slightly, she took her hand away.

'Well, I'm so glad you could come,' she said a little formally, regaining her composure.

'Lovely party, lovely day,' he said. 'Look, I want to talk to you, as far away from that – spectacle –' he pointed to Iona Spring holding court under the oak tree surrounded by a gaping audience '– as possible. Terence Blue is too soft to be a rapist.' Pauline looked at him sharply but he was not making any sniggering innuendo. 'He's a pussycat under all that macho performance, I bet you a quid there's more to all this than meets the eye.'

'Ah Joey, you were always the last of the big spenders,' said Pauline teasingly. 'I remember all those cappuccinos you used to buy me, cappuccini.' Then she added carefully, loath to talk about what Molly had told her, 'You may be right though, about Terence.'

They walked down towards the river, through the guests who filled the garden now. The sun sparkled on the water and small craft chugged by, people staring up at the party. For a moment they stood in silence.

'Well how are you Pauline?' said Joseph at last, and she saw that he was staring at her. 'You know, you look absolutely beautiful. If it doesn't sound rude, you've aged very well.'

'Thank you,' said Pauline.

'Tell me,' he said. 'Do you still want to fly?'

Pauline felt deeply uncomfortable at this reference to the past that was gone. 'I was just dreaming about my father in those days,' she said rather tightly. Joseph smiled an odd smile at her. And then he broke the moment and got quickly down to business.

'Well has Anthony talked to you, what do you think?'

'About what?'

Joseph Wain frowned at once. 'Ah, then he hasn't. Well we only met on Friday afternoon and he's been at Stratford of course. Still, I'm rather surprised he hasn't even mentioned it.' For a moment he frowned again. 'Anyway: I'm just beginning work on a fantastic television project. I've got – we now own – the core of six one-hour scripts, wonderful wonderful stuff about treachery in international politics – it's frightening how much of it there is about apparently – and these scripts are – or will be – excellent, quite excellent, outstanding in fact: America, England, Bosnia, the UN, South African diamonds, Mandela's government, nuclear testing in the Pacific – the lot, absolutely perfect for the international market, and we're going to make it as the first really international television production, stars from every one of the countries involved but set in London with the sleaze set. It's to be called *The Immoralists* and we've been talking about Anthony for the English lead, as the British Prime Minister.'

'Oh,' said Pauline. 'Well, that'll be nice for him.'

'But there's almost as big a part,' continued Joseph, 'as the Prime Minister's wife, and I've suggested you.'

Pauline's heart – she couldn't help herself – lifted, leapt up. 'Go on,' she said, noncommittally.

'Well as you can imagine there's talk on the board of the company about a second English star etcetera – you know, the usual stuff – what the Americans will put money into . . .'

'Yes of course,' said Pauline. 'I understand how it works. But it was good of you to try.'

'But they're wrong and they're stupid, if they get their way they'll blow it all by having someone absolutely useless like the appalling Iona Spring playing the part, Jesus. Anyway, I've been trying to persuade them that there's a lot of publicity mileage in having a couple – I mean a real-life, married couple like you and Anthony – and Anthony's certainly star enough to carry the English side of a project like this. The thing is Pauline,' and Joseph's head moved closer to hers so that they looked like all the other scheming groups on the lawn yet he spoke quite formally, 'I think you *are* a star. I want you to come and have lunch with me next week and talk about this properly away from all these praying mantises. I know you can do this because I've never forgotten you when you were young, you had star quality then, you had that – thing – whatever it is. And I don't believe that ever goes away.' It was true that for a while, back in the sixties, Pauline's performance was talked of everywhere and the world seemed to be, briefly, at her feet. Nobody could move through the West End without seeing pictures of her long, bare, and somehow vulnerable back, on the black and white show poster that had long ago become a collector's item.

Suddenly Pauline looked at Joseph in alarm. 'But you don't mean I'd have to take my clothes off?'

'Well there are some sex scenes of course.'

'Joseph *I'm too old*. You know I'm fifty-six. What fifty-six-year-old woman would take off her clothes in front of a camera?'

Joseph looked at her shrewdly. 'Actresses your age are always complaining there aren't any real parts. This is a real part. Any self-respecting fifty-six-year-old would kill for it. And I want you to do it. She is the heroine, she saves the world.'

Something somewhere inside Pauline Bonham moved slightly, something in her heart, or her soul, some small sliver of ice cracked slightly, moved slightly as if – unbelievably at fifty-six – spring might still come.

'Oh Joey,' she said simply, looking not at him, not at anything, her eyes somehow hooded and focused inwards. 'Pull this off. I'd give anything in the world for you to pull this off, anything at all, you don't know what I'd give for one more chance.'

She turned to face him at last. 'I mean anything,' she said.

At about two o'clock Ho the Chinese cook gave a little sign to Pauline and Viola.

'Would you like to go in through the French windows

and help yourself to some food,' they said, moving among the guests, smiling and kissing. Ho and his two helpers had placed plate after plate of delicious-looking food on long tables in the huge sitting room: crispy won tons, crispy duck and pancakes and spring onions and plum sauce, chicken cooked in lemon, vegetarian spring rolls, fried prawns, sweet and sour pork, large bowls of rice. Everyone was used to how hungry actors always were but even the directors and the writers and the casting directors swooned and fell upon the culinary delights. Bottle after empty wine bottle piled up in a corner of the kitchen; there was already a crate of empty champagne bottles outside the kitchen door. As if on cue, Mr Cooper the vintner arrived: 'Just in case,' he said to Pauline innocently, a large case of wine held out in front of him as he suddenly stared in amazement at Iona Spring under the oak tree.

'But – I've just been reading about her in my newspaper not half an hour ago,' he said unbelievingly to Pauline, 'all about being married to that rapist and all the drinking parties and that, and how he wouldn't let her wear knickers.' He still held the heavy case of wine as if he'd forgotten he was carrying it in the shock of clapping eyes on a film star.

'Well why don't you put that case down and go and introduce yourself to her?' said Pauline smiling at him, and the vintner, unable to believe his good fortune, pushed his way through the crowds.

And Pauline, looking around her very successful garden party, saw how some of the very successful men, the directors and the writers, had again formed a little group now around Joseph Wain. Where the real power was.

Harry Donaldson popped a fried prawn into his mouth as he made up a plate of food that he hoped would interest Michael. He turned, with the plate, to see Portia Bonham – Anthony and Pauline's oldest child – walk out through the French windows and into the crowded, sunny garden. She was wearing a white dress and she stood there for a moment, surveying the scene. Harry, watching her, put the plate of food back on to one of the long tables, not knowing he did so. As Portia, tall and thin, stood there in her white dress, so still, so – disdainful, almost as though the scene angered her – Harry felt a kind of odd falling feeling in his head, a memory of a night long ago that he didn't want to remember. The white dress and the anger. He closed his eyes briefly. As he opened them he saw Portia lift her hand, wave to somebody, move gracefully across the grass. Harry rubbed his hand across his face, turned back to the food.

Looking round the long, successful gardenful of people talking and laughing Emmy Lou felt, once again, out of things. Only her fierce belief in herself sustained her at such gatherings: she watched almost in fascination as Iona Spring held court; it turned into disbelief as she heard a BBC director talking to Iona about Strindberg. As she turned away to look for her friends, Frances and Harold and poor Michael, she bumped, literally, into a short, very plump woman whose (luckily empty) glass rolled on to the grass.

'Oh my God, sorry,' said Emmy Lou and bent to pick up the glass. The plump young woman smiled, accepted her glass back and then looked at Emmy Lou more carefully.

'You played that lovely neighbour in a wheelchair in the West End, I remember you, that was such a good performance in all that shit.'

When Emmy Lou smiled, as her friend Frances had noted often, her whole face lit up, all the lines and pulls of disappointment suddenly turned upwards and surprised the observer. She smiled now at the plump woman, who was obviously an American, who went on: 'I was at Cambridge and I had already decided I wanted to be a director but while all the other wankers were drooling over Shakespeare and Ford and Pinter I used to haunt the West End whenever I could and see the rubbish and try and decide why it was successful, why it made money, that's how I saw that garbage and that's how I saw you.'

Emmy Lou laughed. 'I'm taking all this as a compliment!'

'So you should. My name's Pamela Angel – and I *am* a director now and I'm directing a play on the fringe and we're starting tomorrow and we've lost one of our actresses and oh my God it would be such a good part for you. Look this is totally bizarre, I don't even know your name – could you read the play? We only pay expenses of course, look what *is* your name? Forgive me for not remembering.'

'Emmy Lou Brown—'

'Are you free now Emmy Lou Brown? Like literally tomorrow?'

'I'm free,' said Emmy Lou, dispensing with all the small face-saving talk about waiting to hear about another job.

'OK Emmy Lou Brown, who's your agent?'

Emmy Lou told her. Pamela Angel whipped out a pen and notebook from her voluminous handbag, made a note, pulled out a script, snapped the handbag shut again.

'Would you read this? The part of Alice? And come and see us at the Holborn Centre tomorrow at ten o'clock? There's no salary as I say but we pay expenses and I *promise* you this is a play in a million.'

'I'll be there,' said Emmy Lou.

'O lordy lordy and heaven be praised, what a bit of luck. In that case I'll phone my producer who's having a nervous breakdown and tell him to stop this minute.' And Pamela Angel gave a little salute of the hand and disappeared back into the crowd, rummaging in the voluminous handbag and then coming up with a portable phone which she started dialling. The whole exchange had taken about two minutes. Emmy Lou saw her again through the crowd almost at once, gesturing with the portable telephone and talking to the Artistic Director of the National Theatre. Emmy looked down at the script in her hand in something like disbelief, hugged it to herself, then went to fill her glass and find her friends and tell them that it did matter where you went and where you were seen, after all.

Molly's young man Banjo had found another musician he knew, Chris, sitting right down by the river smoking a joint. They were soon sharing a second joint and talking about the music Chris had composed for the Royal Shakespeare Company's productions some years ago. Molly, talking to an actor she'd been in a TV series with, sought out Banjo with her eyes, saw him sitting there, so peaceful and content, talking music and she smiled back at the television actor, who suddenly thought, *Molly McKenzie's beautiful I never noticed*. And Molly McKenzie, chatting to the actor, smiling, was thinking, *I am happy: I can feel the sun on my arms and I have my work and I have my Banjo and I'm happy.*

'I saw that production of *A Midsummer Night's Dream* with Molly,' Banjo was saying down by the river, 'and I remember that music really well. I've always thought I'd like to sample it, that stuff you had with the bells for Titania you know? I'm making an album now, have you got a copy of it? Would you let me sample it on my computer? It would work great with one of my songs. I'd pay you of course.'

'I have to talk to you young lady,' said Anthony at Molly's shoulder, 'about *work*,' and smiling apologetically at the actor she was talking to he led her into the house.

Harry Donaldson, holding a prawn, called to Pauline, 'Darling this is *delicious*, where were you last Saturday? We missed you at the reunion.'

'Well that reunion's been on every front page in town,' said Pauline smiling at him. 'Let's hope this is not such a public one though who knows –' and she lowered her voice '– with the appalling Iona Spring sitting under the oak tree like Little Miss Muffet. Ah Harry, I'm so glad you brought Michael. But, oh God he looks terrible, poor thing. He's going to die soon isn't he?'

'Yes,' said Harry.

They both stared in silence for a minute at where Michael was sitting, also in the shade of the oak tree, talking to Frances who was making him laugh.

'Harry does this mean – have you had – have you—?'

'It's a long, long time since Michael and I were lovers,' said Harry, 'but yes. I finally did it last week, I get the results the day I fly to Morocco on holiday later this week, I thought that would be fitting.' He smiled at her brightly.

'Oh Harry.' Pauline awkwardly put her hand out to Harry, rested it on his arm, not knowing what to say.

'Ah Pauly.' And he took her hand in his, held it there in the sunny crowded garden, among the calling and the laughing, quite silent.

'You know,' said Harry, recovering, 'you look so beautiful, your eyes are shining, do you know that? You've aged better than all of us Pauly, do you realise? And I was talking about you the other day, I met a circus performer.'

Pauline's face closed up just a little.

'Mmmmmm' she said, looking about her garden.

'He was an old man, I'd say he was about eighty, I'd – I'd met him years ago actually, and he was telling me he'd worked in France and lived in a caravan, and I did wonder if he might have known your father, you know, two Englishmen working in circuses, or is it circii, in

France, but I couldn't remember any details of your father.'

'What was his name?'

'His name was Roger,' said Harry.

For the second time in half an hour Pauline's heart gave a violent lurch.

She gripped Harry's arm hard, surprised him. '*Was he gay?*' she said.

He stared at her. 'As a matter of fact, yes.'

Pauline's face looked quite odd, something strange in her eyes that Harry couldn't read, and just then someone pulled at her. 'Darling Pauline such a wonderful party, such a wonderful day.'

'Wait there,' Pauline hissed at Harry quite unnerving him. She kissed the new arrival, 'Darling lovely to see you, Benedict will get you a drink,' and she waved at her son who was passing, 'and help yourself to food while there's still some left,' turned back quickly to Harry.

'Harry my father was gay and he worked in a circus in France and I've never met him.'

'What do you mean *you never met him*? He was the hero of the class!'

'I – made it up. But it was true, he was in a circus and – and his name was Roger – Harry what was his other name?'

'Oh come *on* darling,' said Harry laughing at her, yet his stomach gave a tiny, unpleasant somersault. Was it *Pauline's father* who had saved him in York by the railway station?

Almost fearfully Pauline asked her last question in a small voice. 'Was his name Roger Popham?'

Harry sighed then. 'Yes,' he said.

So there, in the middle of the laughing, chattering – even now shouting – crowd of people, Harry told Pauline – *I don't want to tell her, though, how I met him long ago* – about his visit to Copperfield Hall. She became paler and paler as she stared up at him, listening intently.

Finally she said, 'I have to meet him.'

Harry didn't say anything for a moment, stared about at the crowded garden. People pushed by, called out, someone kissed Pauline. 'He's a very old man Pauly. I had the feeling that for him –' he tried to choose his words very carefully, '– the past is over.'

Anthony took Molly right to the top of the house, to his study. He shut the door, put his arms around her, and kissed her. 'Oh Molly I've missed you,' he said burying his face in her hair. Briefly Molly allowed herself to be in his arms, felt all the familiar feelings. She was ashamed, and at once disturbed, to feel how quickly her whole vulva seemed to expand and moisten almost instantaneously, felt at once how hard he was against her. He was actually trembling. But she pushed him away.

'Don't do that Tony,' she said shakily, pushing her hair back, retreating.

'Oh Molly,' he groaned. 'I knew. I knew at the reunion.'

'It's a long time ago,' she said, 'for God's sake it's years and years ago, so much has changed since then.' She stopped, took a deep breath. 'It's just that – everybody remembers things from when they were young, but that's all a long time ago, when we were young and working together and everything seemed romantic . . .' and he heard that her voice shook, '. . . we've both had lots of affairs since then – Tony I know you have affairs –' as he opened his mouth to protest '– I'm living with someone else. That was when we were young.'

'But you haven't forgotten, have you?' He put out his arm, to touch her again. He wanted to feel her mouth with his fingers, knowing what it could do. But she was adamant.

'Tony I won't even talk to you if you don't sit down. Over there.' She pointed to the chair by his desk. Reluctantly he sat down, and she sat on the small arm-chair opposite, but he leant forward urgently.

'It was seeing you again,' he said, 'it all came crowd-ing back.'

'We were young,' she kept saying, 'it was when we were young and playing all those parts together.'

'We're still young,' he said, 'and look at you anyway, cavorting about with a man half your age. No, no, I'm sorry –' as Molly stood up quickly '– sit down again my darling, I'm only jealous. Oh God Molly. I want you with all my heart, you remember how it was, not like with anyone else.'

'I know,' said Molly quietly, and if she had been look-ing up she would have seen a gleam of triumph in his eyes but she was sitting with her hands tightly together looking at the floor. 'Tony it'll never be like that with anyone else, but you're talking about sex, I'm happy now with Banjo in all sorts of different ways, I'd never be unfaithful, I love him in a completely different way than I loved you.'

'But the sex isn't as good is it?' He was leaning towards her urgently and she could see the bulge in his trousers, 'and the thing is, something's happened, I've only just found out, I think I may be able to arrange for us to work together again, something big. You *know* how well we work together, this is the chance of a lifetime, and it'll be like before. It'll be just like before, like it was in Birmingham.' He was breathing fast. Molly stared at him, felt the old familiar sexual feelings come back so strongly that she could hardly breathe, clenched and unclenched her hands, didn't speak – and that is how Pauline found them when she opened the study door looking for Anthony, running up the stairs to tell him about Joseph's conversation, and about her father: not in each other's arms but in a room where the tension and sex could have almost been touched. She turned at once and walked away.

'No, *no* Pauly,' called Molly jumping up at once, her cheeks suddenly crimson, and Anthony got up also, swore under his breath. Molly ran along the passage and down the stairs, but Pauline had disappeared. She had quietly gone into one of the spare bedrooms and locked the door. She might have wept, or raged perhaps but she didn't do either of those things because her mother was passed out on the double bed, a glass lying on the floor beside her, a trickle of brandy on the light cream rug.

Pauline sat beside her mother and held the old wrinkled hand in hers, for comfort.

Down in the garden the noise was even louder as people

got drunker and drunker. One of the shy but cocky young men had vomited into the Thames and Viola, ashamed of her classmate in all this glittering crowd, was wiping frantically at his waistcoat with a serviette. Banjo and Chris got up to help her, saw how upset she was.

'Don't be cross with him,' said Banjo amiably, 'he was probably nervous having to meet all those people, I know I would be if I was an actor.'

'Aren't you an actor?' said Viola curiously, looking at Banjo's face, feeling that she knew him, letting go of her classmate at last, leaving him to wander unsteadily up the lawn.

'God no, me and Chris are musicians. I'm Molly McKenzie's – um – partner.'

'Oh yes, of course I know who you are. I've known Molly since I was a little girl, she was at drama school with Mum and Dad, and then I played her daughter in a TV series,' and Viola blushed suddenly, somehow thinking it sounded as if she was pointing out Molly's age in comparison with his own. 'Yes of course, I've seen you before,' she said to Banjo shyly.

'I expect you have,' said Banjo. 'I've been around for a while.'

'Have a joint with us,' said Chris.

'Oh I'd love to,' said Viola, recovering, smiling at them both, taking the cigarette they passed to her, 'but my dad has pointed out that if I'm going to be a famous actress I have to keep circulating and circulating, round and round and round, I might not get so many useful people in one space ever again.' She inhaled quickly and deeply then handed the joint back, laughed at herself, ran up the lawn.

The first long shadow of the autumn afternoon fell across the river.

People lay about on the grass now, some had fallen asleep even, and the machine with the Smarties had stopped dispensing. A television director was still wondering to Iona Spring if she'd be interested in playing a Strindberg heroine for the BBC early next year and as she stood up at last and stretched very seductively she said she'd think about it. The television director paled with excitement. Anthony's agent talked in a serious huddle to two comedy writers. Ho and the two Chinese women collected plates, picked up the odd fork and pork bone off the lawn. Frances and Anthony were talking about Terence Blue and the reunion.

'Dad can I borrow the car?' said Benedict, flicking his hair.

'What the hell for?' Anthony held a large glass of whisky, glowered as he saw Molly's young man coming up the lawn towards them, fell slightly against Frances, looked crossly at his son.

'Darling, do let him drive me back to the Hilton, I'm absolutely exhausted.' Iona Spring was at Anthony's shoulder.

'Absolutely not!' said Anthony, turning quickly to her, outraged. 'For God's sake Iona, he's seventeen.'

'Drive me, darling, that's all I said.'

'What's the matter,' said Pauline, freshly made-up and smiling, 'what is it Iona?'

'She wants Benedict to drive her back into London, I said it's out of the question.'

Benedict was almost white under his summer tan with rage and humiliation. 'Stop treating me like a child!' he shouted at his father, and guests turned to listen. Anthony grabbed at Benedict's arm before Frances, standing next to him, could stop him. Benedict pulled away, swung his arm back as if to hit his father. Banjo, who had reached the top of the lawn, grabbed Benedict's arm, yet quite gently it seemed, or Benedict felt, for he stopped at once, looked at Banjo in puzzlement for a moment. Then he turned and walked back into the house.

'Jesus Iona,' said Anthony, and drank back the remains of the whisky that hadn't spilled

'He's gorgeous and he's got to start sometime,' said Iona to Anthony cheekily, 'although frankly I think you've got a dirty mind if you think I'd do anything with a *boy*. Perhaps you're jealous darling, now that you're old and balding and he's so beautiful.'

Anthony's face turned bright red. He swivelled around quickly and walked into the house also.

For a moment nobody said anything. Pauline had not spoken, but now she said, 'Have another drink everybody, Iona I'll call you a taxi.'

'No no,' cried the Strindbergian, 'I'll drive you Miss Spring, it will be a pleasure and we can talk about the Strindberg play further.' There were several drunken guffaws, quickly silenced. Iona gave a little, real, sigh. Then she followed it almost at once with a big theatrical one.

'Darlings I am exhausted, and no doubt the press will be waiting at the other end. I must go, and I would be eternally grateful Mr –' she struggled and remembered '– Mr Hibberd, if you would drive me.' She waved and was gone, the director in her wake. She hadn't until that moment moved from under the oak tree all afternoon, she had looked beautiful continuously for nearly five hours, and the scent of Guerlain hung there still, in the air.

Suddenly Pauline began to laugh, and Frances, standing there looking after Iona Spring in amazement began to laugh too. They leant against each other now as if it was 1959 still, they laughed and laughed and laughed, so that everybody around them, unable to help themselves, began to laugh too.

'*Strindberg!*' cried Frances, tears rolling down her cheeks. '*Strindberg!*'

Laughter everywhere, in the summer garden.

'Poor poor Terence Blue,' said Pauline finally, wiping her eyes, 'have a drink for God's sake, everyone,' and she and Frances giggled and murmured to each other still, and the chatter began again, the odd clink of a glass.

But the party was, in a way, over. The shadows lengthened up across the grass from the river, the women in their pretty summer dresses shivered a little, looked for jackets. One by one people came up to Pauline and Viola standing together: to say thank you, to say how much they'd enjoyed themselves – the food, the wine, the company. Anthony appeared and smiled goodbye too, got into conversation with a plump casting director; his agent joined them, they huddled together, planning something.

Molly and Banjo came up to Pauline and Viola; Molly and Pauline were not actresses for nothing, smiled good-bye to each other politely and Pauline thanked Banjo for intervening in the fight.

'How did you stop that son of mine so – simply?' asked Pauline curiously.

'I got no aggression in me man,' said Banjo, parodying himself, and then, quite simply, 'I think people can feel it.' Molly's eyes suddenly filled with tears and she turned away to Frances and Harry for a moment, hugged Michael gently who stood so pale on the grass beside her.

And then she quickly turned back to Pauline, the best friend of her youth. She didn't kiss her but she put her hand urgently on Pauline's arm. 'Pauly, Pauly listen, please. It wasn't what you think, *please*.'

Banjo had leaned over to kiss Viola on the cheek, so no one saw Pauline O'Brien turn sharply away from Molly McKenzie, violently pushing the hand away from her arm.

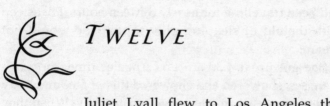

TWELVE

Juliet Lyall flew to Los Angeles that Sunday and so missed the Bonhams' garden party; missed seeing Harry Donaldson who she was trying so hard to contact but who hadn't returned her calls; missed seeing Anthony Bonham's beautiful son Benedict take a punch at his father; and missed seeing Iona Spring, the third ex-wife of Terence Blue the famous film star. Or as she and Harry Donaldson knew so well, Iona Spring, the fourth ex-wife of Terence Blue the famous film star. Missed also the sun setting over the Thames and the long shadows across the garden.

Juliet stared out of the plane window, waved the hostess and the champagne away.

Of course she could do it.

That same flicker of doubt lay there, somewhere at the back of her mind.

About the time they flew over the white-capped vista of Alaska she fell uneasily asleep, the latest copy of

Vogue falling from her lap; woke as dusk fell, saw the horizon catch fire, a wild red panorama, unimaginable colour unless you'd seen it: there, above the world. *The world was hers. She must not lose what she had now.*

She was met at Los Angeles airport by a chauffeur, arrived at the hotel to a large bouquet of white roses and a note from the director Bud Martin saying he was looking forward to seeing her for breakfast at 8 am. She had been travelling for nearly thirteen hours, fell asleep with the aid of sleeping pills so that she would not dream.

She got up at 4.30 am Los Angeles time, did yoga exercises, showered and showered till her face and body made some sense, made herself up expertly. When they buzzed her room at 8 am she was ready. She emerged from the lift looking like what she was: not a film star – they were ten a penny in Los Angeles after all – but an acclaimed and admired actress of a certain age with a still extraordinarily striking bone structure to her unforgettable face.

She walked, knowing this.

The grey-haired but balding director, seated in the lounge, watched her walking towards him. There was something enigmatic about her, some – he couldn't quite put his finger on it – secret. Although he called it 'English reserve' it wasn't that, he knew it wasn't quite that. The tape from Horton had been waiting for him when he arrived back in Los Angeles. It could work, he knew it could work, it didn't matter if the woman was English. But it was a risk. Most of the part he knew she could do easily, he'd seen her work enough to know, and with those bones she still looked wonderful on camera.

But to put it bluntly he had to know what kind of a woman she was in bed.

Not of course for himself, he liked young bodies – she was old after all and he didn't like old women's bodies with their used-up quality and flabbiness that couldn't be hidden and falling breasts. But for the film. Under that enigma what would he find? For he would eventually find it, of course. Not this morning, but eventually. He had to find it for the part to work: age and sex in women – an interesting concept in Tinseltown. Well, that would be the challenge.

Bud Martin stood up, a big, powerful man. One of the most famous and successful and feared men in Hollywood smiled as the English actress Juliet Lyall came towards him.

'Good morning Miss Lyall,' he said and he took her hand in his.

They sat and talked in a small, private dining room over orange juice and thin pancakes with maple syrup and coffee. The foggy Californian sun shone in across the end of the table, across a beautifully arranged jug of magnolia blossom whose scent filled the room.

'You've read the script?'

'I have. It's a wonderful part of course.'

'It requires such – intangible qualities. I haven't been able to find what I'm looking for and I sure have spent many hours looking. It has to be somebody who – an actress who understands.'

'Yes.'

'You know what all those scenes with the young guy are about?'

'Of course.'

Bud Martin stared out into the smoky sunshine. Avocado trees grew there, just outside the window. 'Age and desire,' he said slowly. And then he turned back to her, looked at her carefully. 'Age and desire,' he repeated softly.

And Juliet Lyall smiled at him, that elusive, enigmatic smile.

Lonely people are always early.

Emmy Lou Brown often got to people's houses for dinner at exactly the time she was invited. If she was embarrassingly early she went for a little walk, looked inside other people's houses, studied other people's lives.

Emmy Lou did voice exercises and a fitness routine every morning. Every morning without fail, every morning since she had left drama school over thirty years ago. She saw herself as a craftsman: her body, she said, was the only equipment she had. Other actors had started keenly in the same way but mostly they'd given up, got lazy, were heard to say that voice exercises were for students; Emmy Lou's keenness rather embarrassed them. Emmy Lou was a member of the Performers' Club where classes and workshops were held. At first many people thought the club a good idea: classes to keep actors honing their craft. But gradually it became clear that often people went there hoping to do a workshop for a director who would notice them, hoping that they might perhaps catch somebody useful's eye, that something might happen that might lead to work. So that instead of a training centre it was like everything else in the business: *a place where someone might see you*. She knew in her heart who frequented the place: the green room was a sad place, mostly full of out-of-work actors. It was a vicious circle: it was only in the big companies that actors could train, when they were working already. Anthony Bonham could have gone, but didn't, to a voice class with one of the best teachers in the country every day of his life.

But in spite of its reputation Emmy Lou went to the Performers' Club three times a week at least: took voice classes, used the gym, attended workshops. It made her feel, in the long periods that she was out of work, that she was still an actress. It was all she had.

She was early for the meeting with Pamela Angel at the Holborn Centre. She was too nervous to sit in the coffee bar there so she walked around the streets. She'd read the play on the train going home from the garden party: it had quite simply bowled her over. She *knew*, was absolutely certain, that this was an important new play. She'd been asked to look at the extraordinary part of an old homeless tramp who'd once trained to be a teacher, a wonderful part. There was nevertheless a niggling, almost superstitious feeling at the back of her mind: if I do this part then I am old, I will have left the younger parts behind for good. But she knew she'd be able to do the part well, it was a first play by a new writer, there would be interest in this production. *Tramp*

tramp tramp went Emmy Lou's feet and Emmy Lou's thoughts down Red Lion Street as big lorries hurtled past.

She had worked on the script till one o'clock in the morning and she read well: for Pamela Angel the director; for the writer, a fierce young woman with very, very short orange hair called Eurydice Smith; and for an extremely young man called Colin who was the producer. Over thirty years Emmy Lou had honed almost to perfection the feeling in the air in an interview room: there were some variables she couldn't allow for like had they offered the part to someone well-known or someone's lover, but all things being equal she almost always knew. And this time she didn't even have to wait.

'We could say we'd let you know by the end of the week ' said Pamela Angel shaking her hand, giving her a big warm smile, 'but we need you now, this afternoon, and I'd like to offer you the job now, I'd love you to do it, and I've never forgotten that performance I saw you give in the West End. We'll ring your agent if you agree.'

Emmy Lou smiled back: 'I'd love to do it I think it's a great play,' she said, smiling also at Eurydice. Eurydice smiled glumly, and Colin shook Emmy Lou's hand.

'See you this afternoon for the read-through,' he said. 'Thank God we found you.'

Out on the street again she thought with rising excitement that although this was a play on the fringe it could probably lead to other things, felt an extraordinary feeling of relief that she would be working again at last. On the tube, deciding to go home and change before rehearsal, she had, by the time she got to Highbury and Islington, transferred the successful play to the National Theatre, had it chosen as Best New Play of the Year and then had it made into a movie. It wasn't until she got almost to Finsbury Park that she realised that she called this thing she was so grateful for *work* – but that she wouldn't be paid for doing it.

In a film studio in north Wembley the money was better but the enthusiasm was somewhat different: it was the first day of Frances' two days on her advert for the Wise Insurance Company playing The Plump Woman.

Frances had also got up early, like Juliet Lyall thousands of miles away, no actual exercise but a shower under alternate hot and cold water until her body became at least a little alive, because the car was coming at 6 am. It was the third commercial she had done and she knew that they picked her up in a car – not allowing her, as with some jobs, to find her way by first light on public transport – *not* because of respect for her person but because they were so anxious about the advert – about their client, about time, about money. They wanted the 'talent' as it was called, usually dismissively, where they could put their hands on it.

So she sat back in the comfortable car, pulled at her padded bra, reminded herself to think of the money she would earn and not to get angry no matter how she was treated. There'd be a laugh in it, somewhere.

At the small studio The Thin Woman turned out to be an Australian actress she had worked with years ago

with an unfortunate name in Frances' opinion: Davinia
Fook, although it sounded slightly better in Australian.
Davinia had been struggling to bring up a son on her
own since he was born. They sat in the make-up room:
the two actresses and two make-up girls, warm and
cocooned, early morning radio playing softly in the
background. The rest of the crew except the first assistant had not yet arrived.

'How's your son Davinia, he must be grown up now?'

'Twenty-four. He's a sound technician, loves it. How's
your jolly husband, a dentist wasn't he, did you have
any kids?'

Frances' mouth fell open. 'Sorry,' she said to the
make-up girl who was applying a thick foundation.
'Davinia, is it *that* long since I've seen you?'

'I came to your wedding party,' said Davinia, 'don't
you remember? You met him in Hull didn't you when
we were making that TV saga about fishermen and their
wives.'

'Good God!' said Frances. 'That was about twenty-
five years ago, I was only married to him for a year.'

'Oh dear, sorry! What happened?'

'I'm surprised you don't know,' said Frances, 'most
people do.'

'No.'

'You know he was a dentist.'

'Yes.'

'Well . . .' and despite herself, despite the pain of the
time, Frances began to laugh. 'I'm sorry,' she said. 'It's so
long since – well since I've even thought about it. He
was a drug addict.'

'A drug addict? That dentist? Oh – he seemed so – jolly and, well, conventional!'

'You mean he wore a suit?'

'Well – I suppose I do, I'm not sure what I mean. I just remember thinking good old Fran, a secure future, every actress's dream.'

And Frances laughed, but rather sadly. 'I was brought up on two pieces of advice: You Can't Get a Man with a Gun, and,' (and she began to sing):

> *'the girl that I marry will have to be,*
> *as soft and as pink as a nursery,*
> *the girl I call my own,*
> *will wear satin and laces and smell of cologne.*

'That was me. Thinking I was going off into the sunset. Alas. We had pink curtains and pink carpet all right, but no nursery – actually, I've still got some of the pink carpet in my flat in London!'

'Heroin? Cocaine?' asked Davinia.

'Nitrous oxide.'

'Nitrous oxide, whatever's that? I've never heard of it.'

'Laughing gas,' said Frances.

'*Laughing gas?*' Davinia and the make-up girls couldn't help it, laughed at once.

'He was a dentist. He had access to laughing gas – you know, it used to be used as a dentist's anaesthetic, anyway that's what it was. He used to stay after work and gas himself—'

'What – and just – laugh!'

'Yeah.'

'And then come home?'

'Yeah.'

'Well – that sounds – um – cheery.'

'He was a depressive. He used to get very depressed. So he'd rush off to the surgery for a laugh, he'd often still be laughing when he got home.'

'I think that sounds quite jolly,' said Davinia giggling. 'So how did it all – end up?'

'The surgery –' and now Fran was laughing again too '– the surgery was in an office block down a side street in Hull. A cleaner got suspicious because she'd come past night after night and hear in the silence of the office block a man laughing his head off. Regularly. Finally she called the police.'

'What happened?'

'He was suspended from dentistry while he had – um – psychological treatment.'

'What did you do?'

'By then I was out of work, I was working on the jewellery counter of a big Hull department store. Came home to this morose man every night.'

'Shame,' said Davinia, 'I mean he was only making himself laugh after all, doesn't seem terribly criminal.'

'But the morose man, the one without the laughing gas, used to hit me for flirting with the customers on the jewellery counter. All these front teeth are capped.'

'Oh God,' said Davinia and one of the make-up girls simultaneously. There was silence for a moment in the warm room, and the make-up girl quite instinctively smoothed Frances' hair.

Slowly they changed the subject, talked about Davinia's trips to Australia, about their days in the Yorkshire TV studios, about Terence Blue. And soon they were laughing again. The older make-up artist said she'd always fancied Terence Blue and he could rape her any time. Davinia Fook said her aunt in Wales who hadn't emigrated to Australia with the rest of the family had gone to the local Sunday school with Terence Blue's Aunt Hyacinth Blue, protesting the truth of this story when the others hooted with laughter in disbelief. Frances contributed a résumé of the reunion. Capital Gold played Roy Orbison singing 'Only The Lonely'.

Part of the studio was set up as a café. A trayful of large raspberry ice-cream sundaes was placed by the props man in a hired refrigerator; the wardrobe mistress fiddled with the collar on the paisley dress Davinia was wearing; Frances' red Carmen-rollered curls were tweaked. The first assistant ran importantly about, wearing headphones.

'Have you seen the director this morning?' Davinia asked Frances.

'No, is he still wearing poncy purple shirts?'

'Look!' said Davinia, 'at where he keeps his mobile phone.' Frances looked. Somehow the director had fitted his mobile phone into the front pocket of his jeans so that the jeans bulged but not quite in the right place and the two actresses collapsed into giggles. The director – whose shirt was again purple – stared at them with distaste: *menopausal women*. He came up to Frances and said crisply not good morning or welcome but, 'please actually eat some ice cream during rehearsals, it's important for camera angles that we see the spoon going in.'

'Fine,' said Frances.

He wanted Frances to have finished swallowing a very large spoonful of ice cream, cream, raspberry jam and chocolate twinklies by the time Davinia said, 'How do you protect yours?' (so that the camera could linger on Frances' bosom without her throat going up and down in a swallowing motion just above it). They rehearsed five or six times. Suddenly they heard a voice screaming, 'IT'S THE FROCK, IT'S THE FAULT OF THE FUCKING FROCK.' Frances was hurried away, re-dressed, re-groomed, the first assistant chivvying the wardrobe mistress along just outside the door, *are you ready darling . . . how near are you darling . . . we're waiting darling . . .* and finally COME ON FOR FUCK'S SAKE!!!

Back on the set Frances ate her eighth extra-large spoonful of ice cream and cream and raspberry jam and chocolate twinklies, her ninth, her seventeenth. The director and the cameraman talked angles and lighting. At one point the director's mobile phone rang in his jeans; he spoke quite loudly for a few moments about Bold washing powder. Finally they were ready for a take: the camera turned, the sound man said *sound running*, someone clapped the clapperboard, the director called *action*, Frances ate her raspberry sundae with relish, Davinia Fook said, 'How do you protect yours?'

'We'll do that again,' called the director wearily, 'that was rubbish.'

'Excuse me,' said Frances. She got as far as the room being used for wardrobe, vomited quite quietly into the hand basin, and then returned to her work. 'I would like my make-up checked,' she said firmly. She saw the director raise his eyes heavenwards.

At lunchtime, while they were being provided with lamb stew or lentil salad from a catering van parked in the yard, a man in a suit came quietly out of a viewing room and walked up to Frances.

'Miss Kitson,' he said, 'I'd like to congratulate you.' He had a slight accent, Frances couldn't quite place it. 'Inexperienced directors don't know how to treat actresses,' he said, 'I thought your stoicism magnificent.'

Frances smiled at him a little wanly. 'Thank you,' she said.

'I represent the client.'

'Ah,' said Frances, 'the client.' Absurdly, or so it seemed to her, he picked up her hand and kissed it and then he was gone. Frances and Davinia Fook exchanged glances; Frances toyed with a little bit of lettuce.

That day's shoot finished at 11 pm: Frances had finally refused to eat the ice-cream sundae unless they were doing a take. The director called her a jumped-up little thespian. Frances called him a fucking wanker.

'There're taxis outside,' said the first assistant at last to Frances and Davinia, and gave them their calls for the next morning in the City where they were to stand looking upwards at the powerful thrusting headquarters of Wise Insurance.

The foreign man suddenly appeared again.

'I'll take Miss Kitson,' he said, 'I go her way.'

As she climbed wearily into a chauffeur-driven limousine Frances realised by his voice that he was the one at the interview who had asked for her to breathe in front of the camera; promised herself if he touched her she'd vomit over him and punch him in the balls. He was, however, the soul of politeness: asked her about her career, told her his name was Milton Werner and that he lived in Switzerland much of the year, knew where she lived, dropped her off without laying a finger on her.

'Thank you,' she said gratefully, as she got to her door.

'Goodnight, Miss Kitson,' he said, 'and thank *you*. I apologise again for the manners of the director.'

She fell into bed, was asleep almost at once. But when the alarm went off the next morning, she realised she had been dreaming about a wonderful, kind, rich, mature, good-looking, generous, unmarried, under-standing foreigner. Except that in her dream he lived in Bosnia.

A taxi came again at 6 am; this time the film unit had special permission to be parked in an alley used for load-ing near Threadneedle Street: wardrobe and make-up cramped together in one small caravan next to the light-ing lorry; the camera car and the props wagon and a huge building truck were jammed in a corner. Frances marvelled again at how many *other* people were required to make any piece of film, apart from the actors in it.

'Miss Kitson and Miss Fook as soon as you are both ready please.' The assistant director began his litany of cajoling and persuading although everyone including him knew perfectly well that there'd be hours and hours spent waiting before all the fragments of this particular complicated shoot were in place.

It was complicated because the camera had to work on a special platform which had been erected over the past two days halfway up the big Wise building; for one shot it would be shooting downwards at Frances and Davinia who would be looking upwards in awe at Wise Insurance. It turned out that the director was afraid of heights which afforded Frances a great deal of pleasure: she asked deliberately obtuse questions, while he was up on the scaffolding, about what was required of the actresses. These questions had to be relayed by the assistant director on his walkie-talkie to the director on his, as he stood swaying in his purple shirt halfway up the building on the platform discussing shots with the lighting cameraman.

'How close should our faces be together as we look up?' Frances asked the assistant director, and then:

'How long would you like us to look up for?'

'Should I be on left or right of frame?'

'Is there a special point of the building we should be focusing on?'

'Should I look up proudly, or just neutrally?'

'The sun's shining right in our eyes, what shall we do?'

One by one these questions were repeated by the assistant director on the walkie-talkie, considered by the swaying director. Answers were sent back by walkie-talkie which finally crackled and cut out.

'Oh dear,' called the assistant director finally, 'he's just been sick, sorry.'

Frances grinned upwards. 'Shame,' she said.

The angle of the sun caused enormous problems: no one had thought of it. At lunchtime Milton Werner again appeared beside Frances.

'As we're breaking for an hour,' he said 'let me take you at least briefly for a decent lunch.' The assistant director and Davinia Fook stood aside respectfully.

In an expensive looking city restaurant full of men in suits he took her jacket.

'Just as well I'm not playing a carrot,' said Frances. Milton Werner looked bemused.

'I once played a carrot on a pop video. You could hardly take a carrot for lunch in the City.'

Milton smiled. 'I'm sure I could,' he said.

Over lunch they talked again about her work, a little about her life, a little about his. He talked about Switzerland. *He has kind eyes*, thought Frances.

'I have to see rushes tonight,' he said in his pleasantly accented English, 'but as I've got to stay in London over the weekend I wonder if you'd like to recommend something I could take you to at the theatre on Saturday night? If you are free of course. I am probably being presumptuous.'

It was absurd, she knew it was absurd, how Frances's heart leapt up, how she smiled, how she – totally despite herself and her good sense – had a flash of wondering what it would be like to live in Switzerland. Somehow still, as a leftover from adolescence even though she knew it was ridiculous, a date on a Saturday night meant more than any other.

'Thank you,' she said, 'I'd like that, no, no more wine

thanks, it'll fall out of the bottom of my head if I have to spend hours and hours staring upwards this afternoon. Have you seen *Three Tall Women*, do you think you'd get tickets? Well I suppose if you could take a carrot for lunch in the City, you can probably get tickets for a sold-out show.'

'Yes I expect I can,' he said smiling again as he paid the bill. 'I noted your telephone number from the cast list and I will telephone you.'

All that afternoon until the light began to fade Frances and Davinia craned upwards, looked up proudly, heads together, at the phallic and towering Wise Insurance Company. The purple shirt of the director was not seen for a while; he later appeared where the women were standing.

'I need to watch from here,' he said, 'it's very tricky and you don't seem able to get it right.' He was very pale but had not discarded his mobile phone which still bulged dangerously near to his private parts.

Frances said, 'You've got some vomit on your collar.'

Davinia added cheerily, 'In Australia, especially if it's on a purple shirt, we call that a technicolour yawn.'

As they'd planned at the garden party, Pauline Bonham had lunch with Joseph Wain.

He took her to a small restaurant which was so exclusive that not many people knew it existed; it was owned by the TV company that Joseph was head of. Each of the booths was private: you could not hear what anyone else in the restaurant was saying. A waiter glided in and out discreetly. Pauline had an odd feeling of wanting to reach out and touch Joseph Wain's springy, surprised hair again; did not of course, he was not her Joey of the past.

Joseph checked their order, poured some wine for Pauline, a glass of Evian water for himself. He sat back in his chair, powerful and sure.

'So have you and Anthony talked about it?'

Pauline, stylish as ever, mask in place, could never look embarrassed. But Joseph watched her carefully as she looked down, turned her rings, once.

'He had to go back to Stratford early on Monday. We – we didn't get a chance to talk, to discuss things, he won't be home till the weekend.'

Joseph looked almost annoyed.

'Come on Pauline, this is the chance of a lifetime, for both of you.'

Pauline sighed. 'We had an argument.'

'After the garden party?'

'During the garden party.'

'Oh dear. Those successful things must be hell to organise.'

'No, no I like it. Oh—' Pauline who never ever spoke about her personal life to anyone, felt trapped. 'The thing is – there was so much to do afterwards, clearing up and the odd person stayed and stayed, you know how it is, and Anthony passed out – he'd had a fight with Benedict—'

'I saw that, very classy of that young hippie guy to stop it all I thought.'

'Yes,' said Pauline shortly. 'Anyway – Anthony passed out, I slept in the spare room, I was at the shop before he woke, he was gone before I got back. So we haven't talked about it actually, no.' Pauline spoke coolly but Joseph saw it was agony for her to even discuss this. He frowned.

'We don't want domestic battles getting in the way of this, it's too important.'

Pauline said nothing, looked down.

The waiter brought oysters, bowed slightly, left.

'You're not – excuse me for prying like this – in the middle of a marriage break-up or anything?'

Pauline picked up a fork, popped an oyster in her mouth; in a moment her composure was completely regained. 'Joseph, I make it a rule never, never to talk about my personal life but I will make an exception with you – in the circumstances,' and she smiled at him. She knew how important this conversation was. 'You're married Joseph, I expect you know how it is.' She presumed he was still married.

Joseph Wain did not answer, waited.

'Anthony and I have been married for over thirty years, there are plenty of things wrong as there are with most marriages, but we have a very comfortable life indeed. And for Anthony, a divorce would kill him – his family is his safety net from which he can go out and fuck the world.' Joseph looked surprised either at her completely unexpected language or her sentiments. 'I know about his affairs Joe, I know every nuance of his behaviour after thirty years believe me, but a divorce would break Anthony's heart.'

'Does he know every nuance of yours?' asked Joseph curiously.

'No,' said Pauline. 'He doesn't.'

Joseph looked at her and saw that her eyes, for just a moment, had that strange hooded quality about them again that he'd seen by the river, that he remembered from the days when they were young. The world was shut out.

She had already begun to mask her feelings well when he first knew her. Just once he had seen her cry. It was during rehearsals for the West End show in 1964: it was her big, big chance but it was a difficult part, she was working long hours, exhausted, nervous, not sure of getting it right. All this inner turmoil was hidden almost always, but one day Joseph had found her in the rehearsal room at lunchtime. Everyone else had gone to the pub. To his utter amazement the cool and contained Pauline O'Brien was weeping in a corner. She was mortified when she saw Joseph, pretended she had a cold, actually fumbled for a throat pastille.

What is it Pauly? he had said.

I can't do it I can't do it, she had answered him, but I know I *can* do it but it's not right, I know it's not right I want to *fly*.

Joseph had said: what like your dad, on a trapeze?

Oh leave me alone, Pauline had shouted, *how would I know*? and then she had run out of the room. It was then that Joseph had instinctively guessed that her father was only a dream.

But when the play opened, she had flown, truly, and Joseph had seen it. And the critics had seen it.

Years and years ago.

Seeming now to busy himself with his oysters he kept

watching her carefully. He knew her much better than she realised, even after all these years. But then in a moment or two the hooded look went from her eyes and she looked herself again, and smiled at him. He was satisfied.

He tucked into his oysters with enthusiasm. 'This is my baby,' he said, 'that's why I've got almost absolute power over the casting, that's why I'm determined to have you. There's plenty of time, it's not till next year, we have to wait for Anthony. But I must be honest: I have to have both of you, in order to have you. I've always thought you were a better actor than Anthony but that's beside the point.' He shrugged. 'Anthony's the star.'

'Believe me, I understand perfectly,' said Pauline, smiling slightly.

'Good. Right. Well then, I'll tell you the story.' And he sat back in his seat again. 'This is a story about political intrigue all over the world. Just you watch the government trying to stop us showing it. The rot starts at the top . . .'

'No no no no *No*.' Molly McKenzie was almost jumping up and down in exasperation.

She stood in her bra and pants in one of the private fitting rooms at Harrods. The costume designer sat on a chintz-covered sofa; the wardrobe mistress and the Harrods dresser looked slightly flustered, both knew Molly's face from her many television appearances, didn't want any scenes with somebody well-known.

Coffee and Perrier water and infinitesimal triangular chocolate biscuits stood on a small table.

'He said sexy, the director said sexy,' said the thin but ageing designer, 'we talked *particularly* about this part. Surely she can be sexy, even if she is middle-aged and somebody's aunt. Have you met Waylon Jones?'

Molly tried to control not only her anger but her growing sense of bewilderment at the clothes she was being asked to try on. She stood with her hands on her hips perfectly well aware that they were considering her figure, thinking to themselves that she looked good *for a woman of her age*.

'I've also read the script,' she said, 'have you?'

The designer looked affronted at her question. 'Of course I have.'

'Well the Aunt may be sexy but she's not vulgar – gold belts, cherry red jackets, short skirts – it's ridiculous, I know they've changed the names but this is a real person who's a primary school teacher from Aberdeen married to a social worker, not someone out of Dallas with wide shoulders!'

'Ah.' The designer relaxed. 'Of course this *explains* it, you haven't seen the *new* scripts.'

'What new scripts?'

'You haven't seen the latest scripts have you? They've suddenly made a whole lot of changes, apparently they *finally* decided that rather than contact the family and get permission and all that stuff they'd make some big changes so that the story gets completely unrecognisable.'

'Changes like what?' Molly's tone was ominous and

she remembered how Wardrobe and Make-up always knew about all sorts of changes: script changes, cast changes, writer firings, before they filtered through to anybody else.

'We-ell . . .' the designer sat back, his pink tie over his black shirt matching the pale pink in the Harrods chintz. 'You knew of course they'd made the parents of the two sons *much* more attractive than they are in real life so that they couldn't complain about their portrayal. They're a rather seedy couple actually, well in my opinion, you know two-up-two-down in Stirlingshire – well now both sets of parents are *very* glamorous, they won't recognise themselves now and your part, the Aunt, has been changed, you'll *love* it Miss McKenzie, it's got much more bounce to it, I thought – I thought you knew,' he hurried on, seeing Molly's face, 'she's going to have an affair with the father of the bride.'

'*Her brother?*' Molly stared at the designer openmouthed.

'Well he's now her brother-in-law, oh you know Miss McKenzie how it is, so they can bring in the guilt stuff when the bride is stabbed. And of course it's no longer in Stirlingshire, it's in Knightsbridge – the real family'll never guess.'

'What, they'll never guess that a play about a bride being stabbed by her brother-in-law while she's changing into her going-away outfit is the story of their daughter? What are they going to think? That it's just an ordinary story of everyday folk?' Molly stalked, as best she could in bare feet, across the Harrods carpet to the courtesy telephone, picked up the receiver – 'press nine

Miss McKenzie,' said the Harrods dresser anxiously – and dialled her agent's number.

'Listen Anastasia,' she said without preamble, 'they've completely changed the fucking script of this murder thing and I'm here in my undies in Harrods hearing about it!'

'Darling,' said Anastasia Adams, 'I've been trying to contact you, they've just biked the new scripts over here and I've just had a look. It's great, your part is great, bigger than before, not a cameo any longer and they've even upped the money, most unusual, you have an affair with the bride's father and you're in bed with him upstairs after the wedding when the stabbing happens in the room next door.'

'Jesus wept,' said Molly.

'It's a showier part,' said Anastasia, warningly. 'It's what you need, you were the one complaining about the boring parts for middle-aged women.'

'But – they aren't going to get permission from the actual family it happened to!'

'What are you talking about? This is fiction, a play, a three-parter for television, like *Cracker*, it's sure to be a hit, you've got a better part than you first supposed! What's the matter with you?'

Molly felt the Harrods carpet underneath her feet, knew the others in the room were watching and listening.

'OK,' she said at last. 'Thanks. Talk to you later.'

She put the phone down, stood with her back to them. It was late-night shopping: down below, through the small-paned window, she could see all the people hurrying along the Old Brompton Road in the last light. Some cars, moving at a snail's pace along the busy road, already had headlights on. For a second the memory of Pauline coming into Anthony's study and finding them sitting there flashed into her mind. Then she turned around, shrugged in her underwear and, calculating quickly, went over to the pink designer and kissed his cheek.

'Sorry darling, red jackets, gold belts, snakeskin shoes, sequinned tights, anything you like.' Then she turned to the Harrods dresser and with her most charming, warmest smile said, 'Does Harrods supply alcohol to its fitting rooms if I ask nicely?'

When she got home, having made her peace in Harrods with extremely expensive champagne, Banjo was sitting on the sofa in the sitting room holding a baby.

Molly's stomach jumped in fear.

'Hi,' she said, throwing her bag down on one of the armchairs.

Banjo looked up at her, smiling. 'This is Sam,' he said. 'Pete and Nancy have just gone to get some dope, I said I'd babysit, they'll be back in a minute, I've asked them to dinner, I've made a nut-roast.'

'Great,' said Molly, kissing the top of his head. 'Hello Sam,' she said to the baby. Sam gurgled happily on Banjo's knee.

'How was the fitting?'

'Wonderful,' said Molly. 'They've turned it into a load of crap, I'm to ditch the Scottish accent, I now wear diamantés and miniskirts. It'll be a hit.'

Banjo laughed, bouncing Sam up and down on his knee. 'Good,' he said.

Pete and Nancy came back and the four of them sat round, the three young ones smoking dope, Molly drinking wine.

Pete told them all about watching Sam's head appear into the world.

'Unreal,' he kept saying. 'Unreal.' He shook his head over and over again.

'It was real enough,' said Nancy smiling complicitly with Molly, 'pethidine's great though, I'm going to have more.'

'What, pethidine or babies?'

'Both!'

Molly covertly watched Banjo's face.

Pete and Nancy, who'd been at Goldsmiths College with Banjo, were both on the dole. Pete had been made redundant from his job in a schools music unit. Nancy wanted to be a singer. She had a beautiful voice, clear and high, and Banjo often used her on the tapes he put together. They would sit for hours in his basement studio in the house in Clapham, singing, sampling, harmonising. A couple of years ago Banjo had had one huge hit and he still got royalties; all the equipment in the basement had been bought because he'd composed 'Till I Die' for an unknown pop group who'd suddenly had a massive hit with it all over the world. Molly knew he sometimes rued the day he'd given it to them, and not to his own small group, but he seemed happy enough, chuntering along, doing occasional gigs, composing. Before he'd written 'Till I Die' he'd often been on the dole; once when times were very difficult he'd played his saxophone in Piccadilly Circus underground station. Something in his eyes that night: he wouldn't discuss it with Molly, but he wouldn't go back.

Banjo and Pete and Nancy got more and more stoned, lay back on the sofa giggling. Molly knew she was quite drunk, wine on top of the Harrods champagne. Sam slept peaceably in Pete's arms.

Later Molly excused herself. 'We don't rehearse any more,' she complained, 'we just have to *do* it, I have to learn lines in a vacuum, I'm learning a sex scene and I don't even know who I'll be in bed with!' The others laughed.

'Lovely to see you all,' said Molly, 'come again soon. See you asleep Banjo.'

In her study she, literally, held her heart, rocking backwards and forwards on her chair.

This was the third baby among Banjo's ex-student friends, they were all in their thirties now, all having babies. Except Banjo. She had seen how he stared long-ingly at Sam, looked curiously at his tiny fingers.

That grey, depressed day long ago, wheeling Portia's pram with Pauline, passing the waiting mothers as it got dark in the November afternoon, still haunted Molly. She knew it had to do with her mother and herself; knew it was obviously somehow connected with her decision, not finally made, but always there in the background, not to have children. All through the long affair with Anthony, which had dragged on desperately and miser-ably for another year after they left Birmingham; through countless other affairs with men, married and unmarried; as she became successful and was able to buy this house in Clapham (taking the same phone number with her, she remembered in shame even now, in case Anthony phoned); all that time she had thought she simply never wanted children.

But when Molly's mother had finally, after threatening all her life, surprised them all and committed suicide four years ago, Molly nearly had a nervous breakdown – would have had a nervous breakdown if it hadn't been for Banjo. Not the actual act, committed at last: Molly had died of fright too many times in her childhood, come home too often calling, nervously, *Mum?*; dreamed too often of finding her mother hanging from the ceiling or lying in the bath.

But because she had realised that she could be a parent at last – and it was too late. She was literally too old. And in her heart that she held now, as she rocked at her desk, she knew that Banjo would have to have children, to be happy. That's why the notes they left each other didn't say any longer their old words from years ago *I love you I love you I love you will you marry me . . .?* but only the sadder, bleaker *I love you I love you I love you . . .*

Soft laughter came through the door from the sitting room, Banjo's gentle music seeped in under the door like a potion.

Molly rocked and rocked, and held her heart in her hands.

Anthony had phoned her yesterday. He asked her to go to Stratford-upon-Avon one night next week, see *Othello*, then go to dinner afterwards and talk about the job he wanted her to know about.

'It's absolutely urgent that we should meet,' he had said. 'This is the chance of a lifetime for both of us. Come down Molly darling, come and stay.'

She had said she would phone back. She knew what he was asking.

Molly rocked and rocked.

In the night Banjo turned to her, talking in his sleep. She felt a fierce sexual longing, so strong it woke her completely. She pulled him to her, clasped him to her. Banjo stroked her gently in his sleep, snoring slightly.

Next morning she phoned Anthony and said she would come to Stratford.

THIRTEEN

It was early, just past eight in the morning, hardly anybody in view, when Harry passed the headstone of John Angus Trade in the cemetery.

Last night, because he'd of course finally told them about the Aids test, Emmy Lou and Franny had taken him out to dinner. They'd all drunk a great deal and gossiped a great deal. Franny's laugh had echoed around the restaurant, louder and louder as if to shut out thinking. Safer guests had turned away.

He walked alone, down by the last tombstones. Would there be somebody here? Today of all days. Without warning his body was suddenly covered in perspiration, he felt dizzy, he couldn't see properly, felt he would fall. He swayed for a minute on the empty path, somehow crossed to the edge of an old grave in the straggling grass, sat on its broken top and put his head in his hands. His heart was racing, pounding against his chest and banging in his ears as if his head was a drum:

he felt he was losing consciousness. *I'm going to die I'm going to die,* was all he could think, *I'm going to die.* At last he understood properly what Michael was going through – how could he not have seen it? How could anybody think of anything else at all, thinking of death? It filled his mind like a heavy black stone. Still with his head in his hands, not sure if he could see or not, he prayed to a God he hadn't thought about seriously for years: *please God*, he prayed, *don't let me die yet, don't let me die yet, don't let me die.*

There was no answer.

After a while he opened his eyes, was almost surprised to see himself sitting on a piece of a broken grave, that it was a chill autumn morning, early sun just catching the trees on the other side of the cemetery. He got up clumsily, felt how his shirt was cold and clammy, brushed tomb-dust from his trousers. He looked around, but there was no sign of life around the desolate gravestones in the uncut grass. *There must be someone, someone here, for me to hold, someone.* But there wasn't anybody at all except that far away, where the first sunshine shone, two girls in school uniform played with a fox terrier.

Very slowly, after a moment or two, the sweat still drying chill on his body, Harry Donaldson walked back to the cemetery gates and caught a bus to the hospital.

In the same waiting room on the second floor where he gave his name there were a few women but mostly the sober tense young men. They were quiet now, those voices raised to screaming in a club or a bar: a different reality. Harry had the absurd feeling of wanting to weep, for everyone.

His name was called. He was motioned to sit down across the desk. The same weary Indian doctor brushed his hand across his eyes, looked at Harry's card, looked at the papers in front of him. He wore a name-tag: Dr Aziz.

'Mr Harold Donaldson?' he said, and Harry saw that on one grim, green wall there were hundreds of little holes, as if ants lived there.

'Yes, that's me.'

'Well –' Dr Aziz stared down for a moment '– I'm glad to tell you that your HIV test was negative.'

Sunshine burst in Harry's head. He tore his eyes away from the holes in the wall, stared at the doctor.

'Are you *sure*?' he said and the doctor smiled a tired smile.

'You all say that,' he said, 'whether you're positive or negative, *are you sure*? Well Mr Donaldson that's what your blood says.'

'And it *is* my blood, there hasn't been a mistake?' But Harry saw Dr Aziz's face, saw how exhausted he looked, how he was trying to be pleased, for Harry.

'God man, sorry,' said Harry, getting up from the chair, 'but – oh how I thank you. I don't know how you can bear going through this day after day.' The doctor said nothing, conserving his energy for the next person on the list, who – he looked down at his papers – was positive.

Just as he was going out of the door Harry turned back.

'Dr Aziz. I just want to ask you one question.'

'Yes?' said Dr Aziz.

'What are all those little holes?' he said.

The doctor looked bewildered. 'What little holes?'

Harry pointed to the green wall. Dr Aziz stared for a moment and then his face cleared.

'Oh,' he said. 'In the beginning this was the records room, we used to pin the HIV positive results up there in rows, we were short of filing cabinets. But it became impractical, the wall overflowed. And anyway everything is computerised now.' He gave a funny little smile to Harry.

'Good luck,' he said.

Harry almost danced home to pack for Morocco, did actually tap dance along Camden High Street just next to a flower seller who looked bored, *tap tap tap in my two high shoes*, he sang. He went into one of the little art galleries along Parkway that he often looked into. He chose a painting he'd had his eye on for some time: it was a painting of an almost unknown beach along the Suffolk coast that Harry had once visited. The sun shone on the green-blue sea and in the distance a liner, or a tanker, merged with the horizon. He got the dealer to wrap it, and he posted it to Dr Aziz from the Parkway post office. He just wrote: *for the wall with the holes in, thank you*, and signed his name.

As he got in, the phone was ringing. Instead of leaving it to the answering machine as he had been doing since the day of his test, he picked it up, throwing his coat on a chair like a toreador.

'Hello,' he said, his voice strong. 'Hello whoever you are.'

'Harry? Darling how funny you sound, it's Pauline Bonham. I wondered if today wasn't the day you got your results. I've been thinking of you.'

'Dear Heart Pauline, daughter of a trapeze artist! Pauly, Pauly, I'm negative, I've just got back from the hospital and I'm negative. I'm fifty-eight and I don't deserve it but I haven't got Aids.' He gave a kind of war-whoop down the phone and she realised he was crying.

'Harry that's wonderful, Oh God I'm so glad.'

'Get into your posh pink car Pauly, come and meet me, we'll go to lunch, I'll buy you champagne, I'll buy you a diamond ring – anything!'

'Anything?'

'Anything!'

'Aren't you going to Morocco today, what time's your flight?'

'Not till late tonight, come on Pauly, don't make excuses, Franny and Em are both working, I need to see a beautiful woman.'

'How're you getting to the airport?'

'Dunno – limousine, broomstick, hot air balloon – anything.'

There was a slight pause on the other end of the phone.

'Harry, if I come and collect you will you take me out to Copperfield Hall and introduce me to – oh *take* me Harry, please, please take me. I – I'm too nervous to go by myself, I tried to go by myself earlier in the week but I just – couldn't.'

Some old caution pulled at Harry, even in the middle of his elation, not for himself but for her.

'Pauly,' he said slowly, thinking of the old man sitting in the garden, 'he might not – he's old Pauly, he might not – want a daughter. It might be too late.'

'I'll take the risk.'

'It's just –' Harry tried to choose the right words, '– he might not acknowledge you. Or he might even have forgotten. He's over eighty I'm sure.'

'And then I'll take you for champagne and then I'll take you to the airport.' She seemed not to hear him.

What else could he do but agree? The sun was shining and he didn't have Aids. 'OK Pauly, OK OK OK, what time?'

'I'll pick you up about four. Pack your bag. And darling – I'm so glad.'

He rang Emmy Lou's answering machine and shouted NEGATIVE NEGATIVE so that she'd know as soon as she came home from rehearsal, and he phoned Frances who was back at British Telecom.

'Sales,' she said.

'Eureka!' he said.

'Oh Harry!' she said, and burst into tears.

And of course, he had to tell Michael. Very slowly he picked up his coat again.

In the late afternoon they drove into the grounds of Copperfield Hall where the sun was still shining across the grass. Although the roses were really finished now, they still remained there, overblown pink and yellow blooms not quite falling off the bushes, still hanging on for one last day, clinging to the branch. Pauline bent down to smell one of them, her hand brushed the flower; its petals fell to the ground.

'Are you quite sure you want to do this?' said Harry.

'Quite sure,' said Pauline coolly as they walked towards the big front door, 'and don't introduce me in my married name. You can rely on me, I won't rush in and cry FATHER and throw my arms around him.'

Harry grinned, but still felt trepidation. 'OK,' he said. 'He's expecting me, and a friend. I phoned to ask if it was suitable.' He rang the bell. Pauline stood beside him, her eyes hooded and expressionless.

Mrs Beale welcomed them. And the old man was waiting for them expectantly, hovering around the reception hall, under the large painting of Beerbohm Tree as Macbeth. His white hair shone and he'd put on a suit and he smiled with pleasure.

'Dear boy,' he said, holding out his hand to Harry, 'I couldn't be more delighted, how lovely of you to return.'

'I wanted to introduce you to a good friend of mine,' said Harry. 'This is Pauline O'Brien, we were at drama school together.'

'Roger Popham,' said the old man putting out his hand in turn to Pauline. 'Delighted to meet you my dear, any friend of this young man is a friend of mine. I've asked for tea in the garden, if you don't think it too late for afternoon tea, the weather is still so lovely. Won't you come outside, I'll lead the way, shall I, make it easier.'

Pauline had turned quite pale in her elegant cream suit, stood there for a moment on the red carpet looking after the old man as he slowly led the way into the garden still talking animatedly to Harry. *Wouldn't he have known her name? Surely he remembered her mother and her stepfather.* She heard the word *Noël* float back across the big lounge. In a corner an old woman sat weeping very quietly; *Mummy*, she murmured, *Mummy*, wiping away tears with what looked like a tea towel.

'Come on Pauly,' called Harry over his shoulder.

In the garden, tea was brought, not from the wagon but on a special tray; the old man had ordered it specially, paid for it specially. Pauline offered to pour, her hand was shaking. She looked covertly at Roger Popham, yes you could tell he had been good-looking, and he was tall like her. She was amazed no one could hear her heart. She even wished for a moment she'd brought her mother. But it was after three o'clock and Mrs O'Brien would be passed out by now, quietly snoring.

As she passed him his tea she said more abruptly than she'd meant to, 'Tell me about the circus Mr Popham.'

He looked at her. 'Of course Harry must have appraised you of my adventures,' he said. 'I travelled for years with the Great Zelda Brothers' Circus, all over Europe.'

'I came to see you once,' said Pauline.

'Did you my dear? Where?'

'At Blackheath.'

'Ah. Blackheath. No my dear I – I didn't come to England that time, with the circus.' He didn't say any more, suddenly seemed closed up, stared out at the garden where the water on the pond lay quite still, like glass. Birds were already coming home to the tall trees and shadows crept up now across the lawn.

'I think you knew my mother,' said Pauline, and Harry shot her a warning glance, *not so fast*, his eyes seemed to say.

'I expect Roger knew everyone,' he said, 'he seems to have known everyone.'

The old man came back to them, pulled his mind back to where he was sitting with his young friends. He took out a handkerchief and wiped his mouth, put it carefully back in his pocket, cleared his throat.

'We did you know, all seem to know each other when I was young. But of course,' he added courteously, 'I expect it's the same for you.'

'No,' said Harry, 'I don't think it's the same now, I think television changed all that, I don't think we do know everyone any longer. Do you think Pauly?'

'No,' said Pauline. 'I expect we don't.'

The old man launched into a story about auditioning for a new Noël Coward play, how the word went around that every pretty young man ('for I myself was pretty then I believe') – *yes*, she thought again, *my father was beautiful* – should present himself at the audition, how they stood in lines outside the stage door and were seen, about one every minute, on stage in front of the footlights, unable to see anything or anybody out in the dark auditorium. But The Great Man was sitting there, shadowed in the dark, choosing. Pauline studied Roger Popham's face as he spoke, trying to find something of herself in him; she felt disoriented, odd, as if this wasn't really happening. After some time Harry gently brought the conversation back to the circus.

'Tell Pauline about the circus,' he said to Roger, 'she's crazy about circuses.'

If the old man felt he was being asked to perform he gave no indication of it: it was his profession after all. He told Pauline about a biting, scratching, Russian-born chimpanzee that he could calm by singing 'I'm Dreaming of a White Christmas' in English. Sometimes he tried another song, 'Danny Boy' or 'You Are My Sunshine' but for some unknown reason only 'I'm Dreaming of a White Christmas' would do. He told them of the way the Great Zelda Brothers' Circus always journeyed in a convoy in large, slow trucks and caravans in the middle of the night when the world was asleep, through empty roads, across silent railway yards; how the animals sometimes cried at the moon as they travelled: muffled, eerie animal cries in the darkness, *I hear them sometimes still*, he said. He told them about putting up the Big Top in town after town, the muscles and the sweat of the strong circus men always enticing the local women whatever country they were in, while small boys ran under the big ropes in excitement. He told them about playing the Whiteface in the clown troupe, the one who got slapped. He told them how proud he was when the Zelda brothers offered to teach him to work on the trapeze, how they gave him their secrets, how he whirled through the air under the big canvas roof and felt he was flying. He told them how their caravans were painted with flowers and self-portraits in brilliant colours, and how an elephant died of a broken heart, and how a trapeze wire snapped and the beautiful young daughter of one of the Zelda brothers hurtled to the ground and died at once in the sawdust and no one was sure if the wire hadn't been interfered with on purpose: death and treachery and love. His two listeners were entranced, leant forward, could almost have sworn they heard an old barrel organ in the far distance, as if the Great Zelda Brothers' Circus travelled still.

The dusk shadowed their faces as they sat there and Pauline said, very gently so as not to disturb his mood, 'When the circus came to Blackheath I – my mother brought me to look for you, she used to know you. We met Zarko.'

The old man stirred slightly as if he were still far away. 'My Zarko died,' was all he said. And very quietly he hummed. And the tune was 'I'm Dreaming of a White Christmas'.

After a long silence Pauline said, 'My mother is Ellen O'Brien. She used to be Ellen Fast.'

The old man turned to her very slowly. 'Of course she did,' he said, dreamily, exhausted now, 'of course she did.'

A door banged. 'Goodness Roger, whatever are you doing sitting out in the chill air, it's getting dark, I didn't realise your visitors were still here, surely you heard the dinner bell hours ago? You mustn't get cold dear you know that, come indoors.' Mrs Beale's voice called from the lounge.

Harry and Pauline jumped up guiltily, felt the chill in the air, ushered the old man inside. He walked very stiffly, looked quite pale under the electric light in the lounge, held Harry's arm.

'You change into your pyjamas and get into bed,' said Mrs Beale, 'I'll bring something warm to your room.'

'We'll take him to his room,' said Harry apologetically, 'I'm so sorry, we lost track of time.'

'I do talk,' murmured the old man to Harry as they walked slowly along the corridors, 'I will talk.'

When they reached his room he opened the door and then pulled himself together with an effort, turned to them.

'It was so good of you both to come,' he said. 'I don't have many visitors.' Pauline's eyes suddenly filled with tears.

Harry bent and kissed the old man's cheek, a gesture that surprised Pauline though she supposed it should not have.

'It was good of you to have us Roger,' said Harry, 'I'm so sorry we kept you outside like that, it was very thoughtless of us. But – I am so glad to have seen you again.' Pauline saw that the old man looked at Harry for a moment, the expression in his eyes unreadable.

Then as Roger Popham turned and took Pauline's hand in his very cold one he suddenly said anxiously, 'Did your father get the francs?'

For a moment Pauline looked at him uncomprehendingly.

'The francs,' repeated the old man, very urgently now as if making one last effort, 'the parcel of French francs. It was illegal, of course, to send them.'

And then Pauline understood. 'Yes,' she said, her

hand resting in his, 'yes, he got them. We went on holiday to Brittany.'

'Good,' said Roger Popham, 'good.' And he sighed very deeply and turned and shuffled into his room, closing the door behind him.

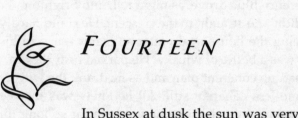

FOURTEEN

In Sussex at dusk the sun was very low in the sky, lighting long, uneven ribbons of cloud from beneath so that the sky was grey and gold in streaming, ragged lines. Terence Blue stared at the effect as he drove; a book he'd had as a child, an illustrated *Legends of King Arthur* drifted into his mind, drifted out again. He had been banned from driving six months ago on a third drinking charge, knew he was taking a risk in his red noticeable car and his face plastered across all the newspapers. But he drove on and, just before the last rays of the golden, glowing Arthurian sun quite disappeared, he finally saw the sea.

Nicola Abbott could hear the sea in the night. Not in the day with the bustle of traffic and tourists coming up from the town but in the night, when the traffic and the tourists had gone. She could lie in her bed in the crescent with the windows open, as she had lain so long ago, and she could hear the English Channel shushing in from France, catching on the stony beach, shushing out again. So that, in the care of the community, she remembered everything that she had been encouraged for so long to forget.

Nicola Abbott, the glittering star of 1961, waited.

And Terence Blue drove, as night fell, into Brighton.

He didn't go straight to the crescent. He could hardly face seeing the house again after so many years. In his red car was a bottle of whisky. He parked near the sea.

He had no coherent plan and as he drank the whisky it became less coherent still. All he knew was that he had to see Nicky, whom he hadn't seen for so long till the reunion, and that she would be waiting.

The red car finally swerved fast up the hill, stopped outside Nicky's house. The curtains weren't drawn, it appeared to be in darkness, but he could see light coming from the back of the house that he had known so well. He could also see the one chair sitting there, a lonely shadow in the front room. Something like a sob choked from the back of his throat though he did not know it.

And then Terence Blue got out of his car, took a key from his pocket with his shaking hand and, as he had done so joyfully so long ago, opened the door of the house where he had lived briefly with his first wife, Nicola Abbott.

'Nicky?' he called, so that she would know it was him.

She was sitting in the kitchen, hadn't cleared away the remains of a meal, and stayed motionless as she heard Terence walk down the hall. He stood in the kitchen doorway and stared at her, at her grey hair, at the damaged shoulder.

Then he moved into the kitchen, blinking in the harsh light, there was no shade on the bulb.

'Hello Nicky,' he said.

'*Hello Terry*,' said Nicky Abbott in the voice that nobody forgot and she stared up at him with an unfathomable look in her eyes.

Terence Blue kept moving towards the grey-haired woman who sat at the kitchen table.

'Nicky.'

She said nothing more, stared at him, at his face. He had come. They were back in their house. She remembered everything.

And then Terence Blue knelt down beside the chair and put both his arms, carefully, around Nicola Abbott, knowing not to hurt her damaged shoulder. Both arms around her carefully. He kissed her grey hair, said her name over and over and over again. He was weeping, she felt his tears on her face, she could taste them on her mouth. And then, unable to stop himself, he pulled her fiercely to him, pressed her to him, felt her small body against him, held her tight.

Not once, in over thirty years, had anybody held Nicola Abbott in their arms, pressed her body to theirs. Now Terence Blue, the famous film star, half drunk, knelt in a kitchen in Brighton and held her violently. And, finally, he put his hand on her breast.

The effect was electrifying. The knife was beside her on the table, looking innocuous next to a loaf of granary bread and some tea bags. With a husky, harsh, almost animal cry she took up the knife and plunged it into his back.

In the quiet Brighton crescent the neighbours heard screaming, saw Terence stagger into the street before he fell with multiple stab wounds in his back on to the pavement, restrained Nicola Abbott although she was actually sitting blankly in her kitchen, called the police and an ambulance. Terence Blue was taken away with tubes coming from his arms; Nicola Abbott was led to a police car. Just before the ambulance pulled away from beside the house, just before she was put in the police car, neighbours peering from windows and doorways saw Nicola Abbott suddenly run forward to the back door of the ambulance. Such was her strength as she held on to the door-handle that it took two policemen and a policewoman to pull her away. The police officers understood at once that this was not normal strength, understood as at last they pulled her away, as the ambulance sped away siren screaming, as they saw the blank look on the woman's face as she got into the police car, that she must of course be mad.

The house with the one chair in the uncurtained front room became quiet again, cordoned off until the morning, a lone policeman standing outside; the blood of the famous film star Terence Blue congealed on the kitchen floor in the light of the harsh, unshaded light bulb which nobody had thought to turn off.

The newspapers the next day had a field day. Terence

Blue was all over the papers again, a rapist on remand, this time stabbed by another woman.

Some clever sleuthing by reporters elicited the fact that this other woman, Nicola Abbott, had also been at the now notorious Drama Academy reunion. A film critic with a long memory made a lot of money by being the first to write an article pointing out that Nicky Abbott had been, briefly, one of the most glittering actresses in London in the early 1960s before disappearing into obscurity. Other newspapers grabbed the story greedily, scrabbled round for old photographs of a young, innocent girl in her first and only (*and* said the film critic, *if you see it, unforgettable*) movie, *Heartbreak*.

There were no photographs available of Nicola Abbott as she looked now and there seemed to be some confusion as to where she had been taken after the brief hearing in the magistrates' court. Telephones hummed with intrigue and delight: it was assumed by the media that this was Terence's second rape attempt and that that was why he'd been stabbed. Photographers and journalists camped outside the London Clinic where he lay unconscious, interviewing everybody who went in or out much to the annoyance of London's top brain surgeon who was performing a long and delicate brain operation on an Arab prince and needed quiet and calm. The street outside the clinic was like a gypsy camp, cameras and press vans and people eating sardine sandwiches. Terence's condition was described in the press release as critical.

Articles on multiple rapists appeared in the *Sun*; on the arts page in *The Times* Terence's films were analysed for signs of his disintegration. Juliet Lyall was frantically trying to contact Harry Donaldson who was now in Morocco; Anthony Bonham kept giving a bemused 'no comment' to reporters who contacted him.

Iona Spring, hearing the news literally as she arrived back at Los Angeles airport from London, took a calculated risk. She arranged, for more money, for a further article to be published in a different English newspaper. It was headed: LIFE WITH SEX-FIEND STAR. And underneath in slightly smaller lettering: THE STORY SHE DARED NOT TELL, BY WIFE WHO GUESSED HE WAS A RAPIST.

And Nicola Abbott, so recently released into the care of the community, was put on remand back into the care of the state; taken to a huge crowded hospital for the mentally ill where she was registered by the authorities in the name on all her papers, in her real name Mary Shand, thus confusing journalists on the *Sun* and other newspapers.

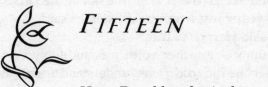

FIFTEEN

Harry Donaldson lay in the sun by the pool of a hotel in Casablanca. He was in paradise. Sex, safe sex, with four different – and yet somehow the same – young men in twelve hours. His body felt tired and yet glowing, and he enjoyed the way his balls ached. He had that feeling that came upon him in his most self-satisfied moments when work and life were going well: he was in his prime. He was smoking some exotic Moroccan hashish one of the boys had found for him. He didn't care how strong it was, he wanted to be out of it at last; he wanted more than anything else to be stoned, have sex, and think about nothing at all.

But he had been away less than a day. His mind still drifted back to London: to Michael, to Fran and Emmy, and to Pauline finding her father.

Sitting in the car on the way to the airport after they'd had dinner together at the *Aubergine*, Harry had watched her profile as she drove. Although they'd had a short conversation as they drove away from Copperfield Hall, all through dinner as they drank champagne as promised, as she smiled with real delight at Harry's story of his Aids test, she never once mentioned Roger Popham again and he thought perhaps she wasn't going to.

Then just as she turned the Mercedes off towards Terminal Two she had suddenly said with a little half-laugh, 'So you see Harry, it was true about the circus, after all. My father was a trapeze artist like I said.'

'Indeed,' said Harry, 'all true!'

'Do you think –' and her voice was suddenly very quiet '– Harry, he did, didn't he, understand I was his daughter?'

And Harry, watching her profile as she manoeuvred into the right lane, had answered carefully, 'Of course he did Pauly, he asked you about the francs.'

And then he suddenly realised that Pauline was *crying*. He had never seen her cry before. 'What is it Pauly, what's the matter? I'm sure he understood.'

Pauline didn't speak, suddenly stopped the car on an illegal corner, turned to Harry, tears running down her cheeks. 'I've waited so long,' she said, 'to meet my father. And I understand – of course I do –' feeling in her pocket for a handkerchief '– of course I understand he's old and it can't probably be important to him but – oh Harry, I'll never know what he was *like*, I'll never know him, it's too late.' Headlights of other cars washed over her face and her tears as they passed, and then it was dark again.

Harry sighed because he didn't want to tell the story

but he saw that he must. Very slowly he reached for her hand. 'I know what he was like Pauly. I knew him when I was young. He was very kind and he was very brave. Listen . . . I'll tell you.' Lights flashed across their faces over and over again as he told her about the waste ground in York in the night so long ago.

In Casablanca now, Harry drew again on the joint, looked at the blue blue Moroccan sky. It was the past, it was all the past, *the past is another country.*

Hours passed perhaps. The sweet scent of the cigarette somehow mixed in his nostrils with the smell of sex, the sun shone down. When one of the waiters brought him a portable telephone he stretched out lazily, his hand touching the waiter's.

'Harry, it's Juliet, I'm sorry to track you down like this, your agent gave me your number, have you heard about Terence Blue?'

Fuck her. Her voice jarred the peace of his Moroccan pool. He could not bear to speak to her. *And why did she always just say 'It's Juliet'? He could know twenty other Juliets for all she knew.*

'Harry? Can you hear me? Have you heard about Terence?'

At last he spoke. 'Everyone's heard about Terence Blue Juliet.'

'But did you know he was stabbed last night?'

'Good God. Why?'

'You should have said Good God who,' said Juliet.

Harry sat up immediately. The smoke of the joint hung on the air but his mind was suddenly very clear.

'Who?' he said, but he knew.

'Nicky.'

'Oh Jesus Christ,' said Harry Donaldson. 'Is he dead?'

'Critical.'

'Where is Nicky now?'

'Back in the loony bin I suppose, I don't know, no one seems to know.'

There, by the pool of a gay hotel in Morocco, Harry suddenly felt the feeling he'd had for days, he now realised, of wanting to weep.

'The past always finds us I suppose,' he said, but more to himself than to her. For a moment neither of them spoke. Then Harry said at last, 'Poor old Terence.' And then, 'Poor, poor Nicky. After all these years and that's all she wanted to do.'

He could have said, *look what you did Juliet*, but he did not. For then he would have had to say also, *look what I did*.

The waiter, aimlessly polishing a table, caught Harry's eye, smiled from across the pool. Harry sighed.

'But why are you phoning me Juliet? What's the point, what can we do?'

'Harry, don't you think there'll be an even bigger court case now if Terence doesn't die, or even if he does die? And the press, and everybody going into every-thing, I – I can't bear the fact that I might be brought into it, all those days raked over, do you know where the stabbing was? It was in that house.'

'In Brighton?'

'That house in Brighton. I don't want to have to think about all that all over again, it interferes with my work,

I'm very tired, I have to go to Hollywood . . .' Her voice broke.

'Juliet, Juliet, listen,' said Harry carefully, 'all that was over thirty years ago, who cares? Nobody'll care. At the very most, if they knew, they might feel sorry for Nicky, maybe even think you behaved badly, which you did. But who's going to tell them Juliet? We were the only ones there.'

Juliet was crying. 'But the – pregnancy,' she said.

Harry wanted to say, *Whose pregnancy Juliet?* but did not.

She went on. 'Even the thought of the rape case made me nervous, that's why I've been ringing you, you know what the press are like, they'll say anything for news absolutely anything and Terry is the hottest news there is at the moment and anybody connected to him, you don't know what it feels like, opening a newspaper, not knowing what it's going to say about you. Do you know the press have been at the theatre and waiting at my house?' and he heard her shaky breathing coming to Morocco all the way from London. 'They know Terry and I were engaged once, my photograph has been in the paper next to his, it's intolerable, absolutely intolerable – I even heard my agent talking to someone in America about how they could nose around and find a lot of dirt and make a film of his life story.'

'Terence's?' Even Harry did not like the idea of this. 'Surely you're exaggerating.'

'You're not a star,' said Juliet, 'you don't understand the pressures, you don't understand. I can't cope with all this, photographers at my door and reporters shouting questions at me as I go into the theatre. I've – I've been offered a damehood in the Christmas honours, imagine some smutty little story about me and Terence and Nicky coming out at the same time.'

Harry was not a cruel man, although he had been cruel beyond forgiveness to Juliet many years ago. But he couldn't help himself, perhaps it was the dope, or the young waiter hovering in the corner: he began to laugh.

'Is this international phone call about a Royal Honour?' he asked, chuckling. 'Are you to be Dame Juliet?!! Are congratulations in order? Come on Juliet, a bit of *paparazzi* now won't hurt you but nobody really cares, it's all in the past, it's between Nicky and Terence now, that's all.'

'You don't understand!' insisted Juliet. '*It's not all in the past*, I've carried it with me all this time. He ruined my life, you know he did. Why should I suffer even more, all these years later? It won't be you who has to read headlines about yourself all over the *Sun*.' Her voice rose. 'It's all Terence's fault, all of it, everything that happened. And yours Harry.'

The lazy doped smile went from Harry's face.

'All my working life I've always been frightened something like this would happen, hasn't he done me enough damage, didn't he damage me enough?' It was true of course, Harry knew. Terence Blue, the famous film star, had done irrevocable damage, if blame was to be apportioned. But Harry Donaldson and Juliet Lyall could be blamed also if someone wanted to write a sleazy story about their past in a tabloid newspaper.

'What do you want me to do?' said Harry. 'I'm in

Morocco on holiday.' And for some reason he suddenly saw himself in the cemetery almost unconscious with fear, and realised that was *only yesterday*.

'When will you be back?'

'For God's sake Juliet, I've only just arrived as you know very well if you've been talking to my agent. I won't be back for two weeks.'

'Will you contact me as soon as you get back?'

Harry was silent. He couldn't think of anything he'd less rather do. He disliked Juliet Lyall intensely.

'But Juliet what's the point? What can I do?'

'What if Terence dies? I've got to have someone to talk to,' said Juliet wildly. 'Why were they back in that house? I've got no one I can talk to, I can't tell my psychoanalyst all this, and I've got to go to Hollywood and make this film and it's – I don't know if I can *do* it – Oh God Harry I need you to talk to, you're the only one who knows what happened, what Terence did to me!' She sounded insane. Nicky Abbott was the one who was supposed to be insane.

'All right all right Juliet,' he said quietly. 'I'll contact you when I get back.' He should have said something kinder, something comforting, like he would have to Emmy or Fran, his friends. But he remembered, and he could not.

He heard her put the phone down at last.

He leant back on his sun-mattress but the feeling of paradise was gone. Perhaps Terence Blue would die. He handed the phone back to the waiter who had been hovering. Their hands touched again and the waiter grabbed Harry's wrist, looked at him with laughing brown eyes.

'For nothing this time, if you like,' said the waiter.

Harry felt his penis rise yet again and as if to annihalate the past he got up violently to go into his room. 'OK for nothing, quickly, quickly.' Harry tore at his own shorts as he opened his door with his key and the waiter, still with the portable phone in one hand, sank gracefully to his knees beside him and opened his mouth.

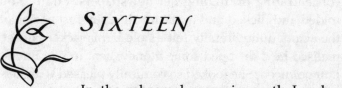

SIXTEEN

In the rehearsal room in north London Emmy Lou too was in paradise: she was working.

Her hair pushed back under an old hat, her eyes shining, she leant forward because she could see in the distance a pound coin. Nobody else had seen it.

Pamela Angel spent a lot of time improvising with the actors, but not the self-indulgent improvising that Emmy Lou had come across in the past: Pamela gave each actor a specific action which was not known to the others, all these actions eventually had to meld together and become part of the scene they were rehearsing.

The street people, many of whom, like Emmy Lou's character Alice, had spent part of their lives in mental institutions, were waiting for the Hare Krishna night food van to arrive at Lincoln's Inn Fields. Emmy Lou had sat for a long time in a corner folding some newspapers and watching the others. It was when she saw the pound coin that her eyes shone. She didn't get up quickly and run, she kind of sidled across the room with great cunning, still holding a newspaper, meandering and chatting to herself. At Finsbury Park tube station near where she lived an old lady settled every morning with plastic bags and a pram. Emmy Lou had hardly noticed her consciously – and yet she had noticed everything. The way the old woman flicked her eyes around, the way she hung out her tongue slightly when she was concentrating on folding her newspapers. Emmy Lou folded and flicked and made for the coin. Just as one of the actors quite literally felt a hole in his jacket pocket, realised he'd dropped some money, bent to see, Emmy Lou pounced. She looked so comically pleased with herself that the other actors lost concentration, laughed, and the actor with the hole in his pocket said rather peevishly, 'I say, that pound is actually mine, I need it for my lunch.'

The rotund Pamela Angel hooted with delight, clapped her hands, 'Hey, hey, brilliant Em, brilliant, keep it in. OK now let's go back to the text.'

Emmy Lou glowed, her cheeks were pink, hair stuck out from under the old hat, her eyes were still shining. She looked wonderful.

It was still the first week but already they worked long, long hours, it was a good but complicated piece, set in the past as well as the present. But there were problems. The author had been invited to sit in on rehearsals. Over any line that was changed, or even questioned, Eurydice Smith fought bitterly.

'It's my play,' she would say, 'every word there I've sweated blood over.'

Emmy Lou had some sympathy with her. She'd seen arrogant actors damage plays. This *was* a good play, but sometimes Pamela suggested something even better and Eurydice was unwilling even to try it out.

'It's a fantastic play Eurydice,' said Pamela Angel patiently, 'that's why we're doing it, but it's also your first play and plays sometimes change in rehearsal, actors sometimes bring new things, extra things, it's a partnership, especially new plays that haven't been performed before. All new plays go through this process, ask any author, ask Shakespeare, ask Tennessee Williams.'

'Tennessee Williams hated people changing things,' said Eurydice. 'It's my play, I know the characters, I don't want actors messing it about.'

On the third day Colin, the ridiculously young producer Emmy had met at her audition, was called in. Emmy Lou saw him go over to Eurydice, take her by the arm. She shook him off.

'I only want to take you for a drink Eurydice,' he said. 'I want to talk to you about the press night, and about giving interviews next week to *Time Out* and to the *Independent*.'

'As long as they don't mess up my play,' she said, following Colin reluctantly. He popped his head back in as she passed him on her way out.

'Lock the door!' he hissed.

Emmy Lou thought he would go far.

From then on Pamela Angel was adamant, and Emmy Lou saw that she had iron in her heart, that nothing would get in her way.

'Everything's cool,' said Pamela, 'we'll have the first fortnight without her until we're more settled with what we're doing even if we have to rehearse on a rubbish dump. Then she can come back. She has to understand the process.' Emmy Lou didn't know whether Colin had locked Eurydice in a cupboard or what, but anyway she wasn't there glowering every morning first thing, and without her rehearsals forged ahead.

Emmy Lou, in particular, shone. Her character Alice, although not the biggest part in the play, somehow almost at once became the pivot around which the action happened. She sat folding her newspapers, with her tongue out in total concentration, flicking her eyes from side to side, sometimes humming totally incongruously, 'In My Sweet Little Alice Blue Gown' from her childhood. Emmy Lou found some of the scenes unbearably moving, admired very much what the dreaded Eurydice had written: the journey of the characters from real recognisable people with families and jobs and loved ones, to people on the street. Alice had been a trainee teacher but had had a breakdown and lost not only her job but her fiancé who had found it all too hard to deal with. He had asked the sick woman for his ring back, on a postcard, so that other people saw the cruel message, *everybody knew*, Alice kept saying, *I had no privacy for my pain, everybody knew*.

Emmy fell into bed at night exhausted, hardly ever dreamed anxious dreams like she often did (if she did dream she dreamed of Alice and not herself), jumped up as soon as the alarm went off, did fitness and voice exercises, as always. She had to travel on the tube in the rush hour: she didn't care. They often didn't stop for a proper lunch break: she didn't care. She overheard Pamela Angel and Colin discussing the fact that the National Theatre was showing interest in the play and her heart almost burst in joy and anticipation.

She told Frances a little of all this on the phone on Saturday night: *a week ago I was at the garden party and not working and now I'm happier than I've been for years.*

Frances in exchange told her of the mysterious Swiss businessman Milton Werner.

'We're going to the theatre tonight,' said Frances, 'he got tickets for Maggie Smith, we've already been out to dinner, he just phoned me suddenly last night, said he'd booked a restaurant, and we went to the Greenhouse, he even said he'd like to drive to Stratford next week to see Anthony in *Othello*.'

'Are you sleeping with him?' said Emmy Lou, to the point.

Fran laughed. 'I only met him at the beginning of the week! And I've only had one date and tonight's the second, this is real life you know, not the movies! He sort of kissed me, after the dinner, but not a real kiss, certainly not anything else . . . I think he's married, he's certainly been married, talks of a son, but I'm not sure that he is now but that might just be wishful thinking. I . . . God Emmy I forget until it happens again, oh I'd like a partner, someone to be with.' For once she forgot that Emmy Lou had been without a partner longer than she had, but Emmy Lou seemed only pleased.

They chattered on, talked about Harry whom they'd

rung in Morocco and his wonderful news, about the stabbing and Terence's critical condition, arranged to send flowers to the hospital; talked about the play again, talked about Milton again, sharing their lives as they'd always done, until Emmy Lou noticed the time.

'Heavens, I've got to work on my lines, I've got to be in early in the morning, we're rehearsing Sundays as well. Franny you will come to the opening night won't you, I need you there.'

'Well I'm coming of course O ye of little faith, I've already booked. I booked as soon as you got the job and told them I was only coming because my favourite actress was in it, I booked four tickets, Harry'll be back from Morocco and he might want to bring Michael if he's well enough, and my Swiss and me. Of *course* I'll be there.'

'Thanks Franny, I've spent a fortune writing to everyone, casting directors, directors – you know – asking them to come, but I expect it'll just be my friends, like you. Good luck with your sexy Swiss.'

'Wouldn't it be wonderful if he could take me away from all this!'

'All what in particular?'

'Well mainly British Telecom.'

They both laughed.

And Pauline Bonham waited up, that Saturday night after the garden party, for her husband to come home from Stratford-upon-Avon.

Those who knew Pauline Bonham, all that cool confidence and expensive style, would have been surprised to know what her husband Anthony knew: how little belief she had any longer in her acting. It had been too long since she'd known how good she was. She still did the odd job, a good television role if she was offered it. Her confidence had been particularly damaged several years before when a well-known actor, five years older than her, preferred not to have her as his wife in a new series when the director had wanted her. *She's too old and she hasn't been around much lately,* the actor had said, *I want somebody who's more flavour of the month, not a has-been.* He had enough power over the casting for her not to get the part. Pauline remembered him playing a small part in another West End play when she was a star. A well-meaning casting director, drinking too much champagne in the sun in France had passed on the remark about the has-been. Pauline, of course, had only shrugged, smiling slightly in the sunshine. These were the vagaries of her profession, especially for women, she knew that, and had seen Anthony more than once veto the casting of an actress in something he was doing, almost always because of her age, or because of her looks.

But having been so successful when she was young somehow made it harder.

It was soon after that, after she heard the remark about the *has-been*, that Pauline had quietly gone, when Anthony was away making a film, to Harley Street. She had arranged not a major facelift, but a clever subtle pulling back of the skin around her eyes: not because she thought any longer that it would help her career but as a kind of defiance. *You know Pauly you've aged very well*, Anthony had said casually sometime after his return.

And now, but of course she hadn't told Joseph Wain this, she didn't know if she could do it any more. She needed Anthony to help her.

Despite herself, knowing perfectly well he was not disinterested, she had begun after a while to rely on Anthony's advice, his opinion of scripts. This year he had persuaded her to turn down a new play in Leeds that she had surprisingly been offered.

'It's not good enough for you darling,' he had said, 'and to go away for months to Leeds for God's sake, what's the point, and the money's terrible.'

The play had been a great success, much talked about, finally came into the West End and not for the first time Pauline brooded on her lack of acting confidence, knew perfectly well Anthony preferred her to be at home smoothly running the family to which and from which he came and went.

But this time, with Joseph Wain on her side, surely Anthony would be glad for her?

But she would bring it up with him very carefully, since he had not yet mentioned the new series himself. Of course they had hardly exchanged a word since she'd found him and Molly panting at each other in his study *and to think that Molly had had the nerve to come here, try to talk about all that, as if it was over and I almost believed her. Jesus I even thought we might* – Pauline quickly poured herself another large vodka; she would go on to Campari automatically when she heard her husband's car arriving, as she always did.

So when he came home from Stratford the weekend after the garden party she was sitting up waiting for him, drinking Campari. He was tired and wanted a big drink and in particular didn't want a late night conversation with his wife although they had not really spoken to each other, except quick telephone calls about business and family matters, for a week.

She poured him a large whisky, patted the sofa beside her.

'Come and sit down Tony, you'll never never guess what's just starting on BBC2, Nicola Abbott's only film *Heartache*, the BBC must be beside themselves with self-congratulation, what wonderfully coincidental timing!'

He came and sat beside her on the sofa, looked at the screen with curiosity. 'The press have been on to me all week, asking me again about the reunion,' he complained, 'because of the stabbing. Why can't Terence do things quietly without involving us – my God doesn't Nicky look young!'

The young Nicky Abbott was mesmerising.

Although they'd both seen the film when they were young they were both completely silent, engrossed. Anthony put his arm round Pauline's shoulders and she shifted slightly to lean against him. It was the story of a young girl who had been adopted, trying to find her real mother: well-made but old-fashioned now. Harry Donaldson had a small part in it too, playing someone older than himself with a not very good wig. But Nicky's performance, the big eyes and the voice that nobody forgot, hadn't dated at all.

When the credits rolled they both realised the other was crying, and laughed.

'Oh she could act!' said Pauline wiping her eyes. 'She was wonderful. What could have happened to her, all these years?'

'Jesus Pauly, I *thought* it was her at the reunion and then I thought I must be wrong, I didn't check properly, what a mistake, I'd have loved to talk to her again.' He blew his nose, then stretched and yawned. 'Remember when you and I and Nicky and Terence went and did that performance from the Academy of – what was it? – at that Shaw Festival in Scotland, you remember?'

(*Of course I remember*, she thought looking at her husband, *that's where you first made love to me and I wouldn't let you go all the way because I was still a virgin and I was scared of getting pregnant and somehow I still thought love and sex and marriage went together and you went stalking back to the film star's daughter and didn't pay me any attention again until I was the Most Promising Newcomer.*)

'Yes I remember,' she said, '*Arms and the Man* in Edinburgh. And Juliet came to keep an eye on Terence, because she was so crazy about him. And that film star's daughter you were having an affair with came to keep an eye on you hoping you would announce your engagement soon – what was her name?'

'You know perfectly well that it was Lavender,' said Anthony so morosely that they both laughed.

'Oh Nicky was a wonderful actress.' Pauline leant back in the sofa. 'What can have happened all these years ago? And then to come to the reunion, and then to stab Terence a few weeks later, it's absolutely bizarre.'

'What more do they say in the papers? I didn't see one today. I played squash with Othello and then we had two performances of *Hamlet*.'

'You'll have a heart attack,' said Pauline mildly. 'They just say that Nicola Abbott – there's no recent pictures of her, just pictures from this film all over the newspapers, the BBC mustn't have been able to believe their luck with this scheduling – they just say she's under medical care and no statement is to be released in the meantime. They keep saying Terence is very serious but stable, do you suppose that *stable* is good news? They didn't use that word yesterday.'

Anthony shrugged. 'The papers I read yesterday said it is assumed he raped Nicky too, or tried to.' Anthony got up for another drink.

'Oh God aren't they disgusting, it's all speculation,' said Pauline. 'Terence loves women, women always fell into his arms.'

'Including you if I remember rightly,' said Anthony quite crossly.

'He only kissed me,' said Pauline soothingly. 'A long long time ago. Anyway nobody knows anything really, poor Terence I hope he pulls through. He hasn't been accused of rape again, except by the press.'

And then, very carefully, she added, 'Anyway Molly says he couldn't have.'

Anthony, pouring whisky, had his back to his wife, stood very still. He didn't look round. 'When did Molly say that?'

Pauline turned her head then, looked along the sofa,

saw that Anthony stood very tense by the drinks cup-board. 'Oh she came round,' she said.

'*Came round?* Here? When?' *Did Pauline know that Molly was coming to Stratford next week?*

'Oh – when the rape happened, before the garden party.'

He busied himself with ice. 'You didn't tell me. You want another of those ridiculous Camparis?'

'No thanks.'

'Why did she come to see you?'

'Well – it was odd really, I forgot I hadn't told you, I think it was you she was after actually, but you were at Stratford. She said that Terence had told her only a few weeks before that he was impotent. She said she'd told you.'

Now Anthony came back to the sofa with his glass. 'She did – imply – something like that, that's right, at the reunion. I'd completely forgotten. But – whatever did she come and tell you for?' All the natural caution of a serial adulterer came to the fore.

Pauline sat back very deliberately on the sofa: all the antennae of the wife of a serial adulterer were carefully attuned.

The old old pattern of their lives.

'I think she thought she might be able to – help him,' she said carefully. 'Go to the police or something.'

'Oh what a lot of rubbish. She can be very tiring some-times, Molly. It's nothing to do with her. Terence'll have the best lawyers in the world, he won't need Molly.'

'I think that's what she thought too, in the end.'

'It was very odd of her, to come and see you . . .' He

drank his whisky rather quickly. 'How's Benedict?'

'Quiet.'

'What should I have done Pauly? Let him go off with the appalling Iona Spring?'

'Oh I don't know Tony. Pity you were so tired and emotional.'

'I was *not* tired and emotional. I was looking after my son. You would have done the same if you'd happened to be usefully there at the time.'

Pauline, who had been there at the time, recognised a row brewing, changed tack.

'Viola wants to talk to you about agents again in the morning. And she's got a plan, with the other students, wants to discuss it with you.'

'What plan?'

'She'll tell you about it. They want to put on their own show on the fringe, as soon as they finish their course. She keeps talking about performance art.'

'Oh for fuck's sake, not Performance Art for Christ's sake, not my daughter.' He actually groaned. 'Anyway there's absolutely no need for Viola to do that, she'll get work, I was talking to Suzie Tonks about her only on Friday.'

'I think she – I think they feel they want to have some control.'

'Does she know how much it costs to put a play on even on the fringe these days?'

'We've talked about it.'

'I hardly call that having control.' And then Anthony sighed. 'And who goes to fringe performances, except other actors to see their mates. Performance Art indeed.'

He leant back in the sofa, closed his eyes for a moment. 'Oh God Pauly I do worry so much about her. I know you think I'm a dreadful male chauvinist and all that stuff and of course I am, but even I know it's a terrible profession for women. We should have worked harder to warn her off it.'

'Too late darling. We can only support her now, hope she's one of the ones who makes it.'

'She is good,' said Anthony fiercely.

'I know.'

'But someone like Emmy Lou Brown is good. And look at her.'

'I know. She looked old, I thought, at the garden party.'

'She is old,' said Anthony.

'She's at least two years younger than you Tony.'

'Yes but she's a woman. I'm in my prime.' Pauline laughed. Anthony reluctantly joined in. 'But you know what I mean.'

'I know only too well what you mean,' said Pauline.

Anthony lay back on the sofa, put his arm around his wife again. 'I'm glad to be home,' he said.

She said nothing but they sat together in companionable silence. *Now this should be the time for him to mention the television series*, she thought.

But Anthony Bonham said nothing.

'I found my father,' she said finally.

'Mmmm?' Anthony was nearly asleep.

'I found my father.'

He jerked his eyes open.

'You mean your real father?'

'Yes. Harry Donaldson of all people found him. He met him by chance.'

'Jesus we all know Harry would fuck anything that moves, is he into old men now?'

Pauline only smiled. 'He met him at an Old Age Home for actors – did you know there were such things? – anyway he took me there to see him a couple of days ago.'

Anthony sat up now.

'Well?'

'Well – it was strange of course.'

'Well – did you tell him you were his daughter?'

'I didn't actually tell him, he was very old, I didn't want to give him a heart attack. But – yes, I think he guessed. Yes, he knew.'

Anthony digested this. 'So what happens next?'

'I – I don't know. I though I'd wait till I talked to you.'

Anthony looked alarmed. 'You weren't thinking of bringing him to live happily ever after here? Set him up at our place with your mother?' He sounded quite comically distressed.

'No no, keep calm, I think he's got his home where he is. But I thought I might at least – bring him here, introduce him to the kids, get Mum round even.'

'You mean before three o'clock in the afternoon?'

'Before three o'clock in the afternoon.'

Anthony placed one hand idly inside the silk blouse she was wearing.

'Well do,' he said, 'it'd be interesting to see the old girl meet him again. Did he talk about the circus?'

'Yes,' said Pauline, 'yes he did,' and she turned into

his arms. From his chest he heard a muffled sound and realised that his wife, who never cried, was crying.

Later, in bed, he pulled Pauline above him, felt the strength of her, felt her straining backwards as she always did; just as he came she moaned quietly.

He fell asleep almost at once.

But Pauline Bonham lay with hooded eyes, awake in the darkness.

Next day over lunch, with Viola and Benedict there, she herself brought up the subject of the television series.

'I had lunch with Joseph Wain last week,' she said.

Anthony suddenly looked very alert but said nothing.

'He said he'd talked to you about the new TV series he's doing.'

'What new series?' said Viola looking from one to the other. 'Are you going to play another big huge lead Daddy?'

'It seems there's also a big huge lead for me,' said Pauline, smiling at her daughter.

'*Really?*' cried Viola in delight.

'Now just a minute.' Anthony put down his knife and fork. 'It's all very early stages yet, the scripts aren't ready, contracts aren't anywhere near to being signed. I don't know that the wife'll be a good enough part.'

Pauline watched her husband very carefully indeed.

'Ah,' she said. 'You think it might not be?'

'You know the parts of wives,' he said.

'Oh indeed I do.'

'Dad can I borrow your car?' said Benedict who had been surly all morning, not looking at his father, the memory of his humiliation in front of Iona Spring still painful.

'Why don't you borrow your mother's?'

'The old Mercedes is a sissy car. It's pink.'

Anthony frowned and then caught himself, decided to make peace – the appalling Iona Spring wasn't worth it – and also to change the subject. He smiled at his son. Anthony's car was the latest BMW.

'Sure you can,' he said. 'And as soon as you reach the magical age of nineteen you can have one of your own.'

'A convertible?' Benedict's face was red with surprise.

'A convertible if you like.'

Benedict got up from the table smiling for the first time for a week, Iona Spring forgotten. 'Thanks Dad, thanks for dinner Mum, see you tonight.'

'Where're you going?'

'To Jeremy's. He's got a new computer.' And Benedict was gone.

'Now listen Dad,' said Viola, 'I don't nag you, but what about my new car? I'm twenty-four and I'm driving a mini.'

'You're a girl.' He dodged the flying napkin. 'You know why Viola darling,' he said, 'you've had a year in America before you went to drama school—'

'I *worked*!' said Viola. 'I was a waitress.'

'And I sent you five hundred dollars a month!' said Anthony. 'And you're going to ask me for money to put on a fringe show and I slave away for you all—' Both women laughed. 'What's all this about a fringe show anyway, and those dreaded words Performance Art?'

'Don't be so old-fashioned Daddy, it's just a term, just

an expression. We want to look at a play in another way, that's all.'

'What play?'

'*Look Back in Anger.*'

'Oh Jesus Christ!' exploded Anthony. 'Don't be so ridiculous, what, *Look Back In Anger* with singing and dancing?'

'It's already got singing and dancing in it if I remember,' said Pauline mildly.

'It's our turn,' said Viola. 'That play's over forty years old, we want to look at what made it relevant when it was written, see if it has relevance to now. People are always doing that to Shakespeare.'

'What, dress up as ironing boards and make noises like irons? I never heard such ridiculous nonsense!' said Anthony. 'It's a play of its time and I certainly won't – Oh God,' he got up suddenly, 'I've left stuff in the car, I've got to work this afternoon, I'm doing a broadcast in the morning before I go back to Stratford, *Benedict*!' and he strode out of the room.

'He'll come round,' said Pauline.

'What TV series Mum?' said Viola.

'A big, huge, expensive, international television series called *The Immoralists*.'

Viola's eyes goggled. 'And you're going to be in it?'

'Yes,' said Pauline, and something glittered in her eyes. Viola looked at her carefully.

'That's great Mum,' she said. But uncertainly. She knew quite well what had happened to her mother's acting career; had had, since she was a teenager, a framed black and white poster with Pauline's bare back on it on the wall of her bedroom, next to Bob Marley.

'Are you sure Mum?' she said.

And Pauline gave her daughter a strange look across the remains of their Sunday lunch, across the last piece of the apple pie that Pauline had made from the autumn apples in their Chiswick garden. Her daughter Viola, in all that happened to her afterwards, never never forgot how her mother had looked that Sunday afternoon, as Bonnie Raitt echoed in from the CD player in the sitting room and the Sunday papers lay spread across a chair in the corner of the big kitchen.

'Listen to me very carefully Viola,' said Pauline. 'I love you very much but there is nothing in this world, not Portia, not you, not Benedict, and in particular not your father, *there is nothing in this world that is going to take this last chance away from me.*'

In the London Clinic Terence Blue was not conscious.

The blade of the knife had ruptured one of his lungs. His agent, his personal assistant, his driver, his secretary, his accountant, hovered outside his hospital room. Sometimes there was a policeman.

Just once, just for a moment, he opened his eyes and immediately remembered what had happened. He thought he perhaps caught a glimpse of his second wife (that is, his third wife) Elvira.

But he did not see, there was no sign at all of, his first wife, the radiant shining actress Nicola Abbott.

His eyes closed again.

SEVENTEEN

As she drove to Stratford-upon-Avon Molly played the music loud, blocking out thoughts.

She didn't know why she had come so early. *Perhaps I wanted to see Stratford again*, she said to herself, *scene of many of my youthful triumphs*. She walked just as the light was fading through the Stratford estate, the land the theatre still owned; past the Avon river where white swans sailed. The theatre had built flats for actors, bought small houses near the theatre for actors; although she'd heard they'd had to sell some land to pay for the new Swan Theatre, the Royal Shakespeare Company still dominated the town. Molly had worked here when she was much younger, played Lady Ann in a production of *Richard III*, and Celia in *As You Like It*; had an affair with the assistant director who'd wanted to marry her. Molly had been horrified: she had only recently finally extricated herself from Anthony for good; she wanted happiness and fun, not marriage. The assistant director moved into television; years later he turned down Molly for a lead in a new TV series, *and so our actions follow us*, she thought. She shrugged by the river, *that's our profession*, remembering, watching the swans.

In the estate huge, old, gnarled trees grew low across the grass, weighed down near to the earth by their own age. Molly, walking, ran her hand over the ancient bark. Tourists always touched the trees she remembered, they always hoped William Shakespeare had walked here and touched them too. Molly had recently heard a theory being expounded that William Shakespeare was actually the pen name for Elizabeth I, but she patted one old tree again anyway, for luck. She had a drink and a sandwich in the old pub she'd known so well, read the *Evening Standard* she'd brought with her from London. Terence Blue, they said on the front page, was still very seriously ill. Poor Terence, such appalling things happening to him all of a sudden, what could all this be, about Nicky? Molly had sent flowers, rung the hospital every day. At the bottom of the page there was a non-committal Home Office statement saying Nicola Abbott was on remand, had not pressed a rape charge and was undergoing psychiatric tests; nothing more, no blurred photographs of someone turning away from the camera. Molly sighed, turned to her horoscope: *you will travel*, it said, and indeed, here she was.

Othello was on in the new Swan Theatre. Molly actually gasped aloud when she saw the auditorium. Perhaps it was only during Victorian times that the proscenium arch and the rows and rows of seats had given theatres such a claustrophobic feeling. For the

Swan stage reached deceptively simply up and back into the audience which surrounded the acting area on three sides, each seat comfortable, spacious even. She presumed the theatre could never make a profit, was amazed in these troubled times that it even existed. It wasn't that actors earned vast sums here, they came here for the kudos not the money and earned much more money elsewhere, the minor actors got peanuts. But the production costs must be huge – there were about twenty actors in this production, God knows how many theatre staff were involved, and even if most of them were working in the other Stratford theatre as well, a full theatre every day of the week surely could not pay for them. *What a sign of the times it is* she thought *that I'm sitting here worrying about the finances of the Royal Shakespeare Company.*

The play astonished her. It was a thrilling production of the kind she seldom saw. Molly sat forward in her seat. Times had changed from when she was young and Laurence Olivier had painted himself dark brown, including, so it was said, his penis, and carried a rose between his teeth. A tall, immensely dignified African actor with a deep resounding voice played Othello; Anthony's Iago, darkly evil, displayed sick envy mixed with a kind of physical fascination that so exotic a being moved amongst them. It was stunning.

Molly was surprised the interval came so quickly.

In the bar she heard her name called, looked around, saw Frances Kitson standing with a rather smooth-looking man who looked like, she decided, a foreign business magnate. Which is exactly what he was, Molly found, when Frances introduced her to Milton Werner.

'Are you by yourself?' said Frances curiously.

'I came to see Anthony.' And then she added, because she felt slightly guilty, 'We have some business we have to discuss.'

'Oh – of course.' Frances remembered, Molly and Anthony had once had a big passionate affair, everyone knew about it. But it wasn't still going – surely? Surely not?

She changed the subject. 'I met Milton while I was making an advert,' she explained. Milton bowed over Molly's hand, and Frances made her laugh with stories of the purple-shirted vomiting director.

'Dear old Fran,' said Molly laughing still as the first bell rang, seeing how Franny's laugh made other people around them involuntarily smile, 'you do sock it to them!'

'Oh I do,' said Frances, 'that's how I survive.'

Molly noted how Milton looked at Frances. There was something – Molly bit her lip and turned away for a moment – hungry, about the way his eyes took in her plump body as he listened to her. Frances didn't seem to notice, smiled at Milton with openness and warmth. Molly too smiled at Milton, she was glad Frances had a lover, if lover he was. Molly had also been working in the North when Frances had finally left her dentist husband; never forgot how her friend tried to make a joke of it all as she hid her mouth behind her hand, waiting for new teeth.

'Emilia's a good part, isn't it,' she said to Frances.

'When you're old enough,' said Frances dryly. 'It's the

kind of part I played in rep when I was twenty-one when people like you were playing Desdemona!' and Molly laughed, understanding her: Frances had got the old parts, which didn't look like good parts when you were young.

'Isn't Anthony *wonderful*,' said Frances for the third time.

'He's extremely wonderful,' offered Milton in his softly accented English, 'he is a very fine actor. I understand you ladies trained with him.'

'We did,' said Molly.

The second interval bell rang.

'Were you there also at the reunion of disaster?' asked Milton.

Molly laughed at his turn of phrase. 'It wasn't *actually* disastrous,' she said, 'it was quite enjoyable, meeting everyone.'

'It was pretty disastrous for Terence Blue!' said Frances. 'Oh I do hope he'll be all right. Did you see Nicky Abbott Molly?'

'Just so briefly, I heard her voice and I turned round and then she was gone. God, I remember her as the best actress I ever saw, did you notice that *Heartbreak* was on the television on Saturday night?'

'I know *Heartbreak*,' said Milton Werner unexpectedly. 'Do you mean – was that wonderful actress she who stabbed?'

'That was she who stabbed,' agreed Molly.

His dismay was so genuine that Molly found herself actually patting his arm, to console him, *what a nice man Frances has found*, she thought. The last bell rang and they returned to their seats.

for big stars from each country, including America even though it's television and I've heard that Marlon Brando is interested. Nothing like this has ever been done before. It's a six-part series about corrupt international politics, it will be filmed all over the world, they're even hoping Mandela might appear in it – frankly I can't imagine why it hasn't been thought of before. It will mean absolutely international recognition, like a movie, only better than a movie.' He chuckled across the table. 'I will frighten you if I tell you how many hundreds of millions the projected viewing figures are, and I'm to play the British Prime Minister.

'And the thing is Molly darling, I want you to be my wife.'

For one absurd moment Molly stared at him.

'You'd be perfect,' he went on, 'and no one knows better than me how well you and I work together as a couple.' He leant across the table, took her hand in his.

'I want you,' he said

All sorts of complicated emotions muddled and jostled around Molly's head. She felt confused, gulped at the wine. Anthony poured more from the second bottle that had miraculously appeared, took her hand again.

'You do realise what a chance this is? It's a good part – it won't be as good as the Prime Minister of course but it is a good part. Of course the scripts aren't ready yet and I'm not signing them till I've seen something more but I've seen the breakdowns, it's great stuff. You do realise what I'm saying?'

'I do,' said Molly. 'But – do you have a say in all this? They may have their own ideas.'

Anthony smiled across at her. 'They want me a lot,' he said.

'I'm not surprised about that, after tonight's performance,' said Molly almost helplessly.

The waiter appeared with small dishes of crème brûlée, Anthony did not even bother to let go of Molly's hand.

'After this,' he said, 'we'll go back to my house for coffee, I'll show you the breakdowns and I'll make the coffee, you'll need coffee, if you're driving back.' And very gently as if they were alone on a desert island not sitting in a busy restaurant he leant across the table and ran his hand down the side of Molly's face, along her neck and down on to her breast. His concentration on her was absolute: he literally didn't care whether anyone was watching or not.

Her nipple hardened under his hand, and her heart sank.

The long Indian summer had done strange things to English gardens. Down the narrow, dark path to the old cottage just outside Stratford that he had rented (*Catch me living in actors' accommodation with everybody knowing your business*, said Anthony) there was the strong scent of honeysuckle still, and tendrils caught at their clothes.

He opened the door, pulled her inside, did not even turn on the light. He pulled her to him, pushed off her jacket so that it dropped on the floor in the dark doorway, kissed her face and her neck and her hair. She could feel his heart beating.

'. . . Tony . . .' she said helplessly. The scent of honey-suckle still, in the room, as he closed the door with his foot.

He actually picked her up off the ground for a moment, held her tightly in his arms, then lay her on the wide couch beside the fireplace and knelt beside her. And then, as he had always done, as they had discovered together on a single bed in Birmingham in the days when they were young, he took both of her wrists and pinned them above her head with one hand; with his other hand, in a way many other women who had known him including his wife would not have recognised, he very gently and very slowly undid her dress. It was the same 〜 n dress she had worn to the reunion.

He took 〜 pple between his fingers, as it hardened and grew he watched her face, again with that absolute concentration; he watched her face as his hand moved downwards and undid his trousers; he watched her face as he pushed her legs apart, then left his hand there, feeling the moisture. Still her wrists were caught above her head in the almost graceful gesture of submission that had excited him over thirty years ago and, perversely, excited him now. Now he was much keener for the younger women to do the work: he would pull them over him, make them ride him, thrust them upwards. And Pauline, of course, always liked it like that.

But in some memory of his youth, and the passionate days and nights with Molly that had been part of it, he stared still at Molly's face in the light from the window as he held her wrists with one hand and pushed her legs further apart with the other, keeping his hand down there, moving it slowly.

'Listen to me Molly darling,' he whispered, 'listen. We'll work together again, like we used to, the way we used to, only this time,' and he pressed her wrists hard down on the sofa, 'this time Molly it won't be hundreds watching us, wondering what it is between us, this time it will be millions watching us . . . watching us darling . . . like I'm watching you now Molly, you know what I'm watching don't you Molly darling. ' She felt his hand, moving less slowly now. She lay there pinned by his arm, knowing he was watching her face, knowing watching her mouth excited him, the way she could not keep it closed because it was opening to take him inside her and she could not wait a█████gh he made her, even as her body moved from side to side on the couch, more and more urgently her body turning from side to side.

'Now then Molly darling,' he whispered, his voice husky. And he finally released her hands. And as if she was someone else her open mouth reached for his urgently, kissed him with passion, her body arched towards him and then with an almost angry groan of inevitability and a kind of pain she bent her head downwards, caught his cock in her mouth and sucked on it hungrily, her mouth opening wider and wider to take him in, their movements becoming wilder and wilder as their bodies finally, remembering everything as if it were yesterday and not thirty years ago, joined together and exploded.

*

She drove back to London in a daze at four in the morning.

It was the first time she had been unfaithful to Banjo in the eight years they had been together and shame gripped her. To even *think* of throwing everything away. Her body that so betrayed her still shook as if she were cold, but she was not cold. She was ashamed. Not just because she had had sex with Anthony after all those years. Not just because she had betrayed not only Banjo, but Pauline again. But because she knew that what had excited her was the thought of that old combination that had excited her so long ago, that Anthony *knew* excited her, used deliberately to excite her because it excited him also: *sex and work* – almost a kind of secret exhibitionism, the secret known only, but oh so well, to the two of them.

And as she turned off the motorway, took the south turning, headed towards Clapham, another, deeper shame closed upon her. She had chosen to go to Stratford-upon-Avon that night because she knew that Banjo would be away with his band, and would not be home till morning.

A few hours later she telephoned Anastasia Adams (Ltd).

'Listen Anastasia, have you heard there's a big new international TV series being made, something called *The Immoralists*?'

'Yes, very exciting, very early stages yet though but it's got lots of parts and I'll keep my eye on it. Where did you hear about it?'

'I had dinner with Anthony Bonham in Stratford last night.'

'*Did* you darling? They say he may play the lead.'

'Yes, he says they want him. He feels he might be able to angle for the part of the wife for me.'

'Was he *serious*?' And then Anastasia coughed rather peevishly into the telephone, realising what she had said. 'Sorry darling, but quite honestly they'll want a bigger star than you I should think, I mean for the American end they're talking Brando. Was he serious?'

'He said he was serious.'

'Good God, this would change your life, it's the most ambitious thing that's ever been planned in this country, or in Europe, or in America. Are you *sure* he was serious?'

'He said he was serious,' repeated Molly.

'My God, my God, I'll get on to them at once,' said Anastasia excitedly.

Slowly Molly put down the phone, then turned as she heard Banjo whistling up the stairs.

'Hello darling,' he called.

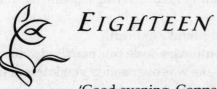

EIGHTEEN

'Good evening, Copperfield Hall.'

'Good evening, is that Mrs Beale?'

'Yes.'

'Mrs Beale, it's Pauline –' she used her stage name, the one Harry had used to introduce her '– Pauline O'Brien, you remember I came with Harry Donaldson to see Roger Popham last week.'

'Ah. Miss O'Brien . . .'

'Mrs Beale, I feel I can tell you now, and I'd like to come back to Copperfield Hall and tell him properly too if you agree: Roger Popham is my father.'

'Your *father*?'

'I know how strange it sounds, he knew my mother when she was young. She married someone else, Ronald O'Brien, but I've known since I was nineteen that a man called Roger Popham was my father, that's why we came to see him and I – oh Mrs Beale, it's extraordinary for me after all these years as you can imagine, and I don't want to either shock him or upset him but – don't you think it might be – pleasing – for him to know he had a family who would at least like to – meet him?'

There was a silence on the other end of the phone.

'Mrs Beale – I know he was a homosexual. These things – well, these things happen.'

'Oh my dear.' Mrs Beale pulled herself together. 'I've phoned Mr Donaldson several times, I thought he'd like to know, but kept getting his answering machine. Roger died two days ago.'

She heard Pauline's intake of breath.

'It was very peaceful.' Mrs Beale was practised at this. 'He died in his sleep, he was over eighty you know and extremely independent, it was a very good way for him to go, he would have hated to have to rely on us more than he did.'

Pauline was literally unable to speak.

'I shall miss him very much,' continued Mrs Beale. Then she added, 'We don't necessarily make much of funerals here as you can imagine, especially if there is no family, and in this particular home there so often isn't.' She had often pondered on this: old actors soldiering on, with no one but one another. 'But there'll be a short service at our local church tomorrow morning at eleven o'clock. Perhaps you and Mr Donaldson would like to attend.'

'He's away,' said Pauline automatically. 'But yes – thank you, I – I'll be there, thank you for letting me know.' She put the receiver down.

I would think it all a dream, she thought, *if Harry hadn't been there with me.*

She looked out over the Chiswick garden in the night, over the dark river.

Next morning she drove to Copperfield Hall, left the Mercedes in the driveway, walked the short distance to the church in the still, warm sunshine. At the church gate she caught up with an old lady who was slowly walking along and had just dropped a long brightly coloured scarf. Pauline picked it up for her.

'This is my funeral scarf,' said the old lady. 'You notice it is very bright colours. I don't know why you are wearing black. Roger wouldn't have liked that.'

'Would he not?' said Pauline.

'He agreed with me,' said the old lady. 'We should add colour to the gathering as we have done all our lives. I of course am an actress. Are you?' She stared up at Pauline.

'Yes. Yes I am.' I *am*, thought Pauline. They walked slowly up towards the church porch.

'You notice how they try to call us "actors" these days.' The old lady stopped, faced Pauline. 'What rubbish. We didn't even get on the stage until hundreds of years after the men, they played our parts for years, didn't want us really.' Her voice was very loud and resonant, as if she was on a stage, not in a churchyard. 'It's always been so much more difficult for us, much more of a battle for us to work, fewer parts, we've had to fight so hard just to exist. And now they want to lump us all together and call us "actors" as if we were the same, as if we didn't have our own, and different, history. Nonsense.'

Organ music wafted out into the sunlight. The tune was 'I'm Dreaming of a White Christmas'.

'Perhaps we should go in,' Pauline suggested.

'Wait.' The old lady settled the long bright scarf carefully, around her shoulder and over her arms. Then she said, 'Would you be so kind as to give me your arm? I just find those three steps up a little difficult.'

Pauline and the old lady were two of the five mourners in the church. Mrs Beale came bustling in to make a sixth just as the minister came to the small pulpit.

Dearly beloved we are gathered here together today . . . The service began.

Pauline Bonham, née O'Brien but in truth Popham, did not cry at the short service that celebrated the life of Roger Popham, actor. But as she stood and sang 'Abide With Me', Roger's favourite hymn (*we all like having a good sing at that one my dear*, he had said to Mrs Beale), she found it was her voice that led the singing, the voices of the old people wavering underneath her.

> *Abide With Me; fast falls the eventide;*
> *The darkness deepens; Lord With me Abide*

She sang on, her voice high and clear still, leading the singing for her father. And as she sang she thought, *it was true: my father did fly on the trapeze in the circus, just as I'd always said. And he told me about it, after all. I am so glad that I found him. And Harry has told me something about him that makes me know he had courage. Whatever happens now I must remember: I am my father's daughter.*

And as her voice soared up she felt some kind of odd affirmation of herself at last.

And something else too: a warning perhaps for others.

> *I fear no foe with Thee at hand to bless;*
> *Ills have no weight and tears no bitterness.*
> *Where is death's sting? Where, grave, thy victory?*
> *I triumph still – if Thou Abide With Me.*

Afterwards, having helped the old lady down the three steps and left her talking to a friend, she walked with Mrs Beale back to Copperfield Hall.

'What an extraordinary thing,' said Mrs Beale, 'Roger being your father. You didn't tell him, the other day?'

'I – I let him work it out,' said Pauline. 'I think he – understood. But –' the thought had been niggling at her mind '–we shouldn't have talked so long, let him get cold, perhaps we – perhaps I shouldn't have—'

'No,' said Mrs Beale firmly. 'He was a very old man.' And then she sighed. 'But it made me feel sad, that you knew him for such a short time. Do you have a family?'

'Yes, yes, three children, I hadn't told them yet, I wanted it to be a surprise, it would have been so interesting for them to meet him and hear about his life, they come from a show business family. And about the circus. Oh, I am so very sorry –' her voice faltered only slightly '– to have met him so late.'

'He was very sociable,' said Mrs Beale, 'as you saw. But he was also very – contained. He might have found it hard to suddenly acquire a family at this stage.'

'I did think of that,' said Pauline. 'Also –' she smiled suddenly '– my old mother is still alive and may well have plagued the life out of him – oh dear that is an unfortunate phrase,' but they both laughed.

'I was late,' said Mrs Beale, 'did the organist play his favourite song?'

'"I'm Dreaming of a White Christmas"? The one he sang to the Russian chimpanzee?'

Mrs Beale turned and beamed at Pauline. 'He told you?'

'Yes,' said Pauline, somehow getting comfort that she too shared a memory about her father.

'He was a great favourite here with the ladies. Not many men survive so long. We'll miss him a lot.'

'Mrs Beale – can I ask you – something I've been wondering about – did he have financial problems?'

Mrs Beale sighed. 'The world would be amazed,' she said. 'Some of these old actors live on the smell of an oily rag, truly. They save up for the packet of ten Silk Cut that they are forbidden. If they are only on a state pension, as lots of them are, and have no assets, as most of them don't, then almost all their very meagre old age pension goes straight to the Hall, of course it has to. The Actors' Benevolent Fund gives us some money, and your union Equity occasionally supports us when they can and occasionally some rich old actor leaves us money in their will. It's a very good home this I think, and the old people keep their dignity in a very special way, but it is very difficult for some of them.'

'And – my father?' She found the words hard but wanted to use them.

'He had almost nothing, he didn't get a full old age pension because of his time abroad with the circus. He had a credit card that he'd had for years which we tried to get him to be very careful with, I think occasionally he would use that for a bottle of whisky or a rail ticket or a Christmas gift. I expect he owes a few hundred on it though I wouldn't be surprised if most of that were interest.'

'I'll pay it,' said Pauline quickly, 'I'd be glad to.'

Mrs Beale smiled at her. 'Thank you, ' she said, 'that would be nice, for Roger.'

They turned into the Hall gates.

'I suppose Harry must've known he was staying here, and come to visit him. He told me he'd met him years ago.' Pauline saw that all the roses had dropped their petals now.

'No, he was just – looking over the Hall one day and he and Roger got chatting.'

'Looking over the Hall? Does he have an elderly relation in the business?' Pauline thought of Michael who had been a dancer, but this wasn't a hospital.

'For himself I think,' said Mrs Beale gently.

'Himself?' Pauline couldn't have looked more shocked. 'Himself?' she repeated slowly. 'But he's only young.'

'He has no family I think. I expect he was just checking.'

'How strange,' said Pauline. 'I mean – thinking of being old like that when he's still young.'

Mrs Beale, who had met people of all ages who were frightened of old age and loneliness, only smiled.

'Would you like a cup of tea? Your father's wake? I'll put a shot of whisky in ours, in his memory.'

'Thank you,' said Pauline and they walked in where the red carpet welcomed them and the large picture of Beerbohm Tree hung on the wall by the reception desk. An old lady stood querulously waiting for a cup of tea, leaning on her zimmer frame under the painting of a girl by Ellen Terry. *And we will all come to this*, thought Pauline. *But I hadn't thought about it*.

As she drove away from Copperfield Hall, from the funeral of her real father, Pauline O'Brien Bonham understood that something irrevocable had happened to her.

Whatever the cost, before it was too late, she was going to reclaim her career.

As an Actress.

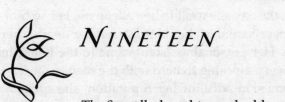

NINETEEN

The Seagull played to packed houses every night: it was still almost impossible to get a ticket; now in the autumn there were still many tourists, particularly American, who wanted to see the Russian masterpiece played by the best English actors.

Every night Juliet Lyall got to the theatre early, did her relaxation breathing, her voice exercises. She also played her other role, the star of the show: arranged for her dresser to give out cakes during the intervals if a member of the company had a birthday, made sure she always said hello to the understudies.

She received flowers from admirers of one sort or another night after night; her dresser was always deciding which ones to keep, which ones to send to the Great Ormond Street Hospital for Sick Children, which to discard. Every night after the show, people came to the Number One dressing room: people Juliet knew, people she'd heard of, people she'd never heard of at all.

Japanese University professors, her hairdresser, American academics, directors and actors from the National Theatre and the Royal Shakespeare Company, a woman she'd been to school with in Wiltshire, film people from Los Angeles. Her dresser handed out champagne, Juliet was truly gracious. Sometimes, later, she could be seen at one of the restaurants actors frequent after performances.

During the day she went to her osteopath, her accountant, her psychoanalyst, her hairdresser, her dentist, her masseuse. Her personal assistant came to the house in Chelsea every morning to help with the mail.

Sometimes, mindful of her reputation, she spoke at celebrity lunches, opened new buildings, appealed for money for Bosnia. Her agent turned down most of the work offers she received daily; she occasionally agreed to read a book on BBC radio for Woman's Hour or Book at Bedtime. The contract for the American film had been agreed in principle; she and her agent went over the small print; it was very, very lucrative indeed. And every night, the admired performance. It was a very busy life.

And underneath all this, underneath all the glittering prizes, Juliet Lyall felt panic rising within like some sort of inexorable tide that she could not control, that she feared would overwhelm her.

She must not think about the past. The past is over.

But too many of the reuniting students had glimpsed, or said they'd glimpsed, Nicola Abbott at the reunion; remembered her from thirty years ago; willingly talked to the press about her. So that it seemed to Juliet that

Nicky became a star all over again. Bitter thoughts twisted away inside her: why should they remember Nicky Abbott who only lasted a year? Who never opened a fête or spoke at a lunch or even endorsed a tin of Heinz Baked Beans? She had played Nora in *A Doll's House* in the West End, that was all. And the film, the one film *Heartbreak* that stayed in people's minds so long.

And then, a few days after she'd phoned Harry Donaldson in Morocco, Juliet Lyall, nominated for Best Actress in the West End that year, was pipped at the post by somebody else, somebody *younger*. She had been at the awards, confidently expecting to win, had a short, graceful speech prepared. The TV cameras lingered on her face as she applauded the winner and smiled and smiled. But disappointment and rage ate at her (although she immediately arranged for flowers to be sent to her rival). She wept in Cheyne Walk. Her husband was, of course, in Switzerland.

The secrets she hugged to her heart rollercoastered around each other, leapfrogged over each other, in her mind, in the night, in the empty house in Cheyne Walk: the coming film, the letter from Buckingham Palace, muddled with the daily bulletins about Terence Blue in the newspapers and the old, old photographs of the absurdly young Nicola Abbott and her conversation with Harry Donaldson in Morocco.

Her psychoanalyst said, *you are not talking freely to me.* She sat before him, numbly.

And then the unthinkable happened. One night Juliet Lyall, one of the most respected and well-known British actresses, dried on stage. Forgot not only her lines, but also where she was in the play, where she should be on the stage. She almost fainted with fright: the old Actor's Nightmare had come true. Somehow the play went on; the other actors, seeing the look of absolute panic on her face, moved her about the stage; she at last picked up the thread; the play continued. Almost nobody in the audience noticed a thing.

But Juliet's supreme confidence, with her all her life, was gone. Every performance was a nightmare as she came to the same part in the play and feared she would forget again. The other actors, some of whom disliked Juliet very much, nevertheless felt for her, tried to support her, watched her like a hawk every evening on stage. For they superstitiously knew that the sickness passed from actor to actor when least expected: it could be their turn one day.

Juliet's days and nights, so ordered and so full, became a nightmare of panic and distress. Her osteopath became worried, booked extra appointments, clicked her neck; her psychoanalyst sat with her, felt her despair, but was unable to touch her thoughts. Her masseuse, a kind and sensitive young woman, could feel the extraordinary tension in Juliet's body, tried to stroke it out, put her hands gently on Juliet's head, *relax, you must relax*, she said over and over again trying to smooth out the terror that seemed to be there.

At last, one night after another frightening show, suddenly leaving the theatre at once, suddenly refusing to see the Japanese professors and the American academics (*so sorry, she has a previous engagement*, said her dresser, *so sorry*), Juliet sped home in a taxi. In Cheyne Walk she picked up the phone before she had taken her coat off and dialled a number she had never forgotten. *Let him be there, let him be there.*

'Grover here, good evening.' He answered, as always, courteously.

Juliet could hardly speak for a moment. 'Grover, it's me. It's Juliet.'

'Juliet?' The voice sounded very surprised but also, almost at once, amused. 'Juliet Lyall?' He knew quite well it was her although she hadn't contacted him for nearly four years, had vowed last time she saw him never to again.

'Grover, can you come?'

'Now?'

'Now.'

'After all this time?'

'Yes.'

'After vowing you'd never call me again?'

'Yes, yes.'

'I have a – client in the next room.'

'Grover please. I'll pay whatever it costs. Please please *please* come.' Juliet Lyall was begging. 'I need you.'

Grover was brisk. 'Have your chequebook ready. I'll be there in an hour. Are you on still on HRT?'

'Yes of course. Why?'

'Never mind. See you.'

Juliet sighed with relief, dropped the phone, dropped her coat where she stood in the hall, dragged herself upstairs to the main bathroom. She ran a bath, put in some Dior bath oil, poured herself a whisky. The nightmare dissipated only slightly as she drank, as she soaked in the warm water. The doorbell rang at last.

Juliet answered the door in her white dressing gown. Grover came in with his small bag, kissed her cheek briefly, walked immediately upstairs.

'Long time no see,' he said on the stairs.

Juliet did not answer.

'The play's doing well,' he said, as they entered the bedroom.

'But I'm exhausted,' was all Juliet told him.

'Lie down,' he said.

She dropped the dressing gown, under which she was wearing nothing, on to the floor; lay on the bed, on her stomach, at once lying spreadeagled as if her body remembered exactly. Out of his small case Grover took bottles of oils, lay them beside the bed. He quickly stripped to the waist, knelt across Juliet, began to massage. He was very, very good at it; long, strong, even strokes all over her body. She was so tense that he gave a low whistle, he had to go over and over her shoulders, pummelling and then stroking hard, pummelling and then stroking hard. He moved slowly down her back, breathing evenly as he kneaded the vertebrae, one after the other, downwards, downwards. Juliet's legs opened wider.

'Wait.' He slapped her buttocks, not too hard.

He massaged her legs, pummelling the muscles, pulling down the calf muscles, pushing at her ankles, wrapping his fingers around and between her toes. He moved back up her body, took more oil, pummelled her buttocks, pushing and kneading. Juliet gave a little sigh, was unable to stop opening her legs wider. This time he did not slap her, ran his fingers along her anus and underneath to her clitoris. She moaned very very softly.

'Turn over,' he instructed.

She turned over. In the lamplight he saw that she still had a good body but her stomach muscles were slacker, the breasts drooped, fell slightly to either side.

'Getting old Juliet,' he said indifferently, oiling her nipples. 'Four years has made a difference.'

She did not answer. Her body began to move in a kind of rhythm. He ran his hands over her breasts, over and over again, pulling at the nipples, pinching them, stroking down to her stomach and her groin. He saw her eyes were closed, her breathing shallow, she was moaning very very quietly, she never made much noise, *yes* she whispered, and then again, but only whispering still, *yes, yes – oh – oh yes*. He was good at his job: he stroked her clitoris again with the oil and then slipped his fingers inside her, moving deeper and deeper, catching her rhythm.

Then she came with voiceless gasps and shudders, her eyes still tightly closed. It was a long, long time since he had serviced her but he knew if she was on HRT she could probably come again and again; he relaxed his fingers only for a moment and then plunged deep inside her again.

Juliet Lyall had four orgasms, her first for four years, her first since he had been there last time. She briefly forgot the nightmare at the theatre, forgot Hollywood, she briefly forgot Nicola Abbott and Terence Blue, all the pain and panic left her for a few moments as she flew away from her life, silently shuddering over and over again.

After a few moments she subsided, lay there, her breathing deepened, and then the world slowly came back. When she finally opened her eyes Grover had already dressed and was packing his oils.

She sat up at once, pushed her hair out of her eyes, reached for her chequebook.

'Thanks,' she said coldly.

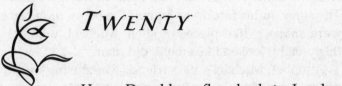

TWENTY

Harry Donaldson flew back to London from Morocco bronzed, satiated, rested, healthy – and with a heavy heart.

He had had a call twelve hours before that Michael had suddenly taken a turn for the worse.

He was to start the Thomas Hardy serial, in which he would be kept very busy for several months, in two days' time. He knew the make-up department would berate him for being so tanned; had told himself that such a peculiar old character as he was playing could look like anything, and anyway he had kept his face out of the sun whenever he could. But it had been so seductive, lying there, sometimes he simply could not move. He knew he had behaved unprofessionally. Actors couldn't get casually sunburnt on their holidays, like other people.

As they landed at Heathrow it was raining and was suddenly terribly cold. He could see hail. The headline on the *Daily Express* said: AUTUMN STORMS LASH BRITAIN. On the tube coming into London he decided to call in and see Michael before he went home; jumped off at Earls Court, hailed a taxi.

The ground-floor flat in Camberwell had its curtains drawn although it was after eleven in the morning. He used his key, calling *Hello* gently as he did so.

Michael lay asleep in the big bed and Harry was shocked at the change that had come in the two weeks. The sores on his face were bigger, the bones of his face were sharper, like pieces of shell. Michael, who was thirty-eight, looked like an old, old man.

Annabel, Michael's best friend, was dozing on the couch, jumped up in confusion when she saw Harry.

'Oh my God sorry, is it two o'clock already?'

'No no, I've just got back, thought I'd call in.' He kissed her.

'Come into the kitchen and I'll make you a cup of coffee,' said Annabel, rubbing her face, looking back over her shoulder, watching Michael's breathing carefully for a moment before they left the room.

In the kitchen she quickly told him what the doctor had said: that the virus had reached Michael's brain, that he was on the last, downward run, to death.

'There's absolutely nothing more we can do Harry,' and her eyes filled with tears. 'They're giving him morphine now. He only knows us occasionally.' He saw how exhausted she was. 'We just have to be with him now,' she said in a small voice.

He put his arms around her, let her cry, stroked her back for a few moments. Then he went back into the bedroom and sat by the bed, took Michael's hand gently in his own. He heard the rain on the road outside. Michael stirred, woke, saw Harry.

'Hello darling,' said Harry.

Michael gave a small smile. His eyes seemed to have sunk down into his head and yet they were young eyes, the same brown eyes. In this old, old man's face a young person stared out. 'Was it good,' Michael said, 'in San Francisco?'

'I was in Morocco darling, and it was very good, but it's good to be home, to see you. How are you feeling?'

Michael considered. 'I'm not bad,' he said. 'I think I'll be up and about in a few days. I'd like it to be sunny.'

'Tell you what,' said Harry, 'when you're feeling a bit stronger, and when I've finished my telly series, we could go somewhere, get some sun. It's always sunny somewhere in the world.'

'Where's Fiona?' said Michael.

'Fiona?'

'We need to get the binoculars for the birds.'

And then Michael closed his eyes again.

When Annabel came in a few minutes later Harry said, 'Who's Fiona?'

'I don't know, why?'

'He asked where she was and said they needed the binoculars for the birds.'

'Oh Harry, his mind wanders all over the place, he says all sorts of incoherent things. God it's so unfair,' and she began to weep again. 'Sorry,' she said, 'I'm so tired, I was up with him most of last night. I massaged his feet, it seemed to help somehow. '

Harry sat there, one hand holding Michael's, the other holding Annabel's, a mixture of rage and frustration and sorrow in his heart. *No cure. No cure. No cure.*

'Who's coming at two?' he asked finally.

'Fred's been coming in most days, since you've been away. He can be here till seven.'

'Then I'll sleep here tonight,' said Harry, standing and picking up his case. 'You have a good long rest this evening. Get drunk. See you later.'

He caught a taxi home to Kentish Town, he heard the swish of the tyres on the wet road as he half dozed, thinking of Michael, the beautiful, golden boy.

He was annoyed with himself for not switching his answering machine off; when he went away he always turned it off, let his agent know where he could be found and this time in all the excitement he'd forgotten. So it flickered and flickered its red light, call after call.

He ran a bath, flicked the switch, the tape rewound. He fast-forwarded the first calls which were from Juliet before she'd found him in Morocco.

But rewound when he heard a woman's voice he didn't quite recognise.

Mr Donaldson, it's Mrs Beale from Copperfield Hall. I'm very sorry to have to tell you that Roger Popham died in his sleep last night. I thought you might like to know, he was very taken with your visits. There'll be a very small funeral on Friday if you should be able to come – he didn't have any family so it will just be a short private service, at the church down the road near the Hall. Perhaps you could ring me.

Harry put his head in his hands, sitting naked on the edge of his bath.

As he sat there the messages ran on, inconsequential pieces of his life. Till he heard Frances' cheery voice welcoming him home, telling him to phone her about Emmy Lou's opening night, and about her new Swiss Gentleman Friend, chattering on, making him smile, good old Fran, he loved her. He got up, jumped into the bath.

The last message was from Pauline.

Harry darling, it's Pauline, I think you're coming back about now. Mrs Beale said she'd phoned you, I went to the funeral and I'm glad I did. Thank you for what you told me Harry, about meeting my father when you were young. I hope you had a lovely time. Phone me when you've got a moment.

Harry lay back in his long Victorian bath. It was nearly two o'clock. He had yet another costume fitting at Berman's at three. Maybe he could see Pauline before he went to Michael's, he wondered if she was sad. He must talk to Frances, he'd missed her, and to Emmy Lou about her rehearsals, she'd sent him a funny postcard and sounded so happy, it had warmed his heart. His agent had reminded him, when he phoned him in Casablanca yesterday, that the publicity people on the Thomas Hardy series wanted to speak to him urgently as soon as he got back. He would have to phone Juliet eventually. How quickly real life returned. He was just rather reluctantly pulling his sunburnt body out of the bath again when the telephone rang. It was Annabel.

'You'd better come,' she said. 'The doctor's just been. Michael's gone into a coma. The doctor says he thinks he's only got a few hours to live.'

*

Before dawn the next morning Michael Rawlings, ex-dancer, lately under-manager in linens, died of complications with pneumonia. Died of a breakdown of his immune system through the HIV virus's attacks. Died of Aids. He was thirty-eight years old.

Harry had cancelled all his appointments, rung Frances and Pauline and his agent briefly, jumped back in a taxi. The heavy rain made the traffic slow and bad-tempered. After talking to the doctor he rang Michael's home in Macclesfield. His mother, after some conversation with a man's voice in the background, said she wouldn't be able to come to London until next morning. But long before she finally arrived the undertaker had taken the body, and Michael's friends, who had shared the caring of him over the last few months, had arranged the funeral.

Harry rang Michael's home again at about seven thirty in the morning.

'It's got nowt to do with me,' said Michael's father. 'I don't want to know anything about it. She's already left.' And he hung up. Harry grieved for his friend and the cruel illness that made parents reject their children, all that *extra* pain for so many of the men who were suffering in this way; he went, not having been to bed, for his fitting with the by now frantic costume designer, went back to the flat to meet Michael's mother who asked him to find her a clean hotel, took her to something appropriate in a taxi, fell into bed at last and lay awake for a long, long time.

After the funeral the next morning, at the read-through

for the Thomas Hardy series, everyone laughed at Harry's rendering of his character. After the reading the actors and the producer and the executive producer and the assistant producer and the two accountants and the director and the casting director and the designer and the production manager and the first assistant and the second assistant and the third assistant and the production assistants and the floor managers and the runners and the make-up artists and the wardrobe assistants and the script editors (the camera crew would only join them when they started filming) had a buffet meal. Harry declined the wine, accepted the rebukes of the make-up department, *even your bald patch is sunburnt Harry and we start filming on Monday it's very naughty of you*, shook hands with a score of actors who were to be in the series, kissed the four actresses, saw Michael's pale, pale face with the sores eating into it, *where's Fiona we need to get the binoculars for the birds*, Michael's last words to him.

The producer shook him by the hand, said how glad he was to have Harry on board.

'Oh by the way,' he said, 'I went to see *The Seagull* the other night, wonderful show, and I went to see dear Juliet afterwards – you know of course she's off to make a film in Hollywood when the play finishes next month, anyway she asked me to be sure to remind you to telephone her, she asked me most specifically.'

'Ah,' said Harry.

He was dragged along for a further costume fitting. It was as if the day would never end.

But when it finally did, he didn't want to go home; on

some strange impulse he went along to the theatre on the off-chance and got a returned seat for *The Seagull*.

There was something – odd – about Juliet's performance. Nothing he could quite put his finger on. He could feel the audience entranced in the play, laughing in the right places, weeping too. But there was something there on the stage that unnerved him, that he recognised: the feeling that something would break. And he felt afraid, in the theatre, as all actors do when they instinctively know that something is wrong, up there where magic comes from.

He walked reluctantly around to the stage door, was sent down to the Number One dressing room. There were several people there, hovering, nobody Harry knew; the dresser gave out glasses of champagne. Juliet appeared from the bathroom in a striking, voluminous, yellow silk dressing gown. She had taken her wig off and fluffed out her hair, she still wore her stage make-up: she looked every inch a confident, successful actress. As she entered the big room she took in Harry's presence at once and he saw that she almost fell.

Thank God, he heard her say and in a few practised moments she had cleared the dressing room, dismissed her dresser, smiling and smiling. When they had all gone she turned at once to the mirror. It seemed to Harry she almost ripped off her make-up, she made wild, heavy movements, smearing cream on her cheeks and her forehead. She stared at herself in the mirror and then out at Harry, who still stood there, leaning slightly against the wall. She stopped wiping at the make-up, half of it still there. She turned round.

I'm frightened of doing this film Harry, she said. *It was never my fault what happened to Nicky, it was Terence, he ruined my life.*

And then in front of his eyes she collapsed, fell to the floor of the Number One dressing room before he could catch her. The yellow silk dressing gown billowed out suddenly and then gently settled about her, part of it slightly masking the pale, smeared face.

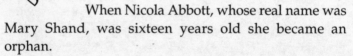

TWENTY-ONE

When Nicola Abbott, whose real name was Mary Shand, was sixteen years old she became an orphan.

Her mother, Mrs Shand, had cancer. Mr Shand had left the two women to their fate years ago by jumping, quite literally, in front of a train. The mother and the daughter lived in extremely genteel poverty in Richmond in a basement flat down an elegant street of Georgian houses. At secondary school, in *Saint Joan*, a school production that was put on three nights running in the Assembly Hall as it was on the A level syllabus, the same qualities that later mesmerised viewers of the film *Heartbreak* were already visible in Mary Shand's performance of the Maid of Orleans: the shining intensity, the unforgettable voice. Her English teacher, Miss Grace, who realised that things were very difficult at home, took a special interest in her talented and very very bright pupil, put the idea of the possibility of drama school into her mind. Mary studied every hour of the night and day as if her life depended on it, as indeed it seemed to do.

Miss Grace lived with her elderly mother who had been a schoolteacher also. Miss Grace spoke to her mother of Mary Shand over their evening sherry; they had both known many, many adolescent girls.

'She is so talented and so very bright, but I fear for her,' she said to her mother, 'there is something so – fragile about her, as if she might break.'

'Girls survive on the whole,' said Mrs Grace robustly. 'Almost all girls survive, they find ways of dealing with the world.'

'No,' said Miss Grace slowly, 'not all. It's something you can almost – touch. I am not sure I should have suggested drama school. Such a life could be too stressful for her. But what will happen to her when her mother dies? She must have some future to hold on to.'

One week before her already overwrought daughter's A level examinations, Mrs Shand – thin, wide-eyed, emanating the particular smell that goes with cancer and death – begged her doctor to give her enough morphine not just to ease the pain but to let her die. Intense and still, just in from school with her school books still in her arms, Mary Shand heard her mother screaming, if you can call the terrible sound that Mary heard screaming. The doctor did not know the daughter had come in; after a while she heard him let himself out the front door as usual. When Mary went into the bedroom her mother was almost asleep. She looked at Mary with an unfathomable look in her eyes. Mary forced herself to walk over to the bed, sit beside her mother. When Mrs Shand fell asleep Mary picked up the pillow from the other side of the double bed and put it over her mother's nose and mouth. She didn't push down on it. She just kept it there, her hand holding it firmly. She kept it there still when the streetlights came on: Mary could see them shining through the Venetian blinds. She kept it there when the churchbells rang as they always did on a Monday night at 8 pm for five minutes. She kept it there when she heard them switch off the new television set in the flat next door. Finally she must have dozed off: she woke stiff and cold in the darkness. She left the pillow over her mother's face, cleaned her teeth, changed out of her school uniform into her pink nightie, went to bed.

In the morning the pillow was still there.

Mary Shand removed the pillow at last and rang the doctor: Mrs Shand was pronounced dead, the doctor said gently to Mary: it was a blessed release.

Mary sat her A levels.

While waiting for the results, which turned out to be almost alarmingly excellent, Miss Grace, who had arranged for Mary to come and stay with her and her elderly mother, helped fill out applications for all the drama schools and to apply for grants for financial assistance; but anxiously, seeing again the girl's fragility.

Even old Mrs Grace could see.

'Yes,' she said. 'I saw them occasionally, you are right. When I was a teacher this was the kind of girl I feared for also.'

Mary Shand became a student at the London Academy of Drama the following spring.

'We would like you to live with us still,' said Miss Grace gently.

While Pauline O'Brien told everybody about her father the trapeze artist, and even the dedicated Emmy Lou Brown went to parties and kissed boys sometimes, Mary Shand did voice exercises and read plays, ferociously as if they were food. While Terence Blue cut a swathe through the girls at the Academy, Mary Shand hardly noticed him: she learnt to use a fan, and walk gracefully in long skirts and corsets. With Miss Grace and Mrs Grace she talked about Shaw and Shakespeare and the new Pinter plays and the influence of John Osborne on the development of British drama. The two older women could see that Mary loved passionately what she was doing, shone at what she was doing. Miss Grace knew nothing of Mary's thoughts or secrets, may have erred in thinking that Mary was only interested in the same things that she, a fifty-two-year-old unmarried English teacher, was interested in but she had no daughter of her own. She and her mother watched over the young girl as carefully as they could. Miss Grace urged her to get as much sleep as possible, believing sleep to be a cure for many things.

Then, without reference to anyone, Mary Shand changed her name to Nicola Abbott. She said she wanted to call herself after her favourite comedian; she pointed out in great seriousness to Miss Grace that it was useful to have a surname that began with ABB when cast lists these days were often listed in alphabetical order and Miss Grace had to concur rather bemusedly that in that case Abbott was more useful than Shand although she herself would at least have chosen Chaplin. She gave the girl books about Ellen Terry and Sarah Bernhardt, wondering whether perhaps she should also give her books about sex or love though it was clear that the only love Mary knew about or understood was the love of her profession.

In the 1961 spring finals at the Drama Academy, in the performances given to members of the public and interested agents and casting directors keeping an eye out for new talent, Nicola Abbott quite simply shone – even though there were more good actresses than usual in the class of '59: Emmy Lou Brown, Molly McKenzie, Pauline O'Brien, Juliet Lyall. Eleven big London agents wrote to Nicky, saying how pleased they would be to represent her; Miss Grace excitedly asked the advice of a friend of hers who directed in repertory but Nicky never went into repertory. An established director, recognising a strange and almost alarming talent, decided to take a tremendous risk and cast her as Nora – a part longer than Hamlet which everybody said was the ultimate test of an actor's stamina – in his new West End production of *A Doll's House*. At first he tried to tame the intensity of her performance which seemed un-English and disturbing; finally he decided to cover it with just the thinnest veneer of sophistication and Victorian manners. Nicky worked with him intently, intuitively; he was a homosexual and came as near to falling in love with a woman as he ever did in his life. His gamble paid off: he was called innovative and daring in his new production and Nicola Abbott was hailed as a star. A new, young feminist radical from Australia – the words feminist and radical not yet in vogue – hailed Nicky's performance: *at last the play is about a woman's right to her own life: this is a performance for the new decade, for the sixties.*

But 1961 was not part of the swinging sixties.

1961 was still part of the fifties; the Prime Minister Harold Macmillan was quoted in the newspapers as saying he believed *mistress* was a French word. Nicky and Miss Grace had pored over John Osborne's play *Look Back in Anger* which caught at changes in the air, but in 1961 they and Molly and Juliet and Emmy Lou and Frances and Pauline had never heard of the Beatles or the Rolling Stones or Peace and Love or a contraceptive pill; they were very ignorant about sex, abortion was illegal, and people who wore flowers in their hair came from the South Sea islands.

Terence Blue knew quite a lot about sex however. At drama school, freed at last from his dour Welsh Chapel upbringing, he had quite simply overwhelmed not only the girls in his class but every girl in the building and some of the tutors as well. He purchased condoms from a barber's shop and kept on practising. Molly McKenzie and Frances Kitson and Pauline O'Brien and Emmy Lou Brown and Izzy Fields all had some of their early – sometimes incredibly innocent – sexual experiences with Terence Blue. By the time they graduated Juliet Lyall had fallen wildly in love with him after a night in the Drama Academy theatre, when he kissed her on the empty stage and held her in his, by now very experienced, arms.

320 BARBARA EWING

When people saw Terence Blue's piercing blue eyes they assumed he'd changed his name in order to draw attention to them, but Blue was his real name, he came from a long long line of Welshmen whose eyes had been unforgettable, just as a family of good suitmakers became Taylor. Casting directors and producers saw at once that he had something special: he played leads in films as soon as he left drama school. It may have been true, as many of his contemporaries ascertained, that he couldn't act on stage but he seemed to know instinctively how to act in front of a camera. He didn't ever play small parts but, unlike Nicky Abbott's film *Heartbreak*, Terence's first films were not of memorable quality. Several of them, English horror movies, were extremely forgettable. Or so it seemed: later the horror films became cult films and to his surprise Terence – although by then extremely famous anyway – also became a cult hero in his fifties.

Terence Blue and Juliet Lyall got engaged soon after the class of '59 graduated. Sex was still an area of ignorance and fear and unwanted pregnancies; supervised contraception was only available to married couples. Crossing her fingers and relying on condoms Juliet threw herself into sex with Terence as though it had only just been invented. She loved him to distraction: she only had to catch sight of his blue eyes and she went, literally, weak at the knees; for the first time in her life of betrayed mothers and stepmothers and mistresses she was happy. She and Terence didn't actually live together, already they were working in different parts of the country. But they met whenever they could, made love continually, anywhere they could find the privacy. Her eyes sparkled with new knowledge and with love. She knew they made a stunning couple – saw them becoming a famous English institution in the theatre: *Dame Juliet Lyall and Sir Terence Blue*, she rolled the names around her tongue.

Juliet's father, a film producer and a friend of Laurence Olivier, had promised his daughter that he was working on getting her a wonderful lead in a new film that he was involved with which would be made in a few months' time. It was called *The Red Dress* and he had already let her see the unfinished script. He assured her it would make her a star.

So when, in the summer of 1961, Terence Blue made his fiancée Juliet Lyall pregnant by mistake, she had an illegal abortion.

The abortion was as messy as – she knew from conversations with other actresses – such things almost always were: a back room near Victoria Station and a shifty man with some chloroform and some extremely alarming-looking sharp instruments, and she blamed Terence because although he paid the £250 required for the abortion – an enormous sum, most of the money he made on his first film – he seemed upset about it, said he would like a child, didn't see that the pregnancy would have ruined her career. (But he certainly wouldn't for a moment, she thought, have wanted it to interfere with his.)

She went back, pale and exhausted and bleeding, after having the abortion on a Sunday morning, to the repertory company in York where she was in a new play every two weeks. Harry Donaldson was also in the company and felt sorry for her as everyone else in the company did but it was a common occurrence among actresses, after all. Everybody knew this, that all over the country actresses who'd been caught walked about as best they could – the show must go on of course – having paid a large amount of money to be operated on in secret rooms; bleeding for weeks, for months; afraid to go to a doctor because what they had done was against the law.

So Juliet Lyall made the audience laugh with her performance of Elvira in *Blithe Spirit* in the evening, rehearsed the part of Gwendolyn in *The Importance of Being Earnest* during the day, used up packets and packets of sanitary towels, had long tearful phone calls with Terence Blue who was filming at Shepperton, told him she hated him, told him she wanted them to get married, waited for her father to change her life.

And then Terence Blue, who went one night to a performance of *A Doll's House* in the West End with an older actress with whom he had begun a somewhat steamy affair while Juliet was in York, fell in love with Nicola Abbott.

No one was more astonished than Terence. He almost didn't know what had hit him: he was an expert in sex, not love. He had known Nicky at the Academy of course but there had been a kind of boringly intense aura around her; it hadn't occurred to him that Nicola Abbott was a sexual being at all. Fascinated beyond belief with what came across on stage as he sat there in the audience, stupified, Terence Blue fell in love for the first time in his life.

He babbled some incoherence of farewell to the older actress and went backstage by himself. Nicky was alone in the Number Two dressing room – the Number One dressing room was occupied by the actor who played her husband, who was very much more well-known and infinitely better paid.

She was sitting in front of the mirror in a dressing gown, the top part of an old stocking held back her hair from her face, the wig she had been wearing stood on a wig block beside her.

'Oh. Hello Terence,' she said quite shyly, smiling at him in the mirror that had light bulbs all around it as she removed her make-up. And she stood up.

For a moment Terence stood there too. And then slowly he walked over to the dressing table.

'Nicky,' he said.

He took the tissue from her hand and very carefully wiped off the rest of the make-up. Then he searched on her dressing table for something, found some rose water lotion and a piece of cotton wool and smoothed it over her face, removing the last vestiges of the cleansing cream. He took the stocking top from her hair with one hand, with the other he fluffed up her hair slightly where it had lain flat. Nicky didn't speak, just stood there, her face totally inexpressive while he did this. Then he very gently took her face in both his hands and kissed it: the eyes, the nose, the cheeks and, finally, the mouth. He put his lips on hers, waited until he felt them relax, then very gently opened her mouth slightly with his tongue. He ran one of his hands down from her face to her neck to the opening in her dressing gown. He felt her tense but, as he kissed her still, he stroked just the top of her small breast very very lightly with his fingers until he felt her relax again and this time she put one of her hands up and very uncertainly touched the top of his back. A voice called *Goodnight Nicky love* and footsteps went past the dressing-room door, but Terence held her as she jumped slightly at the sound. Still he stroked the top of her breast, still he kissed her. Then very slowly, very carefully, still standing beside the mirror with all the lights around it, he moved his hand down, took her nipple between his fingers.

The effect was almost electric, and Terence never, never forgot it.

Nicky was a small person but the strength with which she suddenly pushed against him with a husky, harsh, almost animal cry almost knocked him off balance for a moment. He leapt back against the make-up table, pushed open the dressing gown: she was wearing a funny little singlet that came just past her waist, nothing else, she had small breasts and long thin legs and he could see her dark pubic hair. Terence knelt down on to the floor of the dressing room pulling Nicky down with him, he pulled the singlet over her head, kissed her passionately then put his mouth down to her breast. She instinctively grasped at him through his trousers almost in desperation, giving tiny, husky cries. He tried to undo the trousers, the zip stuck for a moment, then she rather inexpertly tried to help him and her hand was there as his penis almost bounced out, liberated, as if it had a life of its own. By now his trousers were caught round his legs, his shoes were in the way, his socks were in the way, his shirt and jacket were in the way, for a practised lover this was ridiculous but neither Terence nor Nicky thought of ridiculousness. Nicky leant across Terence, her mouth over his, her hands on his face; his hands felt the hair down below, his fingers pressed in, felt the tiny swollen clitoris, stroked it gently, stroking her, as she moved against his hand. *Nicky*, he whispered, *Nicky*, but she did not answer, simply pressed harder and harder against him. The strange, husky soft cry was almost continuous as she held on to him, pushed against him. At last he freed himself for enough time to get off his shoes and his trousers at least and then, moving astride her, he very very gently tried to put his cock inside her. Her eyes were closed but suddenly she opened them, and smiled up at him, the strangest, most beautiful smile in the world. He pushed to reach inside her, gently at first and then with more urgency, harshly almost; then she suddenly gave a great cry and almost at once began to move with him, move with his rhythm, clutching at his chest, at his arms, at his knees, gasping, gasping, gasping and then, when he felt he could not hold on any longer she called out in her husky, unforgettable voice – and even as he came Terence realised it was the first thing she had said since he'd walked towards her at the make-up table and he never forgot the words: *yes now it is over – yes*.

Charlie Evans had lost a leg in the Second World War; even though it had been replaced by a wooden one it hurt when it rained, just as all the stories said. As stage door keeper he didn't have to walk much, only last thing at night, to check that the dressing rooms were locked and the lights were off before he left the theatre. He was surprised Miss Abbott hadn't handed in her key, she was often one of the first out after the show, she had to catch a train to Richmond, it wasn't like her to linger though she'd had a visitor tonight, that young man with the rather long hair and the very noticeable blue eyes. Slowly and rather lumberingly he walked along the backstage corridors checking the doors of the dressing rooms; actors were impossible, always leaving lights on or doors open. Luckily this was a small cast and he didn't have to go right up to the second floor. The Number Two dressing room was down a few steps, nearer the stage. He knocked on the door, and then opened it as was his habit, *Miss Abbott*, he said, *you're late tonight, are you all right?*

In the Number Two dressing room Miss Abbott still in her dressing gown sat at her make-up table. The boy with the blue eyes stood beside her and they both seemed to be looking at themselves in the mirror. His hand rested very lightly on her shoulder.

It seemed to Charlie Evans that neither Miss Abbott nor the young man saw him at first, hadn't heard him, hadn't noticed him come in. And then at last she raised her eyes to Charlie's in the mirror and said so strangely, *what time is it?* He looked at his watch and told her and she murmured slowly, still without moving from where she was sitting, *sorry Charlie we'll leave now, I'll be sure to turn the lights off.* So he lumbered back along the corridor to the stage door, wanting his cup of tea.

*

And so the tragedy began: Nicola Abbott's tragedy, but also Terence Blue's. For Juliet Lyall there were many rewards, so for a long time it didn't seem to be her tragedy. For the rest of his life Harry Donaldson, who was not a cruel man, had to remember and live with the fact that, inevitable as it all probably was, it was a cruel action by him that set what had seemed to be the final act of the tragedy in motion.

Until the reunion proved it was not yet over.

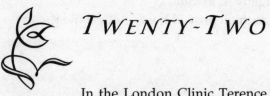

TWENTY-TWO

In the London Clinic Terence Blue began to hover for longer on the edges of consciousness. There was almost always darkness but sometimes he could smell flowers: chrysanthemums perhaps, or something like the lemon balm that grew in his Hampstead garden.

All the time, in and out of consciousness, he knew that Nicky had stabbed him, he remembered clearly what had happened, but in his darkness he made a strange connection. The stabbing was like the first time he had touched Nicky: the odd cry, the strength of her as she pushed against him when he touched her, it was in that way that she had plunged the knife into his back, he recognised it, *the passion of it*.

As his mind drifted away again he tried with an almost superhuman strength to hold on to the memory: he must not lose the connection. Somewhere in the darkness he understood that no doctor could know what he knew, about Nicola Abbott.

*

And then he began to dream.

He dreamt not of the stabbing and the grey-haired woman, but of his past.

The nurses sat beside him in the night.

Terence, they said gently. Terence. Come back Terence.

But what he heard was something else. The words he heard were: *he doesn't know the meaning of love.* But in his dreams he said: *Yes. I do know the meaning of love. I will prove it.*

Very slowly, Terence Blue recovered. He sat up, received visitors. They saw that he was pale, and abstracted. They said to one another it was very understandable in the circumstances.

And in his mind, in the hospital bed, he held on to his dream. *Yes. I do know the meaning of love.*

Not: *she tried to kill me* – as if to Terence the stabbing was somehow in the order of things – but: *Yes. I do know the meaning of love.*

I should never never never have let them take her away from me. When I held her that night in her dressing room after A Doll's House *I took her life in my hands forever and I knew that. That is the meaning of love.* Like Pauline and Molly in the sunny garden by the river it didn't strike him as in the least odd that he was thinking so intensely about things that happened over thirty years ago. As if time was a circle, catching him up in its arms as it passed him again, not a straight line stretching away from him.

I shouldn't have listened to those psychiatrists, they tried to shut me out from her life, they said I was bad for her, that she would recover only if I kept out of her life, so I did. Then they said she was better, that the past was over for her as long as she didn't have to see me and be reminded of it.

But I could hardly bear to drive up to that house in Brighton, I had to be drunk to do it.

What must it have been like for her to be living there again all on her own where the memories are? What were they thinking of, sending her there if they didn't want her to remember things? I should have stopped her going there again, even after so long, but they said the house was hers under the divorce settlement and that I had no rights at all.

But psychiatrists don't know everything I know what happened.

And he understood that whatever the cost to himself she must be kept out of court, there couldn't be a big sensational court case about this – EX-ACTRESS NICKY: ANOTHER OF TERRY'S LOVERS – he could not allow it.

And there was another thought also during the long dark nights. *I was drunk when I went to Brighton. I haven't talked to her for more than thirty years. I should have talked to her before I held her.*

And I should never have put my hand on her breast.

That was like rape.

I frightened her. I wanted to hold her too much.

And then, finally, in deep, private shame: *it's time to stop drinking.*

Terence Blue never once thought of Nicola Abbott as a mad person. What he thought was: *after this ridiculous rape trial I will get her back.*

Some people may have thought that Terence Blue was mad himself.

Finally he was glimpsed briefly in a corridor of the London Clinic by a reporter: TERENCE BLUE WALKING said the headlines. He talked with his accountants about finances, with his American agent and his two American lawyers about sueing the film company who had gone ahead without him on the film he was about to make. His secretary dealt with all the mail and all the flowers and hid from him the pile of abusive letters that called him a double rapist. He talked to his English lawyers about Simone Taylor and the rape case: she's nuts, I didn't do it, he said tiredly, I couldn't possibly be convicted in this country, I want to go for it, get it over as soon as possible, I didn't do it, so I won't be convicted.

A photographer rented a room across the road from the London Clinic: with a telephoto lens and a ladder he managed to get a photograph of Terence in a dressing gown with an arm in a sling smiling at a nurse. Press clamoured still at the doors of the Clinic: Terence Blue was still more newsworthy at the moment than Princess Diana and Hugh Grant put together – a combination at least one columnist had suggested was devoutly to be wished for.

But Terence refused to talk to the press. The journalists felt very hurt, Tel was almost one of them, had been one of the boys, drinking with journalists all over the world late into the night.

And he continued to refuse to lay charges against Nicola Abbott.

The Crown Prosecution Service said they would lay them without his cooperation, they had the neighbours as witnesses of Terence running into the street screaming and of Nicky Abbott sitting in the kitchen quietly holding a knife.

Finally Terence simply disappeared from London altogether and nobody knew where he was, though sightings were reported in Tokyo and Sydney and on Richard Branson's private island. Iona Spring even gave the press the address of his hideaway in Suffolk: he was not there. As Nicola Abbott had seemed to disappear into thin air also, the baffled press, although still sending reporters to South America and Spain just in case, could do nothing but wait for the most notorious rape trial anybody could remember.

It was suddenly announced by the Lord Chancellor, having spoken to the lawyers concerned and moving extremely quickly under government pressure, that the trial would be brought forward to early December. The legal fraternity had noted with horror that the complainant had already spoken to the American press. The kind of prolonged media circus that almost overshadowed the actual trials of Mike Tyson and OJ Simpson in the United States would under no circumstances be allowed to be repeated here.

It was still only October. Journalists rather grumpily turned back to Princess Diana; a few half-hearted pictures of Hugh Grant turning away from the camera returned to the front pages.

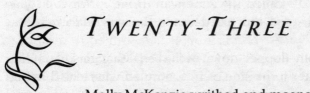 # TWENTY-THREE

Molly McKenzie writhed and moaned.

One of her hands reached up behind her for the bedhead rail, tightened around it then released as she cried *Aaaaagh*.

Malcolm Evans, who had also cried *Aaaaagh! Yes! Aaaaaagh!*, paused for a moment then got off her. As rehearsed, he pulled a towel round him to hide his underpants as the camera lingered for a moment on Molly's released hand then panned down on to the bed where she lay looking satisfied. She lay in a large bed, just the very top of one breast tastefully displayed, and half a bare leg. She too was wearing panties but the camera couldn't see that. Malcolm Evans, playing her brother-in-law, now stood with the towel safely around his allegedly naked private parts, watching the scene of wedding breakfast merriment (which wasn't actually happening) in the dark courtyard below and the camera moved in to him as he turned back into the bedroom.

'I hate weddings,' said Malcolm Evans.

'I love them!' said Molly, smiling coyly.

Then the assistant director gave a sort of strangled *eeeeeek* noise in place of the bride's scream, the bride not having been called for filming today. Malcolm Evans looked towards the door, looked alarmed; Molly sat up in bed cleverly holding the sheet around her body.

'What was that?' she said.

'CUT,' called the American director, Waylon Jones. 'Good, good, much better take, the sex was more believable.'

Molly flopped down in the bed, Malcolm Evans came and sat on the side of it, continued where he'd left off with his story of making a film in Russia. The camera crew conferred, someone called out *gate's clear*, the camera was moved outside for the next shot, Malcolm Evans got on to the bit about the mafia organising the catering and getting food on the black market. Molly listened, nodded, tried not to yawn. It was 11.45 at night and she was exhausted; night filming always seemed to take forever, this was the fourth night in a row. The assistant director came over to the bed.

'Malcolm you're cleared for tonight luvvie thank you, Molly they'd like you to stand by in case they get to your shot in the dark you know, the one where you watch the ambulance disappear.'

Molly sighed heavily.

'OK,' she said, and a dresser who had been hovering slipped a dressing gown round her before she got up from the bed.

She dressed, muttering to herself *I'm mutton dressed up*

as lamb, in the cherry red jacket and the short skirt; the dresser did up the gold belt, gave her the gold chunky earrings and bracelet and necklace. Then Molly returned, yawning, to the make-up caravan where they re-did her hair and her make-up. They were on location at a pretty little country hotel outside Henley-on-Thames: the tragedy of the warring brothers and the stabbed bride, who were all now residents of Knightsbridge and having a pretty country wedding, was taking place at night rather than in the afternoon so that eerie, scary night shots and shadows could give the film more atmosphere. *As if atmosphere will help this pile of shit*, Molly had said darkly as she left Banjo in bed at midday when the car came to Clapham to pick her up and he had answered sleepily, *smile and think of the money* and she had kissed his tousled hair. His saxophone lay in the corner of the bedroom, underneath his jersey and his T-shirt and his jeans.

The assistant director finally came to Molly's caravan about one in the morning.

'Sorry love, we're not going to get that shot in, we have to wrap before one-thirty tonight or the crew are on double overtime, your car will be in the hotel courtyard when you're ready, but Waylon would like to see you in his caravan for a quick word when you've changed.'

Molly wearily took off again her cherry red jacket and her short skirt and her chunky jewellery, her dresser hung everything in the wardrobe caravan. Molly declined the make-up girl's offer to clean her face.

'I'll do it at home thanks,' said Molly, 'I'm buggered.'

As she walked up the steps to the director's caravan she saw the sound recordist standing together with his assistant nearby in the darkness. She didn't like this man, the way he slipped portable microphones down inside her dress, not waiting for her dresser as he should have; Molly was not in the least prudish, just objected to the way he pushed inside her clothes. When the young actress playing the bride had asked her nervously if it was usual to have male sound recordists putting things inside your bra, Molly had complained to the first assistant. She knew she had made an enemy of the sound recordist.

'Goodnight,' she called politely to the two men, and they waved as she entered the caravan.

Waylon Jones was smoking a cigar, drinking whisky; the smoke from the cigar filled the room.

'Like one?' he asked, indicating the whisky bottle.

'No thanks,' said Molly, hating the smell of the cigar.

'Sorry we had to keep you, I thought we might have got that scene in tonight, sit down for a minute will ya.'

Molly felt a slight twinge of alarm. She thought the scene in the bed had gone as well as a-pile-of-shit scenes could go. Was he unhappy with her work?

She sat across the table from him.

'Sure you won't have a whisky?' He waved the bottle at her.

Molly took the other glass on the table, poured herself a very small drink.

'Now listen,' said the director. For a moment he just sat back puffing very slowly on his cigar, surveying her.

She drank the neat spirits, felt it on her throat, smiled

politely although she was almost dropping with exhaustion, she wouldn't get home till 3 am, could he fire her now if he was unhappy with her performance?

'They've called you a car of course,' said Waylon Jones. 'But I tell you what. Why don't you come back in my car to my hotel and we could have –' he paused, took a drink, looked at her speculatively, and Molly was not to know he was thinking of a day on *The Little Love Boat* in the sunshine '– a little – tired – fun. You older women, you want it more, don't you?'

Molly's face didn't change for a moment. She didn't move or speak for several seconds. On the whole the rule of thumb was: one did not insult a director (even if he insulted you) when one was in the middle of filming. She knew too many stories of parts cut, close-ups gone. This was her first job for five months. So she sat there for several seconds, quite motionless, looking at the director. Then she smiled at him, put the glass to her lips, drained the whisky and stood up.

'Thank you for the offer Waylon,' she said. 'I'm very flattered of course but I have a *very* jealous lover, you don't want another murder to deal with. See you tomorrow. ' And she smiled at him again and walked out of the caravan.

Outside, the two sound men still waited which was strange, all the camera crew were usually away in minutes when a wrap had been called. As she walked past them to where she knew her car would be waiting the sound recordist said, loud enough for her to hear, 'Good. We were right.'

Molly stopped. 'What do you mean?'

'You just won us two hundred quid.'

'What?' She pushed at her hair, puzzled.

'It was a bet,' he said, shrugging. 'He bet you would, that you'd be dying for it at your age. We bet you wouldn't, that you were past it.'

Molly felt the colour rush to her cheeks in the darkness of the hotel courtyard.

'Well there you go,' she said shakily, 'you owe me a drink,' and the men laughed.

In the car being driven back to Clapham she was still shaking with anger. She tried to laugh it off to herself as she would have once, but somehow the words *he said you'd be dying for it at your age, we said you'd be past it* stayed there in her mind, and his words to her *a little – tired – fun.*

As the driver neared Clapham she was filled with such a longing to see dear good uncynical Banjo, feel his young arms hold her tight in their bed, the man she loved most in her life.

But Banjo was out, his saxophone gone from the corner.

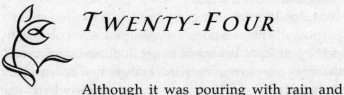

TWENTY-FOUR

Although it was pouring with rain and very cold, Emmy Lou's press night was packed. Somehow word about the new play had got around, the literary manager from the National Theatre had been to the preview the night before and tonight several other people from the National were there. The theatre, really a room above a pub, was only small, could hold about seventy people. Tonight they all cramped together, there were probably nearer eighty and people had been turned away. There was a buzz of excitement.

Eurydice Smith, who had finally been let back into rehearsals, had almost lost her sullen look. She was too good a writer not to see in the end what Pamela Angel and the actors had done, how they had taken her already remarkable play and made it fly. She wished all the actors good luck nervously, pulling at her short orange hair.

Emmy Lou was nervous and yet not nervous. She had worked so hard, loved her part, knew she was good in it. She knew also that this was an important chance for her.

That made her nervous and yet exhilarated at the same time. She never thought any more that she was playing someone 'old' – she was playing Alice, she had become Alice. In the tiny cramped dressing room where the men and women all changed and made up together, bumping into each other as they tried to put on socks and make-up, she pushed her hair down under her hat, rubbed dirt into her face.

Milton Werner, in the audience, was looking slightly perplexed. This was not Stratford-upon-Avon obviously, yet people had clamoured to get in. It was so cramped, the seats were extremely hard, Frances had insisted they sit down early as the seats weren't numbered and she wanted a good place. He felt particularly uncomfortable in his cream business suit. He had come straight from the Wise Insurance offices as the press night started at 7 pm; the commercial was finished. He would now be going back to Switzerland. He would have to tell Frances and he was sensitive enough to feel that she might mind. He also knew that to his surprise he might mind himself. If anybody had been watching Milton Werner they would have seen him look strangely at Frances Kitson's low-cut dress, at her breasts.

Frances and Harry were talking across him so that Frances' breasts were quite dangerously near. By unspoken agreement they didn't talk about Michael, the death of Michael, the upsetting funeral they'd both attended.

'Harry,' said Frances, but quite quietly, 'I've been meaning to ask you, do you think Molly's still having an affair with Anthony?'

Harry looked surprised. His eyebrows raised in his

rather lugubrious face gave him a comic look. 'I wouldn't think so, you mean after all these years? Why?'

'She was at Stratford by herself to see him when Milton and I went. She said they had business to talk about.'

'Perhaps they had?'

'Listen darling, I *know* Anthony, I've known him for over thirty years. He was – looking at her. He got rid of us double quick didn't he Milton?'

Milton nodded but he had actually appreciated Anthony's style: Milton often had to get rid of people quickly and politely in his own business. 'I thought he did it chivalrously nevertheless,' he said firmly.

'But –' Harry didn't want this to be true, for Pauline's sake '– Molly has her toyboy, she's been with him for years.'

'Yeah I know. Well – maybe I'm wrong, there was just – something in the air. Oh look there's Izzy Fields and her husband, good God they've both got bicycle helmets they must be mad, Izzy! Izzy!' and the two women waved across the small space.

Then Frances turned back to Harry.

'Did you see,' she said, 'that Juliet's missing the last fortnight of *The Seagull*? It was in the late edition of tonight's *Standard*. It said she was suffering from nervous exhaustion, she was taken by ambulance from the theatre the other night after the show and it's just been announced she won't go back, can you imagine Juliet Lyall of all people suffering from nervous exhaustion? She's made of granite!'

Harry remained very still for a moment. And then he shrugged, and Frances thought how quickly his tan had faded, he'd been back from Morocco for less than a week yet he looked quite pale, but of course Michael's death had affected him very much.

'She's making a film in America in a fortnight,' said Harry, 'perhaps she couldn't handle everything, we're none of us getting any younger Fran.'

Frances laughed, squeezed Harry's arm affectionately across Milton. 'Not us lot darling,' she said, 'we're not weakening, we're as tough as old boots, the class of fifty-nine, *especially* Juliet. Oh and listen, I went up for another advert today and you'll never guess what it was for, Triumph Telephones, the opposition to British Telecom!'

Harry laughed and Milton smiled. 'Ah my dear Frances telephones are obviously your *métier*,' he said, 'did you advise them you were employed by one of their competitors in another capacity?'

'I was a jibbering idiot Milton darling, I should have asked you what to say, you represent clients, you know what goes down well, but there was no notice, I was just suddenly called in. I couldn't decide whether it was a plus or a minus me being one of British Telecom's employees, I kept starting to tell them and then changing my mind.' Fran's laughter bubbled up. 'It must've looked as if I had St Vitus's dance or something, you know, I thought they might think I could be very useful as a spy and then I thought they'd just think I was an unsuccessful actress, then in the end I did tell them and they looked nonplussed.' She was laughing at herself, leaning against Milton slightly as she did so. The lights in the theatre started to go down. 'Is your filming going well?' whispered Frances.

'Yes,' said Harry, 'it's rather good and frightfully English, I think it will go far, preferably America and West Germany where the royalties are highest.'

Frances smiled, they both leant back into their seats, the buzz of conversation faded, the theatre was in blackout.

When the stage lights came up after a few seconds Emmy Lou was sitting in a corner of the acting space in an old battered hat. She had dirty bandages around one of her legs. She had a small, rusty shopping trolley and she was folding and re-folding old newspapers, her tongue moving in time to her folding. These were her possessions.

She kept doing this for a moment and then, quite unforgettably to the people who were there that night, she said quite simply, in control, so that the audience did not laugh, in a voice that seemed to come from somewhere deep inside her, *I trained to be a school teacher.*

The play, *Lives*, ran for almost two hours without an interval. The audience sat forward, entranced, fascinated by the stories of these street people; heard not the clink of glasses from the bar below, nor the underground trains that sometimes rumbled past deep beneath them. At the end, most unusually in a small theatre, they stood as they clapped, one woman was openly weeping as she stood there.

Harry and Frances were incredibly excited for Emmy Lou, she had been staggeringly good even though both of them were very familiar with her work and her way of acting. Milton Werner was impressed too, saw how in its way this was after all something good, like the production they had travelled all the way to Stratford-upon-Avon to see.

They discussed the play enthusiastically in the bar afterwards with Emmy Lou whose face had become, as Frances always noticed with Emmy, almost beautiful as she smiled and accepted compliments from people milling excitedly about. Harry hugged and hugged her; both he and Frances, her closest friends for so long, took genuine generous delight in her success.

'The National Theatre's been in,' Emmy Lou whispered to Harry, 'Pamela Angel says they're terribly keen to do it, it's good for Eurydice isn't it, oh Harry I never thought I'd say this but if I can join the National and play this part *everything* will have been worth it, after all.' Harry hugged her once more, felt as if he could weep for her, for this good time at last.

Izzy Fields appeared at Emmy Lou's shoulder, clutching a bottle of wine for her. 'You were wonderful Em,' she said as she hugged her, 'wonderful, best thing I've ever seen you do. They're all talking about it at the National I hear.'

'I know,' said Emmy Lou, 'isn't it wonderful, I would so love to work there,' didn't see the little anxious look in Izzy's eyes.

Izzy's husband, Peter the school teacher whom she'd known since her days in rep in Salisbury, wasn't like an actor, he didn't kiss Emmy Lou but shook her hand up and down enthusiastically. 'I liked you a lot,' he said and she smiled.

'Thanks Peter,' she said.

They all went to a nearby Italian restaurant, and there

too people came up to Emmy Lou, congratulated her. Milton Werner quietly insisted that the evening was on him, ordering good wine, presenting an extra bottle to Emmy. Frances glowed. It was a good evening, one of those evenings actors remember.

Afterwards Emmy Lou and Harry ran to the tube station in the rain under Harry's big black umbrella, Emmy Lou held Harry's arm as they laughed and ran, a plastic bag with her wine bottles banging against his legs and the flowers that Harry and Franny had sent her clasped by Emmy against her raincoat.

Their platforms were on different sides. Just as they were parting Emmy Lou said, 'I'm so sorry darling, about Michael. I tried to get time off, for the funeral, but it was just impossible, it was the technical rehearsal that day. Was it – awful?'

Harry stood there where the wind blew up the platform from the tunnels.

'It was awful,' he said. He wasn't going to say anything more, didn't want to spoil this evening but then Emmy Lou touched his arm, looked up at him. 'Oh Em, it was just – as bad as it could be. Annabel was inconsolable obviously. But the worst part was Michael's mother. You know how his parents weren't – very supportive, imagine his mother, only coming to London once the whole time he was ill, his father wouldn't accept it was happening at all, he wasn't there of course. She didn't seem to cry, or show any emotion until just as we came out of the church and she suddenly – the coffin was just going back into the hearse to go to the crematorium – and she—' Harry stopped and Emmy Lou saw his face quite twisted with the effort to talk normally. 'She – made a funny little movement, I can't forget it, as if she was going to, I don't know, touch the coffin, throw herself in – who knows – and then she turned on us and sort of screamed, *you're all dirty, you're all dirty* and started to cry.'

'Oh God.'

'And the vicar – just as well she didn't know he was gay too – he sort of took her arm and –' Harry shrugged '– mumbled away about God's Love Embracing Us All and then Annabel kind of threw herself at his mother and screamed I loved him I loved him and we had to haul her off.' Finally Harry began to laugh on the underground platform. 'It was like – you know a dreadful scene from some dreadful B movie, women screaming, men holding them back, even atmospheric rain pouring down. I'm afraid we left her with the vicar, Michael's mother, I'd brought her to the church in a cab and we'd invited her back to Annabel's for a drink but it was all too impossible. We all went home and they got pissed. I had a read-through and had to make people laugh the next day, it was like being in hell.'

They heard the guard call LAST PICCADILLY LINE TRAIN, kissed quickly and Emmy ran. Just as she jumped on the tube Harry called loudly after her in a parody of themselves and their profession:

You were wonderful darling.

Frances and Milton drove home to Frances' flat: as always he parked under the streetlight outside and thanked her for an enjoyable evening. He had always kissed her decorously on the cheek under the light, nothing more.

'Your friend was very good,' said Milton.

'I know,' said Frances, 'she's a wonderful actress and doesn't always get the chance to show it, this'll be so good for her. And it was lovely of you to take everyone to dinner like that – it wasn't necessary Milton, but it was lovely.'

'I have enjoyed meeting other actors through you,' he said. 'It is not like that for me in Switzerland and I am – well Frances, I am returning home tomorrow. We completed the commercial today.'

'Tomorrow?'

'Yes it is tomorrow.'

'Will you be back?'

'Ah – it is possible. I do not yet know.'

A sudden bleakness descended on Frances who for almost four weeks had had a different kind of life. It wasn't much perhaps but she had had someone to go out with, plan with, be with. And more than that. She had seen what a kind man he was, and had begun to care for him.

'You didn't say,' she said finally.

'No,' he said, 'I didn't say. I should have. I apologise Frances.'

For a moment they were silent and then Frances sighed. 'Well Milton, let's be reckless, come in and have a drink if this is goodbye.'

'No more drink,' said Milton carefully. Conflicting emotions seemed to flit across his face in the light from the streetlight.

'Come on Milton, I won't eat you, a cup of coffee at least.'

'Very well.'

He stood rather stiffly in her kitchen as she made coffee, they took it into the sitting room. Frances sat beside him on the sofa, put her coffee on the floor, took a deep breath and kissed him very firmly on the mouth. He responded ardently for a moment, and then pulled away.

'I am not sure this is a good idea Frances,' he said and his voice sounded strange.

Frances, who was breathing rather heavily, gave a little laugh. 'As I said Milton, I'm not going to eat you, I've only kissed you.' She was still catching her breath from his kiss, her bosom heaving.

And Milton Werner, who for his own sake had only stared, never touched, could hold back no longer as her bosom rose in front of his eyes. He took Frances' face in both his hands and kissed her more passionately than she had ever been kissed in her life. Then he fell upon her breasts with a sort of strangled cry. To her great astonishment he ripped her dress, actually ripped it in his hurry to get at her.

'Milton—' she began, but it was too late. He tore desperately at her dress again as he pushed his face against her large breasts. He sucked and whimpered and then he cried out *you are so beautiful*. He began heaving and rocking in a most extraordinary manner, Frances was pushed back into the side of the sofa, pinned down by a man in a suit heaving like a rhinoceros. He cried out very loudly and then became completely still.

The whole exercise had taken about forty-five seconds.

There was silence in Frances' sitting room except for Milton Werner trying to regain his breath and the loud ticking of the Victorian clock on the mantelpiece which Frances had bought long ago from a secondhand shop while playing in a Christmas pantomime at Crewe.

She gave a tiny sigh.

And then despite herself she began to laugh.

'Poor Milton,' she said, trying to hold her dress together as she laughed. 'You've come all over your suit, you'll have to get it express dry-cleaned in the morning before you fly away.'

Milton Werner pulled himself up off the sofa; as he did so he knocked over the cup of coffee, still steaming, that Frances had placed on the floor; it ran all over her light pink carpet. *The girl that I marry will have to be as soft and as pink as a nursery*, the old, stupid words went round and round in her mind. Milton didn't know where to look, gestured hopelessly at the stain on the floor, averted his eyes from the stain on his cream trousers.

Frances got up too, pulled her torn dress around her still exposed breasts. She went into her bedroom, took off the dress, put on an old dressing gown, wondered, *poor Milton*, how to retrieve the situation so that he didn't feel too humiliated.

But when she came back into the sitting room Milton Werner had gone.

After some moments she took a cloth and some water, rubbed desultorily at the carpet. Then she put some milk in a pot on the stove to make herself a cup of cocoa. She

would have liked to phone Emmy or Harry, someone to
share such a ludicrous experience with, but decided to
wait until morning, till she could laugh more whole-
heartedly, she'd feel better in the morning. She would
call it My Night With Milton.

Frances Kitson, good old Frances as her friends
always called her, fifty-seven years old and one of the
survivors of the class of '59, would have given almost
anything to meet a man who would love her.

In the next morning's newspapers the play *Lives* and
Emmy Lou received glowing notices in small corners.

The *Sun* and the *Mail* and the *Daily Express* all picked
up the story of Juliet Lyall's nervous collapse which the
theatre had been trying to keep quiet but which someone
had now leaked to the press. The *Sun*'s headline
screamed: LUVVIES' REUNION JINXED? and underneath in slightly smaller letters it said: BLUE'S EX-FIANCÉE
JULIET LYALL IN BACKSTAGE DRAMA and BLUE SIGHTED IN MARBELLA?

And in Juliet Lyall's drugged mind the words danced.

It is beginning, she said aloud in the room in the private hospital.

TWENTY-FIVE

When the whole world changes, people often automatically still do the usual things: Nicola Abbott still caught the train to Miss Grace's house in Richmond the night in 1961 when Terence Blue came to see *A Doll's House*. They walked, the two of them, down through Soho to Charing Cross and across the railway bridge to Waterloo station. Terence's arm rested quite lightly across Nicky's shoulders, as if they always walked together, as if it was all decided. There was time to catch the last train. They hardly spoke at all.

Till, at the train, last doors banging, the big hand of the platform clock moving through each minute, Terence said, *I love you Nicky. I will love you for the rest of my life.* He was twenty-four. The midnight guard blew his whistle but still Terence heard quite clearly Nicky say, in the voice that nobody forgot, *I will never never never let you go.* She was nineteen.

And the last train to Richmond pulled slowly out of

Waterloo Station and into the darkness. They hadn't even arranged to meet again.

Every night after the show, sometimes dashing in from filming even as the curtain was coming down and the applause filled the theatre, Terence appeared at the door of the Number Two dressing room. Sometimes people came round after the show, congratulated Nicky on her performance. She thanked them shyly in her dark voice; they would note the blue, blue eyes of the boy waiting by the door and how the eyes of the young actress devoured him. Nicky would be always in her rather prim, pink candlewick dressing gown: underneath it was, but only Terence knew, just the funny little singlet. Terence locked the door now, Charlie Evans the stage door keeper knew they were there now. On the floor of the Number Two dressing room, what Nicky had known instinctively she learnt now from Terence; there under the spotlit mirror, there with the smell of make-up and cleansers and wig glue and corsets and the Victorian costumes that she sweated into every night: the tools of her trade. And there in the theatre one night she told him what she had never told another person so that the words came out in relief at last, one night when they were almost ready to leave and they stared at themselves in the mirror, about the death of her mother.

Charlie knew they would be out in time for the last train to Richmond; he sighed sometimes, went back over the racing results, rattled his keys in his pocket. Sometimes his leg hurt and he would mean to be short with them but then he caught the look on Nicky's face and he had the most extraordinary feeling of memory, of when he was young, as if for a moment she gave him back his past.

'Goodnight,' he would say gruffly, but somehow not cross, after all, 'see you tomorrow. ' Charlie was, like many stage door keepers, an inveterate gossip, seeing and knowing what was going on in the company better than anybody else. For some reason he could not exactly put his finger on, he told nobody.

Of course this strange trysting could not last, lasted perhaps for ten nights, not more. The director flew in from America, wanting Nicky with him at dinner after the show; she began filming *Heartbreak*, picked up in a studio car from Richmond at five o'clock every morning. Terence was sent on location to Fort William in Scotland where the rocks leapt high into the air and where he stood on clifftops like some latterday blue-eyed Heathcliffe, thinking of Nicky. And began, despite another appalling script, to be a star.

Miss Grace and Juliet Lyall did not yet know what had happened.

Nicky was sick one morning on the set of *Heartbreak*, vomited quite unexpectedly and quietly over a chintz-covered armchair; they rushed in the studio nurse but Nicola Abbott said she had had oysters for dinner the previous night. She knew anyway that she was pregnant; believed it had happened the first time Terence had come to her dressing room. There was no such thing as the Pill and Terence may have had a condom in his back pocket but quite simply never thought to use one.

Nicky rejoiced; she would have her own, own, real, beautiful family at last, they would live in a house with a garden. Now that she had spoken about it aloud, just a hint of a thought about her mother's death filtered into her mind; just there, on the margins of her reality she sometimes now caught at the streetlight shining in through the Venetian blinds on to the double bed where a schoolgirl in uniform sat holding a pillow. Now she would be a mother, like her mother. How odd. Then the thought was gone.

She sent Terence a telegram to Fort William.

For a moment Terence felt as if his heart had stopped when he received the telegram. He was delighted, joyful. But he remembered what had happened to Juliet. This time things must not go wrong, he loved Nicky too much, they must get married at once, he must tell Juliet of course, somehow he must deal with his Welsh religious family who thought him engaged to Juliet Lyall, and would be devastated by the shame of a hasty marriage to someone else. His father was a strong, white-haired, still physically powerful man of the Chapel: right and wrong were absolutely clear to him, and he had always made them absolutely clear to his only son. He would be very, very angry. For it was 1961 still. Although Beat poets recited their poetry in pubs and in a few years the Rolling Stones would explode it was still shameful for an unmarried girl to get pregnant. Not only Terence's family but Miss Grace and her mother would have been absolutely horrified if they had known.

Nicky told Miss Grace she had found a flat in town. What she and Terence actually and quietly did was buy a house in Brighton, as Laurence Olivier had suggested expansively to young actors in theatre green rooms. Nicky arranged the mortgage while Terence was in Scotland, discussing it with him excitedly from telephone boxes. Miss Grace had expected to help her furnish the London flat, choose curtains and tasteful pictures and furniture; felt instead Nicky drawing away from her, closing her down was how she described it to herself, hurt for the rest of her life: *she closed me down*.

'She has survived,' said old Mrs Grace briskly, 'leave it. As I told you, most girls survive.'

Terence, unbeknown to Nicky, went to York to talk to Juliet, to break off his engagement. He swallowed nervously on the train. Their work had mostly kept them apart the way it so often did with actors; he had told her nothing on the telephone. He knew how very badly his behaviour would appear to anybody, but he had never been in love, had had no conception until now of the meaning of the word.

Juliet, still pale, still often bleeding from the abortion although it was now over four months ago, wept when she saw him. *Where were you?* she cried, told him she could not bear him to touch her, then clung to him with such ferocity that all night, lying decorously beside her in the one bed in her digs, he could not say it, could not bear to hurt her more. *I want us to get married now*, wept Juliet, and later, *I don't ever want to see you again*. Terence was not cruel, only young and cowardly: he did not know how to deal with the situation he found himself in.

So, confused, he told Harry – good old Harry Donaldson, their queer friend from the class of '59. Terence asked Harry if he had time for a drink; they sat in a quiet pub far from the theatre and Terence told Harry almost everything: the Number Two dressing room, the last train to Richmond, the rubbishy film in Scotland, Nicky's pregnancy, the film *Heartbreak* that would make Nicky a star.

He did not talk about Nicky's mother.

Harry knew about *Heartbreak*, had had a day's filming on it before he came to York, had already witnessed how extraordinary Nicky's performance was. On and on the monologue went in a low voice, Terence staring at his cigarette but just occasionally looking up at Harry with his blue eyes glowing. Not for the first time in his life and certainly not for the last, Harry wished people would keep their life stories to themselves, not involve him so that he had to share their experiences, think about them, even give advice. He was still coming to terms with being a homosexual, not knowing how to proceed, cruising places in York he'd been told were meeting places where it was probably unsafe, not to mention illegal, to do so; he was very unhappy and confused. He wondered how people like Terence could possibly think he had answers.

'Well, you'll have to tell Juliet,' said Harry.

Just at that moment Juliet came towards them in the bar: dissatisfied, pale.

'Where were you?' she said to Terence sorrowfully. 'I've been to nearly every pub in York looking for you,' and Terence, not looking at Harry, weakly patted her arm in apology, bought more drinks, stayed in the bar drinking heavily when the others went off to appear in this fortnight's play *Widowers' Houses*. He flew back to Scotland with his mission still unaccomplished first thing next morning, having lain in an uneasy sleep beside Juliet who sometimes clung to him weeping but who also literally could not bear to feel his body that had given her such pleasure, and then such pain, next to hers: a kind of sad schizophrenia.

And so it turned out that only Harry Donaldson knew that Terence Blue and Nicola Abbott got quietly married the next Saturday morning.

'Be our witness at the Pimlico register office,' said Terence on the telephone to York from Aberdeen. 'We want it to be you, there's a night train after your show and we'll whiz up from our new house in Brighton and get married at ten so you can get back for your matinée, I checked the trains.'

'For fuck's sake Terry,' said Harry, 'what about Juliet? You're still engaged to her. How can you do this?'

'Listen,' said Terence, 'we've got to get married quickly, obviously we do, you haven't met my father, she's nearly three months pregnant, we've got to do it this weekend when I get back from Scotland. But I've got four days off in three weeks' time, I'll come and see Juliet then.' Then added with a flash of twenty-four-year-old self-knowledge, 'I know I seem to be behaving like a shit but I'm not a shit you know. I'm in love with Nicky, I've never been in love before, it makes things absolutely different. I know it seems a bit of a mess now but I know somehow that when it's all cut and dried and irreversible, I'll be able to tell my parents too. I'll be able to explain everything properly to Juliet, Nicky, my parents, everybody. You'll see Harry, by the end of the month it'll be all sorted out.' And then he said an odd, old-fashioned thing. 'Harry I give you my word.'

So Harry reluctantly agreed. Along with a cleaner who was often asked to do these things he signed the papers in the Pimlico register office and congratulated his classmates Terence Blue and Nicola Abbott; saw how it was with the two of them. Terence was wearing a dark blue suit that somehow brought out the blue in his eyes; although it was a cold day Nicky stood signing the register in a simple cream dress and carrying one red rose, she looked absolutely wonderful. Happiness shone from them as they looked at each other. Harry thought that he saw for the first time in his life what happiness was. For a moment, standing alone at the train station afterwards, a pain of longing overwhelmed him. Would he ever feel like that, even briefly, himself?

That same weekend, after the last performance of *Widowers' Houses*, Juliet Lyall drove herself home in the car her father had given her, hiding the bleeding as best she could, to see her father who had phoned and said he wanted to talk to her.

'Is it about *The Red Dress*?' she asked excitedly.

'Come home,' said her father.

He lived with his fourth wife, this one younger than Juliet, in their eight-bedroomed house in Wiltshire; his first wife, Juliet's mother, lived in France. Juliet wanted to tell her childish stepmother that she needed some help, that she had been bleeding after an illegal abortion for weeks and weeks and weeks, that something must be wrong. But her stepmother pouted at her father, wanted him for herself as soon as lunch was over, was not interested in a stepdaughter older than herself. Over that Sunday lunch, her father told her the news: the executive producers on *The Red Dress* had been shown the rushes of *Heartbreak*. They were absolutely adamant they wanted nobody but Nicola Abbott for the new film.

Juliet wept with disappointment and rage and envy and anger, and in desolation too: she could have had Terence's baby, after all. She phoned and phoned the flat he stayed in when he was in London, there was no reply.

Back in York on Monday morning, during the last run-through for the next play, *A Midsummer Night's Dream*, a story of self-deception and enchantment and misunderstanding and love, she pulled angrily at Harry Donaldson in the coffee break, making him follow her.

'Nicola Abbott, Nicola Abbott, it's all I ever heard from the day I started at drama school.' Juliet was shaking with emotion in the theatre rehearsal room, a cold room with two paraffin heaters. She and Harry sat apart from the others, on two chairs in a corner near one of the heaters, holding their hands round their mugs of coffee, wearing jerseys and scarves because it was so cold; they weren't having a dress rehearsal in their costumes till the evening.

'And where's Terence?' she added, tears coming into her eyes. 'He's always disappearing, I thought he'd be back in London this weekend but I've phoned and phoned him and he's nowhere, we may as well get married and he can have a damn baby.'

And, in the cold rehearsal room at York on that Monday morning in winter, Harry Donaldson did what he regretted for the rest of his life.

He thought he was doing it to be fair, to clear things up, doing what Terence wasn't brave enough to do.

But in many dark nights afterwards he knew it was something else.

He was used to Juliet, had worked closely with her now since 1959, but he didn't like her. He thought she was a selfish and confident actress on stage, he disliked working with her, had disliked it from their first term as students together. She *grabbed* the stage was the way he described it to himself, grabbed it and filled it with herself, often so there wasn't room for other people.

But there was something deeper and darker.

He wanted to see what would happen.

'Terence married Nicola Abbott on Saturday, she's pregnant,' he said.

TWENTY-SIX

Some weeks after her father's funeral Pauline O'Brien Bonham very carefully polished a valuable eighteenth-century chest of drawers in her workroom. It was hard work, and it gave her great satisfaction. The workroom at the back of the antique shop always smelt of old wood and furniture polish, a warm and reassuring fragrance, something solid and permanent about it that Pauline liked. Her hair fell across her face as she worked; the gas heater purred, the rain fell on the roof. How quickly the winter had come, how quickly the long, hot summer had become just a memory. A series of Mozart quartets were playing on Classic FM, interspersed with irritating advertisements that she closed her mind to.

And as she worked, she thought about Joseph Wain.

And her husband. Who had not once mentioned *The Immoralists* and Joseph Wain's plan for them to work together.

And the best friend of her youth, Molly McKenzie.

She had dealt with sexual betrayal all her married life; it hurt her less each time. But the first, most important one was always there.

After Portia was born, those Monday mornings when Anthony, family duty done, would race back to his exciting work in Birmingham while Pauline, only the previous year the toast of London, dragged the nappies and the pram to the local laundrette, had been almost unbearable. One afternoon, desperately depressed, she made an unannounced visit with Portia to see her husband. The landlady had seemed surprised to see her and a baby but had shown her in to Anthony's room.

That room, in Birmingham, had haunted her for years.

Molly's tights, and the baggy green cardigan she'd always worn at drama school, lay entwined on the narrow bed with Anthony's jockey shorts, and a packet of contraceptive pills lay on the windowsill. That was how Pauline found out.

Pauline replaced one polished drawer back in the old chest carefully, just as carefully removed another.

At the time she thought that she would never recover. She wanted to leave Anthony, but he worked hard, persuaded her it was an aberration because he missed her, took to phoning her every single night after the performance to see how she was. *It's all over darling I was a fool, I am so truly sorry and I love you*, he would say. None of the other betrayals, the small, regular, tacky treacheries, hurt her anything like the first one had; sometimes she was able to persuade herself they weren't happening at all.

By the time she finally realised the pattern of their lives, Anthony was starring in a very popular television series about life in an office of which more and more episodes were made by popular demand; they were richer than most actors they knew and had moved to Chiswick to the beautiful house by the river. And she was expecting Viola and she hadn't been on stage for nearly five years. The swinging sixties were almost over: the Rolling Stones had already given free concerts in Hyde Park, young girls had ironed their hair on ironing boards to look like pop stars. But Pauline felt as if, in some unaccountable way, although she'd lived through them, she'd missed the swinging sixties, she was too unhappy, and too busy at the laundrette and the kindergarten and the doctor's surgery, and with Portia's bad bout of whooping cough that seemed to last forever. Sex, drugs and rock 'n' roll weren't so easy for a pregnant ex-actress with a demanding young daughter. With whom she'd never really had an easy relationship: *my fault* Pauline always said to herself, *I loved Portia of course but I resented her coming*.

There began to be the rewards of course, as she'd implied to Joseph Wain when they'd had lunch together: the reasons for staying, not going, were as complex as marriage itself. They began to have a very good life indeed, and she would have had to be blind to see it wasn't like this for most other actors. People began to ask Anthony Bonham the famous actor and his wife to all sorts of interesting dinners and parties and occasions, Pauline often found herself with a painter or a writer or an MP of the kind she could talk to, found herself beginning to belong to a certain part of London artistic and intellectual society that she enjoyed, would have missed. And at first she was vain enough to be pleased to see how often she and Anthony were in the newspapers, photographed with a playwright or a Prime Minister; her vanity was pierced however when – Anthony's star rising and rising – she began to be known as *Mrs Anthony Bonham*. Where was her own identity? *Pauline O'Brien: Actress*. Yet like her mother before her she did not complain out loud. This was her life: she must get on with it.

But she recognised something then. The ice in her heart – her inheritance from her cold stepfather – sharpening when she could not find her real father, hardening when she walked into the bedroom in Birmingham, seemed somehow to become part of her. She had tried to melt it but she could not. Her inscrutable mask became part of her stylish, fashionable, persona.

But she and Anthony loved their house, both deeply loved their children. When their son was born Anthony was a big hit at Stratford as Benedict in *Much Ado About Nothing*; the *Evening Standard* had published a wonderful picture of him in costume on the front page, holding the young Benedict in the air.

Pauline had started her antiques business on the advice of a sculptor she met at one of those fashionable parties, whose wife already had an antique shop. She was almost at once successful, that stylish persona was useful in the antique business and being married to a famous actor helped. Really, she had no thoughts of leaving. And Anthony was in many ways an entertaining man, was getting better and better at his job as he had the chance to stretch himself more and more, and still in many ways interested her more than any other man she met, although for Pauline their sex life had never really recovered. The thought of her husband and her best friend fucking – she made herself articulate the word, *fucking* – together would not go from a corner of her consciousness; hovered there: icy, curious.

She had her first – and only – affair with the sculptor who had told her to start her antiques shop; she felt guilty of course, but she couldn't help enjoying the sex in particular. *Oh is this what it can be like?* she said to him rather shyly, nude on a sofa in his studio in Greenwich as he knelt before her. She was younger then, in her late thirties; he had loved the long curves of her body (his wife was very short); had smoothed the long back once admired all over London, had spent hours caressing her buttocks in particular, his hands feeling over and over the firmness and the roundness, had finally penetrated her from behind very gently at first so that he did not hurt her and she had surprisingly found that she had not disliked it. *I'd like to know more about sex*, she thought, *I'd like to have more affairs. I think.*

But the sculptor and his family moved to America where his round, curved pieces were very popular; Pauline bought all his wife's antique stock before they left. And somehow she didn't have other affairs after all, as if she wasn't, really, that kind of person. Until now perhaps when she found herself over and over again thinking of Joseph Wain and the wild, beautiful hair that used to stretch up to the sky and the days when they were young. But, of course, it was unthinkable: he was trying to cast her in *The Immoralists* but it was professional business, it was work. He was always slightly formal with her, now.

She sighed now and stretched, just for a moment ran her hands over her now older body, bent again to the chest of drawers.

She knew, with absolute certainty, as she had said to Joseph, that Anthony might have affairs till he died but he would never leave their life: he needed the security.

But the thought of *Molly* around again disturbed and angered her: Molly who had come to visit her in the sunshine as if it had all been over so that Pauline had stupidly allowed herself, just for a moment, to think they might be friends again. It felt as if Molly had cheated her twice.

Just as she was removing the third drawer in the antique chest the phone rang.

'Pauline,' said Joseph Wain, 'the scripts for *The Immoralists* are nearly ready. We're going to be getting down properly to casting and contracts.'

'Ah,' said Pauline very carefully, 'scripts and contracts.'

'Now listen Pauline. I understood you that day of the garden party, and when we had lunch together. You want this badly don't you?'

'I want this more,' said Pauline, 'than I think I've wanted anything in my life.' Then, suddenly, harshly, 'if you're asking me what I'll do to get it Joey, I'll do anything.' (And because of what she'd been thinking about before the phone rang a thought flashed through her mind: *I'd have an affair with Joey. He loved me once.* And then: *I want to, Oh God I want to so much*.) She heard her own sharp intake of breath. There was a silence on the other end of the phone for a moment. Perhaps he heard her thoughts.

'That's what I understood,' said Joseph finally. 'But I was talking to Anthony again at the end of last week and he seemed to imply you weren't so keen, that you were busy with the shop, he was making suggestions of other actresses he thought might be more suitable. I wondered what that was all about?'

Pauline felt the blood of anger rush to her face. *Bastard bastard bastard*. 'Hold on Joey,' she somehow said. Her face was suddenly so burning, *bastard bastard*, that she pulled off her woollen jersey even as she began speaking again.

'Listen Joseph, I'm sorry to put you in this position: was one of the other actresses a woman we were at the Drama Academy together with, Molly McKenzie? I wouldn't ask you this if it wasn't of immense importance.'

'Yes,' said Joseph. 'Molly McKenzie, I know her work of course, she's very good, he did mention her, yes.'

There was a cracking, breaking sound. Pauline's hand had smashed through the fragile base of an eighteenth-century drawer.

'Are you all right?' said Joseph Wain.

'I'll settle it Joseph,' was all she said. 'You can rely on me absolutely.'

'I leave it to you then.'

'But – but, don't do anything more the mate's way, through Anthony. Please at least let my agent know it's on the cards, if we can – sort everything out.'

'Of course I will Pauline, I'll do it today. But remember what I said – I'm fighting for you, you know what this business is like. You will have to sort it out properly with Anthony very quickly, he could quite easily mess this up for you, it's him the others want, they've all been to see *Othello*, he's absolutely right for this.'

'Trust me Joey,' said Pauline, her voice harsh again and she put down the receiver.

She kicked the pieces of the drawer away from her, she did not notice the pain in her hand, she dragged her raincoat from behind the door so violently that it tore along the shoulder, she ran out into the rain. She walked very fast along the river not knowing where she went, once she thought she saw Hammersmith Bridge, found herself finally in Chelsea as dusk fell. Knives twisted in her heart: she saw again Molly and Anthony in the study at the top of the house the day of the garden party, the palpable feeling of sex in the air although they sat across the room from each other, a feeling so strong in the room that she could almost have held it in her hands. *What was it they had that she was excluded from? What did they* do *to each other?* And now Anthony was trying to take this last chance away from her and give it to Molly McKenzie; Anthony Bonham was doing this to his own wife: this was the man she had married and *lost her career for*.

Suddenly, down by Chelsea Bridge, Pauline vomited violently into the Thames. The rain became heavier and heavier but she did not notice.

Sometimes when it had been raining the river rose. Once when they were children Portia and Viola and Benedict

Bonham had actually seen the River Thames creeping right up their back lawn; they had screamed in terrified delight, then watched in fascination as the fingers of water fell back.

It was late when Pauline got home. Benedict, feet up, eating crisps in front of the television, looked actually alarmed when he glanced up and saw her.

'You're soaking Mum,' he said. 'The river came up the lawn.'

Pauline did not answer.

'You look a bit funny Mum.' And then after a pause because she still did not answer him he added, 'What's for dinner?'

'Fish and chips,' said Pauline. 'Go and get them,' and she threw him the keys to the Mercedes with a five pound note. Ordinarily he would have complained, talked about homework, insisted he hated driving the sissy pink Mercedes; tonight he stared at her again and decided not to.

At three o'clock in the morning as the rain pounded on the river still, Pauline conceived the bizarre and unlikely plan that was to change her life.

Sometimes she rubbed her bruised hand but she did not know that she was doing so. She walked up and down and up and down in her long bedroom by the river. She would do it. *She would do this*: nothing would stop her.

She finally heard – with a start of guilt that she had not realised earlier that her daughter was still out – Viola come in at nearly 4 am. It was so unlike Viola not to phone if she was going to be late or was not coming home that Pauline put on her dressing gown, went downstairs.

But as she put her hand up to switch on the kitchen light she saw a white shape on the lawn: her younger daughter stood motionless in the rain where the river had reached up across the bank. Pauline stood motionless herself, her hand still on the light switch. There was something so intense about the way Viola stood, matching her own intensity, that Pauline wildly wondered, consumed for a moment with guilt and a kind of madness, if she'd spoken aloud, phoned somebody, made her thoughts flesh by mistake so that in some way Viola knew what her mother was planning. Finally her daughter turned and walked slowly through the rain back to the house. Pauline turned too and went quickly upstairs in the darkness to her own bedroom. Her heart beat so fast against her breast it was like a drum; she suddenly remembered walking into the Big Top on Blackheath all those years ago, the way her heart beat then, waiting to find her father.

And she had found her father, after all.

She stood by the window looking down at the flooded river; still the rain fell. With part of her mind she heard Viola getting ready for bed, running water, opening and then closing a door.

Pauline went on standing there by the window. Finally the first light appeared behind the trees right across the river. The rain had stopped. A lone sparrow shivered on the lawn.

'You were late darling,' she said to Viola later,

carefully making coffee for breakfast, trying not to look at her daughter's white face, realising it mirrored her own, 'You could have crashed your Mini in the rain.'

Viola looked up. Totally self-absorbed in her own chaotic thoughts she saw, almost at the edge of her consciousness, that her mother's face was white and drawn, and something else. Glittery.

'Sorry Mum,' was all she said. But for just a moment mother and daughter stared at each other across the kitchen table. Then the phone rang and someone wanted to buy the polished wooden chest of drawers.

'Oh – one of the drawers is broken inside,' said Pauline, remembering suddenly, looking at her bruised hand in surprise but the customer did not care.

Pauline bent and kissed Viola briefly. *I love you Viola. Whatever happens never forget that.* Viola, huddled over the kitchen table, thought her mother might have guessed, decided to at last tell her what had happened. But when she finally looked up to talk to her, her mother had gone.

At the shop, the chest of drawers sold, Pauline took a deep breath.

She was fifty-six years old.

She put out her hand to pick up the telephone. She knew she would have to move fast.

Then suddenly she realised how audacious her plan was, how many quantum leaps into the unknown would be required. She laughed aloud in the empty antique shop, laughed and laughed but it was real laughter, the way she used to laugh when she was young. In an antique mirror she caught a glimpse of herself: her mouth open, her pale face, but her eyes were crinkled with real humour, real laughter thank God. It was all right: she was not mad. Thinking, though, that she looked too pale after no sleep she felt around in the bottom of her handbag, found a lipstick. *This is rather red, did I ever wear that?* she thought, looking at it. She forgot that Viola had given it to her, that hot summer's afternoon with Molly on the lawn.

Carefully she applied it to her lips, watching herself in the antique mirror.

She remembered other red lips: the painted red lips of Zarko the clown up on Blackheath so long ago, Zarko the friend of her father in the circus. Her father's lover, she supposed.

Her own lips were red now and lifted her face, made it different, brighter and brave. She picked up the telephone.

She would fly like her father, after all.

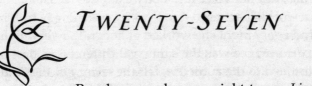

TWENTY-SEVEN

People queued every night to see *Lives* in the room above the pub. The reviews for the new play had been unanimous:

> Eurydice Smith is a new and exciting talent. Here is an author who has, without saying it in words, written a crueller indictment of homelessness and the un-thought-through concept of community care than all the opposition spokesmen put together. She has shown the human cost of policies that were enacted not for social but for economic reasons. Every member of Her Majesty's government should be made to see this play, and be ashamed.

Emmy Lou's reviews had been the sort actors dream about:

> Emmy Louise Brown seems to reach inside her

character and show us a real person and it is someone you will never forget . . . don't miss this
intelligent and moving performance . . . wonderful,
certainly one of the best performances I have seen
from an actress this year.

In her small white flat in Finsbury Park Emmy Lou
glowed and shone in the mirrors, smiled at Sarah
Siddons, did her voice and body exercises as usual. She
was a working actress.

And every night she worked at her craft. Every night
her performance was the same, yet different, as part of
her listened to the audience, felt the energy of the audience, adjusted to that other part of the full circle of her
work: the audience. She felt them listen, felt them sigh
inwardly, felt the silence. Sometimes they laughed: she
timed when to wait, when to speak. Sometimes they
coughed and shuffled: automatically she adjusted, drew
them in again. With one part of her consciousness she
felt them, worked with them; with the rest of her consciousness she was old Alice the tramp.

It was this, this art, that she had dedicated her life to.

Her agent, from whom she usually heard so little,
rang her almost daily, told her how many people had
praised her performance.

'We know the National Theatre is interested,' Emmy
Lou told him.

'AND I've got you an audition for a commercial this
afternoon,' replied her agent.

Emmy Lou sighed, but went along.

There she heard them talking about a new exciting

filming process: they would soon only need a few shots of the actors against a particular computerised background, could fill in the rest of the performance on computers, would hardly need actors at all in the future, only their image, briefly.

She didn't get the job, as usual.

It seemed strange to be praised in all the daily newspapers and yet still sign on at the dole office with the salesmen and the young West Indians and the university students and the frightened middle-aged men who had always been secure before: as if the two halves of her life didn't connect, were disjointed. Pamela Angel paid their tube fares and said she hoped to give them all forty pounds at the end of the four-week run.

And every night she played Alice, the old lady with the plastic bags and the newspapers who had nearly been a schoolteacher.

The season was completely booked out by the end of the first week. It couldn't be extended for more than a month because another small theatre company had booked the room above the pub. And it couldn't transfer anywhere because the National Theatre were negotiating to buy the rights.

'They'll do it later,' was all Pamela Angel would say to her cast. 'They want to do it in the New Year, we're still talking.'

On the last night Harry and Frances went again to see their friend; the play had changed slightly as the actors grew into their roles, was clearer, better in parts. Pamela Angel was the kind of director who came to almost every performance, gave notes to the actors, talked to them long into the night when some of them were anxious to get to the bar. Some of the actors grumbled, found ways of dashing out straight after the show, *my agent's here darling*, but not Emmy Lou. She worked always, never let her performance quite settle; her friends saw there was something intangible there, luminous and true.

On that last night The Three Stooges, as they sometimes called themselves, went out to dinner afterwards; after they'd had quite a few drinks in the pub below the theatre Harry decided, *I insist darlings I insist I insist*, on taking them to one of his favourite Indian restaurants.

'It'll sit on our stomachs,' objected Frances, 'we're too old to eat Indian food at eleven-thirty in the evening.'

'Nonsense,' said Harry, 'this is vegetarian and light, you'll see,' and he brandished two bottles of very good white wine from the depths of his raincoat pocket.

'Isn't it even *licensed*?' groaned Frances.

'Trust me,' said Harry. Emmy Lou hummed along the road beside them. They were all slightly and pleasantly drunk. She'd made a small private farewell to Alice, as the other actors called goodbye, cajoled Pamela Angel to remember to send them their forty pounds, collected make-up and coats from the crowded dressing room. She knew she and Alice would be meeting again.

In the restaurant they ate *poori*, light pancakes filled with vegetables and spices; the women exclaimed with delight, Harry smirked and poured the wine.

'Here's to you Em,' he said, raising the thick glass tumbler the waiter had brought for the chardonnay.

'We'll be at your next first night too,' and Emmy smiled and smiled.

Frances told them again about Milton and their sexual debacle although each of them had heard a version of the story on the telephone.

They laughed, the three of them, sharing again their rackety and yet brave lives, huddled over the wooden table drinking the wine, trying to cheer Frances, knowing she had been hurt. Harry put his arm across her shoulder often.

'Darling Franny,' he said, 'be reasonable, you couldn't have gone to Switzerland, we need you here, you're our family, what would we do at Christmas? And it's your turn this year, you can't get out of it that easily! We all belong together, we're family.'

And Emmy Lou said, 'I couldn't survive without you Franny.'

And Frances shrugged and laughed her infectious laugh, good old Franny, and they drank more wine.

'I can dream,' she said.

'Darling I didn't want to be the one to tell you, but he was – odd,' said Harry.

'Was he?' said Frances, looking at them both in surprise.

'He wasn't, Harry,' said Emmy Lou, 'he was kind.'

'Yes but – he was a little odd,' said Harry.

'Well he was – in a way,' said Emmy Lou, 'the longing way he looked at you, I saw him at dinner that night, staring at your bouncing bosom. But that's not odd, it's natural.'

Frances began to laugh again, then looked down for a

moment at her body with a kind of puzzlement. 'Why should they affect people so much?' she said. 'Oh God – oh it was so – so *instant*, oh poor man, I should've said something comforting but I went to change my ripped dress and he disappeared – my yellow dress too,' she finished plaintively.

'Saw the commercial last night,' said Harry, 'you'll be able to buy ten yellow dresses soon. You made me laugh, you're outrageous talking about your Wise Insurance "assets", no wonder poor Milton was orgasmic!'

'Oh good, it's started has it? That means the money'll start coming in. D'you think it'll become a favourite and be shown lots of times and I'll get frightfully rich and become a Media Person and be able to leave British Telecom for good?'

'Certainly,' said Harry. 'Along with Emmy who will be the star of the National Theatre. ' And the two women looked at each other with a kind of suppressed delight, *it could be true, it could be true.*

'But I did like Milton,' said Emmy, 'all the same. He was awfully kind, he made my first night so – memorable. And he really did like you Fran.'

'Did he,' said Frances wistfully. 'Do you think he did? I thought he did. But perhaps it was only my bosom.'

'And what happened to the Triumph Telephone advert?' asked Harry, wanting to change the subject.

'Oh they've postponed it, but they said they'd let my agent know if it came up again. Oh listen Em I completely forgot to say, I heard two chaps talking in the audience tonight, about *Lives* and how much it would cost to be put on at the National, I just caught the end of the conversation but they were talking hundreds of thousands!'

'I don't care about hundreds of thousands,' said Emmy Lou simply. 'I just want the chance to be paid for doing it. Oh God, imagine getting off the dole, what a pleasure to sign off at last, it's been seven months this year, I've had interviews in booths, and lectures about Restart courses. They said I'd have to retrain for something after six months, you know, and I said I only know how to be an actress, it's what I trained for, it's what I've been doing for over thirty years I said and they said well you could work in a shop so I asked to go on a Chinese course.'

Harry and Frances both stopped eating simultaneously, looked at Emmy Lou.

'Chinese?' said Harry. 'Darling am I drunker than I think I am?'

'Well, I said I thought that with China opening up to the West there'd probably be a lot of opportunities for actors who could speak the language and that that was probably a very good way of deploying my skills. The woman looked totally confused, she was Spanish, she went away and talked to a colleague for a while about whether I could do Chinese, they said they'd be in touch and I thanked them, pointedly reading the Claimant's Charter on the way out. Haven't heard from them since. Do you know they play Beatles songs in the dole office these days, muzak?'

'Muzak?'

'Muzak. "Yesterday" with strings.'

'In the dole office?'

'In the dole office.'

'Good heavens.' Harry sloshed the remaining wine from the second bottle into their glasses. 'Well things have changed since my day!'

'How long since you've been on the dole Harry?'

'God.' He paused to think. 'Eighteen, nineteen years maybe.'

Emmy Lou sighed deeply. 'It's not like before. Acting isn't a profession that they understand any more. You wouldn't recognise it Harry. We're just part of the great mass of unemployed and redundant. Our only advantage I suppose is we've *always* known what it was like to be unemployed. You should see the people in there now, the people who never thought it could happen to them, you should see their –' Emmy looked down at the table for a moment '– you should see their faces.'

'Em,' he said firmly, 'you'll be out of there soon, probably never to return, once they re-do *Lives* properly, not that it's not done properly now, but you know what I mean, in a proper theatre with proper resources.'

'And I'll get paid!' said Emmy Lou, and she smiled and smiled.

Harry told them about filming his Thomas Hardy serial, the long long hours in studios and on location, his beard memorably falling off while a fight was being filmed with horses and dogs and pigs.

'All because of my beard, the whole huge scene had to be filmed again, dogs in the right place, horses in the right place, one of the pigs bit the script editor who nobody likes, I could feel it coming off but I couldn't do anything, I was being attacked by vagabonds at the time, my God there was a lot of swearing and the make-up girl was in tears!'

They talked a bit about Michael's death, they leant their elbows on the wooden table gossiping into the night as they often did, until they saw the Indian waiter yawning by the door.

Frances stopped a taxi in the street, Emmy Lou had missed the last tube, was staying with Harry.

Later, he knocked on the door, came into his spare room in his paisley pyjamas as Emmy was snuggling down under the duvet, under the David Hockney print on the wall. She thought suddenly, *he looks old . . . we're getting old . . . thank God I got this last chance.*

'Goodnight Emmy darling,' he said, 'I'm proud of you.'

'I do love you Harry,' said Emmy Lou, and he turned out the lamp. Just as he went out of the room she murmured, 'I feel like a quite different person when I'm working, as if I am – myself – at last. And I only get that feeling when I'm playing other people. Isn't that strange?'

'It isn't strange to me because I understand exactly what you mean,' said Harry. 'And this is your part, and this is your chance.'

So that when, two days later, a letter arrived from Pamela Angel in the mailbox downstairs in her Finsbury Park flat, Emmy Lou was unprepared for the contents.

•

My Dear Emmy Lou,

You know how I admire your work, you were wonderful as Alice, I will never forget your performance. But the cold hard facts of the matter are that Dame Helen Storey wants to play it and she would be a draw at the National in a way that it wouldn't be possible for you to be. I am so sorry and hope you won't be *too* disappointed. I am of course thrilled to be going to the National to direct and very sorry I can't take my original cast with me. I will of course advise your agent but I wanted you to hear the news from me first. Thank you for all the hard work you put in, I'm sure we'll work again together one of these days. And I enclose a cheque for forty pounds, your share of the profits.

With much love,

Pamela Angel.

Emmy Lou only read the letter once.

From the window of her flat she could sometimes see the old couple in the block across the road. He would bring his wife a cup of tea on a tray. Today they were not sitting by the window; all Emmy Lou Brown could see was a rather wilting pink geranium in a pot.

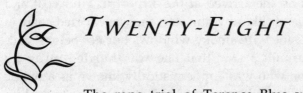

TWENTY-EIGHT

The rape trial of Terence Blue was set down to begin on 3rd December.

The Lord Chancellor and the Director of Public Prosecutions announced again that Great Britain would not countenance a Show Business Media Grotesque. That it was with deep disapproval that they noticed that the complainant had spoken to newspapers in another country. That the best traditions of British Justice would nevertheless be upheld; that the trial would be held in camera if the British media over-extended their coverage to the detriment of either the complainant or the defendant and that the early holding of the trial was to avoid just this.

At the beginning of November Simone Taylor suddenly flew in to Heathrow. Somehow the press was alerted to the fact. She was not allowed to speak to the press about the rape of course, indeed the press were not supposed to know she was the complainant, but since she had opened her heart to the *New York Post* it was common knowledge in the media.

So there was extraordinary coverage of her arrival in all the newspapers; she was seen on all the television news bulletins, yet nobody could actually say why. There was no doubt that she was, at this moment in time, a Celebrity, a Mystery Celebrity: *Simone Taylor, Cosmetics Executive*. Cameras clicked and whirred and flashed as she arrived at the airport in a fur coat and dark glasses like any film star; she was hurried away in a limousine with smoky windows but not before waiting journalists saw that she was hurried away by someone who was euphemistically known as a public relations consultant. Among journalists who knew him he was known as a shit and they rushed to their telephones.

BLUE RAPE: MEDIA HARLOTRY BEGINS? the papers bellowed next morning. The rights to her story were bitterly fought over by rival newspaper groups. Serious newspapers discussed in their pages once again the ethics of 'pocketbook journalism'. There was also much discussion about anonymity for the accused in rape trials as well as for the victims; there was a good deal of sympathy for Terence Blue in some quarters, though not, on the whole, from women.

Simone Taylor, it was reported, was not this time staying at the Dorchester; she was to be found in a suite at Claridges. She herself remained inviolate, spoke to no press.

But once again members of the class of '59 found themselves in the limelight; there was an immense hullaballoo when it was realised that Frances Kitson, she of the large bosom and the far from innocent smile in the Wise Insurance TV commercial, had also been at the infamous reunion.

So that Frances found herself one morning, to her great surprise, on the front page of the *Sun* which described her as a younger, naughtier, and more attractive version of Ena Sharples (*Ena Sharples!* she complained to Harry, *what about Jane Russell or Rita Hayworth, they had red hair*); she was asked to be on a celebrity TV quiz show with a pop singer and a nun; the same day she suddenly got the part in the Triumph Telephones commercial. It was going to be a series of six adverts, probably more; she would make an enormous amount of money, much much more than she had ever earned as an actress in her life.

She phoned Harry and Emmy Lou.

'Is there anything more bizarre than me becoming the most famous I've been in my whole life because Terence Blue raped or did not rape Simone Taylor!' she said. 'What an *extraordinary* profession we belong to. We shall have the biggest Christmas tree and the biggest Harrods turkey and the biggest Harrods Christmas pudding and the biggest Tesco's mince pies because they're the best, and the most expensive Christmas crackers from the Victoria and Albert Museum Shop that you have ever seen, and I'll get the champagne from Harvey Nicks. After all these years, who would've believed it!'

Emmy Lou's muted voice on the other end of the telephone, trying (Frances knew) to be enthusiastic pierced her heart.

'Em, dear dear Em, there'll be other things. Fuck the National, Fuck Pamela Angel.'

'Of course,' said Emmy Lou.

Pauline Bonham was hardly seen, in her house or in her shop; nobody seemed to know where she went.

Viola Bonham needed advice, longed to talk to her mother. But after all those years of almost always being there, suddenly Pauline wasn't. And when, occasionally, she was there – standing at the stove or talking on the telephone or making some coffee – the glittery look in Pauline's eyes was still there as if her mother had become, Viola suddenly thought, an ice-maiden version of herself, fitting in with the cold weather, with the frost on the trees and on the river, so early this year after all that sunshine. And she had taken, Viola noted, to regularly wearing bright red lipstick. *She looks as if she's part of 'lesbian chic'* thought Viola crossly. *Whatever is she thinking of? I only meant her to wear it occasionally like if she was going to a party, not at breakfast time.* Her father was so busy he hardly noticed anything that was going on in the house at all: he was playing at Stratford most nights and filming a TV series in Devon about the Second World War most days. They were also preparing at Stratford to make a film version of their *Othello* production, so successful had it been, and some weekends now he didn't come home. And now, sometimes, *nor did her mother.* So Viola, struggling with the difficulties of her own that she found herself in, watched the cold mist drift across the river in the early mornings and thought about the meaning of love.

Viola Bonham had always told herself she would never fall in love. When she was young she thought she lived in A Happy Family; by the time she was sixteen and doing her O levels she understood. It was hard to love and despise and admire her father all at the same time. She saw what marriage did to people, and in particular to actresses. And she told herself she would never fall in love.

But she had fallen in love, after all. Only . . . but she turned her mind away again, for the hundredth time.

'You can't be *serious*!'

Elvira Pugh, crime-writer, ex-wife of Terence Blue, was hardly ever shocked, but she stared at her old friend Pauline Bonham in amazement, saw how she stood very straight, very strong, found herself thinking, *My God she is still so beautiful*.

'I am deadly serious Elvira, I was never more serious in my life.'

'How do you know?'

'A – little bird told me,' said Pauline.

'Terry – *impotent*! I find that impossible to believe. No, it's absolutely impossible – he must've just been having an off night. Anyway he's been terribly terribly ill, he nearly died.'

'This information pre-dates the stabbing,' said Pauline stubbornly.

Elvira got up from the long polished table in her dining room where the two had been sitting with their coffee as they talked, walked to the window. She stared out through the rain at the gently rolling Berkshire fields that stretched out, it seemed from this window, for eternity. After some moments she looked back at Pauline who was wearing a bright red lipstick and staring at Elvira intently.

'And you want to use this – information to – bargain with him?'

'Yes.'

'To blackmail him?'

'No, no, that's *not* what it is. You misunderstood, or I explained it badly. I want to use it to help him at his trial. But in return he must help me.'

'But he'll never agree to such a plan Pauline.' Elvira actually gave a little laugh. 'I mean frankly can you imagine Terence agreeing to that?'

'As a last resort? If he thinks he'll be convicted?'

'I think he'd rather go to prison.'

'Do you think so?'

'Anyway he is totally convinced he'll get off because he didn't do it, he says there's no case to answer.'

'The pre-trial committal thought there was, you told me.' Pauline's voice was cold.

'I know.' Elvira turned angrily. 'Do you know that little shit Simone Taylor had bruises all over her breasts, which were seen by London doctors? Or so she says. Stu got all the American papers for me.' Stu was Elvira's present husband who had previously been unhappily married and sometimes couldn't believe his luck in finding Elvira. He was a very rich farmer and horse-breeder who named members of the Royal Family among his acquaintances and who, when Elvira laughed aloud in bed (as she did sometimes, thinking of a new twist, a new plot for one of her books), laughed too, in his sleep, in sympathy. Elvira loved him deeply.

She sat down edgily again at the long table. 'Terence was here about a week ago, Stu and I asked him down here, we wanted to look after him for a few days – he's still far from well you know – and to see how we could help him. And his main priority seemed to be not his health, and not his rape case which he's certain he can't lose – he kept talking in that infuriatingly simple way of his about "British Justice" for God's sake – but to keep this other bloody stabbing case out of court. He's obsessed about it, says Nicky mustn't be brought in to it.'

'But why? What would he care about Nicky Abbott for, no one's seen her for thirty years, and she tried to kill him for God's sake!'

Elvira sat down again at the table, finally looked up at Pauline. 'You're not going to believe this Pauly but – Nicky Abbott was his first wife.'

'*What*?'

'He married her in 1961.'

'Good God!' Pauline stared at Elvira, open-mouthed. 'Good God!' she repeated. 'How long for? What happened?'

'I don't know. He wouldn't say, just told me they'd been married. And that she mustn't be brought into court, that everything was his fault. He seems to be trying to convince himself that the CPS won't bring a prosecution in the stabbing business, that they can't do it without his evidence – but they will you know, he just doesn't seem to understand the law. He seems desperate to protect her – yet he admits he hadn't seen her, till the reunion, for more than thirty years. And can you believe it, *he's stopped drinking.'*

Elvira looked down at her empty coffee cup, shook her head slightly and Pauline remembered the many battles Elvira and Terence had had about his intake of alcohol.

'You know, when he told me last week that he'd actually been married when he was young you could've knocked me down with a feather in the true sense of that cliché, I nearly fainted. And of course I asked him all sorts of questions. But he wouldn't talk any more about it, how long they were married, what happened to her, it was as if –' and she paused for a moment '– as if he'd, I don't know, choke if he said any more. Just one thing he said – and I felt as if he were trying to explain to me, or apologise to me. He said that the first time he'd seen Iona Spring, standing in a corner of a room at a party she had reminded him, for a split second, of Nicky when she was young. He said, "Just for a moment it all was – there – again" and his face looked so sad somehow that I wanted to cry.

'And, to think of all those jolly years we had together – they were jolly, on the whole – and I never knew I was his third wife, not his second. I knew Betty Bailey was just an aberration and I thought of myself as his only wife – you know, his real wife. Until the appalling Iona Spring came along of course. And so when he told me, I felt so strange. As if the past had got muddled somehow. I mean he's always been such – well until now I've always thought him such a simple person, someone you could see through – I thought I knew him so well, I could read him like a book. After all there's not that much to know about Terence, once you get out of bed, except that he's got a sort of Welsh stubbornness. But there was this other secret Terence underneath, all that time, it quite shook me Pauly, to be honest. And now you tell me he's impotent for God's sake!' Elvira stared out again at the rain and was silent.

Pauline waited.

'Stu and I are desperately worried about the rape case, he seems not to understand the seriousness of it somehow. He's got this ridiculous logic, says he's told his defence he won't go into the witness box. "There's no need," he kept saying, "I didn't do it and nobody can prove that I did. It offends me to be accused of rape, and I don't see why I should go into the witness box and be in all the newspapers giving a kind of credence to her story, I won't do it." God Pauly, the courts don't work like that, I know how the courts work, it's my business to know, I'm a crime-writer for God's sake. But the only thing he's agreed to is that his counsel can call someone to say how Simone used to be crazy about him, that maybe this is all a figment of her imagination – though how you get bruises all over your body from a figment of your imagination is beyond me.'

'You don't think at all –' Pauline paused, choosing the words carefully '– you don't think – it – might have happened. That perhaps he was drunk?'

Elvira looked at Pauline. 'Don't be silly,' she said coldly.

'Well I'm going to talk to him,' said Pauline firmly, 'and put my plan to him, if you'll tell me where he is?'

Elvira seemed for a moment to be pondering some-thing. Then she said, 'I think your plan is utterly ridiculous. But all right I'll tell you. Somebody has to help him somehow to see the seriousness of the situation he's in, that he must defend himself. But literally, Pauline, no one knows where Terence is except me and that secretary he's had for a hundred years, Virginia whatever-her-name-is. It's the only way to keep such a thing secret, nobody must know, I haven't even told Stu. He's hiding out in a farm near Darlington, it's the only way he can get some peace.'

'I'll go this weekend,' said Pauline, 'there's not much time, I must talk to him before the trial.'

'Indeed you must,' said Elvira dryly, 'if you intend to be part of it.' But something about Pauline, the red lips, the pale face, made her feel uneasy. 'I hope you know what you're doing Pauline,' she said, and her tone was disapproving.

Pauline got up from the table violently.

'Listen Elvira, *listen to me*.

'For thirty years I've taken all the shit that Anthony has thrown at me: the affairs, the total lack of support for me as an actress, keeping the family together while he went off on his adventures, bad sex. I took it because I grew up in the nineteen-fifties and that's what I thought wives were expected to do. But now I'm nearly fifty-seven and I want to change my life before it's too late. I've thought and thought and thought about all this. I know it's an audacious plan but why shouldn't I be audacious? Just because I'm getting old? Are only the young allowed to be audacious? *I want to be an actress*

again. If Terence's rape trial goes smoothly and there's no
case to answer, fine, we can forget I ever mentioned this.
If he's in deep trouble maybe I can help him. And then
he can help me, that would be the bargain. Don't be disapproving of me Elvira, I'll get plenty of that if I go
through with this, you're my friend, I need your help
and support because *I want to change my life*.' She stood
there, across the table, breathing heavily and staring
wildly in a way that Elvira hardly recognised.

'And if Terence – does agree, you'll leave Anthony?'

'Yes yes yes.'

Elvira contemplated her friend and then quite unexpectedly she laughed. 'Well that'll be a surprise for Mr
Anthony Bonham that in some ways he richly deserves.'
And she smiled at Pauline. 'I was always so glad when I
was with Terence that I wasn't an actress but I do feel –'
and she laughed her big throaty laugh again '– that if
you're going to be an actress, do it in style! Of course I'll
help you Pauly, sit down. Standing there in your red lipstick you look like a baddie in *Dallas* or something!'

'I know,' said Pauline, 'it happened by mistake and
then I decided I rather liked it,' and at last she grinned
rather shakily at Elvira and sat back down at the long
table.

'Right,' said Elvira. 'Let's see what we can plot and
plan before you go to see Terence. I wonder, you
know –' and she drummed her fingers on the table for a
moment '– if Nicky Abbott isn't the clue to everything?'
And she leant across the table to her old friend and her
eyes sparkled with a kind of cheeky malice.

'The appalling Iona Spring will look such a fool if

Terence gets off after all her sordid little press exclusives about being married to a Sex-Fiend Rapist that she'll never work again. That will give me enormous pleasure! I'll be delighted to assist in this matter.' Then she slowly tipped backwards in the chair, thinking. 'Now where were we? Nicola Abbott. She's the clue, I'm sure she's the clue.'

Her smile across the table to Pauline was dazzling.

'I'm good at this you know. I do it for a living!'

Pauline drove back to London early next morning.

At St Catherine's House in Kingsway she stood among the registers and the people, pulling out marriage registers for 1961, laboriously checking, quarter by quarter, for what she wanted: Nicola Abbott and Terence Blue. She stood at the desks beside other people, turning page after page; she found she was shielding the information with her hand, as if someone might watch or pry or guess. She found nothing.

Suddenly she remembered something, suddenly from over thirty years ago another name dropped into her consciousness.

'Shand,' she murmured aloud: 'Mary Shand.'

And finally found an entry: the wedding of Mary Shand and Terence Cecil Blue in November 1961. When the copy of the marriage certificate arrived in the post a few days later, Pauline's eyes widened in amazement as she read the name of one of the witnesses.

'Harry darling, it's Pauline, haven't seen you since the day of Michael's funeral. Could I take you to dinner?'

'That'd be nice,' said Harry, 'or I could take you, or we could take each other, or any combination you like. I'm rather off funerals at the moment as you can imagine after that debacle but I would like to hear more about your – about Roger Popham and that funeral. Oh Pauly, I've been meaning to phone you, I've just been so busy with this Thomas Hardy thing, I'm away filming half the time. When can you make it?'

'Tonight?'

'What now?' He looked at his watch, he'd just got back from the studio and was in the bath. It was 7.30. But Harry liked changes of plan, sudden invitations, movement in his life. 'OK,' he said cheerfully, 'and I'm not called till the afternoon tomorrow, so I won't have to run home like Cinderella.'

'Good,' said Pauline, 'I'll pick you up in an hour.'

'In your posh pink car?'

Pauline laughed. 'In my posh pink car,' she said.

She told him what more she had learnt about Roger Popham. About the small funeral, about the old lady wearing shiny colours who didn't want to be called an actor, about the sad credit card bill that Mrs Beale had sent her: a small on-going amount with an off-licence, a couple of train tickets with British Rail, accumulated interest: a total of ninety-three pounds. They were on the second course and the second bottle in a small, expensive Italian restaurant before she said firmly, taking out her lipstick, applying it at the table, 'Harry darling I understand you were a witness at Terence and Nicky's wedding.'

Harry was so shocked he dropped his fork on the floor. He picked it up very slowly and Pauline saw that he was composing himself, drawing himself into himself.

She put her hand on his arm urgently, she could not allow him to escape.

'Darling listen. I know something of the story. He did tell Elvira a little, just recently, but she thinks not all. I—' she took a deep breath. 'Harry forgive me, I feel I owe you such a lot but I can't explain it all now – I need to know, I have to know what happened, I—' she paused and he remembered how she never spoke about herself, the way her eyes hooded allowing no one else to see. 'I'm leaving Anthony but I *have* to know this story first.'

'You're leaving Anthony for Terence?' Harry's face looked goggle-eyed in amazement. Pauline thought suddenly *Oh God it's Joseph Wain I want but I don't know any more how people do these things. And of course I'm old now . . . I don't expect these things will happen to me.*

'No,' she said quite slowly. 'No not for Terence. For me.' And Harry caught the wistful, unguarded expression that flitted across her face, just for a moment. Then she leant across the table again. 'Listen, Harry – if I give you my word I'll eventually tell you everything will you tell me now? About what happened to Terence and Nicky?'

And Harry smiled. Pauline thought it was one of the saddest smiles she'd ever seen.

'You don't have to give me your word Pauly,' said Harry. 'I've wished all my life that I didn't know so much about people's lives as I do.'

The waiter brought a clean fork, changed the ashtray (Pauline had been smoking which Harry never remembered her doing), poured more wine into their glasses. Harry didn't pick up the new fork. He pushed his plate aside, held his glass in his hand and looked across the table at Pauline.

'The reason I've never talked about this is because I'm so ashamed of my part in it,' he said. 'You've heard of bitchy queens, and that's what I was. I think I was jealous of . . .' and he paused for a long time, 'happiness.'

Pauline stared back at him and she looked puzzled, and impatient. 'Harry darling don't be ridiculous you're quite one of the nicest people I know.'

'No I'm not,' he said, 'but thank you.' He stared round the small restaurant as if he wasn't quite sure where he was: at the aubergine starters on the counter, at the tiramisu and the trifle on a trolley. 'I kept on looking for that kind of happiness but I never found it.' Finally, with the small, sad smile still there, he said, 'I seem to always be telling you stories about the past Pauly.'

And then he began: *once upon a time . . .*

Later that week the trial of Nicola Abbott was set down in the court lists. As the victim had declined to lay a charge in such a serious matter, the Crown Prosecution Service was bringing to trial Nicola Abbott (54), unemployed, for the attempted murder of Terence Blue, film star.

TWENTY-NINE

Juliet Lyall, the much-respected and much-loved English actress, recovered (said the newspapers joyfully) from her nervous exhaustion, was flying the British flag, filming in Los Angeles.

She might just as well have been on Mars.

Prozac and Mogodon, combined, kept her upright. Which was mild, after all, for Hollywood where she could have had lines of coke by the swimming pool every day before breakfast if she'd felt so inclined. She lived in chauffeured cars and frenzied studios and behind closed doors of carpeted silent hotel suites that seemed cut off from the rest of the world.

The director, Bud Martin, looked at the early rushes in disbelief.

She had, when she had returned to Los Angeles to begin filming, seemed herself: cool and British. But the camera made her seem cold not cool; the enigmatic British reserve seemed, in the viewing room, to be an empty shell, signifying nothing. The first tentative sex scene they had filmed was rubbish: he could never use it. He mused alone in the dark of his small private movie theatre. *He'd made a mistake.* Something that had been there in the work he had seen her do that had decided him to take a risk with her had fooled him, deceived him. He had taken a risk and a guess over her ability to do the particular kind of love scenes so important to this film, and he had been proved wrong. *She couldn't do it.*

Age and desire. Bud Martin knew himself very well: understood why seventeen- and eighteen-year-old girls were the only women to arouse him; his power and his fame bought him the one thing he didn't have: youth. The film explored, better than most Hollywood films, if this might or might not be the same for ageing women . . . age and desire . . . and any actress should have killed for a chance to play the part.

And the young Clint O'Hara, the actor he had cast opposite her, should have been any ageing actress's dream: he was not only young, he was good-looking and personable and even intelligent; had gone to some trouble to watch some of Juliet's film work so that he would know something about her. She didn't have to fuck him off-screen for God's sake if she was one of those actresses who wanted to remain faithful to her husband and it certainly wasn't in any way a pornographic film they were making, she only had to be – to seem to be – roused by him, *affected* by him. There were only intimations of desire, not the fulfilment of it; this was a good intelligent script, not a dog, the original had even been written by a woman for God's sake (though they'd had to get in a professional to tidy it up). But it was a very very good script.

But proximity to Clint O'Hara seemed not to raise Juliet Lyall's temperature one iota.

She could be gay, a lesbian, a dyke. He'd thought of that at once, there were plenty of them around though they tried to keep it quiet. But she was married and, what's more, it had been all over the papers that she'd once been engaged to that well-known and now infamous Lothario, Terence Blue. Terence Blue wouldn't fuck a dyke for fuck's sake.

Perhaps it was the nervous exhaustion: her small breakdown before she began filming. But actresses were always having small breakdowns; the doctors, hers and theirs, had said she was perfectly well again.

He had cast her because she had seemed to offer something intangible; *intangible: eluding the grasp*. But of course he had hoped that this unknown quality would be realised, perceived, found. But it seemed that it didn't exist. Had he only imagined it?

Bud Martin stirred angrily in the dark of the viewing theatre. He had a particular aversion to being made a fool of; he had fought bitterly with the studio heads, who had wanted an American actress, to get Juliet Lyall.

His fingers drummed on the arm of his chair. He could fire her. Or he could take one more chance to find out more about her. His fingers drummed and drummed as he sat there alone in the darkness.

*

He telephoned a man he knew in London. The man rang him back within twenty-four hours.

Bud Martin rearranged the shooting schedule so that Juliet Lyall wasn't called upon to do anything for some days.

Then several nights later, after nine hours filming, he went unannounced to her hotel suite.

She was sitting huddled on her bed surrounded by copies of English newspapers, watching CNN news; she looked up, bewildered, to see him brought not only into her suite but into the bedroom by the manager with only so much as a knock on the door. When the manager had gone – bowing slightly, for the film company paid him so much money that he would unlock doors any time they wanted – Bud Martin switched off the news and walked towards the bed. He stood some way away from her, frowned at the newspapers everywhere. Stared at her.

'What are you looking for?' Indicated the newspapers. 'What is it doll, what's happened?'

It wasn't the absurd use of the word *doll* to a woman of fifty-six that made her drop her eyes from his; something else.

'I'm – just reading news from home,' she said.

He got up, opened the bar, took out a bottle of whisky which was almost half empty. He knew the bar was replenished every morning.

He raised his eyebrows. 'It's whisky you like is it?' he said, and filled two glasses. He had a particular American drawl that almost always sounded slightly amused.

'Do you always walk uninvited around actresses' hotel rooms in quite this manner?' she asked coldly. 'I believe my door was locked.'

As he handed one of the glasses of whisky to her he pulled a chair over to the side of the bed and said, without any further preamble, 'Are you going to tell me why your performance is shit, why you can't give me what I'm looking for? You're an experienced actress, you must know it isn't working.'

Her eyes flickered, she tried to get up off the bed but he leant over and pushed her, but very gently, back.

'Or am I going to have to find out my own way?'

Juliet remained silent.

'Answer me,' he said, but still the drawl, still the amusement.

'I haven't been well.'

'All the doctors, yours and ours, gave you a clean bill of health, said you'd be fine. You said you'd be fine, that *The Seagull* had been strenuous, that you'd had a rest, that you were fine. We don't pay the kind of money we pay for you not to be fine when you've said you'd be fine. A huge part of the success of this film depends on you. I could fire you tonight but I still believe you can do it. I just want to know what's happened. Are you on anything, apart from the whisky?'

'A few pills,' said Juliet coolly, 'nothing by the standards you're used to.'

'What pills?'

'Is it your business?'

'It most certainly is my business. How many?'

'A few. Nothing for you to be alarmed about.' He let that pass, in the meantime.

'Anything else?'

'What do you mean?'

'Dope, cocaine, crack, heroin?'

'Don't be silly Bud,' she said 'I am not a drug addict.'

'Had any sex, since the evening with Grover?'

Juliet could not have been more shocked if he'd hit her. There was only the light from the lamp by the bed-side table but she knew he could see the blush that at once spread over her face, down her neck.

'I think that *is* my business,' she said, and her English voice was like ice.

'Do you?' he answered. For a moment he stared at the whisky. 'You know that scene you did a few days ago, with Clint?'

'With your young stud. Yes.'

He looked at her angrily. 'With the actor Clint O'Hara.'

'I know the scene you're talking about.'

'The rushes are rubbish. You don't want him, even with part of you. And that's what the film is about for God's sake, that – risk-taking. When you came to see me first, I told you what the film was about didn't I?'

She did not answer.

'Didn't I? What did I say was the theme, the key?'

'Yes, yes, I remember.'

'Say it.'

'Age and desire,' said Juliet with distaste.

He picked up her tone at once. 'Why do you find that distasteful? This is a class script and you know it.

Do you know how many actresses we saw for this part? Over one hundred and fifty, real stars, actresses much more well-known than you, actresses in their mid-fifties who would have given five years off their fucking life to play this part because there's not many parts like this for women of your age, women who are *getting old*. I don't like to be made a fool of. You're a very experienced actress. We pay you not to be embarrassed if it's embarrassment you're talking about. But it's ridiculous to be embarrassed at your age, I don't understand you.'

Juliet took a long long swallow of whisky. 'Nothing embarrasses me,' she said.

'Including sex?'

'Sex isn't at the root of everything,' said Juliet. 'That's such an immature, American way of looking at things.' Outside the long window, outside the double glazing that reduced the city sounds to a murmur, Los Angeles was lit up, hummed below them.

Bud Martin got up, went to the telephone, still watching her. 'It is at the bottom of everything,' he said, 'in a way.' He spoke into the telephone for a moment and then came back to the bed.

'Let's leave sex out of it just for a moment. When you did *Dreams* on Broadway I loved your performance because of what it promised about the woman if only it could be found. That's the quality I thought you could bring to this. That quality was also on the film test you sent me. But in this film that quality has to be pushed further – that –' he struggled with the concept for a moment '– that elusiveness, that enigmatic quality has to break, reveal something. Otherwise it's nothing, there's nothing there. In the rushes that – that revelation, that thing that leads to the audience understanding – it simply isn't there. I need to know why.'

He saw that she would not or could not answer; sighed, leant forward, tried again. 'Look Juliet, I'm your director, I'd like to help you if I can, for both our sakes. This isn't a press conference, you don't have to protect yourself from me and I am a man who has kept many secrets. But I will fire you from this film if you can't do it.'

Juliet stared at her glass, said nothing; saw that the glass shook, the liquid moved in the glass, shone in the light from the lamp. Everything was happening as she had predicted in her nightmares. The past would come back. She would lose everything. She wished there was more whisky in the glass. She drained what was there, felt it warming her throat, her stomach. Her heart.

She took a deep, shaky breath. If she was fired it would be all over the newspapers in five minutes. She had nothing, after all, to lose. 'A long time ago,' she said very slowly, 'I behaved very badly.'

'Has that got to do with what we're talking about?'

'I – I don't know. I – I've been reminded of it lately. I – helped destroy a person.'

'What, murder?'

She gave a little uncertain laugh. 'No of course not.'

Bud Martin suddenly stood up. 'Juliet. We all behave badly, especially people in our business. You just have to learn to live with it. I thought you meant you were a child murderer or something really interesting.' He didn't see the look on Juliet's face as he went to answer the discreet knock he had heard at the door.

Bud returned to the bed with a man wearing jeans and a very nicely cut blue jacket. He was not young, or old, just a pleasant-faced person who could have been on his way to work, or to the movies, or to dinner. He smiled at Juliet, a warm open smile. 'Hi,' he said.

'Now then,' said Bud Martin. He stared at Juliet for a long moment. '*We* are going to behave very badly but I understand –' and he flashed her a very quick look '– that you like this way of behaving badly.' The man took some bottles of oil out of the pocket of his jacket, laid them on the table beside the bed, took off his jacket.

Her face was ashen even as a pulse began beating between her legs, even as she felt a rush of moisture there, almost like a pain.

'I don't know what you mean,' she said, and the cliché ran round and round in her head *I don't know what you mean I don't know what you mean.*

The man opened the oils on the table by the bed and Juliet watched him. Her whole body ached to be touched, to be soothed. She still sat huddled against the headboard, but her hand, without her knowing it, went to her own shoulder, moved very very gently down her own arm. Bud Martin saw, stood up. 'That's my girl,' he said quietly but she did not hear him.

The man leisurely took off all his clothes except his undershorts. He did not look in the least alarming. He did not have an erection. He was as impersonal as Grover could be when he wanted to be. He opened one of the bottles.

...d again. The man was astride her again, rubbed the ...to her nipples, gently at first, pinched them gently ...hen pulled at them harder and she arched upwards ...rds his hands, *please*, she whispered, *please*. Her eyes ... very tightly closed.

...*ok at his face.* Bud Martin's voice came from some-...re, *please*, she whispered but louder, *please*, her eyes ... closed, only feeling the man's hands on her. He ...ed at her nipples, less gently as she strained towards ..., more urgently as she tried to push her breasts into ...hands.

...*ook at his face Juliet*, said Bud Martin's voice again, ...y gentle, *and then he'll give you what you want*. This ...sn't part of the routine, part of the service, she ...n't want to look at his face, even as she strained ...wards towards his hands, *please please*, she cried ...rsely, urgent now as her swollen breasts ached and ... legs opened wide, *oh please please please give it to me,* ...e *it to me*. Still the strong hands on the nipples and ... oil.

You must look at him, said Bud Martin.

In desperation she opened her eyes, saw that the man ...d curly brown hair and brown eyes and that he too ...s excited, that he was looking at her, that he strained ...ck as he massaged her nipples still, that his penis was ...ollen, that there was a condom on it. She screamed at ...ce, tried to move from under him: *no no no no, I can't,* ... *me go, let me go, I can't do that!* but in the quiet ...rouded hotel rooms in Los Angeles many screams go ...answered.

I can't I can't I can't, she cried in horror, in terror. And

'Could you take off your clothes please?' he said pleasantly.

Almost mesmerised, Juliet began to undo the buttons of her silk shirt. 'Are you going to give me a massage?' she asked uncertainly.

'Yes,' said the man.

'The kind you like,' said Bud Martin.

Juliet's hand had reached up to undo her bra, froze suddenly. She stared back at the director. 'And you're going to *watch*?'

Bud Martin leant forward patiently. 'I am going to watch,' he said. 'I am going to watch you very carefully, I am going to watch what happens to your face, what sort of sounds you make, how your legs move.'

She stared at him in disgust and almost at once something more than disgust: horror; she held her shirt around her, began to get off the bed. 'I don't want to do this Bud,' she said. 'Please don't make me, I couldn't possibly do this with you watching. It's – it's not this that is the matter with me.' She sat in an ungainly way, very unlike how she usually looked, half on half off the bed, staring at him.

'Your Alexander Korda said he may make actors do things against their will but never against their best interests,' said Bud Martin. 'This is, if you like – a rehearsal. I am going to watch, and tomorrow night we are going to film that scene again and you are going to do it as if you mean it because otherwise I am going to have to fire you and you know how that will affect the career you value so highly.'

'I will call my agents and my lawyers,' said Juliet

tightly, 'and I will tell them exactly what you have dared to suggest to me. Please leave my room at once.' Even as she spoke the man was rubbing some oil very gently into her taut shoulders, leaning towards her slightly, coaxing her with his hands back on to the bed. There was something warm about the oil as he stroked her very gently, some fragrance that caught her. She sighed very slightly, turned her head as if to catch the scent, like a memory there.

'Whatever is the matter with you does have something to do with sex,' said Bud Martin, 'I know that now. If you looked at the rushes of the work you did you would know it too. We have to help you find what it is.' His voice seemed to come from a long way away and there was a different quality to it, more gentle, less mocking.

The man stroked her back very gently. 'Please take off the rest of your clothes,' he said quietly. She smelt again the fragrance of the oil. As if she were a child getting ready for bed but thinking about something else, she quite slowly put her silk shirt down on the bed, took off her skirt, undid her bra.

'Yes,' she said slowly, answering Bud Martin, 'yes. A long time ago.'

As if in a dream she lay on the bed, face down. The man sat astride her in exactly the way Grover did. Long, strong strokes, up and down her spine. Smoothing very gently the tense back and shoulders.

'Why has all this suddenly come up now, disturbed you now?' Bud's voice was very quiet now, and yet nearer, as if he had moved nearer. The man's hands

moved downwards to the bottom ⎡ ⎤ clos
her buttocks, stroking hard and pr   oil i
and pressing, over and over again,   and
Unconsciously she moved her legs   tow
was still, there in the room.   wer

'Do you suppose,' said Juliet at la   L
husky, 'that our past always catches   wh
man had changed his weight, his har   still
now, long firm hard strokes, up a   pu
down.   hin

'It does,' said Bud. 'I'm sure it do   his
But I've always been of the opinion
own it, claim it, no matter what it is.'   ve
'Own our past?'   wa
'It's what we are. It's who we are.'   di
she heard him sigh.   up

Just at that moment the man allow   ho
smooth round her anus and then,   he
stroked her there, the oil on his finge   gi
soft sound. His hands returned to her b   th
strokes, up and down, calming her agai

'Age. And desire,' said Juliet Lyall a
was like a sigh.   ha

'Yes,' said Bud Martin gently, and th   w
smoothed there where her legs parted a   b
small cry she pressed against his hand.   s

'Please turn over,' said the man polit   o
her for a moment.   le

As Juliet turned, her eyes half opening   s
she saw that Bud Martin was nearer, that   u
nearer to the head of the bed. It was too

her arms, a moment ago so sensuous, so soft, flailed at him, hit him, *I can't I can't let me go let me go.*

The man pushed her back urgently now and yet still gently, ran his hands from her breasts downwards to her dark dank hair, smoothing and smoothing over and over again, calming her, calming her, his fingers just touching her clitoris with each strong, gentle stroke.

She opened her mouth to scream again as the man touched her again and then her body decided for her: opened, took him in, this man above her who she did not know, moved with him, rocked with him faster and faster on the bed in the hotel room in Los Angeles until she hardly knew where she was at all, cried out in wild abandon, there in a room she did not know with a man she did not know Juliet Lyall cried out, *oh my God*, she cried, *oh my God oh my God*, and tears poured down her cheeks, *oh my God, oh my God* and she climaxed over and over again with a man she did not know in a hotel room in Los Angeles.

Finally she lay on the bed exhausted, racked by terrible shaking sobs of misery and pain and shame. And memory.

The man got up off the bed, got dressed, and after speaking very quietly to Bud Martin left the room.

Bud Martin waited. He waited for a long long time. At last the sobbing subsided.

'Well doll,' he said, and his voice was back to its old mocking tone, 'think you can remember some of that for later?'

Juliet very very slowly turned her face towards the chair where he sat, further away now, nearer the window. She had pulled a sheet towards her, to cover herself, but she did not know that she had done so.

'How did you know?' she said.

'I talked to Grover.'

'What did he tell you?'

'That you never had real sex. That you were frightened. That pretending it was a massage was the only way you could enjoy it. And that some years ago he made you very angry by suggesting that you should try and face what was wrong with you and get some proper help.'

'It was not Grover's business.' But she was too exhausted to be angry. 'How did you know about Grover?'

'It's part of my job, to know these things. How did it – come to this?'

Juliet looked at Bud Martin across the hotel room.

'I was afraid you'd find out,' she said simply. 'The film was too – real. I haven't had sex – proper sex, since I was twenty-one.'

Bud Martin's face didn't change but he moved away at last and walked to the window. He stared out at the city.

'You mean for thirty-five years you've never done that?' There was a kind of pity in his voice.

'I can't,' she said.

'But you can,' he said. 'What happened?'

'I – I had an illegal abortion that went wrong. I was young. It – damaged me. It messed me up. I – can't bear to have anyone inside me. I – I've been reminded of it all lately because – what I said to you earlier, I damaged someone. It was at that time. It's all tied up with that time. And I've never had to do anything so – so specific on film that might – tell people.'

'Do you really mean you've never had a proper sexual relationship of any kind since then?'

'Yes.'

'But you're married.'

'He's gay,' said Juliet simply. 'It suited us both. When we married twenty-five years ago he couldn't afford for it to be known. He's the head of a big stock-broking firm. Twenty-five years ago they needed wives at dinner parties and company functions if they were to climb the corporate ladders.'

'Didn't you want children?'

'I can't have children,' said Juliet Lyall, 'the abortion had been done so badly I finally had to have a hysterectomy when I was twenty-two. It was all illegal in those days, and I was scared of what I'd done, I – left it too long before I went to a doctor.'

He was looking out of the window, down on the sprawled smog-ridden night and again there may have been a small sigh.

She stared at his back. 'Do you know,' she said, 'I've been going to a psychoanalyst for years. We talk every week. Grover said I wasn't talking about the right things, that's what made me so angry with him. We go back to my childhood, and my father and all his wives, I talk and I talk and I talk. But I never talk about this.'

'Sounds like a fucking awful psychoanalyst,' said Bud Martin.

He was still turned away from her. Something about

the impersonality of his back, turned away from her. She wanted to see his face.

'Is this how you get your kicks?' she said.

He turned back to her at once.

'You misunderstand,' he answered, quite coldly. 'This is how I get the performances I want.'

The next evening, the fifty-six-year-old actress Juliet Lyall re-did the scene with the young man she'd met in the bar, the young man the lonely older woman had met in the bar; sat with him in his old car parked outside, with the camera crew and the sound crew and the lighting crew all moving into her face for close-ups. The actor, Clint O'Hara, leant over her, kissed her, put his hand on her neck, her neck with its lines and its creases; moved his hand slowly, as scripted, towards her breast. Her eyes, which had closed as he kissed her, opened then, looked at the young face. Clint O'Hara had blue eyes. She stared at the boy for a long time.

And then they heard a kind of sigh, a kind of cry, and, uncertainly, her hand reached up to touch him.

And very slowly, tears slid down Juliet's face, in close-up.

'Cut,' said Bud Martin quietly, at last.

As she was changing, back in her caravan, there was a knock at her door. The dresser put a dressing gown around her. Bud Martin put his head around the door.

'Sorry,' he said, seeing that she hadn't yet finished dressing. 'We're just moving off to another location.'

And just for a moment he stared at her, and his voice became the other voice.

'It was good,' was all he said, and then she heard him go down the steps of the caravan to where his driver was waiting.

THIRTY

No no no no no no no.

It wasn't loud, Molly McKenzie's voice, it was low and desperate and unbelieving.

No.

Banjo sat hunched on the end of their bed, his saxophone still in his hands. He looked at her with such pain in his eyes that an outside observer may have thought that she was leaving him.

'Molly. Molly I can't bear to hurt you like this, I can't stand it. But darling we've always known it couldn't go on forever.'

'Why? Why can't it?' She knew the answer but waited for him to tell her.

'Because –' and his voice shook '– because by the time I'm your age you'll be seventy-five. I'll be like you are now, full of life and energy – and you'll be seventy-five. And because – because I want to have children, you know that. Real children. I know we once talked about adoption but I want children of my own.'

'Because I'm already old,' said Molly, 'and you're young, and you don't love me enough for it not to matter.' She knew it was the most unfair thing she could say.

He looked away, fiddled with the keys on his sax. His new chance for happiness sustained him, otherwise he knew he couldn't have gone through with this.

'But – we've been together for over *eight years*,' she said pleadingly. 'Some people aren't married for half that long, we've been happy. Haven't we?' She saw him in her mind, how he'd been lately, gently doped for at least half the time, out of it. And she saw herself, in the honeysuckle-scented dark room, with Anthony.

'I have been happy Molly, you know that.' His face was pale, and taut with tension. 'You taught me most of what I know about love, and relationships, and being with someone. I don't think I was grown up till I met you and I'll always love you, in a way. But I – oh darling,' and it was his turn to plead now, 'I want other things too. I—' he hesitated. 'I don't want a life like yours.'

Molly made a weird kind of groaning sound. 'Banjo I can't live without you, you are my life, you saved me when Mum died, I can't live without you, I can't survive!' Her voice rose in the night, not meaning to.

He put the saxophone down at last, took her in his arms. She had been almost asleep when he finally came home. He knew he had to tell her when she sat up in bed blinking in her green nightdress saying, *I missed you*. She wept on his shoulder, he stroked her hair.

'Who is it?' she asked at last, tears still streaming down her cheeks.

He told his only lie of the evening. 'No one you know,' he said.

Later, in the night, in his arms, she woke crying so loudly that she frightened herself as well as him. Her breathing came in big gulps, fighting for air through her mouth, *I can't live without you*, she said, *I can't live*. And the image of her mother's dead body in the car, in the garage which they had walked into together, came darkly, clearly, into both of their minds.

He was frightened then too and in more pain than he could imagine.

'Then I can't go,' he said, 'I suppose.'

It was the *I suppose* that finally broke her heart: she understood then that hearts break. It was almost sulky, as if he were trapped; she knew then that this was real, and it was over.

She loved him too much, she could not trap him, they would never recover.

She tried to control her breathing. 'I just mean that I love you,' she said more quietly, 'that's all.'

He never wore anything in bed; his bare shoulder was wet with her tears. She fell into a fitful sleep finally; his pillow then was wet with his own.

For some reason not clear to either of them, they ended up on a train to Hastings the next day. They walked along by the sea in the cold, icy wind, Molly walked as if to walk out pain, Banjo pulled his coat around him, felt in his pocket for a joint.

Finally they sat in an empty beach café with plastic

ashtrays and coffee made with warm milk. Molly couldn't talk without tears running down her cheeks but tried still to make sense of it all.

'I know you're right,' she said, 'of course I do. I've seen all your friends having children, I've seen you with them, I know it's got harder and harder.'

He stared at cigarette burns on the table and the faded check of the plastic tablecloth. 'I've tried Moll,' he said, 'I tried to think how it would be, them all having kids except me, how you and I would go and visit and smile.'

'I know,' she said and tears kept falling into the coffee. 'I know.' She tried to warm her hands around the cup. 'There's no role model for us, we don't know anyone who's done it, lived it successfully. Maybe it would never work out for anyone. Of course it works,' she added bitterly, 'if the man is old. But not the woman.'

She had known of course for months and months and months that it would end. And she saw that he had another happiness waiting, that made him strong, in this.

'Is she young?' said Molly.

'Yes,' said Banjo, 'she's much younger than me,' seeming not to hear the irony of it.

'But not twenty years?'

He looked shocked. 'Of course not twenty years,' he said. Round and round he turned the plastic ashtray and he did not look at her.

'How did you meet her?'

'Oh – music, you know.'

'Have you known her for a long time?'

The ashtray stopped turning. 'Actually,' said Banjo, 'I've known her as long as I've known you.'

Molly put her face in her hands.

When they got home they bought fish and chips in the High Street, walked home in the clear, cold evening air.

Molly relied on every ounce of strength she'd ever had, ever built up, every ounce of strength she had ever possessed.

'I think,' she said, collecting up the newspaper when they'd finished eating, putting on the electric jug to make tea, 'it might be best if you moved out tomorrow.'

Banjo looked slightly bewildered. 'Well of course,' he said. 'I guess that would be best.'

'Are you going to move in with her?'

He looked at her steadily. 'I'm going to move in with Pete and Nancy,' he said, 'till things settle.'

'What do you mean, settle?'

Again he looked bewildered. 'Well you know, I'll need to move out permanently from here eventually, sort things out with you, money and – and my possessions and things, decide where to live.'

'Have you already arranged this with them, with Pete and Nancy? Have you already told them?'

'Yes,' he said. And it was like a door closing.

'Take what you need tomorrow morning,' she said angrily. 'I'll send the rest.'

In the night, suddenly, urgently, they made love. And Molly, attuned as she always was to every sexual nuance, knew, even as she came in the arms of her love who was leaving her, how in some odd way it was newly exciting to both of them, because it was over. She cried out, and wept. *Then I can't go I suppose* echoed in her mind.

In the morning, pale and firm when Banjo would have slept on, she helped him pack the things he would need immediately. 'Let me know,' she said, 'where to send the rest.'

Banjo, pale also and sad-faced, kissed her goodbye, held her in his arms.

'I didn't mean it to be as – quickly – as this Molly,' he said uncertainly. 'But I'll phone you darling, we'll always be good friends, of course we will, we're a huge part of each other's lives, perhaps we can go out to dinner next week. ' She turned away from him, shuddered at the thought of them politely eating in a restaurant.

He had a green van when he met her. They had laughed because green was her favourite colour.

He packed the green van with some of his belongings and drove away from the big house in Clapham.

She woke in the night, over and over; several times not thinking of Banjo but of her mother, slumped in the car in the garage. She tossed and turned, cried out, unbelieving, at the pain of it. An expression – a poem? – came again and again into her mind: *if you love something let it go, if you love something let it go*, over and over and over As the first light shone dully behind the curtains in the bedroom something jumped into her mind: their last holiday in Greece, when he had taken the saxophone and played to her on the verandah of their villa in the warm fragrant night. But had also turned away from her several times in the night as if, as if – she forced the thought to come into her mind where she could see it properly – as if he had seen something, as if, almost, something disgusted him. As if he saw her growing old. The sound of the saxophone had soared out over the sea, from the verandah of their villa.

She got up and switched on the light. There was a full-length mirror in the hall. She took off her green nightdress and stared at herself. *Not bad*, they always said, for her age. But she looked carefully. There were flabby bits on her legs, her breasts drooped slightly, she had a slightly protruding stomach. She always felt as if she were a young person, she had the energy of a young person; her hair was blonde, her teeth very cleverly capped; HRT suited her, enhanced her. But as she stood there that November morning and stared and stared at herself she saw, for the first time in her life, staring at her face and at her body (and it was as unbelievable to her as if someone had suddenly said she was a man not a woman, or that she was adopted or had been born on another planet): *she was old*.

She went on with her life in a daze. She still had two more days filming to do with the A-Little-Tired-Fun director; Waylon Jones had turned his attentions to one of the young bridesmaids who disappeared into his caravan in the lunch hours. Molly wandered about the hotel where they were filming, in the cherry red jacket and the short skirt and the chunky jewellery, chattering brightly. She came home and wept, knowing too that next week there would not only be no Banjo, there would be no work.

He had said *he didn't want a life like hers.* What did he mean?

He left kind, loving messages on her answering machine: *how are you Molly darling . . . just phoning to see how you are . . . I'm thinking of you darling, of course.* When the phone rang she never answered, in the end never even listened to the messages, sat in her dressing gown staring at nothing in Clapham.

All the good and quirky things about the man she had loved most in her life came into her mind: how he once, when they first met, bought her a big plastic rubbish bin for her birthday because he saw she needed one and inside the rubbish bin were dozens and dozens of flowers, smiling up at her. She remembered him again, kissing the carpet. She remembered him stopping the fight between Anthony and Benedict at the garden party. She remembered how he'd waited for her to come home from filming very late one Valentine's Day and had, when he saw her get out of a taxi, begun to play on his saxophone in the darkness, something he'd written for her. He'd lit candles on the stairs and she walked up in the flickering light, towards the beautiful sound, and his love. She could not even bear to think of her mother's death and how he had guided her through that labyrinth of anguish and guilt and regret. And the most simple pain of all: she missed his comforting, comfortable, so well-known body next to her in the bed.

The following week, filming over, she dared not go

out, do anything, in case people should see such pain and ugliness and age. She thought over and over again of the young girl, whoever she was: Banjo's new love, who was young. And one morning, quite early, she thought of Pauline O'Brien, her friend. Was this the kind of pain she had inflicted on the friend of her youth? But Anthony hadn't left, was there still. But the idea that it was this, this pain and heartbreak that she had inflicted on Pauline who had been her best friend so appalled her that in a kind of madness she picked up the telephone and dialled the number.

'Hello?'

At the sound of another human voice Molly pulled herself together.

'Viola, that's you isn't it? Hello darling, it's Molly.'

There was absolute silence on the other end of the phone. As if it hadn't been answered after all.

'Viola?' said Molly, puzzled.

'Oh – sorry Auntie Moll.' *Auntie Moll*. What Viola used to call her when she was a little girl. 'Sorry, it was – Benedict, he – dropped a frying pan.'

'Good heavens is he all right?'

'Yes,' said Viola vaguely.

'Darling is your mum there?' *Why am I doing this, whatever can I say?*

'No, no,' said Viola and Molly felt relieved at once. 'No, she's not here, she's busy on something, the shop I expect, I'm on my own, Dad's filming, I should be at class.'

'Never mind darling, I'll phone again, look after yourself.' And Molly put down the phone.

Vaguely she wondered how Viola could be on her own if Benedict was dropping frying pans, hoped she was all right. She loved Viola.

She sat alone in the kitchen, in her dressing gown.

One night she woke suddenly in that way that had become familiar, but she was smiling. A memory dried away from her; very gently she tried to hold it, tease it back into her mind.

And it came back. Banjo had told her one night in bed about his first erection. He had seen it, surprised, wondered what it was, and the funny feeling of it. He was getting undressed. So he hung his shirt on it. It hung there for some time, unsure and drooping a little.

I will die of this pain, cried Molly aloud, *I cannot live without my love. I will die.*

Frances and Harry arranged with each other to phone Emmy Lou every day while she was feeling so bleak. They sent her funny cards and jokey gifts, just so she'd know they were thinking of her and loved her. They had dinner with her, went to the movies. Harry was going away for three more days filming in Dorchester. 'Why don't you come with me Em?'

'No thanks Harry, I'll probably go to the recording of Franny's chat show.'

'It was a hoot, I knew that nun from when I was a kid, but Emmy didn't come,' said Frances when he got back and asked her how it had gone. They phoned Emmy again and again but there was no reply.

'Shall we phone her agent?'

'Oh God it's so melodramatic. She's fine, she must be fine.'

'Harry let's phone her agent.'

'He's probably sent her off to Scunthorpe.' They always said Scunthorpe, having been there for a week with a play once in their final term as drama students and the theatre had been almost empty every night.

Emmy Lou's agent hadn't spoken to her that week.

Frances had a key, had always had a key, was Emmy's family.

Her heart beat so horribly as she and Harry let themselves in after knocking and knocking on her door. They kept calling *Emmy? Emmy?* knowing they would hear her voice in a moment, or find the central heating on, or wet underclothes in the bathroom, that they would all laugh at the ludicrousness of it.

In her white bedroom, under the white crocheted bedspread that her elderly mother had made for her when she first left home, Emmy Lou lay asleep except that Frances and Harry knew at once that she was not asleep.

On the bedside table was an empty pill bottle and an envelope marked: FOR FRANNY AND HARRY. Harry put out his hand; before he picked up the envelope he touched her arm. It was cold and stiff.

Frances thought she would faint: at the silence in the lonely room, at the books on voice production by the bed, but of course really at the cold, cold body of her friend lying so still and small. She stood there, in the middle of the room.

'Oh no Harry, no Harry,' she said.

He opened the envelope.

My dear friends,

I am so sorry because I love you both more than I love anyone else in the world. It is true you were my family for me. But I suddenly found I couldn't hang on any longer. Merry Christmas and have a drink for me and please don't be angry with me or sad about me. I simply couldn't go on, I know you will understand.

Em

The small sad face was slightly turned away from them as if to say: I have already gone.

'It's not fair,' cried Frances, 'it's not fair, *it's not fair*.' She threw herself into Harry's arms, he held her tightly, the two of them stood there, both shaking and crying, beside the body of their friend.

'This fucking profession, this cruel fucking profession it simply breaks people's hearts.' Harry was suddenly shouting, he broke away from Frances and with his arms swept the voice books off the bedside table. To think of voice production books as Emmy Lou's night-time reading was utterly unbearable.

Frances stood rocking with grief in the middle of the room, her arms around herself. Across the street in someone's window she saw an old man bring his wife a cup of tea on a tray. Beside them, on the windowsill, a rather wilting pink geranium stood in a pot.

*

Somehow the papers got hold of the story of an actress's suicide, found that she too had been at the reunion.

So Emmy Lou's face also appeared on the front page of the *Sun* under the headline: JINXED REUNION DEATH. And underneath, in the slightly smaller print: ANOTHER OF TERRY'S LOVERS?

Frances grimaced in pain as she saw the headline in the newspaper shop remembering how both she and Em had of course kissed Terence passionately but innocently too: happy, remembered kisses, part of their youth. She sat in her flat on the sofa where you could still see slightly the coffee stain on the pink carpet from My Night With Milton.

Finally she rummaged around in her old record collection in a cupboard until she found what she wanted, put on an old Dory Previn record that Emmy and she used to sing when they were young, when they believed the world was still waiting for them.

> *Mary Cecilia Brown*
> *Went to town on the Malibu bus*
> *She climbed to the top of the Hollywood sign*
> *And with the smallest possible fuss*
> *She jumped off the letter H*
> *Because she did not become a Star*
> *She died in less than a minute and a half*
> *She looked a bit like Hedy Lamarr.*

Frances sat on her old sofa and wept, for the loss of her friend who told the dole office she would learn Chinese, and for the rest of the song that they had sung so often, and laughed at:

When Mary Cecilia jumped
She finally made the grade
Her name was in the obituary columns
Of both of the Daily Trades.

Pamela Angel sent flowers to the funeral.

Frances Kitson sent them back in a taxi to the National Theatre. On the back of Pamela Angel's card she wrote: NOT WANTED ON VOYAGE.

THIRTY-ONE

The next Saturday night, late, Anthony Bonham drove home from Stratford (dropping off the young actress at Hammersmith again, whose kiss lingered on rather tediously he decided) to find his wife wasn't home. She was not watching television, nor in the kitchen with her Campari, nor in bed and when he finally thought to check he found the pink Mercedes was not in the garage. Benedict was asleep, Viola was out. Anthony was very thrown by this: Pauline always said where she would be; it was one of her efficiencies.

He slouched crossly in front of the telly with a very large whisky, desultorily reading Saturday's *Daily Mail*; it seemed to be full of nothing but show business stories, almost all of them connected with what everyone now called the Jinxed Reunion. The obituary photograph of Emmy Lou Brown unsettled him further: he had been genuinely fond of her, had admired her as an actress, vaguely thought they might find her something in *The Immoralists*. He had seen the good reviews she'd so recently had in *Lives* which were quoted in the obituary. Why should she kill herself? Silly sad girl. Nothing in the world was worth killing yourself over. He threw the paper on to the floor, uneasy.

Where was Pauline?

And Molly? He'd phoned her, he'd even written to her. He knew their last meeting would have stayed in her mind, as it had in his. But he got only her answering machine. He left urgent messages about the TV series, which were not returned. Didn't she realise the chance he was putting her way? And didn't she miss him? She *must* miss him.

And the activity surrounding *The Immoralists* seemed to have slackened. He hadn't talked to Joseph Wain for some days. His agent said it was probably finance. *But I want it settled*.

Where was Pauline? When had he last spoken to her? Wednesday was it? Thursday? He'd told her he'd be home; she hadn't said she wouldn't be here. It was – he looked at his watch – Jesus Christ three o'clock in the morning.

Alarmed now, he went and woke Benedict, with difficulty.

'Sorry Benny old chap.' He knew how hard it was for Benedict to wake up in the morning let alone in the middle of the night. 'Where's Mum? She's not here.'

'Gone away,' mumbled Benedict.

'*Gone away?*'

'She said she had to go away for the weekend.'

'Go away for the weekend? Go away where?'
'Didn't say.'
'Where's Viola?'
'With her boyfriend.'
'What boyfriend?'
'That guy.'
'*What* guy?'
But Benedict had done his valiant best. He was fast asleep again.

The whisky and the travelling and filming all week and the performances of both *Hamlet* and *Othello* suddenly all fell heavily on the shoulders of Anthony Bonham. And he was filming again on Monday morning. Hardly able to take off his clothes, he got alone into the double bed and fell instantly asleep.

The winding private drive up to the old farmhouse in a small village near Darlington was hidden from the main road. So nobody saw the pink Mercedes parked there next to the red BMW convertible. There was another car there also.

Pauline O'Brien sat at the old wooden kitchen table with Terence Blue, who had one arm in a sling still, and another, taller man she had arranged to meet there.

She told them of her plan.

Terence Blue stopped her. 'For Christ's sake. How do you know that? How did you know that I'm –' he forced himself to say the word '– impotent?'

'Oh,' said Pauline casually, 'Molly McKenzie told me.'

She saw hurt fleetingly in Terence's eyes and pressed

her advantage at once. 'Well you know Molly – she tells everybody everything.'

'Molly does?' said Terence, puzzled

'God darling, yes, it'll be all round London now for sure.'

Terence didn't say any more then, looked away, his face bleak and the other two felt a pang of pity for him. But Pauline knew she could not let herself feel sorry for him now.

Terence drained his coffee cup, clumsily poured more from the percolator using his good arm. 'No, no, I can do it,' waving Pauline away. There was a long silence in the farmhouse kitchen. Heat from the Aga warmed the room, enclosed the three of them.

Finally he said, 'You surprise me about Molly. I didn't think she was – that kind of person.'

'Oh she is,' said Pauline and both men heard a kind of venom in her tone. 'Believe me, she *is*.' She took out the red lipstick, applied it to her mouth, looking in a small mirror.

The second man in the kitchen still remained silent, but stared at her, this new Pauline.

Terence drank the coffee. 'Well anyway there's no need for any of this rubbish, there is no way a British court will convict me. I won't be found guilty of rape, I didn't do it, and I'm certainly not going into the witness stand to talk about my sexual problems for the gratification of the world's press. I didn't do it. That isn't the trial I'm worried about.'

But Pauline leant across the kitchen table where they sat and kept on talking. She had enough information now: Harry had given her knowledge of the past and the knowledge was her power. And Elvira Pugh, crime-writer, had made the important connection. *All he cares about is keeping Nicky out of court: Nicky is the most important thing in his life. I suspect this – illness – will be something to do with Nicky. Make him see how he can help her: put it in his mind that he could use the first trial to prevent the second.*

Pauline continued long into the night, talking; her eyes glittered, like ice. 'I was thinking about Nicky Abbott,' she said.

The other man remained silent.

Terence Blue said *I will not do it* over and over again.

THIRTY-TWO

On the first day of the Terence Blue rape trial it snowed very heavily. The roads around the looming Old Bailey had been white, were now slushy; pedestrians had made icy tracks through the snow on the pavements and now it was treacherous to walk. That did not stop the journalists arriving early or the public queuing eagerly at the gallery entrance or huge groups of winter tourists hoping for a glimpse of a famous British film star, all milling about the Old Bailey stamping their feet in the cold.

'I used to save his picture for years,' one woman said, blowing her nose on tissues she kept pulling out of a box. 'We're exactly the same age,' and a press photographer took a photo. She had a woollen scarf tied round her head and fur-lined boots: she looked like a Russian in a food queue, was actually a dental assistant from Ruislip with a bad cold (*Karen Williams, 58*) who had taken a week off to catch the trial.

Dozens of photographers in thick wet-weather jackets wiped the lenses of their cameras, gossiped in groups; journalists cupped red hands around a match, coughed, watched the road carefully. Policemen at all the doorways were photographed by foreigners.

When Simone Taylor arrived, in a startling pink dress and a fur coat and wearing dark glasses, there was a flurry; no one was supposed to know the identity of the complainant but lights flashed in the white morning, journalists crowded around the chauffeur-driven car as she got out. She waved, but with a serious look on her face, at the press; was hurried inside the building.

Terence Blue arrived, not in a chauffeur-driven car, not in his red BMW from which he was banned, but in an ordinary London taxi. Bedlam reigned as the press suddenly realised: Terence Blue, who had seemed to disappear off the face of the earth, was actually here; photographers pressed forward, saw that one of Terence's arms was in a sling, slipped in the snow in their excitement to get near. Show business journalists who had known Terence for years, had drunk with him in bars all over the world late into the night, crowded around him, pushing out the crime reporters and the serious press, *Hi Terry! Did you do it Terry? Where've you been Terry?* and even, seeing the sling, remembering the stabbing, *You all right Tel boy? How're you feeling?*

He stopped only for a moment, more gaunt and paler than people remembered, his attention caught by another taxi stopping, disgorging Elvira Pugh the crime-writer, one of his ex-wives; the journalists saw him raise his right hand in greeting. Just at that moment a group of women arrived on the other side of the road waving a banner and chanting RAPIST RAPIST and a rather muddy snowball suddenly hit him on the shoulder. That would have been the photograph, the one that travelled round the world in seconds, the image of the Famous Film Star brought low.

But Terence Blue understood that. He was a Star. There had to be a better photograph. After the split second of stillness when he was hit, he bent down and scooped up some snow with his right hand and threw it back at the women with the banner. So it was that picture, the picture of Terence Blue on trial for rape but throwing a snowball, the other arm in a white sling, that was syndicated all over the world: to Berlin and Paris and Cape Town and Bangkok and Auckland and Delhi and Dublin. It became a very famous photograph. A photographer had caught the expression on his face: a kind of wry half-smile as if to say, *give us a break, you don't know I'm a rapist yet.*

Elvira Pugh had been in court many times, researching her crime novels that were so popular – although she had preferred to attend courts outside London – learning her craft. She knew very well that a rape trial – no matter the hype surrounding it, no matter the press benches full to bursting, no matter the woman in pink and the still handsome man with the greying hair and the piercing blue eyes sitting in the long lonely dock at the back of the courtroom – she knew that a rape trial is always ugly: degrading for the complainant and the defendant, both. It is bald and ugly and cold. Actions are described clinically; medical and forensic evidence is impassively given, passion or sex or lust or rage are long absent, months later, from the men in wigs describing vaginas and penises and positions and bodily fluids.

Elvira had tried hard to warn Terence.

'It will be horrible darling,' she had said.

'I'm innocent,' he answered and he had shrugged his good shoulder in a kind of stoic resignation.

It is hard for a member of the public to get a seat in the public gallery during a popular or notorious trial at the Old Bailey; Terence's trial, the most notorious of them all, was no exception. The lady in the scarf and the snow-boots (*Karen Williams, 58*) was there at dawn every morning of the first week even though the trial didn't begin each day until 10.30 am. Izzy Fields came one morning on her bicycle through the snow, hoping to catch some of the trial before she went to her matinée, but the court was full. Only Elvira was somehow able to arrive just before the public gallery was opened and get in. She had told one of the ushers she was Terence's ex-wife, he recognised her anyway, from the newspapers. 'Come and see me every morning love,' he had said, 'I'll keep a seat for you.'

So Elvira was there every day: impassive, beautifully and expensively dressed in Italian clothes, smelling of Chanel No 5, an unusual perfume up the concrete steps to Courtroom Number 10. She always sat at the end of the front row, saw the bailed Terence Blue – with whom she and Stu would have had breakfast in Berkshire some hours before, but people did not know this – brought by a uniformed guard each day through a padded door behind which she could glimpse more bleak concrete steps and a liftwell. Each evening, the press saw, a car was waiting for her, and she was gone. And Terence was in a taxi that disappeared into the rush-hour traffic.

Everyone in court seemed to have a cold, not just Karen Williams (58) who carried a box of tissues: the woman judge sucked throat pastilles, the court stenographer sneezed, the voice of the prosecution lawyer, Mr Lee, was thick and deep with accumulated phlegm.

The first witness called that December morning was Simone Taylor. She was examined by her own barrister and cross-examined by Terence's. She maintained her story stubbornly and palely in her little-girl voice: 'Terence Blue came to the Dorchester after the reunion for a drink, everyone saw us come in. Everyone saw us having a meal in one of the restaurants. After the meal he came to my room, we ordered a bottle of whisky from room service; the room service waiter saw him there. Suddenly he jumped on me, ripped my dress. I screamed out, and he hit me, hit me and bit me on my breasts. I have never been so frightened in my life, he forced me to lie there. He raped me, several times. And then he left. Everyone saw him go.'

The defendant Terence Blue stared at her impassively. He was not guilty, his lawyer said over and over again. He did not rape Simone Taylor.

The lady judge, in her short white wig that made it difficult to tell her age, wrote things down in longhand in a big book. Sometimes, coughing slightly, reaching for another pastille, she would say *pause please* while she bent over her pages.

During the prosecution's case, as witnesses came and went, bits of Simone Taylor's and Terence Blue's anatomy were discussed by the court. Photos of the bruises on Simone's breasts were shown to the jury. Diagrams from an extremely respected woman gynae-cologist were also handed to the jury; a drawing of Simone's damaged vagina had been photocopied seven times so that the judge could have one copy and the jury could have one copy between two. A young Indian woman on the jury frowned, then giggled slightly in deep embarrassment.

The case slowly, and often boringly, proceeded: one day, two days, three. BLUE RAPE LATEST said the newspaper headlines every night and every morning. Slowly some facts emerged from all the speculation. There was no doubt that Terence Blue had arrived at the Dorchester with Simone Taylor and had a meal with her there. There was no doubt he'd gone to her room. There was no doubt that Simone Taylor had had violent sexual intercourse and suffered physical damage. But she had bathed several times after the attack, the sheets had been thrown into the bath, she had not reported the rape for almost a day, the rapist had used a condom. It had not been possible to ascertain forensically that her attacker was Terence Blue. But hairs from his head (and no one else's except Simone Taylor's) had been found on the white sofa in the suite on the top floor of the Dorchester.

Day by day, painstakingly, the trial went on.

For some days Molly McKenzie did not get dressed, as if

grieving should be done undressed. She sat in Clapham. She had no routine to keep to that could automatically help her, force her to think of other things. She listened to the radio, watched a bit of television, sometimes she read. Often she had to turn back the pages: she had not taken in what she was reading. She waited for the pain to go away. Surely this kind of pain had to go away eventually.

She heard news of Terence's case on Radio 4 in the mornings, sometimes saw him on TV leaving the court, disappearing into a taxi, at the end of a day's hearing. He looked very much thinner she thought, still very much showing the effects of the stabbing. She even laughed briefly one day at a report that Ronnie McDermott, a Scottish comic who had been a year ahead of them at the Drama Academy, had been called by the defence to describe Simone banging her shoe on the bannister as she lay draped across the stairs screaming I LOVE HIM I LOVE HIM in 1959. The court laughter had to be silenced several times, the complainant was in tears, the judge reminded everybody that rape was a serious crime, and that love was not.

Molly wandered in her dressing gown around the Clapham house that seemed so large and so empty. She had not waited to see where Banjo and his new love might live: she had packed up every single piece of musical equipment still there, every single item of clothing, all the furniture that belonged to him, and, knowing the mode of transport would embarrass that household, had arranged for everything to be sent to him at Pete and Nancy's small council flat in a Harrods removal van.

She knew she was behaving badly, she didn't care. *I am a rejected mistress, not a storage depot.*

She wept every day. Her eyes were permanently red and swollen, she remembered how she felt when her mother died: jagged, unjoined together, sometimes seeing a part of her body – a hand, a leg – as if it belonged to somebody else. Then Banjo had held her, let her talk incoherently, comforted her, over and over again. This time she did not feel there was anybody she could talk to about how she was feeling, Banjo had been the one she always talked to about how she was feeling. She was absolutely alone with the pain

Sometimes she drank large vodka and tonics

She never answered the telephone, not even Anthony's calls about the television series; she knew that she must answer them, that work and such a job as he seemed to be offering, would be her salvation. But she literally could not pick up the telephone.

And gradually, over days and nights, she realised what quality it was that Banjo had given her, shared with her. It wasn't, after all, his youth although she had enjoyed that.

He was a happy person.

The thought, when it was properly formed, so surprised her that she stopped crying.

Banjo was a happy person.

Until now, almost all the thoughts she had of him, all the memories of their time together, made her smile. He saw life as a pleasant thing. He had had a stable, ordinary, uneventful, happy childhood: two sisters and a brother and parents who loved him. He went home to

Essex continually to see them, talked to any of them on the phone for hours about this and that. His granny had been a cook; he had told Molly about going on holiday once to Whitstable: his granny had seen him swimming one morning and had come rushing into the caravan they were staying in saying to his mother *I can see his ribs I can see his ribs* and had immediately made a huge meat pie for morning tea. He was surrounded by uncompli- cated love. And he grew up happy.

And I expect he will make his children happy as he made me happy.

And I am an actress. And what makes me good at my job, and I am very good sometimes, is perhaps the very fact that I didn't have that stable and uncomplicated childhood; that I ran home from school often with my heart in my mouth in case my mother had carried out her latest threat; that when I was at primary school I found strange men in my mother's bed who wanted to buy me sweeties; that I grew up damaged and com- plicated and have had lots of men in my bed too, over the years. They fuck you up your mum and dad even if you don't have a dad. Someone should do a survey of actors' childhoods. Banjo said he didn't want to have a life like mine, but he didn't see: he never had a life like mine.

I am as I am.

I am as I am. Somehow the thought comforted her.

The next day she went to her hairdresser.

'I'm sick of being blonde,' she said, 'I despise those actresses who stay blonde long after their sell-by date,' and burst into tears.

Her hairdresser, Fifi, had known her for years – from

when she was a junior tinter at Vidal Sassoon and her name was Diane Lloyd. She pretended Molly wasn't crying. She pulled bottles and potions from cupboards. She shouted at juniors in her Chelsea salon to bring peppermint tea, tear up silver paper, tidy the *Vogues*, sweep hair off the floor.

And then she set to work.

It was a newer, cooler Molly: light brown hair streaked with honey lights that hid the grey, and a flash of gold at certain angles. When Molly, amazed at the transformation, went to pay the bill, Fifi put her hand over Molly's.

'It's on me,' she said. 'For your new life.'

As Molly opened the door of her Clapham house with her new streaked hair, her nose red from the biting cold, her phone was ringing.

'Darling where were you?' said Anastasia Adams. 'You haven't got your answering machine on and I've been phoning all day.'

'Is it the new series?' asked Molly almost eagerly. 'Is it *The Immoralists*?'

'No it's not. I have talked to them several times, to the producer, a man called Joseph Wain, and he said they were certainly considering you, but that it was a long-term project and nothing had been decided and he'd get back to me. But he hasn't, though I've called him several times and not been able to get him. I'll get back again, after we've talked about this, but listen darling, the Royal Shakespeare Company have been on to me about you for their new season.'

Molly's heart lifted. There were still a few good parts

in Shakespeare for women of her age: vital, interesting. Emilia, as she had seen in *Othello*, Queen Margaret. Not Gertrude, she hoped it wasn't that drifting, obedient woman, she'd much rather play Claudius now that she'd studied the play from his point of view.

'What parts Anastasia?' she asked.

'They are doing a new production of *Romeo and Juliet*. They want you to play the Nurse.'

'The Nurse?' *The Nurse?* She remembered Sybil Thorndike, white-haired in the role, when she was a child. She remembered the old woman, now dead, who had played it at Bristol when Molly, almost straight out of drama school, had played Juliet. 'I think that's a ridiculous casting idea,' she said. 'I don't know what the casting director at the Royal Shakespeare Company can be thinking of, she knows my work. I'm not *old* enough to play the Nurse.'

'Ah Molly,' said Anastasia Adams, 'I think you are.'

Frances Kitson grieved also, for her friend Emmy Lou Brown. One day she went to the little white flat and reluctantly began clearing out Emmy's things. Emmy hadn't left a will, there was a cousin who asked Frances to clear the flat and take anything she wanted; the flat was to be sold.

Frances hadn't cleared out the belongings of someone dead before, didn't know that the smell of the people stayed in the clothes even though the people themselves were gone. When she caught just a hint of the Body Shop tea rose that Emmy Lou had used she instinctively glanced behind her, as if Emmy must somehow be there. She folded Emmy's jerseys and T-shirts, crying sometimes and then taking a deep breath and carrying on, putting shoes in plastic bags for Oxfam.

Harry was filming again in Dorset, had wanted Frances to wait until he got back; she'd shrugged and said sadly, 'I'm off on Friday and it has to be done, it needs to be all finished before Christmas or it'll just make us too sad.' She listened to a short story on Emmy's radio.

The voice books were still on the floor where Harry had thrown them that terrible day.

Emmy Lou had read plays, devoured plays. In the sitting room, next to the picture of Sarah Siddons, there were shelves and shelves of almost every play that had been written in, or translated into, English; she used to scour second-hand bookshops when she was on tour, Frances knew, gleefully finding some battered old edition of 1940s American plays to add to her collection. She reckoned she always knew in about twenty minutes, if someone offered her a part, what it was all about; all their acting lives Frances and Harry had phoned her for advice when parts were offered.

I guess we should keep the plays, Frances thought to herself.

But some memory of Harry's pain made her put the voice books into a black bag of rubbish.

She had bought a buttered scone at a local bakery, she made herself a cup of black coffee with Emmy's Nescafé. It was four o'clock and dark outside and cold here in the white flat. She would keep the picture of

Sarah Siddons of course, but she didn't know what to do with Emmy's little, personal things that lay about the flat: a little porcelain pillbox with *Home Sweet Home* on the top, a small furry black cat that Emmy always took for luck to whichever theatre she worked in, some Victorian scissors, a conch shell, a framed picture of her elderly parents.

And one day someone will go through my things, thought Frances, *and they won't mean anything, to anybody.*

In Emmy's desk by the window were her unemployment card from the dole office, her birth certificate and her diary that just noted impersonally what she had done each day. The diary stopped abruptly the day she got the letter from Pamela Angel.

She found Emmy Lou's make-up box at the bottom of her wardrobe, a square wooden hinged box with little compartments like the one Frances' father had had, like the one Pauline's mother had given her daughter; it seemed old-fashioned now *a make-up box* nobody used them any more. She'd seen so many young actresses in the theatre just pull out their street make-up to apply before they went on stage, and most people were used to television where they just sat in a chair and someone else did it. *A make-up box.* And suddenly she saw them all, all the class of '59 graduating from the London Academy of Drama with such hope in their hearts, carrying their make-up sticks of Leichner number five and number nine and their red rouges and their black eyeliners and their big tins of powder and their lipsticks; all these things carefully and proudly placed in their make-up boxes because they had trained to be actors, they

were in the theatre, they had dreams and the world was
waiting.

The news on the radio said that the Terence Blue trial
would go into a second week; the home affairs corre-
spondent discussing the case said he thought things
looked very bleak for Mr Blue.

Frances had parcelled up almost everything. She
pulled open the drawers beside Emmy's bed: aspirin,
tissues, and a toilet bag. She opened the toilet bag and
saw some batteries and some Body Shop oil. And a small
plastic vibrator in the shape of a man's penis, more or
less.

THIRTY-THREE

Anthony Bonham's agent had become extremely suspicious. A big, powerful man just getting old, just getting tired, George Washington – *yes it's my real name*, he would say wearily, *my mother was a card* – was sixty-nine and knew the business better than almost any agent in London. He was experienced and powerful: he had represented stars since the early days of good British films, nobody crossed him with impunity.

'I think *The Immoralists* has run into trouble Tony, I don't know what it is exactly but something's going on. I can't get sense out of the fuckers, I can't get hold of Joseph Wain, I told them the RSC is desperate to know your other commitments and that the BBC wants you for that new series, but suddenly the scripts aren't ready. I suppose it could be finance, we're talking millions here, much *much* more than any ordinary TV series.'

'Jesus Christ I thought that part was mine,' said

Anthony, thrown. 'I want that job badly, I want that exposure.'

'I know, I know, but I'm an old hand. Something's wrong. It won't be the first series to go down the drain this year, but something as huge as this, I can't think they'd want to let it go. It's the most fucking ambitious thing ever set up in England, it's more ambitious than a movie.' He paused for a moment. 'These are tricky times of course.' No good getting too alarmist, but he felt trouble. 'Well,' he said briskly, 'maybe it'll all work out yet.' But George Washington was a wily old fox and he knew there was something. 'You're absolutely sure you don't want to do *Richard III* after the other plays come to London?'

'Jesus Christ, absolutely positive,' said Anthony, 'I've done my stint for fucking culture, *I want that fucking series.*'

'Then pray for fucking finance,' said George Washington.

Anthony was speaking to his agent from his dressing room in Stratford-upon-Avon on a Friday night before a performance of *Othello*. His dresser knocked at the door.

'It's nearly the half Mr Bonham, anything you need?'

'No, no,' said Anthony vaguely.

He was very disturbed by his agent's news but automatically, for that was his job, he placed his lips gently together, began to hum till they vibrated and once again his head became the soundbox for his voice: *I have professed me thy friend and I confess me knit to thy deserving with cables of perdurable toughness.* The finance for the series would surely be found, it was too good a project to be lost. *There are many events in the womb of time which will be delivered.* By Christ they'd better not be thinking of anybody else for the part, no, surely it was his, all the producers had wanted him. God he was very tired: the filming for the World War II series was tedious and exhausting, running around Devon in the snow was as unromantic as much filming was – cold, wet, disjointed – and then too often to have to do a show at night. The snow had hampered them, the shots didn't match, some they'd had to do again, and he was called again early Monday morning and he was recording television commercial voice-overs on Sunday afternoon. He was tired. He wanted to go home. But he would have to wait until after tomorrow evening's performance of *Hamlet.*

There was a kind of nagging anxiety somewhere just on the outskirts of his mind. He hadn't talked to Pauline for over a week and all he got every time he phoned home was the answering machine. How dare she not be at home last weekend without at least an explanation. Viola had not been there at all either; on Sunday he and Benedict had morosely eaten a cold chicken from the fridge and a homemade apple pie that Benedict had been instructed to remove from the freezer. Benedict had seemed uncurious as to the whereabouts of his mother and his sister, *they're always out these days,* he had said, had removed himself to his friend Jeremy's house and computers for almost the whole day. And Anthony, crossly wandering about the empty house, turning down the central heating which – as if they thought he was a bottomless financial goldmine – was on full in every room, had finally fallen asleep for most of the afternoon, snoring with his mouth open on the sofa by the television, surrounded by the Sunday papers from which photos of Terence Blue smiled up at him. He'd woken with a headache and gone to bed alone again The whole business put him extremely out of sorts.

Pauline had better have a pretty good explanation when he got home again tomorrow night.

From his Stratford dressing room he phoned Molly yet again; her answering machine said she was not available at present.

He tried his home number again. His own actorly tones informed him that he was out.

'Ladies and Gentlemen of the *Othello* company in the Swan Theatre, this is your half-hour call, half an hour please,' and his dresser knocked again at the door.

The next evening Anthony rather brusquely informed the young actress that he could take her to Hammersmith only if she could be ready ten minutes after the show ended; the young actress, who was used on a Saturday night to hanging about with a devoted look while Anthony fielded compliments from visitors and drank a rather dashing amount of whisky, was ready in five at the stage door. She was quite devastated (*she is a tedious girl*, thought Anthony) when he only gave her a quick peck on the cheek when they came to the Hammersmith turn-off.

Pauline was at home as usual sitting in front of the television with a long glass of Campari and soda in her hand.

'Now look here Pauly . . .' said Anthony, cross and yet oddly relieved at the same time.

'Sssshhh,' she said, 'that dreadful old film of yours about Oliver Cromwell is on.'

'What!' Anthony stared at the screen. 'That old rubbish?' He poured his own whisky, sat beside her on the sofa. He'd made that film before they were married, when Pauline's career was more successful than his own.

'Oh Jesus,' he said, 'will you look at those wigs!'

'Oh look there's Frances playing a nun,' and there was Frances, buxom in a nun's habit, pleading with a monk.

They both laughed. Anthony put his arm across the back of the sofa. When a scene began that he wasn't in he said, 'Where's Viola all of a sudden, all the time?'

'She doesn't say. She's suddenly not here very much. She'll tell us when she wants to but – she seems to be in love.'

'*In love*? What the hell are you talking about?'

'She's twenty-four Anthony. She's not a child.'

'She's still a child as far as I'm concerned, especially as I'm still supporting her!'

'Not for much longer,' said Pauline soothingly, 'a few more months.'

'What do you mean in love?'

'I don't know exactly. There's something on her mind but she hasn't talked about it.'

'How can she talk about it if you're never home?'

'You are of course.'

'Don't be silly Pauly, how can I be home – oh look at me on that horse! I think that was my first riding part, I couldn't ride very well in those days, d'you know I've been filming every bloody day this week except

Wednesday when we had a matinée, thank God I missed the War, even filming it is excrutiating. Although I sometimes think a bit of army discipline would make Benedict wake up his ideas a bit, even just wake up full stop would help.'

'They won't have conventional armies in the future, computers'll direct the wars, if Benny's in any war he'll be working in a darkened room not doing foot patrol.'

'They'll always have conventional soldiers mark my words, I'd just like Benny to march briskly five miles occasionally. Where were you last weekend?'

'Mmmmm – oh look, I'd forgotten Julie was in this, and Albert, good heavens how long ago it all is. I was at Elvira's, I thought I said.'

'You did not say. I mean I only have one day a week off, and that only if I'm lucky, so is it too much to ask my own wife to be here, or at least advise me of her whereabouts? It's not like you Pauly.' But his complaints had already become half-hearted: she was here, he was tired. An advertisement for low-calorie dairy spread was on the screen, he went for another whisky, took it back to the sofa, leant back wearily. 'Aaaaaaaah.' He stretched out his legs.

'Looks like Terence is guilty,' he said after a few moments, 'from the papers.'

'Do you think so?'

'Well it all points to him doesn't it, what else could have happened? He told the police she'd passed out and he left and someone else must've done it, who's going to believe that twaddle? This'll fuck his career won't it, rapists just aren't politically correct at the moment.' And he laughed shortly, with a kind of satisfaction. 'They drag on these trials don't they, I'll be glad when I don't have to see Terence on the front page every day, oh *look* at that hat I'm wearing will you!' He put his hand inside Pauline's blouse.

For a split second he felt she had flinched away from him. But then, in that same second almost, she moved, leant companionably against him, laughed at the hat which was indeed unbecoming.

In their bed he pulled her above him as usual, grasped her buttocks, pulled her against his groin as he thrust upwards. She rode him, the way he always wanted it.

The phone rang at her desk in the corner of the bedroom. 'Leave it,' said Anthony, thrusting inside her again and again, *leave it leave it leave it*, in time to his thrusts, *leave it leave it leave it.*

The answering machine clicked on.

Darling, it's Elvira, we've seen the early editions of the Sunday papers, will you phone me?

Anthony pushed upwards once more inside his wife, felt the release, heard with a part of his mind a little sigh above his head, fell back exhausted. He waited till his breathing calmed. God he was tired.

'What the fuck is Elvira doing phoning in the middle of the night?'

Pauline lay back across his bent knees, she didn't speak for a moment, he felt her breathing in and out in and out. Then with a jerk she pulled herself upright, grasping his arms to help herself upwards. In the lamplight from the bedside table he could see, as he opened his eyes for a moment, that her eyes glittered as if, if he didn't know her better, there were tears.

'Stu hasn't been well,' she said. 'Maybe there's bad news about his business in the papers.' She pulled her long naked body away from his, his now flaccid penis fell out; she swung her legs over the side of the bed and padded across the floor to take her dressing gown from behind the door.

'I'll phone from downstairs so's not to disturb you,' she said. 'Go to sleep.'

At the bottom of the stairs of the old house by the river, where the front door and the wide hall met, where Anthony had tripped and fallen drunk at his wife's feet after the reunion, there was a lamp on a windowsill. The small, warm glow could be seen from the front gate and from the top of the stairs. Portia and Viola and Benedict and Anthony always automatically looked for the light if they arrived home late at night: *ah we're home, she's home*.

In the soft light of the lamp Pauline picked up the phone in the hall and dialled a number.

Elvira answered at once.

'It's me,' said Pauline.

'Thank God, we thought you were out.'

'No, no, I was waiting to hear.'

'Where were you? You knew I'd be phoning.'

Pauline paused for a fraction of a second. 'Pretending for the last time I hope,' she said.

'Ah,' said Elvira, understanding at once. 'Yes.'

'What do the papers say?' Pauline's voice was tense.

'It's very very bad. What we expected really. I don't know why we bother to have juries. Who needs juries?

We've got the great British Press who are only supposed to publish unbiased court reporting. Well – underneath what passes for unbiased court reporting they're guessing about how many years he'll get, what it will be like for a film star in jail – there just happens to be an article in the *Express* about Mike Tyson's rape trial and his sentence and what it was like for him in jail and him becoming a Muslim, that sort of stuff.'

'How's Terence?'

'Bad. Terrible. Do you know Pauly, it's the first time he's really understood – that he's likely to go to jail. He's stopped saying "But I didn't do it" as if he suddenly realises at last that that's not the point.' And then suddenly Elvira's voice became very brisk. 'Can you get here about seven tomorrow night? Terry's barrister will be here. Oh – and Joseph Wain. We'll have to work out the sequence of events exactly before the court reconvenes on Monday morning.'

'So we're going ahead?'

'Yes. '

'Terence agrees at last?'

'He agrees. Oh Jesus, poor Terence, it will be so awful for him but there seems no other way. She was raped Pauly, you can tell listening to her, it happened. But *what* happened? God what an almighty mess.' Pauline wasn't actually certain that Elvira wasn't crying but she could not consider that now.

'He agrees –' Pauline repeated urgently, '– to –' and even now she hesitated in a kind of disbelief '– everything? Everything else, I mean?'

Elvira heard the naked urgency in Pauline's voice.

Elvira was doing this for Terence. But Pauline would be doing it for herself. Elvira angrily brushed her own tears for Terence away. Life was like this. Who knew better than a crime-writer?

'He agrees,' repeated Elvira. 'I don't think he's got much choice now. He sees – he sees it will help Nicky of course, if he tells the story right. But I think he also sees now that it's the only way he can help himself. Anyway, yes, he agrees.'

'To *everything*?'

'Yes Pauly, to everything.'

Pauline let out a long, long sigh, as if she had been holding her breath for weeks. 'Aaaaaaah,' she sighed. 'Aaaah, good.'

Elvira heard the sigh. 'You're *sure* you can do it Pauly? It won't be easy, so much will depend on you – and Terence will almost certainly go to jail if we don't get this right, never mind your own hopes and dreams. It's much much harder than you think to stand up there in the way you're going to have to. You'll have to be tough under lots of pressure.'

'I'm tough,' said Pauline. 'Rehearse me tomorrow night. I'll be wearing my red lipstick.'

When she'd put the phone down she stood there for a moment in the warm hall of the house she had so loved. It had been snowing again. From where she stood she could look out across the river, white flakes drifted silently across the lawn in the darkness. Not regret, but memory hovered there in the night on the stairs: the life she had made for herself and her family.

One more Sunday lunch. She had left a note for Viola

in her room earlier in the week: *Darling, do try and be here for Sunday lunch. I'd love to see your face to see if I remember it.* The roast beef and the peach pie waited in the big refrigerator to do their last duty.

There would be other lives.

Pauline O'Brien found she was smiling in the empty hall. And then she walked slowly upstairs in her blue silk dressing gown to the bedroom where her husband snored loudly.

She pored over the Sunday papers while the roast beef was cooking and the snow fell steadily on the lawn outside. Sunday papers were part of the Bonham Sunday. During the week they only had the *Independent* and the *Mail* delivered; they kept tabs on their profession with the Sunday papers. She read reports of the trial in the *Observer*, the *Independent on Sunday*, the *Sunday Times*, the *Sunday Telegraph*, the *Mail on Sunday*, the *Sunday Express* and the *News of the World*. As Elvira had said, everyone of them, the more responsible papers less overtly, somehow seemed to imply that Terence was guilty. Of course he would deny it, Mike Tyson had denied it also. Too many people in the Dorchester had seen Terence arriving with Miss X then leaving the hotel in the middle of the night, many of whom the Prosecution had called as witnesses.

The Under-Manager of the Dorchester, a very reluctant witness (furious that the top people's hotel, a haven of class and service and privacy, was being dragged into the gutter in this way, nothing like this had happened to the Dorchester, he said, since Elizabeth Taylor nearly died of pneumonia there and he was aghast at the publicity), had been scathing of Terence's intoxication on arrival and his rather manic behaviour in the Michelin-starred Cantonese restaurant: shaking hands with all sorts of people whether they wanted to be shook or not.

BLUE VERDICT TOMORROW? said the *Mail on Sunday* in big black letters.

It was clear from the court reports that the most damning witness of all was the Italian room-service waiter. He took to Miss X's suite the bottle of whisky they had ordered. When he brought the tray with the whisky and the glasses and the ice into the room the waiter had been thrilled to recognise Terence and had asked him for his autograph. Terence had his shoes off and his coat off and all the buttons of his shirt undone and his belt undone and his fly buttons undone and he was lying back on one of the sofas when Miss X had answered the door. He had signed a napkin with a pen between his teeth, and had slapped Miss X's posterior while reaching for the whisky. *'E wassa once my 'ero*, the room-service waiter had said in great disappointment, *now he is justa drunk*. There was a sad little coda to the court report in both the *Mail* and the *News of the World*, of Miss X suddenly leaving the court during this last evidence, as if at last it was all too much for her.

At no time in his cross-examination of prosecution witnesses, said the *Independent on Sunday* in a formal court report that somehow managed to sound disapproving, had the defence barrister sought to imply that Ms Taylor might be a willing party to the sexual event, a more fruitful path surely, the paper implied, than merely reiterating that when Mr Blue left the hotel room Ms Taylor was passed out on the bed. There was much covert criticism of Terence Blue's legal team in many of the newspapers: it was felt they had not put up a proper case at all. Simply denying a rape was not a defence. Terence Blue should have taken the witness stand.

It seemed a foregone conclusion that he would be convicted.

Engrossed in the newspapers in the warm kitchen, with the smell of the lunch cooking, a sherry in her hand, most of all knowing that this evening she would be rehearsing her own part in the trial for the following day, Pauline didn't hear the front door open, heard only vaguely voices in the hall, coats being hung up, shoes being removed.

'Hello Mum.'

She looked up finally to see her daughter Viola standing a little shyly at the kitchen door. Next to her, his arm resting round her shoulder was Banjo Mitchell, Molly McKenzie's young man.

'Good God!' said Pauline.

'I know,' said Viola.

Lunch was electric. Both Pauline and Anthony, for different reasons, were completely thrown by the appearance of Molly's lover at the dinner table with their daughter.

Pauline, shocked, at once saw that this could be her final triumph over Molly at last; nevertheless had her suspicions that somehow even this was part of Anthony's grand plan; therefore felt strangely elated that tomorrow he would find out that she had a grand plan of her own. She drank more wine, very quickly. Anthony tried, not very hard and not very successfully, to hide his anger. To have this man at his dinner table, his mistress's lover with an arm round his beloved daughter was deeply sexually disturbing. Anthony literally could not bear it. He ate quickly, anxious to get away to Soho where he was recording voice-overs for four different commercials. Benedict remembered that this was the man at the garden party who had stopped him punching his father and that his father called this man *Molly McKenzie's toyboy*; Viola was shy but determined.

Only Banjo seemed unfazed. Although he was a vegetarian, so smoothly did he bypass the beef and so obviously did he enjoy the roast vegetables and the peach pie and cream, so interestingly did he mention to Benedict about computers and music, that a bizarre kind of normality prevailed across the fraught table. They even managed to have a few sentences of conversation about the Terence Blue rape case, the likelihood of him being sentenced, how a film star would fare in prison.

As Anthony stood up to leave while the others were still eating the peach pie, he said, very crossly, 'How did you two meet?'

'When we were first planning our fringe show,' said Viola, her face animated with love. 'Well I've told you Daddy, it's *Look Back in Anger* but *us* looking back at it, there's music and movement as well as acting, well, we realised we needed some really really special music and we racked our brains about who could help us and then

I remembered Banjo and I knew I could find him at Auntie—' She stopped abruptly, just for a second.

The silence in the room was absolute. Viola recovered first. 'He's doing it wonderfully,' she continued finally, smiling at Banjo. 'You should see what a saxophone and a computer can do together,' so that Molly McKenzie, hovering there in all their minds as they sat there around the table, only hovered still, was not actually mentioned, at the Bonham family's last Sunday lunch.

Anthony was gone, slamming the front door; Benedict, suddenly voluble, pleaded with Banjo to come to look at Jeremy's computers just for twenty minutes, *cyberpunk man that's what we're interested in*, they had an electric guitar there, they could show Banjo what they were doing. Banjo smiled, kissed Viola's hair *only twenty minutes* and was gone. So that Pauline and Viola sat alone at the table, the remains of the Sunday lunch everywhere about them.

'I love him Mum,' said Viola. 'I've never felt like this in my life before.'

'He's – he seems a very nice person,' said Pauline slowly. 'But I – hope you'll take time to get to know him properly.'

'We're going to get married.'

Pauline, for a moment thinking only of Viola, tried to tread carefully around her daughter's dreams.

'Darling – there's plenty of time. Perhaps you could live together first, see how things go.' (*Oh how things have changed*, she thought, *since I had to get married*.)

'He wants to get married now, have children.'

'Viola, darling, remember what happened to me,'

Pauline said urgently. 'You're only just starting out on the most difficult career in the world; this profession needs all of your energy if you are to survive.'

'I can start out with Banjo just as well as starting out on my own.'

'Not if you have children.'

'Banjo will share looking after them.'

'It doesn't *work* like that, you think it will but it won't.'

'It will with Banjo,' said Viola serenely. 'You can't compare him to Dad. He's a different generation and they see things differently, you'll see, we're going to do lots of work together.' She chattered away about their plans.

Finally Pauline could not help herself. 'What does Molly say? What does she feel about all this?' And casually, 'Was it her decision, breaking with Banjo, or was it his?'

'He – he won't –' Viola was uncertain for the first time '– speak about it,' standing up abruptly, clearing the table. 'He says he can't speak about it just now. We'll talk about it one day. But of course –' and Viola busied herself at the bench, scraping plates, gathering cutlery, her own doubts in this area resolved in her own mind, banished, '– it couldn't have gone on, could it?'

And just for a moment, there was the same icy glitter around the eyes of the daughter. 'Surely Auntie Moll couldn't have expected it to go on forever? She must've known it couldn't. I've always loved her of course, ever since I was a little girl but – she's – well she's always been a bit of a bohemian hasn't she, she's never led an ordinary life, she's never *settled*. How could Banjo be happy with her in the long run?' Viola briskly ran hot water to rinse the plates.

'Of course,' said Pauline. And she wondered: as Molly was presumably having an affair with Anthony presumably she wasn't suffering. *But what if she was, what if this wasn't what she'd wanted, what if Pauline's daughter had broken her heart? What if Molly was actually suffering as she, Pauline, had once suffered so desperately in a two-roomed flat in Vauxhall nearly thirty years ago?*

She took out her red lipstick. 'I have to go out in a little while,' she said to Viola.

Nevertheless, as they were stacking the dishes into the dishwasher, as Banjo's green van appeared, as he ran up the path with a scarf round his neck past the snow-covered rose bushes, Pauline suddenly put her arms around her daughter.

'Don't throw everything away darling,' she said, 'for love. It's never worth it, in the end.'

'Of course not Mum,' said Viola, hugging her mother briefly. 'Really, you don't understand,' not thinking just now of anything but her own happiness, running to the front door to let Banjo into the warm Sunday afternoon house, running to meet her love.

Her mother turned the dishwasher on and placed the remains of the peach pie in the refrigerator. She then went quietly, unobserved, to where her pink Mercedes stood in the garage.

She was an actress, and she was going to a rehearsal.

THIRTY-FOUR

Next morning at 10 am the case in Court Number Ten in the Old Bailey was reconvened. Another case was scheduled to begin there later in the day when this one was over, as it was expected to be. The court rose as the judge, her cold obviously worse, walked in; sat, as she put her throat pastilles and her small box of tissues on the bench beside her. The prosecuting barrister had spent the weekend in bed, his voice sounded better. The court stenographer, whose sneezing had been a part of the proceedings the past week, had been replaced.

Terence Blue's barrister stood up again almost at once.

'My Lady,' said Mr Tweed. 'I would like permission to call a further witness for the defence. New evidence has come to light that reflects on my client's case.'

There was a rumble of conversation in the courtroom, people turning to one another in surprise. They thought they had come for the summing up. After some further discussion, eliciting the fact that this new evidence was not an alibi for the defendant, it was agreed by the judge that this was possible.

'My Lady,' said Mr Tweed, 'I would like to call Pauline O'Brien.'

Tall and beautiful and pale, in the same cream-coloured and elegant suit that she had worn the one and only time she had met her father, and wearing bright red lipstick, the actress daughter of a trapeze artist appeared from a side door and entered the court room.

After Pauline had sworn on the Bible, after the judge, blowing her nose, had courteously invited Pauline, as she had invited all witnesses, to sit down in the witness box, Mr Tweed began.

'You are the actress Pauline O'Brien?'

'Yes.'

'How long have you known the defendant Terence Blue?'

'Since nineteen fifty-nine, we were students at the London Academy of Drama together.'

'Miss O'Brien,' said Mr Tweed, 'you have come to this court this morning in Mr Blue's defence because you are privy to some knowledge that you feel means that he is not guilty of the rape of Simone Taylor.'

'Yes.'

'Would you, in your own words, please give that information to the court.'

'Mr Blue,' said Pauline O'Brien, actress, in careful well-modulated actress's tones (not looking at Terence, looking at the jury), 'Mr Blue –' and she took a deep breath and leapt into the unknown '– is impotent.'

In the split second before the uproar in the court room, before journalists, unable to believe their ears, quite literally jumped over the press desks and out into the corridors to use their mobile phones, in that split second Terence Blue, actor, leapt up in the dock.

'That's a lie!' he shouted at Pauline. 'THAT IS A LIE!'

'Silence in court!' cried the judge, banging the gavel as the reporters ran, '*Silence!* The defendant will immediately be arraigned for contempt of court, and I am now going to consider holding the rest of this trial *in camera*. I will not have my court made a circus of in this way.'

There was chaos. Journalists ran everywhere, the prosecution lawyer was on his feet, Terence was being restrained in the dock by the uniformed guard who, as the trial recommenced, had been quietly reading a lurid paperback with a naked woman on the front. The judge was pink-faced with anger. And Elvira noted that Simone Taylor was as white as a sheet.

'This court is adjourned while I confer with my legal colleagues,' cried the judge and she stood up sweeping up her pastilles and her tissues; the clerk of the court shouted ALL RISE above the hubbub. Elvira stood quietly in the crowded public gallery while all around her people talked excitedly, foreigners asking all about them with puzzled expressions for elucidation of the word *impotent*.

Terence was taken out through his padded door past the grilled liftwell, down the concrete steps; the judge walked through her padded door to fawn-coloured carpets, a little lie-down and even perhaps, in the circumstances, a very early-morning gin. It was 10.47 am.

Anthony Bonham was again filming in Devon. The driver who had been appointed to drive him everywhere, including back to Stratford if he had a performance in the evening, was new to the business. He heard the news on his car radio, that the rape case of the famous Terence Blue had been adjourned because of sensational new developments, even mentioned the fact to Anthony who only grunted: he was sick to the teeth of hearing everybody talking about Terence Blue. But the driver didn't know that Pauline O'Brien was Anthony's wife, had never heard of her. Anthony was having a warming whisky in his caravan while his dresser fetched him a scone from the butty-wagon when the first assistant put his head around the door.

'Your wife's caused a sensation!'

'What?' Anthony's glass was halfway to his lips.

The first assistant looked a little confused. 'Well – I presumed you knew of course. The trial's been stopped.'

'What trial?'

'Terence Blue's trial. There's been a newsflash. Your wife's just been in the witness box saying he couldn't have done the rape because he's impotent.'

'WHAT?' Anthony lunged up towards the door, banging his knee on the corner of the caravan table. 'JESUS CHRIST!' at the news, at the pain in his leg.

'Here, here, have my radio,' said the first assistant, leaving swiftly.

Anthony turned to Radio 4 but they spoke of Bosnia.

He found a local radio station but they spoke of a Devon man who had invented a new kind of Christmas rose.

By 11.30 am there had been fistfights between journalists for the press desks in Court Number Ten at the Old Bailey. Elvira had, wisely, arranged for Stu's chauffeur to queue outside the court while she also had an early gin alone and made some phone calls.

Terence Blue was in the police area downstairs where his lawyer impressed upon him in front of a policeman the importance of apologising to the judge, of never interrupting again, or he would be kept not on bail but in custody for the rest of the trial.

Pauline O'Brien had a cup of tea and seemed to be quietly reading the *Independent* but her heart was beating like a drum.

When the court sitting resumed Mr Tweed, barrister for the defence, was on his feet at once.

'My Lady,' he said, 'my client wishes to unreservedly apologise for his outburst earlier this morning. He deeply regrets the incident.'

'I take note of the apology,' said the judge rather sourly. 'One would have thought Mr Tweed that your client would have been appraised of evidence being brought in his defence,' and she gave the defence lawyer a long, shrewd look, and then looked briefly at Terence, staring at the ground in the long dock.

'Before this trial goes any further I want to address this court. You are all, I am sure, aware of the remarks made about this trial by the Lord Chancellor and the Director of Public Prosecutions before it began. If there is a single further disturbance – and I mean a *single* further disturbance – I will have no hesitation in excluding the press and the public from the rest of this trial and holding the defendant in custody. I hope I make myself clear.'

Pauline was brought back to the witness stand in her cream suit.

'Miss O'Brien,' said Mr Tweed briskly, 'you made an extraordinary statement in this court this morning. Would you please elucidate.'

Pauline cleared her throat slightly and pushed at her dark hair. It was clear she was nervous. She wasn't quite sure who to address: the jury, the judge, the barrister. Finally, to the defence barrister she told the story that she and Terence and Elvira had agreed upon.

'I have known Mr Blue since I was a drama student. We have always been good friends, our families have been friends, one of Mr Blue's ex-wives is godmother to my son.

'I sometimes (*it's got to be* domestic *Elvira had said, gardening will make it sound domestic and boring, otherwise you'll sound like a luvvie*) go and work in Mr Blue's garden in Hampstead. Sometimes we both work in it, we both enjoy gardening. Some weeks before the reunion, we were working together in his garden, you remember how hot it was, and we stopped for a cold drink and I suddenly saw that Terence – Mr Blue – who was sitting on the steps leading up to his back door was – crying.'

'Mr Blue was crying?'

'Yes.'

'Why?'

'I asked him why. After quite a long time he admitted to me that he had this problem, that he – had had it for some time, that he was –' and she hesitated for a moment before using such an emotive word again '– impotent.'

Again disturbances on the press benches, but quickly self-regulated as the judge looked across. Terence Blue, sitting absolutely motionless in the centre of the long prisoner's dock, stared down at the floor.

The prosecuting barrister ostentatiously raised his eyes to the ceiling, sighed theatrically, made some notes on a pad in front of him.

'Did he know the cause of this – um –' Mr Tweed seemed at a loss for a moment, '– this – ailment?'

'He seemed to, yes.'

'What did he say?'

It was Elvira who had finally said to Terence what she had guessed to Pauline. *Is it something to do with Nicky, Terence darling, that has caused this – illness of yours?* At last Terence had answered her: *yes.*

And Elvira had sighed with relief, now she could see how the story must be told.

So Pauline embarked on that story. 'At first Mr Blue was not willing to discuss it but at last he said that his first wife whom he had loved dearly had lived for many years in a mental hospital. Although Mr Blue had supported her financially since the early sixties he was never allowed to see her, the psychiatrists at the hospital had advised him that his presence was actually a danger to her. In the spring of this year she had on the best advice of psychiatrists been released into – community care I believe it is called – but the doctors had *specifically* got in touch with Mr Blue and asked him, for her sake, not to try to see her, even now, even more than thirty years later. This – this had deeply disturbed Mr Blue, who – or so it seemed to me – felt some guilt about her illness although he did not – elucidate on this; he wanted so much to see her and his – trouble – had begun at this time.'

'His impotence?'

'His impotence yes.'

Terence Blue stared at the floor.

'Had he seen a doctor about this complaint?'

'He said – he said that he felt very embarrassed, that he had gone and looked up – the complaint – in the library and had been able to find almost nothing about it, as if it didn't really exist, except in his mind. His – reputation is built upon his sex appeal, everybody knows that. He couldn't face going to a doctor.'

'And why are you telling the whole world about it in that case? Isn't this revelation damaging to his career?'

'Not,' said Pauline O'Brien firmly, 'as damaging as being convicted for a rape he didn't commit. I don't know what happened to Simone, who was also in our class at the Academy. She was –' Pauline chose her words carefully, remembering how the Scottish comic had somehow lost sympathy for Terence by making the court laugh at Simone Taylor '– very fond of Terence I think.' And Pauline looked across to the place in the court where Simone, dark glasses and fur coat, was sitting palely, staring at Pauline. 'I don't believe she would – put herself through this if she hadn't been raped and I am very sorry. But I not only don't believe Terence would have raped her, I don't believe he *could* have raped her because of the information I have just given you, and I felt that it was my duty in the circumstances to tell the court what I know.'

'Thank you Miss O'Brien, no further questions,' said Mr Tweed.

Elvira had warned Pauline over and over that now the hard part would begin. Pauline O'Brien Bonham licked her red lips nervously.

The prosecuting barrister Mr Lee did not leap to his feet to begin the cross examination; lumbered upright rather, again sighing loudly. He had had time, when the court had briefly adjourned, to do his homework. He blew his nose, took a long time putting his handkerchief in his pocket.

'Miss O'Brien, or perhaps I should call you Mrs Bonham, you surely do not expect the court to believe this farrago of lies.'

Pauline looked at him. 'A farrago is – a medley I believe,' she said.

Mr Lee stared at a point on the wall above the judge's bench, did not look at his witness. 'A medley, yes, in this case a cheap, ugly mixture.'

'I have only said that Mr Blue is impotent. I do not believe that is a medley.'

'In my long experience as a barrister I cannot remember a time where for sheer cheek a witness has invented so much unlikely rubbish as we have heard from you today. Discussing impotence among the nasturtiums, *please*!' He looked around the court as if garnering support for his disbelief. 'Impotence. What is impotence? A state of mind that comes and goes. The defendant him-self, according to you, said he could only find brief reference to it in medical encyclopaedias. Impotence can be connected to an illness, a by-product of an illness, but it isn't an illness itself, it is a psychological state that comes and goes, I repeat, *comes and goes*. How conve-nient, if we could say it was present at the Dorchester on the night in question, this Impotence. How would you know, how would *anybody* know except the people con-cerned when and where it occurred. It's not like measles you know, this Impotence. Presumably you are invent-ing this story to try to save the skin of a rapist who happens to be –' he loaded the next word '– an acquain-tance of yours. For, Miss O'Brien – or perhaps I should call you Mrs Bonham – I find it hard to believe that the defendant would suddenly tell you all this during a little gardening afternoon, unless – of course – your relation-ship with him was of a different nature than the one you have presented to the court?'

Everybody in the court leant forward.

Mr Lee made Pauline O'Brien sound like yet another show business luvvie cashing in on having an affair with a star. He became extremely personal as he stared not at her but at a point above her head and asked her how successful she was as an actress. He said it was well-known in show-business circles that her career was in the doldrums. He asked if she was hoping for publicity from this case. He skirted daintily around her marriage, asked if Anthony Bonham, the well-known Shakes-pearean actor, was also a close friend of Mr Blue's. Pauline's face became paler and paler in the witness box, her red lips lost their colour as she bit at them in distress. It was as if Pauline was on trial instead of Terence; on and on Mr Lee's sarcastic voice went, attacking her personally, waiting for her to break. Sometimes Pauline's voice shook as she answered but she stuck to her story. *Oh god*, she thought, *this will look so disgusting all over the* News of the World, *this had all better be worth it.* He was a devastating cross-examiner and Pauline, cool, elegant Pauline O'Brien, was not used to being cross-examined, hesitated sometimes, made a mistake, back-tracked. In any other situation, using the pejorative term *luvvie* many times to good effect, Mr Lee might have broken his witness.

But Mr Lee didn't know just how much hinged, for this witness, in her not breaking in front of him.

And Mr Lee didn't know that Pauline was only the supporting role, paving the way for Terence Blue to tell his story and to protect Nicky Abbott.

Elvira had insisted that Terence intervene when Pauline began her testimony. The whole court had heard Terence's interjection *it's a lie*; saw him, the old sex-symbol sitting staring at the floor in the dock with one arm in a sling, sometimes his head resting in his good hand, being described in that shameful, devastating one word feared by men above all other words – *impotent*. In a way Mr Lee's cross-examination of Pauline, although so cruel and so enjoyable, seemed almost irrelevant. People wanted Terence Blue to speak now. They wanted to hear what this famous film star would say.

Just before Mr Lee said *no further questions*, just

before he was ready to flourish to his seat, his face registering disbelief and scorn, Pauline leant towards him in the witness box, gathering herself together despite the way he had tried to tear her apart, despite the way she was now openly shaking. Suddenly understanding just how much hinged not for herself but for Terence on the outcome of this case, she said in a clear voice, 'It has not been pleasant for me to have been attacked in this way by you Mr Lee, in public. But I think it must be much worse for Mr Blue. You wouldn't like to have your sexual inadequacies discussed in court Mr Lee any more than Mr Blue does I expect. How can anyone believe a person would go through this if he didn't have to.' There was a murmur around the courtroom.

'No further questions,' said Mr Lee coldly.

'My Lady,' said the defence barrister, getting up quickly, 'I would like an adjournment in order that I may speak to my client.'

'The court is adjourned,' said the judge, 'until two-thirty this afternoon.'

Only Terence and his barrister and Elvira were in the small, impersonal room beside the courtroom.

'Are you ready?' said the barrister.

Elvira looked with old affection at Terence Blue's pale, drawn face. 'It's out in the open now darling,' she said, 'use it.'

And Terence Blue, one of the most famous men in the world, who had stubbornly resisted, who knew so well how it would be used – IMPOTENT FILM STAR RAPIST:

headlines all over the world for a crime he hadn't committed – felt at last that he had nothing left to lose.

Except Nicky.

And just before he nodded his head in bleak, stoic agreement he thought: *Yes. I do know the meaning of love.*

And so at 2.30 pm, finally, after all and against expectations, Terence Blue was called by his own barrister to the witness stand.

He walked rather slowly and heavily from the dock to the other end of the courtroom; Reuters, ITN, BBC, CNN, they were all there as well as every British crime and show-business reporter that could jam into the press boxes or the public gallery.

When he swore by Almighty God, Terence looked rather bemusedly at the card on which the words were written that he held in his good hand. What his eighty-year-old Welsh Chapel father was making of all this, although he had tried to warn him of some of it, he could not imagine. *Nothing but the truth,* he said, giving the words a kind of resonance and new meaning.

'You may sit down if you wish Mr Blue,' said the judge quietly.

'Thank you My Lady, but I prefer to stand.' He stood there, waiting.

Mr Tweed only said finally, gently, 'Is it true?'

Terence Blue, grey-haired and gaunt and handsome in the witness box, with his left arm in a sling, looked (the *Daily Express* had said that morning) like a wounded lion. He stared down at the wooden handrail; with his right hand he smoothed it for a moment. There was absolute silence in the court.

Then he finally answered, his Welsh voice clearly heard.

'It is – temporarily – true, sir, yes.'

And it seemed to Elvira that a soft, collective sigh seemed to echo round the courtroom, the word *temporarily* somehow putting him in touch with, echoing in the minds of, everybody there. All the men: all the lawyers and the legal clerks and the men on the jury and the hard-drinking hard-bitten journalists; all the women: the legal secretaries and the consultative lawyer for the prosecution and the women in the public gallery and on the jury. *Temporarily*. The soft sigh seemed to enclose the man in the witness box as if they were saying, *we know*. As if they were saying, *we all know how it can be, temporarily*.

'Was it true the night in question, the night of the alleged rape of Miss Taylor?'

'It was most certainly true the night in question. I had just seen, that afternoon, my first wife for the first time in over thirty years.'

The court stirred, but Mr Tweed was like a conductor, not ready yet, for the crescendo; he actually put up his hand as if to say: wait.

'Mr Blue, is it true as Miss O'Brien stated earlier that this – affliction of yours, this temporary affliction, was brought on by news of your first wife?'

'Yes.'

'Tell me Mr Blue, why was your first wife in a mental hospital for so long?'

Terence, prepared though he was for this line of questioning, familiar though he was with the answers he knew so well, agreeing as he finally had that this way Nicky could almost certainly be kept out of court, suddenly stared down – at his arm in the sling, at his black shoes, at the floor of the witness box. And Elvira in the public gallery could feel it: the constriction suddenly in his heart, desire and memory and pain and silence of thirty years.

She caught her breath in fear, she wanted to call across the balcony *Terry, we agreed Terry, we agreed, this is the only way, it's for Nicky too remember. Tell them the truth.*

Terence Blue knew he would tell the truth. But not the whole truth.

At last, he began to speak.

'When my first wife was a schoolgirl her mother was very very ill and in very great pain, with cancer. She would scream to be put out of her misery and one night, wanting to save her further pain she – my wife – I mean my ex-wife – put a pillow over her mother's face until she was dead. She was sixteen. She somehow managed to – put this memory away until – until—' Terence's voice was suddenly husky. The court leant forward, anxious; even the judge had stopped making notes, had moved her body forward slightly on the bench.

'Until,' prompted Mr Tweed very quietly.

'Until we – lost our daughter.'

'How did you lose your daughter?'

'In a car—' he hesitated for a moment. *I cannot tell them how the accident happened, I cannot tell them that.* 'In a car accident. In nineteen sixty-one. I was driving.' A sigh around the court. 'She – she miscarried. And was also very badly hurt in the crash. At the hospital they told me – it was a girl. Of course it was my fault. She was in a coma for several months. When she – when she finally regained consciousness she could only talk – she seemed only to remember – not about the baby, but about her mother. Somehow the incidents became muddled in her mind. She was very, very ill and, as she recovered from the accident, she unexpectedly became for some time very –' his voice faltered '– violent.'

'She was put in an – institution?'

'That's what they were called in the sixties, yes. I thought it would just be temporary, a big hospital in London, just for a few weeks I thought. But she – she seemed unable to recover, or recognise anything, or me. When – when you wait so long for someone you love so much to come out of a coma it is not as you expect, you can't just sit at the bedside and explain and apologise, it – it doesn't work like that. And the hospital was so – impersonal and big and – I – I didn't like things that were happening. I began earning quite a lot of money at about this time so I had her moved to a small private mental hospital, they called it a nursing home, which I believed was less involved in . . .' Terence swallowed several times, '. . . physical restraint. I thought it would be better for her.'

With his good hand, he pulled at his collar. 'But the doctors in that private hospital wanted to give her electric shock therapy. They wanted to – jolt her brain. I would not agree, I would not let them – interfere with her brain, it seemed so barbaric, and just – wrong. They

could not do it without my permission because I was
her husband. As soon as I found a more suitable private
place I moved her again.

'At first I thought this third hospital was a very good
place, she became much calmer almost at once and I
believed at last that she was getting better. But bit by bit
I realised that the doctors there thought – that I was bad
for her, that it was bad for her to see me, that it hindered
her recovery *that everything was my fault*. The psychiatrist
in charge there – he actually owned the nursing home –
who had seemed such a good influence when I first took
her there – well, I found it harder and harder to – to get
on with him.' And Terence sighed with a kind of self-
knowledge.

'Unfortunately I once – hit him and broke one of his
teeth. It was unforgivable of course but I felt so – frus-
trated and angry and useless. He wanted to have me
charged with assault but was persuaded by others at the
hospital to hush it up, but he never forgave me. He made
everything as difficult for me as possible, said that she
did not know me, that she did not want to see me, that
her wishes must be respected and that I should keep
away. I – I of course wanted to move her away, to
another hospital but – she had become so much calmer
there, I would have been a fool not to see that, I really
thought she would soon be better.' Again Terence pulled
almost violently at his collar with his good hand, as if
trying to free himself from his memories.

'And I could see that I couldn't keep moving and
moving her for my own satisfaction. Over and over
again they told me it was best that I kept away. I was

twenty-four years old and they seemed so much older and wiser than me and I felt so much to blame. And of course I knew I must do what was best for her, not what was best for me. I still thought it was only temporary. But after about a year I saw – that they meant it to be permanent.' Nobody in the court could miss the pain in the voice of the man in the dock.

'You support her?'

'Yes.'

'You have supported her since that accident in nineteen sixty-one?'

'Yes. Of course. For years I thought that she would be better. But the years just – drifted into each other, and nothing seemed to change. Finally the psychiatrist told me that she would never get better, that she would have to live in a hospital for the rest of her life, and that if I loved her I would leave her alone. That that would be the way I could prove my love for her.'

Terence's voice faltered. He was silent for a moment but his barrister simply waited and when Terence spoke again his tone was again flat and unemotional, as he had tried so hard to keep it throughout his evidence. 'After about – fifteen years I got a divorce. I never actually saw her, and finally it seemed – only quixotic to stay married after all that time. It seemed that I needed to get on with a life of my own and leave my – my wife to hers. And that seemed to – be the end of it.'

'Although you still supported her?'

'Of course.'

'And she was released into the, um, care of the community at the beginning of this year?'

'You know the current thinking,' said Terence and a note of bitterness crept into his voice. 'In April of this year the manager of the hospital wrote to me, said that it was now – accepted psychiatric practice to try and integrate even long-term patients into the community. We – we had a house in Brighton that became hers after the divorce, I wanted her to be able to sell it for financial security if she ever needed to. But they said she would be *living* there. *Living in that house*.

'I thought it was a *terrible* idea, it was in Brighton where everything happened, I went to see them at once. But the same old psychiatrists were still there, including the owner, the one I had attacked, he said I had no rights over her, that I had been divorced from her for years and that she was his responsibility not mine. He said they knew what was best for her and that there were very good community psychiatric nurses in Brighton who could help her better than I could ever hope to. And – and he said I could not see her, *even then*, asked me specifically not to try and see her, that's why the hospital had got in touch with me he said. He said, even now, even *thirty years later*, I would be damaging to her, and I couldn't help feeling that he – he had got in touch with me to – still remind me that I was to blame. He said that it was best to let her – rebuild her life. Best for her. He didn't want me he said *hanging about Brighton*, that's how he phrased it exactly.'

'And you minded about this.'

'*Of course!*' For the first time Terence's blue eyes flashed. 'Of course I minded, and I hit him again.' There was a murmur of something – approval? laughter? –

around the court, quickly silenced by a look from the judge. Terence seemed not to have heard.

'I always thought, all those years, that I would at least see her again one day, somehow be able to talk to her –' and he hesitated for a moment '– explain things. You see she was unconscious for a long time, months, and – we never talked afterwards. We never ever talked after the – accident. I wanted to talk to her. Finally I asked if I could at least send a car, help her to move to Brighton. They said it wasn't necessary, everything had already been organised.' Terence's voice had become almost inaudible but suddenly it became angry and strong.

'I wondered at the time why the psychiatrist hadn't had me charged with assault this second time. Then I found that the bastard had already sold the hospital for millions to a sports club and that all the patients were being moved out, community care or not. He went to live in the south of France I believe. Don't suppose he wanted any publicity.'

'And your – affliction began? Then, in the spring?'

'Yes. It was as if – even thirty years later – I had some-how failed her still. And this feeling of absolute failure –' he made a tired little gesture with his hand '– manifested itself physically, in the way you now know. In the way –' and he grimaced to himself '– in the way *everybody* now knows.'

'And continued?'

'Yes.'

'So the night you went to the Dorchester with Simone Taylor you could not have raped her.'

'I could not have,' said Terence – and for a moment he

flared again in anger, 'even if I had wanted to. I just wanted to be somewhere, anywhere, and drink and drink and drink. I had just seen my wife after more than thirty years,' he saw again the empty, sunny street outside the Academy, 'and then lost her again.' For a moment he didn't speak. There was not a sound in the court, not a cough, not a rustle.

Mr Tweed had to take Terence where he was leading him.

'Mr Blue, this has been a difficult day for you I know but I would like to ask you one more question. Newspaper reports show that your first wife was the TV actress Betty Bailey to whom you were married for six months when you were already forty but I don't think this is the woman we are talking about. I believe you were actually first married when you were twenty-four.'

'Yes,' said Terence dully.

'What was her name?'

'Mary Shand,' he said woodenly, the name used at the mental hospital, pain back in his heart.

Elvira leant forward suddenly, and her bag dropped on the wooden floor beside her. The echoing bang after the silence in the court made Terence jump slightly and he looked back over his shoulder for a second, up to the public gallery where the noise had come from.

Then he shook himself.

'She is also known, my first wife, as Nicola Abbott,' he said. 'She was – an actress.'

'Who – attacked you in Brighton recently?'

'Yes.'

'Did you go then after all, Mr Blue, to find her?'

'I – thought she needed me.'

'So you had ignored the psychiatrists' instructions to you?'

'I couldn't help it. Yes,' said Terence Blue. 'But I had a feeling that maybe she needed me after all, that maybe all the doctors were wrong after all. That maybe she had come to the reunion because she – did want to see me, after all, that the doctors had got everything wrong.' And he looked down at the floor of the witness stand. *I can never tell them how it was when we were young.* And then he said what he had planned to say.

'I frightened her,' he said. 'It was my fault. She stabbed me because I frightened her.'

The silence in the court was absolute.

Finally Mr Tweed said very gently, 'Mr Blue what happened in Simone Taylor's room in the Dorchester the night of that reunion?'

And Terence made an odd, disjointed gesture with his good hand, across his eyes, as if he needed to do that to bring his mind back to the present. He sighed very slightly before he answered.

'As I said in my statement to the police that was read to the court, we drank a lot in Simone's room, but I was not in a state of undress as has been implied by the waiter who brought us more whisky, I don't know why he said that, it wasn't true. I couldn't *get* drunk properly that night no matter how hard I tried. At some stage Simone passed out, on her bed, sometime late in the evening. She was actually –' and Terence sounded almost apologetic '– snoring. I left her there and drove home to my house in Hampstead. The first I knew of any rape was when the police came to my home at about six o'clock the following evening and said they were arresting me and took me to St John's Wood police station. I did not rape Simone, I understand that something must have happened to her after I left the Dorchester but *I did not rape her.*' And for the very first time he turned to where Simone was sitting. 'You know that Simone,' he said.

She looked at him, dark glasses hiding the expression in her eyes.

He turned away, closed his eyes very briefly.

'No further questions,' said Mr Tweed.

Bits of Terence Blue's life had fallen into place to the people who were sitting in the courtroom, *so that's why he was attacked, it wasn't that he was trying to rape someone else, he had a mad wife.* Even the judge seemed subdued, caught up in the story.

The cross-examination of Terence Blue that followed as the winter dusk fell was something of an anticlimax: there was no new information, only a going-over of the old. He answered everything in a dull, quiet voice.

The prosecuting barrister Mr Lee said, over and over again, that this myth of impotence had been set up so that Terence would be acquitted of rape; even if Mr Blue was found to be impotent in a medical test, *how could it be proved that he was impotent at the time of the rape?* He reminded the jury that there was no question of Miss Taylor not being raped: who did it if not the man who was drinking in her hotel room all evening?

Terence answered all the questions put to him in the same dull voice, always coming back to the same theme:

I wouldn't go through all this and have my private life made so glaringly and humiliatingly public if I didn't have to, it seems the only way of proving my innocence.

'But that's the point, it doesn't prove anything. You are doing it to try to get public sympathy.'

'Would you discuss your sexual inadequacies in public if you didn't have to?' snapped Terence finally. 'Have you ever suffered from this ailment Mr Lee?'

The judge leant forward quickly. 'The defendant is not here to question the prosecuting barrister,' she said seeing Mr Lee's face, but quite gently.

'Mr Blue what do you suggest happened to Simone Taylor?' said Mr Lee in a sarcastic, angry voice.

'I don't *know*!' repeated Terence in frustration and he turned again to Simone Taylor. 'What happened Simone?' he said and his face was puzzled as he stared at her. 'You know it wasn't me.' The woman in the fur coat and the dark glasses stared at him silently.

'No further questions,' said Mr Lee.

'I am adjourning the court until 10 am tomorrow morning,' said the judge.

Simone Taylor was the first to leave the courtroom.

Terence's shoulders were slightly hunched, *but at least Nicky will not be brought to trial now, they cannot charge her now, they will understand now*, as he was escorted back along the courtroom and through the padded door, past the concrete stairs and the grilled liftwell.

Anthony Bonham, alone in his dressing room at Stratford-upon-Avon while the young actor playing Hamlet agonised over the tannoy what a rogue and peasant slave he was, listened to a portable radio, read the rather inadequate court reports in the local evening newspaper, could not believe his eyes and his ears.

Molly McKenzie, reading the late edition of the *Evening Standard* in her empty Clapham house and then watching the court report on the television news, was totally bewildered; kept asking herself why Pauline O'Brien – *of all people* – would stand up in a court of law and repeat what Molly had told her in the Chiswick garden, a lifetime ago, when the sun shone. Pauline had advised her not to do such a thing, had become helpless with laughter at the idea. *What had happened?* Thought also of poor, brilliant Nicky Abbott who had, unbeknown to them all, lived most of her life in a mental hospital.

Frances Kitson also watched the television news alone in her small flat in her dressing gown and with wet red hair. She was called at 5.30 next morning, to begin the first of her Triumph Telephone commercials. She thought again of the days when the world was waiting for them all so brightly, when they stalked the country with their make-up boxes under their confident arms, the new young eager class of '59. '*Poor Nicky*,' she said suddenly, '*for such hopes and talent to end like that*.' And then, with a sudden sob in her throat, the way it came upon her when she thought she was all right at last, 'Poor, poor Emmy.'

Harry Donaldson, on location in Dorset, watched the news on the BBC, saw Terence walking heavily to a taxi.

'*So there it all is, at last,*' he said, aloud in his hotel room. There was no mention at all of Juliet or himself, of the key to everything that had happened.

Terence Blue had chosen not to tell the full story.

In Wells-next-the-Sea, Norfolk, an old retired doctor listened to the early evening news on Radio 4 in amazement. The summary of Terence Blue's evidence that the court reporter gave included the story of Mary Shand, now known as Nicola Abbott.

Finally, for he was a deeply moral man, Dr Michael Hardy walked slowly, his rheumatism made it hard for him to walk, into his kitchen and looked up a telephone number. Then he walked down the hall and picked up the telephone. The early editions of the next morning's papers had been put to bed already but the editor of the *Guardian* was still in his office and spoke to the doctor. The conversation went on for a long time and a car was despatched to Norfolk for a signature.

Next morning all over Great Britain *Guardian* readers found an extraordinary story in their newspaper. The headline read: TERENCE BLUE TRIAL: DOCTOR SPEAKS. And Dr Hardy, now retired, once a doctor in Richmond, was interviewed on *Today* on Radio 4.

He repeated what he had told the editor of the *Guardian* the previous evening: that he remembered the case well, Mrs Shand had been suffering so terribly from cancer. One afternoon she had screamed out in a terrible voice to the doctor to save her from what was happening to her. 'I thought I was alone in that basement flat,' said the doctor, 'I thought the girl was at school. The pain was so great, and Mrs Shand's suffering was so terrible that I administered a lethal dose of morphine and knew she would drift into unconsciousness and death that evening. A pillow over her face could have had nothing to do with it.'

'Do you not think Dr Hardy,' said the interviewer on Radio 4, 'that it is rather rash of you, even at this stage so many years later, to admit what you did, which is, after all, murder?'

Dr Hardy's voice crackled from a studio in Norwich where he was wearing headphones that connected him to the BBC in London. 'I did what I thought was right at the time,' he said. 'I am appalled beyond measure that that child thought she was responsible for her mother's death, and has had to live with that misapprehension for so long, and with such terrible consequences. I had no alternative now but to come forward and the law must do with me what it thinks fit.'

The old man was eighty-four.

THIRTY-FIVE

Anthony Bonham, his wife and his name featuring largely in the newspapers and on television and in public places, grimly went on with his work; was picked up by the film car at 5 am from his Stratford cottage where the snow lay now upon the bare honeysuckle branches; carried his mobile telephone in his dressing-gown pocket, in his coat pocket, had it by him in his dressing room, in the studio car, in his location caravan. He was, anyone could see, apoplectic with rage. He telephoned his house again and again and again: his own voice on the answering machine informed him, again and again and again, that he was out.

He'd had a most appalling moment last night in *Hamlet*. Prince Charles had come on a private visit to the theatre, as he often did, accompanied only by one male friend and a couple of bodyguards who had searched the theatre with dogs earlier in the day, as they always did. During the play scene in the middle of *Hamlet*

Anthony's mobile phone, which he'd by mistake put in an inside pocket in his royal cloak, fell to the ground, and as the stage was raked for this production the phone began slipping ominously, making strange clicking noises, towards the audience, many of whom caught sight of it among the Edwardian costumes, including Prince Charles' bodyguards who had simultaneously stood up and walked noisily and single-mindedly towards the stage as the actors went on valiantly acting. Luckily Ophelia plucked the phone up in her skirt as Polonius cried *lights! lights! lights!* and they came off-stage.

'Thank Christ it didn't ring, you wanker,' Ophelia had said to Anthony, flinging it at him angrily.

Now in the car on the way to Devon he threw the offending, useless machine on to the seat beside him, turned on the news on his radio, heard some doctor droning on about the Terence Blue case on the *Today* programme, turned the radio off again. He picked up the phone again, rang Chiswick, then rang Molly's number. She answered almost at once, as if she was expecting someone.

'My God Molly darling *where have you been*? I've been phoning and phoning you, what on earth's happening, why haven't you answered my messages? The world's gone crazy, something's going wrong with *The Immoralists*, what is Pauline doing making a spectacle of herself, I thought it was *you* who found out Terence Blue was fucking impotent, is she using your evidence or what? And what was your toyboy doing at our house with Viola?'

'Banjo was – with *Viola*?' Her voice shook in disbelief.

'At lunch last Sunday with his fucking arm around her shoulders, what's happened? Darling we must meet, God I want you, I've got to see you.'

Very very slowly Molly hung up on her old lover. She stood in her hall with her hand up to her mouth, totally still, like a statue. *No one you know*, Banjo had said. The phone rang again but it rang on and on in the hall in Clapham as Molly stood there.

That same morning, before the trial was reconvened, the first of the mail started arriving for Terence Blue at the Old Bailey. Hundreds and hundreds of letters from sympathetic women and grateful men.

Dear Mr Blue, By bringing our problem out into the open you have allowed myself and my wife to discuss it . . . My lover and I are eternally grateful to you for mentioning this subject in public . . . I am an experienced woman, I'm sure I could help you if you would only telephone me . . . hundreds and hundreds of letters. Terence Blue had suddenly become a different kind of hero. There were photographs of postmen with sacks of mail standing outside the Old Bailey in the snow wearing Christmas holly in their hats.

At 10 am Simone Taylor was recalled by direction of the judge.

'I am sorry Simone,' said the judge, very gently, leaning over the bench towards the witness box, near enough for Simone Taylor to catch the scent of menthol, 'to ask you back into the box like this. I understand what a terrible ordeal this has been for you but we must be sure. Are you certain it was Terence Blue who raped you?'

'He raped me, it was him,' she insisted in her high, girlish voice. 'How could Terence Blue be impotent? Everyone knows he couldn't be impotent, he isn't impotent, he kissed me, I loved him.' She was now in such a state of terrible distress that even Elvira in the public gallery couldn't help feeling sorry for her. She broke down several times, especially when the defence pressed her about the state of her inebriation that night and whether she remembered Terence leaving. The clerk of the court brought her lots of glasses of water. She never once, Elvira noted, looked towards the prisoner in the dock.

'He came back in,' she wept, 'and he raped me.'

'Came back in?' It was the judge asking her quietly. 'Had he gone?'

Simone looked confused. 'He raped me,' she repeated, wiping away the tears that kept pouring down her face, 'he raped me, I was raped, I *was*.'

Mr Tweed, counsel for the defence, pounced.

'Could someone else have come back in Miss Taylor?' he asked. 'Could you have been too drunk to know *who* came back in?'

In the absolute silence in the court, only the sound of her own tears, Simone Taylor suddenly looked straight at Terence. Terence Blue the famous film star who she had wept over when she was eighteen, who she had never ever forgotten, and whose life she had at last joined to hers. And then with a little shuddering sigh she looked up at the kind judge.

'Could I talk to you by myself My Lady?' she whispered and her voice sounded like that of a child.

Elvira knew from experience that the majesty of the courts was never so great as when the impersonal and the personal come together in the person of the judge sitting at the long bench of power and history and law and knowledge. She stared down at the judge from the public gallery, wondered what she was really thinking.

'Miss Taylor,' said the judge and her voice was both firm and kind, 'I regret that that is not possible. Your lawyers will explain to you why not. I am here only as an arbitrator, and as the representative of Justice.' She turned to the barristers in front of her.

'I will adjourn the court Mr Lee, ' she said to the prosecuting lawyer. 'Perhaps, after you have spoken to your client, you and your colleague Mr Tweed will be good enough to come to me in my chambers.'

And the judge, just for one moment, rested her eyes on the crumpled, fur-coated figure in the witness box. There might, Elvira thought, have been a kind of sad compassion in her eyes, or perhaps it was only the light.

It was early afternoon when the police came to the Dorchester. They asked very politely to speak to the Italian room-service waiter, the one who had brought the whisky and told of Terence Blue's state of undress, the one who had said so sadly, *'E wassa once my 'ero.*

For Simone Taylor had wept more and more hysterically in a room off Court Number Ten where she had been taken with her lawyers. *Perhaps I made a mistake,* she wept in her high, childish voice, *perhaps it was some-*

one else perhaps – and she had finally lain on the floor in her fur coat and cried as she had cried over thirty years ago I LOVE TERENCE, I LOVE HIM. A doctor was quickly called and she was sedated. The woman lawyer attached to the prosecution team held Simone's hand while she slowly calmed down, slowly lay back at last on the brown sofa in the anonymous room. Then the lawyer put her arm gently around Simone's shoulder.

'What happened Simone?'

'I woke up,' said Simone, blankly, expressionless, 'and he had his trousers off and was pushing inside me he smelt of garlic he hurt me and bit me and then he did it and – he kept hitting my breasts and biting them, even afterwards he kept doing it. He kept hitting them and punching them, my breasts. He said he was in the mafia and he would make sure I was killed if I told anyone, that no one could ever ever prove it was him. He said they would all think it was Terence.'

'Who was it Simone?'

'I love Terence. I've loved him all my life.'

'Who was it Simone?'

'Terence Blue could never be impotent, never, I don't believe that, they're just saying that to upset me.'

'Who was it Simone?'

After a long silence she said, 'The one who was Italian who brought the whisky. He came back. He smelt of garlic.'

And then almost asleep, in her little girl's voice, she said, as if it explained everything, *'I could only think about it if I pretended it was Terence.'*

*

Later in the afternoon the judge sat once more with her throat pastilles in the reconvened court, an empty seat where Simone Taylor had been sitting during the trial. More snow, driven by the wind, lifted along the road and fell on the pavements outside the courts as the judge directed the jury that the complainant had withdrawn her accusation against the defendant and that because of certain evidence that had arisen they must now find Terence Blue not guilty.

The rest was shambles.

Outside the Old Bailey, despite the atrocious weather, a huge media posse had gathered. Film and television cameras, radio cars, microphones, foreign press, tourists, passers-by – they stretched right down into Fleet Street and extra police were called in to control the crowds. Discreet to the last, Elvira quickly disappeared in a taxi. Neither Simone Taylor the complainant, nor Pauline O'Brien whose evidence had first turned the trial around, were anywhere to be seen.

Terence Blue emerged at last into the dusk ignoring the falling snow, and smiling broadly; waved with his right hand to photographers, journalists, tourists, well-wishers as lights flashed and people shouted; even accepted a kiss from one of the group of women across the road who had, in front of a camera, ripped up the banner that said RAPIST. Terence, snow in his hair and on his coat, disappeared at last into a taxi accompanied only by one unknown man; press cars gave hot pursuit.

But George Washington, Anthony Bonham's agent, gave a roar of anger as, watching the six o'clock television news, he saw who that one unknown man was, and suddenly everything fell into place. The man with Terence Blue was Joseph Wain, Executive Producer on *The Immoralists*.

The administrator of the mental hospital gave only one statement to the press, who had finally found Nicola Abbott under the name of Mary Shand. He said no decisions had been made about her future. The psychiatrist who had been treating her for so many years in the small mental hospital that had been sold to a sports club, and who had been punched in the face by Terence Blue, had been called to the big state hospital from France. He spoke pessimistically to the rest of the staff about the extraordinary information on the death of the patient's mother that had come out of the now-concluded extraordinary trial; he doubted whether Mary or Nicola, totally non-communicative since her admission after the stabbing of Terence Blue, would understand. 'That bastard ruined her life years ago,' he said to them. 'I know that.'

A police guard on the gates leading down the long drive turned journalists and photographers away from the unfamiliar room with the window, and the bed, where Nicola Abbott sat staring at nothing.

They all met at Stu's farm in Berkshire that evening all travelling by different routes in different cars. The taxi carrying Terence Blue and Joseph Wain had headed for Heathrow Airport, stopped at the intercontinental terminal. There the pursuing press lost them for Terence and Joseph were whisked away through the VIP lounge, not to the Virgin Islands or Bali but, careless of the weather, back to Berkshire in a private helicopter.

They sat at the long, polished table that evening eating a meal that Elvira had cooked by candlelight (while telling Stu that she felt as excited by the outcome of the trial as if she'd just finished writing another thriller), every single person around the table in a state of elation. The host, Stu, although he was the least involved was nevertheless elated also because Elvira was, and he loved her. They laughed and talked around the long table: Elvira and Stu, and Terence, and Pauline with her son Benedict, and Joseph Wain Executive Producer of *The Immoralists*. With them were Terence's English agent and his agent from America, and Pauline's agent from Regent Street who couldn't believe what was happening to her client and was in a state of excitement bordering on hysteria. For once Benedict had forgotten about computers; he had been whisked away from Chiswick, missed the last week of school before Christmas, found his mother's photograph in all the papers, and understood – because his mother explained everything to him very very carefully because he was a boy just learning about sex and she didn't want him to be confused – exactly what had happened. He was sitting beside Terence who was famous and odd and apparently this thing that Benedict couldn't really conceive of: *impotent*, and who seemed, peculiarly, to be drinking Coca-Cola.

'It was *worth* it,' Terence kept saying exuberantly over and over again, 'every single humiliating thing, to find out about Nicky's mother, what a fantastic thing, I only thought I was going to save her from the stabbing trial, fancy that wonderful old doctor coming forward, it was worth it, Nicky will get better now.' Even tonight he didn't drink, hadn't had a drink since the stabbing to the amazement of everyone who knew him. Sometimes his bright blue eyes filled with tears. 'I always thought, because I didn't do it, that I wouldn't be found guilty, but sometimes it's not that simple, justice, is it?'

'What was *wrong* with that Simone Taylor?' asked Pauline's agent breathlessly. 'Why did she do that, was it just to tie her name to a film star I suppose?'

Pauline and Terence, long-ago members of that class of '59, caught each other's eye and Terence shrugged. But Pauline answered.

'No it was more than that,' she said, pouring herself more wine. 'She *was* raped, I think she just tried to change the circumstances. We didn't really know about such things, we were kids, but I think she was obsessed with Terence, it was literally an obsession, and it had lasted all these years. You read about these things all the time only it's not usually people you know.'

'It was partly my fault,' said Terence slowly, and everyone looked at him in surprise. 'I was drunk and shocked about Nicky turning up like that after so long but I shouldn't have gone anywhere with Simone Taylor at all. When we were young she was often trying to . . . to get me to . . .' His voice petered out and he shrugged again but suddenly Pauline understood. She remembered Molly, and all the other girls including herself, who had known the beautiful blue-eyed boy from Wales when he was young.

Stu started passing salmon across the table and calling

out instructions, plates were being handed from one person to another, wine was being poured.

Pauline leant across the table and said to Terence in a very quiet voice, 'And did you?'

Terence sighed, stared down at the white linen table-cloth. 'I made the mistake of kissing her once in the Music Room.'

'At the reunion?'

'Thirty-six years ago in the Music Room. That's what started it all. I saw that she was a bit – unbalanced and I never kissed her again, but it was too late.' He turned his glass round and round in his hand. 'Nevertheless my father would no doubt call this –' and the glass turned round and round '– retribution.'

And Pauline, who like all the others had always remembered Terence kissing her on the stairs when they were young and the world offered them everything, was silent. Benedict, the only person who caught this exchange, stared, fascinated. There were *tears* in his mother's eyes.

'Here's to Terence!' called Stu. 'Welcome back to the world, old boy.'

'Get as drunk as you like on your Coca-Cola tonight baby,' said Terence's American agent (*Baby*? Benedict, who had grown up with show-business inanities, nevertheless could not believe his ears. Terence had grey hair, he was an old man, people only talked like that in the movies), 'for tomorrow your life begins again.'

The American turned to Joseph Wain. 'I love those scripts, I was reading them every night after the trial to take my mind off it, I never thought I'd ever recommend a client of mine do a television series over a movie, not that Terence was taking any recommendations of mine – the motherfucker –' he looked at Terence fondly '– he seemed to have made up his mind to do it if he got off this rape, but this stuff is dynamite, absolute fucking dynamite! It'll work like – as if people were watching the news! And what's this I hear about Marlon Brando? He doesn't do television.'

'I know,' said Joseph Wain, 'but it seems he might do this.'

'Fucking dynamite,' repeated the American. 'Fucking unbelievable.' He reached for more wine. 'And you were great!' he said to Pauline.

'I don't think anything will make me nervous ever again,' said Pauline, as he filled her glass, and she suddenly began to laugh helplessly. 'That barrister, he tried to annihilate me, it was no fun in that witness stand I can tell you!'

'Did you see that drawing the court artist did of you?' said Benedict. 'Sort of standing in court waving your arm around, you looked like Portia.'

Pauline leant, laughing, across the table, tears rolling down her cheeks. 'I know,' she said, trying to control herself, 'sorry I think I must be a bit drunk – he means Portia, his sister, my daughter, who is a PR consultant, not *The Merchant of Venice*,' she explained through her laughter to the others and she fumbled for her red lipstick.

'No, I meant in *The Merchant of Venice*,' said Benedict quite crossly which made everybody laugh again. 'You wanted justice for Terence so you got it in a clever way, Mum stop putting that red lipstick on.'

Pauline looked comically surprised. 'I like it,' she said, peering into a small mirror.

'No no, I mean I like it too,' Benedict said, 'but Mum you're putting it on all *crooked*.'

Elvira looked at her friend Pauline, at her animated, laughing, open face. She knew it was not only justice for Terence that Pauline had wanted but justice for herself. Who would have ever thought in a million years that Pauline would leave her philandering husband and become an actress again? *She never once complained, and I was one of her closest friends. She deserves good things now.* And Elvira rested her eyes speculatively on Joseph Wain. No one knew anything about his private life.

Just then Joseph smiled across the table at Pauline.

'You did it then,' was all he said.

'And it was worth it,' repeated Terence, waving his Coke can in his right hand, 'Nicky will get better now, it was worth it.' Not realising that the laughter died a little then, that everybody was watching him carefully. Nobody knew how he really felt about having the shameful word *impotent* conjoined to his famous name. Not once had he talked to anybody about what he'd been through since that Saturday in late August when the sun had shimmered on the hot pavements outside the London Academy of Drama and he had walked so unsuspectingly through the doors.

'It's probably a bad time to make an announcement about the new series,' murmured Terence's English agent across the table to Joseph Wain.

'Because of the trial?'

'No, because of Christmas.'

'Oh heavens, Terence will upstage Christmas,' said Elvira.

'I think it will be a fitting finale to the trial,' said Joseph. 'We'll announce it boldly on Monday, and then leave it till January, let them speculate all they like. You know my phone didn't stop ringing in the car while we were losing the press tonight – Paris, Berlin, Brussels, Sydney, Tokyo, you'd think I was in the stock market rather than television, every country involved in the series has been waiting with bated breath for the result of the trial. Even Tonga rang! The King wanted to know, because of course we're hoping to film sequences about nuclear tests there, the French won't allow us anywhere near Mururoa of course. Apparently *Diversions* is a huge hit in Tonga!

'Anyway I've arranged the press call for Monday,' he said to Terence and Pauline, 'and then you're free till the end of January, plenty of time for your shoulder to heal properly Terry, you need some sunshine.'

'I want to see Nicky,' said Terence stubbornly, 'I want her to know she didn't do it, she'll get better then, they must let me see her now.' There was again a sudden chill around the table, as if Terence didn't quite understand that he was free but that Nicky's nightmare would never be over. Elvira, his third wife who was still so fond of him, looked at him discreetly, anxiously. *What is he thinking of, still thinking of Nicky Abbott after all these years, it is a tragedy he must leave behind him. He needs a young wife a couple of kids a life in the sun, he can't be saddled with a mad old woman now, it is totally unrealistic it is ridiculous. He has done for her what he had to do, now he must leave it.*

'I hear you and your mother have got a new house young man,' said Stu rather over-heartily to his wife's godson, slicing more salmon.

'Yeah you should see it,' said Benedict, 'I've got a computer room right at the top, in the attic. It's brilliant!'

'Will you miss being right by the river Benny?' said Elvira.

Pauline looked across the table at her son. The soft hair fell in his eyes, as usual, he flicked it back like a beautiful nervous horse, as usual, but his face, instead of being closed off from them, was animated.

'I expect I'll go back there often and see my dad,' he said unexpectedly, 'but he can't cook.'

'He'll have to learn Benny,' said Elvira, 'and so will you.'

'I know and I already can,' he answered. 'I invented a little computer programme that will tell me when things are ready.'

'Surely he doesn't mean a timer!' said Pauline, drinking more wine.

'No, no,' said Benedict, 'what I thought was, say I was cooking stew Mum, it would connect to a computer that would tell a thing to cut up things first.'

'There are already machines for that,' said Pauline, laughing again, 'come and help me in the kitchen sometime and I'll show you!'

'No no Mum what I mean is . . .'

Their exuberant shadows flickered and danced on the walls of the room.

Terence was quieter now, not asleep but leaning on his good arm; the candlelight caught his blue eyes. He thought of the risk he had taken, and of the sackfuls of mail, and of the old doctor. Of course he had resisted Pauline's outrageous plan at first, but now so much more had happened: there was a path now that would lead him back to Nicky at last. He looked at Pauline and smiled, and she smiled back at him. She knew she was probably drunk with the relief of it all, but she knew a whole new life was starting. She saw Joseph Wain looking at her and found herself again wishing again she could touch his strange hair. *I know I'm drunk*, she thought. *I know there'll be horrible things about me in the* News of the World. *But I don't care, I'm going to be a star with Terence!* And then quite unbidden another quite different thought came into her mind. *I want to tell Joseph that I did find my father, after all.*

Now I'll be able to do it, Terence told himself, *now it will be Nicky's turn, to be happy at last. The others don't understand yet, they're so foolish to think I still want young girls, can't they see I've had enough young girls, I want to look after Nicky because* – and he thought again of what he had understood when he was barely conscious in the hospital – *I know Nicky better than any psychiatrist ever could, I should never never have let them take her away from me. I want her to know that I do know the meaning of love.* The others hadn't known his father, the strong, religious, determined old man from the Welsh valleys, who had imparted something to his son, after all.

The agents had their heads together, discussing business.

Elvira leant comfortably against Stu, all was well at last, *yes we'll find Terry a new young wife who'll help him forget the past*, she thought again to herself, *somebody pretty with energy and fun –that's what he needs – to have fun again.*

Joseph Wain looked at Pauline laughing with her son. Her life would now change so much, he wasn't sure if she realised. Those hooded eyes that he knew had concealed her unfulfilled hopes for so long stared out now, clearer and brighter and strong. She looked extraordinarily beautiful.

Outside, across Stu's soft rolling hills, snow lay white. It had got colder, the sky was clearer and stars shone. Sometimes a horse called; once Pauline caught the sound, suddenly thought of her father travelling with the circus from town to town in the darkness, and how the animals cried to the moon.

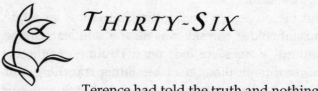

THIRTY-SIX

Terence had told the truth and nothing but the truth in the courtroom. But not the whole truth.

Juliet Lyall, engaged to be married to Terence Blue or so she thought, was still bleeding from her badly done, dangerous, illegal abortion when Terence Blue married Nicola Abbott. Juliet used sanitary towels and lost a lot of blood and played in *Widowers' Houses* at night and rehearsed her part as Titania in *Midsummer Night's Dream* in the daytime. It was months now, but what should she do? You couldn't go to a doctor, the abortion had been illegal, you just hoped things would clear up in the end, that's what they all did, all the actresses, all the girls who had been caught.

When Harry Donaldson sat beside the paraffin heater in the cold rehearsal room of the theatre and told her that Terence and Nicky were married and that Nicky was pregnant, Juliet fainted. She simply fainted on to the none-too-clean rehearsal room floor, Harry caught her or her head would have hit the heater, their woollen scarves entwined as he knelt awkwardly beside her, lowering her to the floor, blushing not at the warmth from the heater but at his own quite senseless cruelty.

She had to know, he kept telling himself as the rest of the cast crowded round. Peaseblossom and Mustardseed sat Juliet up gently in a moment or two, murmured quietly to her.

The show went on: *Widowers' Houses* had closed, *A Midsummer Night's Dream* was opening; Juliet fluttered and fluted as Titania in diaphanous gowns, terrified of blood showing through, smiled lovingly at Bottom wearing his ass's head, charmed the audience in a brittle sort of way, made them laugh. Harry playing Snug the Joiner watched her woodenly, was not very good in his part, answered shortly when the director said he must pull himself together, whatever was bothering him. He ate fish and chips late at night in the street, walking along fast, stuffing them into his mouth, ashamed.

One night he decided he would go to the piece of waste ground, down by the railway station that he'd heard about. That night he was attacked, and a stranger came to his aid.

Next morning Juliet came to Harry's digs while he was still in bed. It was Saturday morning, their morning off. She walked, uninvited, into his room.

'What's wrong with your face?' she said.

One of his eyes was swollen and closed, and there was blood on his face and on the bedclothes. 'Nothing,' he mumbled angrily, 'nothing, nothing. Go away.'

She stood there so pale and so somehow rigid in the doorway of his room that it seemed as if she might snap.

'Take me tonight,' she said, 'after the show. In my car.'

'Don't be silly Juliet.'

'Silly?' She looked at him scornfully. 'You think I'm silly?'

'No, no I don't of course, I just don't think it's a good idea. What's the point?'

'You must have thought there was a point,' she retorted bitterly, 'you're the one who was so keen to give me the news.'

Harry blushed under his swollen eye.

'I want to see them,' she said obstinately, 'that's all. They should've told me. You know where they are, you come with me.'

'It's miles away, in Brighton.'

'Doesn't matter.'

'He's probably filming in Aberdeen,' said Harry weakly, as Juliet stood there.

It was guilt perhaps that made him agree finally. Or still perhaps a perverse feeling of *wanting to see what would happen.*

The roads were icy, they had to drive carefully, it was almost two in the morning when they arrived. They could hear the sea, smell the sea through the window that Juliet opened as they consulted a map, drove around the grassy centre of the street of Georgian houses known as The Crescent.

The curtains were drawn but the lights in the

downstairs front room were on. Terence's car was parked outside.

He had in fact only just arrived, had flown from Aberdeen to Gatwick, driven from there to his bride of one week, who had just finished her own film *Heartbreak*; had opened the door of their house with his key, ran almost, so anxious was he to hold her; lifted her, kissed her, held her in his arms, his hands already on her breasts, her face suffused with happiness and desire as she pressed so passionately against him. And then the doorbell rang.

His face when he answered the door was puzzled, cleared when he saw Harry. 'What have you done to your face Harry?' he said.

And then he saw Juliet. Her face was so pale in the darkness and the light spilling from the hall that it almost shone.

'She had to know Terry,' sad Harry helplessly. 'You should have told her.'

And Terence Blue stepped forward and took both of Juliet's hands in his, as if some of his happiness could flow into her and she would understand.

'I'm sorry Jules,' he said. 'I know. Of course I should have told you. Come in.'

In the front room just off the hall Nicky Abbott wore a white Victorian nightdress made of some warm material, she looked like a child. She was still slightly dishevelled and flushed. She smiled a little bemusedly at Harry and Juliet but said cheerfully, 'Come and get warm.' Unconsciously she held her hands gently together, over her stomach.

'Have a drink everyone,' said Terence, rubbing his hands together in an effort at friendly hospitality. He poured a large whisky for himself and drank it down at once, looked enquiringly at Harry. Harry kissed Nicky nervously, sat down uneasily on the nearest chair, asked for a beer.

'A whisky Jules?' said Terence, facing her at last.

Juliet Lyall, aged twenty-two, stared at Nicola Abbott who took her roles and her man. And then very deliberately she let her coat drop. She too was wearing white, a white dress, far too thin for the icy November evening. But her white dress was stained at the back, with blood. Juliet just stood there and as she stood, as if she had timed it, blood dripped slowly down one of her legs and on to the grey carpet in the room.

'Sit down Jules,' said Terence tensely, 'have a whisky,' but nobody moved still.

'Are you all right Juliet?' said Nicky in the husky, broken voice. 'What's the matter?'

'That's the remains of Terence's last baby,' said Juliet.

And she stood there in her stained white dress, her eyes shining with contempt and anger and pain.

'She wanted an abortion,' said Terence pleadingly to Nicky. 'It was before I met you, she didn't want to have a baby, she thought it would interfere with her career.' He heard his own words, grimaced in a pain of his own. 'But this is all my fault. I should have told everybody everything.' He quickly poured another whisky.

'But –' Nicky stood there in the room but seemed hardly to touch the ground '– do you love her?' The only question that mattered. Still her hands were folded there, over her stomach, but tensely now.

Harry watched as the two women watched Terence. Who looked sadly at Juliet, standing there in the stained dress.

'I'm so sorry Jules,' he said, 'I've behaved so stupidly, and I seem to have been cruel but I – truly, it was just that I didn't want to –' and he grimaced again, hearing how inadequate his words were '– you know how fond I am of you, I didn't want to hurt you. But I fell in love with Nicky and nothing else seemed important.' He drained the glass.

'But we were engaged!' cried Juliet. And then very suddenly, harshly, she added, 'You slept with me.'

She stared at Nicky, glittering, pale. 'He slept with me two weeks ago you know,' said Juliet. 'Don't think you can trust him just because you've been through a pathetic little ceremony. You must never, ever, trust him. *He doesn't know the meaning of love.*' Her arms seemed longer than usual, hung beside her thin and white. 'In my room in York. Everybody knows. Harry knows.'

There was no time for Terence to explain, to say why he had gone to York, that sleeping was all he had done and not much of that as Juliet lay weeping in the bed and he hadn't the courage to tell her that he was marrying Nicky who was pregnant. For he hadn't had the courage to tell Nicky he was going to York at all.

Nicky Abbott Blue, married for a week, ran out of the room and out of the house in her white nightdress, they saw her flit past the big front window like a ghost in the darkness, running and running down the crescent.

Terence ran, and Harry ran, out into the freezing night. *You take the car Terry*, called Harry, as he ran down across the grass.

The car skidded on the newly formed ice, hit Nicky just at the bottom of the hill. She fell on her shoulder and lay quite, quite still.

After the ambulance had taken Terence and the unconscious Nicky away, Harry walked numbly, unable to believe what had so quickly happened, back up the hill and into the house.

And heard Juliet telling her father on the telephone in a high, wild, excited voice at three o'clock in the morning, *'but Daddy I had to wake you, she's unconscious and she's pregnant. She's been badly hurt, yes isn't it terrible, just terrible. But she won't be able to do* The Red Dress, *tell them, tell them quickly, I'll be able to do the part after all Daddy, this will make me a star.'*

And, within weeks, Harry Donaldson saw the glittering career of Juliet Lyall, Actress, take off like a rocket.

THIRTY-SEVEN

Anthony's first fear, when he got home that weekend after Terence Blue's trial was over, was that he would have a heart attack.

After a week of public indignity and his wife's photograph splattered all over the cheap newspapers and only the answering machine answering the phone in his house, he came home late on Saturday night and found the house in darkness, no lamp on the stairs. The central heating wasn't on and Pauline's short, cold letter was on the kitchen table under an empty whisky bottle. For one terrible moment he thought there was even no whisky in the house which increased his chest pains but eventually he found half a bottle in a cupboard in the kitchen.

Pauline's letter stated that she had left him. She and Benedict would be living near Kew so as not to upset Benedict's schooling, they would be away from England for Christmas. Nothing else. What's more, *the fridge was empty*. He drank the half bottle of whisky, passed out in the sitting room.

He had an unbelievably terrible hangover the next morning; he actually went outside and began shovelling snow from the pavement and the drive in the hope that he would feel better.

He didn't.

He jumped into his car and went to the nearest supermarket. He was making himself bacon and eggs and gratefully drinking from the fresh bottle of whisky when the phone rang. It was Portia.

'Hello Daddy.'

'Porshe, do you know about all this?'

'I had a note from Mother.'

'She didn't leave any food.'

'Are you working today?'

'No I'm off till Tuesday. My first long weekend for months. I was going to – take her Christmas shopping.' His voice whined slightly.

'Come over to Ealing Daddy, I'll make us Sunday dinner about four.'

'Do you understand any of this Porshe? How could she possibly, possibly humiliate me like this, it simply can't be possible that she's left me for Terence Blue, it can't be, I know her, I simply don't believe it.' But that weekend she had been away nudged there at the corner of his hungover mind. *I'll never forgive her for making a fool of me in public, never*. 'Where's your mother going for Christmas?'

'Hawaii.'

'*Hawaii*? Rubbish.'

'Hawaii Daddy.'

'With Terence Blue?'

'With Benedict.'

'With Benny?'

'Uh-huh. Shall I expect you then? We'll talk when we meet shall we?'

How crisp his daughter was. Like his wife at her worst.

'Have you seen Viola?' he asked plaintively.

'She's living with her musician.'

'*Living* with him?'

'See you at four then Daddy, bye.'

Anthony rang Molly's number but there was no answer, not even her answering machine.

He sat sprawled on the sofa with all the Sunday newspapers, at least she hadn't fucking cancelled them. His wife's photograph and Terence's were in every paper; he found himself getting angrier and angrier, several of the cheap papers questioned Pauline's involvement in the trial. They all mentioned she was married to one of the country's leading Shakespearian actors. The *Sunday Express* even had Anthony's photograph: an old one, of him as Petruchio in *The Taming of the Shrew*. Not bad actually, he thought, considering it.

But he hadn't yet got the full measure of his wife's revenge.

It wasn't until the following day that a huge press conference was held at the Savoy, and there in a suite called *Patience* overlooking the river Thames it was announced that Terence Blue, at the moment one of the most famous men in the world, and Pauline O'Brien, who had appeared as a witness at his notorious trial, would be starring together in a mega international television project called *The Immoralists,* the biggest, most expensive, most ambitious television serial ever made.

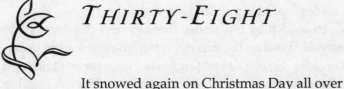

THIRTY-EIGHT

It snowed again on Christmas Day all over Britain, it had been snowing off and on for weeks. People had built snowmen in their gardens or on suburban pavements or outside tube stations, used carrots or parsnips for noses and tea cosies for hats with sprigs of holly sticking out.

Frances Kitson and Harry Donaldson met on Christmas morning at Frances' flat. She had a Christmas tree and all the promised champagne and mince pies and turkey and crackers. But Emmy Lou their friend, the third of The Three Stooges, wasn't there.

'My mother'll be here at one o'clock as usual, I ordered a car for her, no point in doing anything different, I hope she'll remember about Em though, she's inclined to forget things.'

'This year I bought her a mock fur stole,' said Harry,

'look,' and he pulled it out of his bag to wrap in Christmas paper.

'Oh Harry it's lovely.' Frances rubbed her hands over it. 'I hope it wasn't too expensive darling, you know she'll probably put it round her hot water bottle.' She watched Harry folding the stole into the brightly coloured paper. 'If Em was here she'd make us go for a healthy walk now, wouldn't she, before Mum arrives, she was the one who made us look after our bodies because they are the tools of our trade.'

'Yes,' said Harry. But they didn't go.

Instead they lay across the sofa and the floor, occasionally basting the turkey, wrapping more little things for Mrs Kitson, as though she was their child and Christmas was for her. As though they weren't missing Emmy Lou.

The central heating was turned up full, they ate chocolates and drank champagne, laughed at Franny's ludicrous adventures making Triumph Telephone adverts: on the first day a telephone had suddenly burst into flames. They gossiped about the affair that the fifty-seven-year-old leading man in Harry's Thomas Hardy serial – who had a second wife and two young children – was having with the young heroine just out of drama school. As though they weren't missing Emmy Lou.

They discussed Terence's trial and Pauline's sudden elevation to celebrity.

'I'm glad,' said Frances firmly, 'she was such a good actress and she didn't work enough. And what about Nicky Abbott, Harry? Fancy she and Terence having been married all those years ago. Isn't it odd to know that after all these years?'

'I always knew,' said Harry.

'Did you?' said Frances staring at him in surprise.

'Franny I think there's something about you that precludes filming being done in a straightforward way, I'm never around when phones blow up or directors vomit and you're the only person I've ever heard of going on a chatshow with a Croatian nun who turns out to be someone you sat next to at primary school.'

'What, Beryl Makepeace? Yeah, wasn't that a hoot, they used to live near us, Mum swears her mother used to drink! Beryl only went to Yugoslavia when she was nine, course she wasn't a Croatian at all really, her father ran a bar in Dubrovnik or somewhere, handy for Mrs Makepeace.' But she added curiously, 'you never *told* me about Nicky and Terence.'

'No,' said Harry. And she saw something there in his face, some closed-up look, unlike him. *I will ask him about it another time*, she thought.

Mrs Kitson arrived in a taxi at 1 pm as arranged. She tottered fraily in the snow as Frances ran down the stairs to meet her, to pay the taxi; the taxi-driver held the old lady's arm or she would have fallen.

'Merry Christmas Mum,' called Frances, tottering herself down the snow-covered path in her high-heeled shoes.

'The vicar came,' said Mrs Kitson, 'I wished him Merry Christmas but I told him I wasn't leaving him my money.'

Slowly they progressed to the first-floor flat.

'Hello Mabel,' said Harry loudly, kissing her at the doorway.

'Hello Harry dear, I've brought you something nice. Ooooh isn't it *cold*, I didn't want to get out of bed,' taking off her coat, putting on a cardigan.

'You did so Mum, it's Christmas.'

'I'm eighty next year,' said Mrs Kitson. 'One Christmas more or less doesn't make any difference.' She peered short-sightedly in her bag for her slippers. 'Oh I see her Majesty is going to honour your friend, it was in the hush-hush column in the paper, you're not supposed to tell you know, till New Year's Day.'

'What friend?' said Frances.

But Harry guessed. 'Dame Juliet Lyall,' he murmured, 'England's best-loved actress.'

'She may be best-loved,' said Frances, settling her mother on the sofa, 'but she's a greedy actress, grabs the stage.'

Harry looked at her. 'I've never heard you say that before,' he said. 'Perhaps stars have to grab the stage, perhaps that's how they become stars.'

'Harry, you remember Nicky Abbott's acting?'

'Of course.'

'She didn't grab the stage like a glutton, like a greedy, greedy person. She filled it, that's a different kind of acting. If I was a good actress that's how I'd like to act.'

'You are a good actress dear,' said Mrs Kitson. 'I've enjoyed seeing you on those adverts, all my neighbours love them, a bit saucy but you make me laugh. And you made me laugh on that chat-show with Beryl

Makepeace, fancy her being a Croatian nun these days, her mother used to drink in the back garden you know, ruby port. You always made me laugh Franny you know, you're good for my soul, did you know that, I told the vicar.'

'Thanks Mum,' said Frances, smiling at her. 'Did the boys phone this morning?'

'What's that dear?'

'Did the boys phone? Have you got your hearing aid turned up?'

'Yes, yes they phoned, don't shout, it's because you've got the radio on, there's too many noises tuning in at once.'

'That's not the radio, that's a new CD of Christmas carols to make you feel all jolly.'

'Give me a sherry for goodness' sake, that'll do the trick easier,' and they all laughed.

For years now Christmas day had been the four of them. Frances had wept as she set the table for three.

They drank and ate nuts and opened presents. Frances gave Harry an electric juice squeezer that he'd said he wanted. Mrs Kitson gave Harry a ship in a bottle that she'd found in a junk shop. She had knitted for Frances, laboriously with her arthritis, a shocking pink jersey with a yellow cat on it, taken from a pattern. The cat was slightly crooked but it was bright and jolly and Frances put it on. Frances had given her mother a portable phone – *you can even take it to the lavatory* – and they bent over it, to show her how to work it. Harry gave Frances a yellow silk dress like the one Milton Werner had torn, she gasped when she opened it, and kissed him. Mrs Kitson kept stroking the fake-fur stole, *I do like this Harry*, she said.

She made them watch the Queen's speech, as usual.

At the table they pulled crackers, put on hats, ate turkey.

'You know – I don't like turkey really,' Mrs Kitson said.

'But it's Christmas Mum. Look it's snowing outside, we're having a White Christmas like everyone always hopes for, "I'm Dreaming of a White Christmas" etc, you've got to have turkey!'

'Yes dear but I don't like turkey, I can't taste it, it feels like I'm chewing something – you know –' she searched for the word '– anonymous.'

'You should've said last year.'

'Emmy Lou cooked roast pork with apple sauce last year, because I said it the year before.'

Harry and Frances looked at her in amazement.

'So she did,' said Harry, 'I'd forgotten.'

'Don't worry dear, I forget almost everything,' said Mrs Kitson. 'I'm always forgetting people's names, you're lucky I remember yours, I forget the vicar's name even, even though he calls so often, so I just call him Father even though he's a Baptist. You know he wants my money, I say to him Father Vicar you can come all you like and I'll make you a cup of tea but the Church won't get anything. You read about them you know, and doctors. And *dentists*,' she added crossly, shooting a look at her daughter. 'They don't fool me.'

'I think he comes so often because you entertain him.'

'He doesn't fool me,' repeated Mrs Kitson, 'even

when I can't remember his name, actually I think he's lonely the way he turns up week after week, I don't think there are many Baptists left in the world, they've all died. Funny life, being a vicar. '

And then she surprised them again.

'Here's to Emmy Lou,' she said, picking up her champagne glass, 'who didn't cook turkey, God bless her soul wherever she is.' And after they'd drunk she added, 'And to you Franny, I'm so glad you're being a successful actress at last, it's so nice to see you on the telly nearly every day.'

'I'm not sure I'm an *actress*,' said Frances wryly.

'Yes, yes you are,' said Mrs Kitson firmly. 'When you sang you can't get a man with a gun with your father at those shows at Blackpool and places I always knew you'd make it one day, and I know God moves in mysterious ways, but it doesn't matter that it's adverts dear, you haven't finished yet, think of your father and how he struggled, you're on telly almost every day and getting paid for it. You're an Actress.'

Izzy Fields had cooked Christmas dinner for ten people; her two other children had arrived with the grandchildren; there had been a huge decorated Christmas tree, Christmas laughs and tears and food and fights and hugs and delight and sulks and joy. The usual Christmas.

Now, late afternoon, Christmas paper and presents lying everywhere, dishes in the kitchen lying everywhere, people too lying everywhere – on chairs and beds and couches – a sort of peace had descended on the house in Tufnell Park; she could hear the television droning from the sitting room but no one was watching. Her husband had borrowed her bicycle to go for a ride to clear his head and escape the dishes, his bike had a puncture.

She too left the dishes, took a coat off the back of the kitchen door, walked out down the snow-covered path and on to the slushy road.

She had just received another long contract from the National Theatre: a raise in salary; more small parts, a couple of which looked as if they would be quite fun; more understudying. Izzy Fields would be employed as an actress forever, she probably worked more regularly than any other person from the class of '59.

She walked slowly down to Kentish Town Road. It was just beginning to snow again. It had been a happy Christmas, no more rows than usual and the children made it fun. But all the same there had still been that heavy feeling round her shoulders, that burden.

She had not yet recovered from the death of her friend Emmy Lou Brown.

She found she thought of Emmy every day. The sad little funeral at the Actors' Church in Covent Garden, the subdued gathering of friends who all knew exactly why Emmy Lou was dead. The cast list had gone up at the National Theatre for the new year production of *Lives* by Eurydice Smith, directed by Pamela Angel: the part of Alice was to be played by Dame Helen Storey. And Izzy was to understudy her.

That was Show Business.

And walking past the tube station and the little rotunda and the few people there, some of them quite alone, Izzy's eyes ached, tears just behind them. Emmy Lou had stood for all the things Izzy Fields admired in their profession: the talent and the hard hard work and the absolute dedication. All the things that Izzy Fields knew in her heart that she did not have enough of.

Emmy Lou had been, despite the fact that she had not in the end been able to carry the weight of it any more, an Actress.

Izzy Fields walked slowly home to the dishes.

Juliet Lyall spent Christmas Day in her hotel room in Los Angeles. She had declined an invitation to a Christmas barbeque with members of the film company: she pleaded tiredness. The film company had sent her masses of yellow roses, Bud Martin had sent her some exotic orchids, the hotel gave her Christmas dinner in her room. She did not want to go anywhere or see anyone: she was dealing with something inside herself and she needed to be on her own.

She had followed the story of Terence Blue's rape trial, and the story of Nicola Abbott which she knew already, on CNN news and in the English and American newspapers. There had been no mention at all of Juliet Lyall and her part in all this story. It was as Harry had said: who could tell the story except those who were there? And Terence had chosen not to tell. Her damehood would be announced in the New Year honours.

But something had changed, some self-knowledge had come to her at last after that terrible night in her hotel room. Not just the knowledge that she could have sex, after all, like any normal human being. That was gained (she understood as she covertly watched Bud Martin on the set, off the set, disappearing with young girls, occasionally catching her glance, smiling almost slyly at her across the studio floor) at too high a price. Over and over again, tossing and turning on the same bed, she thought of Bud Martin watching her: clear-eyed, harsh, quite still, getting intimate private information about her. Looking for age and desire. As she thought of these things she burnt with pain and disgust and shame.

She understood that her 'cure' had come too brutally and too late; she did not believe she would ever want sex again.

But she could live with that: had lived with that.

She bent over her film script for the next week's shooting; soon the film would be finished; her performance, they said, was stunning: so infused with a kind of bleak pain that there was talk of Oscars even before the work was over. She knew that this film would probably be the triumph of her career and there would be many many rewards, of a kind. They were the rewards she had dedicated her life to, and she knew they had their own importance.

But on Christmas Day in Los Angeles, above the words on the page of her script, the memory of the young Nicky Abbott hovered. And most of all, the memory of the one man she had loved, Terence Blue.

Juliet Lyall had fooled Bud Martin. It was not age and desire she was playing, but memory: waiting there till she opened her eyes and saw a young face, and blue, blue eyes. The memory of what for almost thirty-five years she had tried so hard to push away with her anger so she would not have to think about it: the memory of youth, and love, and how they were lost.

It was that pain the camera saw.

Mabel Kitson tottered back down the steps on Harry's arm at six o'clock when the taxi came for her, its headlights shining in the dark reflecting the white pavements, picking out the number in the street. She waved and called Merry Christmas as she was driven away.

Harry and Frances sprawled again, dozing sometimes as they talked, the television was still on but with the sound down.

'She's amazing, Mabel,' said Harry.

'Yes, I think it's terrific she still feels she can manage on her own. She hasn't *got* any money you know, about six hundred and forty pounds in the Abbey National I think.'

'The vicar's on to a bad thing then,' said Harry morosely and Franny smiled into the pink carpet.

After a while, suddenly out of a drifting silence, she said, 'I saw my ex-husband the other day.'

'The dentist?'

'Mmmmmmm.'

'The laughing dentist?'

'He wasn't laughing,' said Frances, 'he had a wife and two teenage children and they were in Selfridges.'

'Did you talk to him?'

'I started to walk towards them, just sort of instinctively, but then I kind of stopped. I couldn't think what I was going to say. It all seems so long ago, as if it wasn't me, as if – you know, as if there's nothing inside me of the person that I was when I married him. I couldn't believe he would recognise me, well I've got different coloured hair and I don't think he ever saw me with my new capped teeth after he punched me, I'd left by then.'

'You recognised him, he'd have recognised you.'

'I know, I know, it was just a feeling. They say we – completely replace ourselves in seven years, all our cells, our nails, our hair well I must've replaced myself about three times since we split up, except for my teeth.'

'You don't replace memory,' said Harry.

'I know.' And Frances smoothed with her hand the pink carpet of her marriage. 'I think I've forgotten. Then out of the blue I dream again.'

'You don't understand when you're young do you?' said Harry. 'The past is never quite over, after all.' (And just once more he saw Juliet Lyall standing there in the white dress and Nicky Abbott like a ghost running across the frosty grass in the darkness.)

'But perhaps,' said Frances, 'it's only rackety people like us, people who – who don't have ordered lives. Lots of people probably never think about the past at all.'

'It's there though isn't it?' said Harry. 'Waiting for them.'

The silent television pictures flickered. There was

only the sound of the old clock, ticking in the warm room.

Then suddenly Harry yawned. 'Oh sorry, sorry darling, just all that lovely food and drink. And I've been working long hours and I've only got three days off and a lot of lines to learn. And I didn't get enough sleep last night.'

'Out on the tiles?'

'Yes,' said Harry, 'met someone at a club – we went driving, down in the City.'

'Someone nice?'

'Good sex,' said Harry grinning.

'Sex in the City?'

'Sex in the City in a Car on Christmas Eve. But actually, I'm really getting too old for sex in cars.'

'I'm getting too old for sex anywhere.'

'Franny! Don't say that. You're not old.'

'I'm fifty-seven,' said Frances calmly, 'I haven't had a regular sexual partner since I was about forty. Being a middle-aged woman isn't like being gay, picking people up and having sex in a car. Or like being a man, marrying someone younger, starting again. You just take what you can get, if you're a woman my age. I mean think of My Night With Milton,' and despite herself she giggled in a kind of half-hearted way. 'And the funny thing was, if only he'd known, it wasn't really sex I wanted – I liked him, he was kind, I'm really not interested in sex any more, I just liked him, it was a person, to be mine.'

'I'm yours.'

'I know, but – not like that Harry, oh you know what

I mean. I find myself thinking I want someone to – grow old with, be my person, so I never have to have ludicrous experiences with strangers ever again in my life. I'm tired of being a cheery actress on my own who makes everybody laugh, even her own mother. I want –' and she laughed but it was a sad little laugh '– someone to clean my teeth with.'

'I know,' said Harry, 'so do I, so do most people. Or at least I think I do and then the idea of sharing a toothbrush disgusts me – I've been on my own too long, I could never live with someone new.'

'I think of all the couples all over the world having Christmas together. And then there's people like you and me and Emmy.'

'Don't go down that tired old road,' said Harry firmly, 'there are couples killing each other this Christmas day, there always are.'

'I know I know I know,' said Franny, 'have a –' she rummaged in the fast-dwindling chocolate box, changing the subject '– pineapple delight. Is it going to be really good, the Thomas Hardy, win lots of awards like all the Jane Austens do you think? I mean despite affairs and dramas?'

Harry didn't answer for a moment, turned away from the chocolates. 'It's a funny profession Fran. I'm not finding it easy actually. I don't want to turn in my usual eccentric performance, it's an interesting character, I wanted to make him – special, individual. But we hardly rehearse, you work on your own these days. The young ones often paraphrase the language, take away its period flavour somehow. I've got a lot to say but I find myself learning the lines in a vacuum, and I make mistakes. Maybe it's that I'm getting old.'

'Oh Harry don't be silly, you could do it standing on your head.'

'But that's just it, I don't want to do it standing on my head, I wanted to do something – original, something I could've worked on with the director. I'm not sure if I've portrayed the character I wanted to portray, that I saw when I read the book.' He sighed. 'One of the young girls in it is a pop star.'

'So what's new? They think they'll get bigger audiences with a pop star, probably do get bigger audiences.'

'I know I know but she hasn't done any acting before. I've got quite a few scenes with her and she's – it's charming in a way what she does I suppose but it's not –' he shrugged helplessly '– right.' Harry stretched on the couch, took off one of his socks. 'Why is it that people think *everyone* can act, that anyone can do it? Ah shit it's a stupid profession now, it's not like when we started, it's about stars and the Network Centre controller having a say in everybody's casting, and money, and divorce announcements to the press, and gossip, no wonder people have started calling us *luvvies*.'

'Perhaps it was always like that only we were young and idealistic and didn't see.'

'No,' said Harry firmly. 'When we started it was about *acting*, about our work.' He took off his other sock, lay back on the sofa, stared up at the white curlicues on the ceiling. 'Perhaps it'll come round again, acting,' he said. 'Something will happen, telly and marketing will lose their stranglehold, the world will explode, some-thing.'

'In the meantime,' said Franny handing him the last of the chocolates, 'Merry Christmas courtesy of Triumph Telephones.'

The couch turned into a bed where Harry stayed the night.

'Franny,' he said at the bathroom door as she was cleaning her teeth in her voluminous pink nightie.

She made a noise to indicate that she was listening.

'We're both earning quite a lot of money now, and I've got my house. Would you – think of buying a couple of flats somewhere together – not living together –' as her face popped up from the basin in surprise, her mouth covered in toothpaste '– but you know, together, near each other. Next door maybe. '

Frances spat into the basin, wiped her mouth with her face flannel, stood upright and looked at Harry, frowning slightly.

'You mean – grow old together?'

Harry looked a bit self-conscious. 'Something like that, like what you were talking about earlier. We wouldn't be living together but we'd be – there.'

He'd somehow expected her to be pleased, to say yes straight away.

'Can I think about it?' said Frances slowly.

'Darling of course.' But he at once felt sad. Perhaps it wasn't a good idea, perhaps he was drunk, perhaps he should just wait till he was ready for Copperfield Hall, perhaps he should set up somewhere with a friend, a gay friend. *But Michael is dead and all the gays I really know well are either old lovers or ridiculous. Or ridiculous old lovers. I couldn't live with them.*

She kissed him. She smelt of toothpaste and cleansing lotion. Her face looked quite different without make-up, rounder somehow. Harry seldom saw her without her make-up, carefully applied.

'Merry Christmas Harry darling. I do love you, and of course I'll think about what you've said.' She held on to him for a moment. 'Oh Harry. If only Em could've—'

'I know Franny,' said Harry, 'I know.' For just a moment they held each other. And then she went into her bedroom and Harry wriggled down under the duvet on the sofa. He missed his own bed. But it was only once a year. He fell asleep almost at once.

Frances turned off the bedside lamp, lay in her double bed in the bedroom of the flat she had rented for over twenty years, since the break-up of her marriage with the laughing dentist. She did not go to sleep.

She cared for Harry more than anyone else she knew, and she guessed he had made the suggestion because she had said she was lonely. He was a good person.

But hidden in a very secret part of her mind was the vision of lonely ageing actresses at first nights and parties with gay men, the *fag hags* people called them, the animated chatter and the waving and the loud loud smiles.

She was just drifting off to sleep when there was an urgent, noisy ring on the doorbell. She sat up at once, heard Harry stir in the next room, quickly put her dressing gown over her shoulders as she opened her door. In the doorway between the two rooms, as the doorbell rang loudly again, she stood blinking at Harry who had put a light on. She knew that however ridiculous it seemed they were both thinking at once of Emmy Lou, as if Emmy had somehow come back for Christmas after all.

'We are stupid,' she said aloud, 'look, it's only ten-thirty.' But as she went towards her own front door she turned and said, 'Come with me Harry?'

At the main door downstairs a harrassed-looking man in uniform stood holding a huge bunch of yellow and white and pink roses.

'Good heavens,' said Frances.

'Miss Frances Kitson?'

'Yes.' She looked at him, puzzled.

'I am so sorry to arrive so late with these, they should have been here hours and hours ago but I had an accident, skidded in the snow – I had to wait for hours for the AA to come, to get going again.' He stood there in the night, surrounded by roses, the scent of them drifted between the darkness and the light. At last Frances took them from him.

'Will you come in?' she said, bemused still. 'Have a drink, get warm?'

'No, no, thank you, I must get back now, I think the roses are all right, I didn't let them get too hot in the car, I laid them in the snow for a while.'

'Roses in the snow, what a lovely picture.' Frances smiled at him. 'Are you sure you wouldn't come in?'

'No thank you, no, I've rung the wife and she's making me a big turkey sandwich and a treble Scotch so I'll get a bit of Christmas cheer, even this late and I'm looking forward to it I can tell you. Here, there's this envelope for you as well, will you sign, thanks, thanks, Merry Christmas,' and he was gone down the steps that were freshly white. In the light spilling out from the doorway she saw through the silent drifting snow that one side of his car was smashed in. But he'd left the motor running and, tooting once softly, he carefully drove away.

She closed the door, leant against it, and still holding the roses, clumsy, managed to open the large envelope. Harry saw that she had to hold the note away from her, in order to be able to read it without her glasses. She frowned at the letter.

Dear Frances,

Christmas has given me an excuse to contact you again. I have not been courageous enough to speak to you in person but I have become courageous enough to write you this letter. I have been divorced from my wife for ten years which has led to many problems for me as you are now only too well aware. If they seem unsolvable to you then I just send you warm and affectionate Christmas greetings but I also enclose a ticket to Basle on New Year's Eve. I will meet the plane but only catch it if you feel you can. I will of course understand if you do not. I have missed you very much.

Milton Werner

Harry still stood at the top of the stairs. He looked down at Frances.

'Do you know Harry,' she said, looking up at him, a smile breaking on her face like sunshine, 'I think I'll take a trip to Switzerland.'

Her round shining un-made-up face smiled and smiled up at him, through the roses.

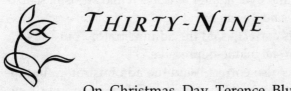

THIRTY-NINE

On Christmas Day Terence Blue drove through the snow in his red BMW convertible – he was still banned from driving but who would have the heart to arrest him now – to see his first wife, Nicola Abbott.

He had, against his doctor's orders, taken the sling from his shoulder for the first time. It was very painful but he didn't want to appear in a sling, frighten her. He took flowers, champagne, and presents wrapped in pretty paper.

After the spectacular end to the trial he had absolutely insisted to the administrator of the hospital where Nicky now was that Nicky would recover once she understood about her mother, that it was important that he be allowed to visit her at last, that at last he could help her recovery. Her old psychiatrist, Terence's old adversary, who had been called in specially had gone back again to Monte Carlo; his final words were: *don't let the bastard near her just because he's a film star, she's my patient, make*

*sure she takes her medication. I'll come back after Christmas
and he can pay again for her to be put back into private care.*

The administrator had of course been following the
Terence Blue trial, was amazed at Terence's steadfast-
ness even after the stabbing, but said he was clutching at
miracles.

'Perhaps there are miracles,' said Terence, 'even in
psychiatry.' The administrator shook his head.

'Over and over again I have been told she isn't schizo-
phrenic,' said Terence.

'That is correct,' said the administrator, 'but—'

'Nor is she manic-depressive.'

'That is also correct,' said the administrator, 'but the
use of categories to describe people who are not func-
tioning is not always useful. You see we have *told* her
about her mother Mr Blue,' he said. 'It makes no difference any longer. She hasn't spoken since your – since
the stabbing. And it is dangerous Mr Blue,' he said. 'You
will have to accept finally and forever what the psychiatrist has told you for years, she had forgotten what
happened so long ago until your most inopportune visit
reminded her. We understand it is hard for you but *you*
must understand and do what's best for her. Look what
happened in Brighton, you put back her recovery for
years. A small private hospital will be the best place for
her, for the rest of her life, we will find something suitable after Christmas. That is how you can help her, by
allowing her that.'

'No,' said Terence, 'you don't understand. I understand what happened.'

The administrator repeated: 'She's in a catatonic state

and we cannot communicate with her, a visit from you cannot help her.'

'She *will* speak,' said Terence.

Finally, because this time Terence simply would not give up, because the psychiatrist he'd punched was not on the staff, because the administrator was quite a kind man (and also a big fan of Terence Blue's movies although he had not told the psychiatrist that), the administrator agreed: one visit. After Christmas when he would be back in his office and could be present at the interview.

The junior psychiatric nurse on Christmas Day reception duty stood up in surprise and then smiled widely, recognising the famous film star who was stamping snow off his shoes in the doorway.

'But we're expecting you next Friday, Mr Blue,' she said. 'The administrator will be back on Friday to see you, it's all arranged.'

'I want to wish her Merry Christmas,' said Terence simply.

She was unsure whether she should let him in. But it was Christmas after all, there were lots of visitors in the hospital today, and they *had* agreed he was to see her. She thought him romantic, and extremely handsome still in an ageing sort of way, but not very realistic. And rather brave to come back to a woman who had tried to stab him to death, not that there were any knives now of course within reach of Nicola Abbott. And he was a *Film Star* after all.

'Could I have your autograph Mr Blue?' she said, giggling prettily.

And when he smilingly obliged she decided no harm could be done from a short Christmas visit and led him cheerfully along the rubber-covered corridor floors, through the locked doors, past visitors with Christmas presents and anxious smiles, past the vacant faces, to the small room with the window and the bed.

As they walked along Terence Blue was silent, carrying his gifts, but the junior psychiatric nurse could hear his rather uneven breathing. Calling, crying voices echoed everywhere along the corridors, behind the doors, but the nurse was used to them, did not hear them. If Terence Blue heard these sounds he gave no sign. The nurse pondered: Mary Shand – or Nicola Abbott as she was called in the papers – was an old woman now, and quite lost to the world. Whatever was a famous film star like Terence Blue hoping for?

'I'm afraid she doesn't talk,' she said, opening the door.

The grey-haired woman sat very neatly, her feet exactly together, exactly underneath her, as she stared out of the window. She turned when the door opened.

To the everlasting amazement of the young psychiatric nurse the patient got up from the chair almost at once. She remained quite still for several moments and then walked slowly towards the man in the doorway, the nurse had her finger ready to press her panic button, *God I should never have allowed this, I'll lose my job.*

No one would have guessed from Terence's demeanour that the woman walking towards him had stabbed him only a few months ago. He showed no fear at all, actually put down the Christmas gifts on a small table by the door and stepped towards her.

'Hello Nicky my darling,' he said to the grey-haired, dark-eyed woman.

For a moment they stood there, about two feet apart. And then Nicky moved slightly, stretched her hand across to Terence. She very hesitantly pulled her fingers across his face. The young nurse in the doorway could hardly breathe.

And then in her unforgettable, breaking voice, sounding more strange than ever because it was so long since it had been used, Nicky said, 'I thought I killed you.'

Her dark, fathomless eyes stared at the man. 'I haven't been allowed to see the newspapers. I thought they were hiding it from me. I thought I killed you.'

The nurse looked on in amazement: *the patient was talking!* And then she looked at Terence. All the calmness had gone from his face and she saw that he was shaking.

'You didn't kill me,' he said, 'but Nicky –' and Terence Blue took a deep anxious breath '– *I love you. I do understand the meaning of love.*' The agitation in his gaunt face was seen by both women and the words rushed out of his mouth. 'I understood it that first night in your dressing room Nicky – I don't know if you've been thinking all these years about that night in Brighton? I wasn't any longer having an affair with Juliet, you misunderstood. Juliet wanted you to misunderstand. But it was my fault, all my fault. I had been in York trying to tell her about you being pregnant and us getting married but I felt sorry for her and I put it off. All these years they would never let me talk to you, tell you, they said you were too ill, that I was bad for you.'

The junior nurse couldn't believe her ears. She knew enough about the trial to know he must be discussing something that had happened more than thirty years ago, long long before she was even born, *good God I should never have allowed this, he sounds mad himself*.

For a long moment Nicola Abbott stared at his face, as if she was balancing his anxious words in her mind. Then she said in the husky voice, and in an odd way she sounded much saner than he had, 'I don't think you understood Terry.'

For a moment she was silent again. 'I'd put all that out of my mind years ago,' she said finally, 'they helped me to do that. After the coma you know I didn't remember things clearly. There were pieces missing. And after a while – well it was all such a long time ago, and we were all so –' and she paused before she said the word '– young.'

Terence Blue's voice cracked with pain. 'You forgot *everything*?'

In the small room there was just his uneven breathing, and Nicky's breathing, and the breathing of the young nurse.

Then Nicky began again, most carefully, to speak: slowly, almost without expression, as if she wasn't used to putting words together. She frowned sometimes at the effort to express herself.

'Terry I got better a long time ago, in a way. Some of the medicines made me calm and after a while I never thought about the past at all. I think there were a lot of patients like me, not exactly ill any more but – but protected from the past by our medicines. It was – perhaps as if we were in a private hotel somewhere, away from the world. But favoured. Because someone was paying.' She stared for a moment out of the small window of the huge state hospital, at other buildings, at snow falling past barred windows. 'But – I wasn't unhappy Terry.'

A long silence in the small room.

'Did you know I learnt Russian?'

Terence shook his head numbly.

'I read Chekhov in Russian, and Tolstoy. They were wonderful.'

'Nicky . . .' Terence's voice was almost inaudible, as if the hope that had sustained him through everything that had happened was draining away. 'Why did you come to the reunion?'

And then Nicky breathed in very sharply and her voice suddenly became agitated. 'Because they sent me back to Brighton, to the same house in Brighton – it made me remember things I'd forgotten – Terry it was still the *same cover on the bed*, even though it was old and faded and my –' she looked up at him '– did you know my cream wedding dress was still on the top of the wardrobe, in a brown paper bag?'

Terence Blue gave a kind of groan though he did not know that he did.

'And after I'd stabbed you, when they took you away in the ambulance like my mother I realised –' she gave a small unsteady sigh but did not take her eyes away from his face '– that after my mother died you were the only person I ever knew how to love. By putting away my memories I had forgotten that.'

'When you held me,' said Nicola Abbott at last, '*I stabbed you because I remembered.*'

'*I know,*' said Terence Blue.

His face was so pale the nurse thought he would faint. But at last he spoke again.

'Nicky,' he said 'I've got something else very very important to tell you. About the death of your mother.'

'I know,' she said.

Silence again, in the small room, as they looked at each other. 'I know, they told me. I remember that day, and the doctor. But – I couldn't – accept it properly. Because I felt that I did kill someone I loved, only it was you.'

And then she said again, like an echo, 'When you held me like that I stabbed you because I remembered.'

She looked at him and he saw such pain in her eyes that he could not bear it.

And then she saw the pain in his.

'Terry, I am so so sorry,' she said. And perhaps it was the future as well as the past that she might have meant, as if she saw his dreams. But did not believe them.

Very very slowly Terence Blue moved nearer to the grey-haired woman, moved nearer to her, smoothed her hair from her face; then at last, slowly because his own shoulder was so stiff, he put his arms very carefully around her, careful of her shoulder that had been so damaged on the winter night in Brighton when the car he was driving skidded on the ice and struck her so long ago; careful, like a man with a moth in his hands.

'You didn't kill anybody at all my darling,' he said. He touched her hair again, but infinitely gently. 'It will take a long time maybe. But I will be here now. We'll see where you are safest, and that's where you will stay.' And then, almost like a vow he added, 'You will see Nicky, that I do know the meaning of love.'

And, at last, as he had in the kitchen in Brighton just a few months ago, because such was his own pain now that he could not help it, he buried his face in her grey hair.

After a moment, very slowly she reached for his hand. And very very slowly and uncertainly she placed it on her breast, where it had been that night in Brighton in 1961, when Harry and Juliet rang the doorbell at two in the morning, that night when they were young.

The junior nurse had never seen anything so shocking in her life. She could feel it in the air, it was *sex*, these old people. She didn't know what she should do, she was sure this wasn't permissable.

She cleared her throat.

But the couple stayed just where they were, quite still in the small room, quite still in each other's arms.

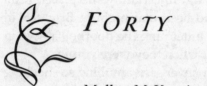

FORTY

Molly McKenzie had no family for Christmas Day. She had made Banjo her family and Banjo had left her for her young friend Viola Bonham, who she had always loved. He left messages on her answering machine saying how he thought of her every day, wondered how she was, hoped they could have a meal together soon. She never answered, not even when she thought she would go mad with grief and loss and pain and betrayal.

She was lucky, she looked young for her age, but now when she walked down the street, the swing in her step had gone. She noticed her knees ached sometimes when it rained, wondered if this was the beginning of rheumatism or arthritis. Little aches and pains came to her, reminding her that in four years' time *she would be sixty*. In four years' time she would travel half price on buses and trains with *a pensioner's pass*.

Her life, her work, her self-confidence, her relation-
ship with Banjo had kept her young at heart quite
literally; she had simply not thought about ageing except
in regard to the parts she was offered as an actress: she
hadn't equated this with her life, not aching joints and
greying hair and loneliness. She thought of all the
women of her age she knew, some with families, some
without: how so many husbands had left for younger
women (in her profession, younger actresses), a chance
for the men to start again, to be young again. But this did
not happen for women. *Age was different, for women.*

She actually shrank from young men who were pleasant to her, her self-confidence gone. There would be no
more young lovers for her, she could not bear the
thought of such a recurrence; maybe she would have no
real lovers again. All these thoughts devastated her,
showed in her face. She had been with Banjo when she
turned the corner into age and had not noticed. But he –
and she remembered again the holiday in Greece when
he had turned away from her – he had noticed.

He had left her, and she had become old.

So Molly McKenzie decided to spend Christmas Day in
a hotel in Hastings.

The morning Anthony had woken her with his phone
call about Banjo and Viola – when just for a moment,
waking so early, she had thought, like a dream, that it
would be Banjo on the phone, wanting to come back to
her – that day she had accepted the part of the Nurse at
the Royal Shakespeare Company's new production of
Romeo and Juliet in the coming Stratford season. Mainly

because she knew she must work or die and that was the only work she had been offered; but also partly because it was the same director who had directed *Othello*.

If I'm going to be old, she said aloud to herself, *I'd better be old in a good production*.

And then, as often happens, she immediately got a good role in a new television play, playing – she had laughed aloud – a palmist. She thought Anastasia Adams meant a psalmist, a religious nut.

'No,' said Anastasia, and then more doubtfully, 'Well I don't *think* so. I think they meant a fortune teller.'

Molly had laughed: *psalmist, palmist what the hell*. Her laugh had echoed in the empty Clapham house – no Banjo to say *what? good!* sleepily and pull her back into bed.

'A nut but a different kind of nut do you mean Anastasia?'

Anastasia was used to Molly, knew she was unhappy. She never encouraged her clients to talk about their private lives, it wasted too much time, but she sometimes heard things on the grapevine and she indulged Molly this time.

'Everyone over fifty is a nut darling, we know that.'

'Every *woman* over fifty,' corrected Molly.'

'Every woman over fifty,' agreed Anastasia.

It turned out indeed to be a palmist and a very good and different part at last; Molly wore scarves and swirling skirts and had a crystal ball and tarot cards and filmed in the seaside town of Hastings, in the snow. *I will not think about when I was here with Banjo, walking along the beach and weeping*. They started the week before

Christmas, had a few days off for the festive season; Molly stayed on in Hastings, but in another hotel so that the company would not know she had no plans, this year, for Christmas.

She kept away from where she had walked with Banjo.

She took her work: her TV scripts, her Shakespeare, and books on *Romeo and Juliet*. She'd had, the week before, a long meeting with the young director who was to direct her at Stratford, he'd had some interesting ideas about the Nurse. *I think she's a piece of all right*, he said, *that's why I had the idea of casting you because people won't expect it. I know it's a famous part but I think we might find some interesting things that haven't been done before*, and she banished white-haired old ladies from her consciousness, read the play over and over, becoming familiar.

She took novels to Hastings that she'd meant to read for years. Very very warily she understood: that this might now be her life. That she was no longer young.

She read of the press conference held to announce the starring of Terence Blue and Pauline O'Brien in *The Immoralists*. There was huge excitement when it was also announced that Marlon Brando, who never appeared on television, was probably going to play the American lead. And into her mind, remembering Anthony's excitement, and Pauline's appearance at Terence's court case, flickered a kind of understanding of what might have happened, of what her old friend Pauline might have done with the private information about Terence Molly had shared with her. *Well good luck Pauly*, she murmured into the cold wind along the seafront.

She kept away from where she had walked with Banjo.

She knew without doubt that because of Banjo, and because of Anthony, she and Pauline were lost to each other.

She didn't cry so often. But she dreamt of Banjo, and sometimes he seemed to embrace her body. But waking, she would feel her mouth held tightly together; sometimes she would catch herself in a shop window and the tight clenched mouth reminded her, she knew, of her mother.

In the second hotel, the evening before Christmas Eve when she moved in, she met a computer analyst.

'Don't computer analysts go home for Christmas?' she said lightly.

'Don't actresses?' he said.

He had recently separated from his wife; she gave him a small bit of information about her recent life upheaval.

They went to bed together on Christmas Eve not too soon after dinner but when they had both had just enough to drink to think it an excellent idea.

There weren't many preliminaries, he had an erection before they even lay down on her bed; when he did lie down he immediately popped up again. He fumbled at once with something in the pocket of his trousers which lay on an armchair and she saw it was a condom. She hadn't seen one for years.

'Jesus Christ,' she said, but not loudly, remembering that it was her room they were in and that the walls of the hotel rooms were not designed for indiscriminate fornication. 'Does this mean I am so old I've gone the full circle and am back on *condoms* again?'

'Yes,' he said, breathing heavily, pushing the condom down on himself in a way that reminded her of someone putting on a glove.

'Listen, I'm part of the Permissive Society. In about 1964 we threw away condoms.'

'You've come out the other side then,' he said pushing at her with his now rubber-covered penis, 'welcome to the era of Aids.'

'I came in at one end with delight at all that freedom' (and she thought of Anthony and the Pill and how easy it all seemed, as if there were no problems once sex was safe from pregnancy), 'then I fucked my life away, and, bloody hell, here I am coming out the other end as if the Permissive Society never existed!'

'Yes yes yes,' he said, excited by her use of what his wife called the *f-word*, 'that's right, yes, fucked your life away,' busy pushing against her, entering her (*entering*, she thought, *as they say, as if this part of me is a doorway to a funfair, not the key to my lonely heart. Oh Banjo*).

'Yes yes,' he repeated, moving faster now, 'yes yes.'

She moved with him in a spirit of cooperation and Christmas goodwill, her head bumped against the books on the bedside table, the television script and the Shakespeare and the novels.

'Yes!' he cried. '*Ah! Ah! Yes!*' his voice echoing into other, more respectable, Christmas rooms.

And to give him a Christmas lift (but not clutching at the bedhead, she decided that was going too far) she gave a little bit of a gasp and a moan also, entering into the spirit of the thing as best she could, in all the circumstances.

She was an Actress, after all.

But when she woke very early on Christmas morning the idea of another meeting with the computer analyst had palled rather, *that wouldn't be a very merry Christmas*, she said to herself as she quickly showered and dressed and packed her script and her books into her bag, *I've been welcomed to the era of Aids and now I think I'll go home and scrub the kitchen floor, it could do with it.* A yawning receptionist said Merry Christmas and made out her bill and Molly heard her own footsteps echoing across the marble floor to the exit.

Luckily her car was parked in a garage; she trudged through the falling snow to collect it. There were still not many people about in the cold Hastings morning and the sea was silent as the snow fell on it. Seagulls walked on the shore, arguing their white territory in shrill voices. In the Citroën, driving back to London slowly and carefully, she listened to Christmas carols from Ethiopia.

Inside her front door a pile of mail lay on the carpet, Christmas cards: she saw Banjo's writing on one and tore it up without reading it. She was glad she had turned her answering machine off. The house was freezing; she put the central heating on, put on her oldest clothes, piled the table and the chairs and the rubbish bin and the vegetable basket into a corner of the kitchen and was already scrubbing at the lino, her knees covered with Ajax, when the doorbell rang.

At the door Anthony Bonham stood clutching a large bunch of red roses and three champagne bottles, his coat and his hair covered in snow. He was either drunk or suffering from a terrible hangover: she could smell the alcohol and his forehead was creased in a frown of pain.

As Molly stared at him, holding the door open, he stepped forward to cross the threshold and by some miscalculation tripped and fell at her feet. He immediately remembered doing this after the reunion in the doorway of his house in Chiswick.

'Oh God,' he moaned.

The champagne bottles rolled on the hall carpet but did not break; some of the red roses lay squashed between the carpet and his body.

'God Molly darling,' he said, lying there, lifting his head from the floor with an effort, 'I couldn't face Christmas with Portia, open the champagne, Merry Christmas,' and his head fell back again. 'We're going to Rome at 8.30 pm from Heathrow,' he said and closed his eyes.

'Who is?' she said, staring down at him.

'You and I are. There'll be a car waiting at Fiumicino.'

'Don't be ridiculous, I'm working.'

'You've got four more days off after today, I checked with your agent, I knew you were in Hastings, I've got a *palazzo*.' His eyes were still closed.

'A what?'

'A *palazzo*. An Italian palace.'

'*What*?'

'Molly darling don't keep asking me questions,' he said peevishly. 'Just open the champagne.' He opened his eyes just for a moment. 'I like your hair,' he said and then closed them again.

And suddenly Molly McKenzie began to laugh. She leant against the open door and laughed and laughed till tears were running down her cheeks. She stared down at Anthony's pained face, at the red roses lying everywhere, at the champagne bottles rolled into corners and she laughed. And she suddenly thought, *how odd: I remind myself of Pauline, this is how she laughed when she was young.* And for the shortest moment, almost subconsciously, a thought flashed into her mind, *I'll always miss her*, and then it was gone.

Anthony, observing out of half-closed eyes that she wasn't going to be responsible for the alcohol, pulled himself up to a sitting position, extracted some battered holly-decorated paper cups from his coat pocket, reached for the champagne. And then as he expertly opened the first bottle he began to laugh too.

'God,' he said, laughing and pouring the fizzing, spilling liquid, 'I'm glad you're here Moll, though I would even have come to Hastings to get you if I had to, Portia was making a vegetarian Christmas dinner.'

Molly slid down the wall on to her floor, still laughing, still holding a scrubbing brush in one hand. Anthony handed her a drink.

'I guess we deserve each other for Christmas,' she said at last, wiping away tears with the back of her hand, catching her hair with the scrubbing brush.

'Of course we do,' said Anthony, misunderstanding, 'we've deserved each other for years, we *deserve* to be together after all we've been through. In a *palazzo*.'

But she shook her head, although she was laughing still.

A neighbour, walking his dog despite the weather, passed the two of them, laughing on the floor in the doorway. Surrounded by red roses they leant back against the wall and laughed together, shoulders touching now, drinking champagne out of squashed holly-covered paper cups as church bells pealed out incoherently all over the icy city.

FORTY-ONE

And on Christmas Day Pauline O'Brien, actress, lay by the blue Pacific Ocean.

She had never seen such blue sea in her life and she was wearing a bright blue sundress that had caught her eye at Honolulu airport, blue like the water, like no colour she'd ever worn before. Anyone in the distance walking towards her would have thought a piece of the sea lay there in the white sand.

They had only stayed in Honolulu one night, Waikiki beach awash with golfers and Japanese honeymooners. They had taken a tiny plane to the smaller island of Maui, to a small remote hotel on a small remote beach. Nevertheless at the end of the unpaved road, through the palm trees, past the brightly coloured hibiscus flowers and the frangipani blossoms blooming in clusters, there was a bar with sophisticated American video machines. So Benedict wasn't completely deprived of the things close to his heart.

She had also brought her mother. Whose face had crumpled when Pauline had said that Christmas would not be celebrated in Chiswick this year; whose old eyes had widened in amazement and something else, perhaps approval, when Pauline said she was leaving Anthony. And then her whole face had sparkled in frail delight when Pauline had finally said, 'You come to Hawaii too Mum.'

Now Mrs O'Brien had found a cool place on the verandah of the hotel where frangipani-laden air drifted about her brandy glass and friendly Hawaiians, passing slowly by, stopped to listen to her stories of tap dancing in England long ago.

'Merry Christmas Pauly, I'm having such a lovely time,' she had said so simply this morning that Pauline had bent and kissed the old lady and saw, suddenly, the young laughing tap dancer from Colchester shining there somewhere out of the old wrinkled face. And Pauline had thought in surprise, *she never complained about how things turned out. It wasn't just my father who was brave.*

Somewhere, as usual, someone was strumming a guitar and people were singing, soft voices in an unknown language; it sounded beautiful and Pauline smiled to herself as she thought she caught the strains of 'Silent Night' in the sun-drenched morning. They said this was the rainy season, but there was no rain, only sunshine. She could feel the sun on her shoulders, and hear the waves breaking gently, soothingly, on the shore just a few yards away. Frangipani bushes laden with flowers grew everywhere, even right outside the windows of their rooms, the heavy voluptuous fragrance wafted into their dreams. Her dreams were odd, languorous, unreal. And when she woke in the scented night, as she often did, as her body adjusted to its journeying, she thought, almost in disbelief, about how it had all happened.

She thought about it again, lying in the sunshine.

All she had done was beat Anthony at his own game.

When she had suggested to Joseph Wain that they might get a very famous film star *instead of Anthony* to play the British Prime Minister in *The Immoralists*, Joseph had looked at her in some bewilderment. When she had told him that she thought she might get Terence Blue to agree to play the part, if she appeared as a witness in his defence at his rape trial and said he was impotent, Joseph's mouth actually dropped open in astonishment and he looked disbelieving and dazed at the turn of the conversation. When the full implications of what she was suggesting hit him his hand went for his mobile telephone. *Wait*, she had commanded, *I'll have to talk to Terence first, and he'll only agree if it looks like he'll be convicted and if he thinks it will stop Nicky Abbott being brought to trial. I've got a lot of talking to do.*

This is the most ridiculous thing I've ever heard of, I'll come with you, Joseph Wain had said, and his car had met hers in Darlington and followed her to the remote farmhouse where Terence was living.

And now she, Pauline O'Brien, was to be in this incredible television series, she and Terence Blue, the golden boy who had kissed her on the stairs when she was young. Those few days before she left England she couldn't open a newspaper without seeing pictures of Terence and herself smiling at each other.

The part was fantastic, the secretly good and courageous woman amongst all the immoralists, she had six fat draft scripts on the table beside her bed on the island of Maui. She had forgotten that wonderful feeling, of a pile of scripts waiting to be brought to life. She read them, immersed herself in them, her creative work already beginning. She would be filming in Africa and Europe and Asia and Tonga and America. At last she would be working again as an actress. She would be alone, but she would be working. Her life, since that morning of the reunion when she stared out at the river in her blue silk dressing gown, had changed completely.

And so, of course, had Anthony's.

He would find at last what it felt like to have his security taken away from him, at work and at home. She shook her head wryly, it would be a difficult adjustment: he liked ironed underwear and shiny bathroom taps and shopping lists. But of course he would manage, somehow.

Perhaps Molly would stay with Anthony. But perhaps she wouldn't. And perhaps Pauline would become the mother-in-law of Molly McKenzie's toyboy. And if Molly stayed with Anthony she could become the mother-in-law of her toyboy too. Pauline began laughing helplessly in a kind of disbelief as she lay in the warm sand: how ridiculous life was, how ludicrous and improbable, how could she and Molly, best friends in their youth discussing life so earnestly, have imagined it would all come to this?

And as she laughed she understood: the ice around her heart was moving, breaking up and moving and beginning to thaw. The way it did when winter was over.

Pauline O'Brien, daughter of a trapeze artist, stretched like a cat, pushed her long body into the warm sand. Along the beach under the palm trees they were now singing 'Away in a Manger' in Hawaiian to the strumming of the guitar. Unexpectedly, almost subconsciously, a thought flashed into her mind, *but I'll always miss Molly*. And then it was gone.

In her bag beside her was the red lipstick and a mirror. She rolled over lazily, put the lipstick on, rolled back again into the sand, drifted into a half sleep.

A hand smoothed her back, very gently.

'Benny?' she asked, sleepily.

There was no answer. The hand smoothed the skin on her long back that had once shone so youthfully from theatre posters all over London, stroked the back that was no longer young, in the warm sunshine. Just for a moment, Pauline lay there still. Nobody had smoothed her back so gently, so caressingly since her one lover had gone to America twenty years ago.

And then she very slowly turned her head, and then her stomach gave a leap.

Joseph Wain was sitting on the sand beside her, two very long American daquiris on a tray.

'Hello Pauly, Merry Christmas,' he said, and grinned. 'Thought I'd pop over from England. How're you feeling? Any regrets?'

Pauline very carefully leant on one elbow; stretched

out and very carefully took one of the drinks. She took a long sip before she answered him, tasted rum and then peaches; her red lipstick stained the glass. Then very carefully she smiled at Joseph Wain. So she would be a person who had affairs, after all. This was her new life. Everywhere around her, bright hibiscus flowers shone and the sea sighed gently. How wonderful everything was. Then to her immense surprise, and deep embarrassment, one tear slipped down her face, past the red lipstick, and fell into the daquiri she was holding.

It was so *long* since anybody had touched her like that.

She looked quickly out under her eyelashes at Joseph but he seemed to be busying himself with his drink. She breathed carefully in and out for a moment to stop herself weeping. Then she took another long sip of the daquiri.

'Frankly my dear,' she said answering him at last, smiling at him: sophisticated, cool, catching his eye, 'Frankly my dear, I don't *give* a damn.'

And then she spoilt the effect by reaching up shyly, as she had the day of the garden party, and touching the short springy hair. He caught her hand and brought it down to his mouth and kissed it.

'I love you Pauly,' he said. 'I've loved you all my life.'

Just at that moment, just as he kissed her hand, before she could say anything at all, a group of Hawaiians started another Christmas song somewhere further along the beach.

And the song they were singing in another language, there in the hot sunshine on Christmas Day on the other side of the world, was her father's favourite song, 'I'm Dreaming of a White Christmas', that he had sung so long ago to the Russian chimpanzee, in the circus.

Pauline and Joseph walked slowly along the beach in the sunshine towards the hotel. The drifting Christmas singing faded into the sound of the sea, the sound of the waves breaking on the shore; coloured birds flashed sometimes between the trees.

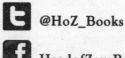